The Eighth House

Karen Sealy

Highbridge Press

This is a work of fiction. Names, characters, places, and incidents are either the product of the author's imagination or are used fictitiously, and any resemblance to actual persons, living or dead, business establishments, events or locales is entirely coincidental.

THE EIGHTH HOUSE

Published by
Highbridge Press
www.highbridgepress.com

All rights reserved.
Copyright © 2000 by Karen Sealy

This book may not be reproduced or transmitted in any form or by any means, electronic, mechanical, photocopying, recording, or otherwise, without permission of the publisher.

ISBN: 0-9678832-5-3

Library of Congress Card Number 00-102383

Cover design by Karen Sealy

Printed in the U.S.A.

Acknowledgments

There are a number of people who, without their input and support, this book would never have come about.

A heartfelt thank you to my sister and business partner Tricia, whose never-ending inspiration, advice, wisdom, and vision not only contributed to the creation of this book, but helped me rediscover a long forgotten talent.

To Adrienne, Francine, Sally, Sheila, Liz, Ruane, Gertie, Carol, Joyce, Annette, Donna, and Shirley. Your feedback and moral support were priceless and for that, I am eternally grateful.

And finally, thank you S.B. You'll never know just how much your words have truly set me free.

THE EIGHTH HOUSE

"The house of Scorpio and Pluto. Represents sex and money: the life force, which sharpens and directs our sexual appetites. The money we acquire by our own efforts - although sometimes by inheritance. It is traditionally the house of death - but often the death of old ways and the beginning of new life."

PART I

EDWARD HASTINGS

CHAPTER I

NEW YORK CITY, AUGUST 1908

Edward Hastings half-heartedly listened to his mother having sex in the next room. The French doors, which separated her bedroom from the kitchen where he slept, barely concealed the daily carnal activity.

He rolled over on his lumpy mattress and yawned.

The two room apartment was already stifling from the late summer's heat, and it was only eight o'clock in the morning. He grabbed the soiled fabric of his sweat stained undershirt and began fanning it against his bony chest. Edward wrinkled his nose against the stench of his own reeking body odor that was stirred up by his fanning.

Splintered floorboards creaked in protest as he shuffled across the room to the kitchen sink. Maybe if he splashed some cold water on his face, he'd feel better.

Roaches frantically scattered onto the drainboard when he pushed a pile of food encrusted chipped plates and cups aside. When the rusty faucet handle refused to budge, he cursed and reached for a small iron skillet. He took a moment to smash some of the slower retreating insects before giving the stubborn lever a few sharp wacks. The loud banging caused the windows to rattle throughout the apartment.

His efforts were immediately rewarded when the handle moved. Water erupted from the faucet after it produced a few tentative sputters and wheezes. Edward stood on his tiptoes and stuck his head under the spigot, letting the cold liquid sting the back of his neck and ears. Then, he shut it off, shook the excess from his dirty blonde hair, and slicked it back from his forehead with his long, skinny fingers.

Treading softly over to the French doors, he pressed his ear against the glass. The sound of the musical bedsprings reached a fevered pitch. He listened with amusement as his mother's moaning swelled to an explosive crescendo. Ten, nine, eight, seven, he counted under his breath. When he reached one, he clutched his chest, threw his head back and in silent mimicry, mouthed, "Oh God! Oh God!", in perfect unison with his mother's orgasmic shrieks. He slapped his hand over his mouth to muffle his snickering. Unknown to her johns, this was his mother's regular routine. He couldn't help feeling sorry for the poor saps who fell for her phoney sexual theatrics. But, as she explained it, the more convincing her performance, the more money they paid.

* * * *

Edward was a product of the crime-filled streets of the Lower East Side of Manhattan and he had always been exposed to the seedier side of life.

Margaret Hastings was a career prostitute. During the first six years of Edward's life, he was left in the care of Mrs. O'Brien, a next door neighbor, while his mother sold her body. But, he didn't mind. Mrs. O'Brien's five children provided him with ample companionship.

Unfortunately, the neighbor's babysitting services ended abruptly when the frazzled woman accidently slipped and fell out the window while hanging her wash on the clothesline strung between the two tenement buildings.

He cried when his playmates moved across the river to Brooklyn with their widowed father.

Without the mothering of Mrs. O'Brien and the camaraderie of her children, Edward was left to his own devices while his mother worked. Most days, he ran amuck through the crowded neighborhood with an unruly gang of street urchins, robbing push carts or rolling drunks who staggered out of the local taverns.

When he reached school-age, Margaret, who was forbidden by her pimp to take any time off, defied his orders and escorted her son to the grey, brick building with the tall windows. To Edward, it looked more like a prison than a public school.

At first, his natural curiosity about learning was enough to keep him interested in his classes. But once he fell into the school's mundane routine, he and his old gang developed the fine art of avoiding the truant officer.

Overall, he was pretty content with his incorrigible, poverty-stricken lifestyle, especially since almost everyone else in his neighborhood was just as destitute. That was, until the day he and his gang snuck into the brand new motion picture theater on Grand Street and watched a five minute silent movie titled, "A Day in The Country."

Edward was captivated by the black and white film depicting the life of the Davis family as the story unfolded before his eyes.

Accompanying the handsome couple were two children, a boy and girl, dressed in their Sunday best.

Edward salivated as he watched the cheerful family sit at a picnic table covered with a checkered cloth to enjoy a meal together.

After eating, the father and son began to play a game together while his daughter helped her mother clean up.

Edward's shoulders slumped when the organ music swelled to a thunderous climax and the words, "The End" flickered across the screen.

The nine-year-old was deep in thought as he slowly walked back to his block. Did people actually live that way? Or was it just make-believe? He posed that question to his friend Petey later that evening.

"Whatta ya, stupid or something, runt? Of course people live like that. Ain't you ever been uptown or nothin'? They got mansions up there on Fifth Avenue. That's where all them rich people live," was Petey's scathing reply as the two friends sat on the stoop of Edward's building.

"Well, how come we don't live like that?" Edward asked as he watched his freckled-faced best friend pick a scab from his grungy knee.

"Cause we're poor, that's why. How the hell can we expect to live like that when my old man is drunk most of the time and don't give my ma no money for the eight of us? And your ma, well, she does, you know... It ain't like she's workin' outta one of them ritzy bordello's over on Avenue A," Petey replied, matter-of-factly, but not wanting to hurt his friend's feelings.

"I guess you're right," Edward had agreed, sadly.

For days after viewing that film, he continued to analyze the bleak circumstances that contributed to his miserable life. He needed some answers that only his mother could provide. So, on a day when she decided to disobey her pimp and take a few hours off from work, Margaret spent the evening with her son on the roof of their tenement. As they drank soda pop together and enjoyed the cool spring breeze that drifted across the adjacent rooftops from the East River, Edward thought it was the perfect time to question her.

"Can I ask you somethin'?" Edward said, after he drained the last of the sweet, dark liquid from the bottle.

"Sure. What?"

"How come we're poor?"

"That's an easy one. Cause we don't have no money."

"Well, geez, ma, I know *that*. But *how come* we don't have no money?"

"Because that sonofabitch Rick takes more than half of what I make a night," Margaret spat with disgust.

"Well, how come you gotta be a harlot? Why don't you get a husband like other women?"

"My, ain't we full of questions tonight," Margaret shook her head. "Why the third degree all of a sudden?"

Edward went on to describe the movie he'd seen, purposely omitting that he'd snuck in without paying.

"Mmm," Margaret paused to take a sip of pop before she continued. "Well, wasn't that just swell. Listen, Eddie. Since you already know more than a nine-year-old is supposed to, I'm gonna give it to ya straight. The reason we don't live like 'Mr. And Mrs. High Society' is simple. I grew up in an orphanage. When I got out, I had no money, no relatives and a third grade education. I had two ways to earn a living; as a maid in one of them mansions you admire so much or as a seamstress in a factory."

"I was a maid for three days. I walked out after the master of the house wanted me to do things that the mistress never mentioned as bein' part of my duties. The factory job lasted two months until the pig who was my boss threatened not to pay me if I didn't show him a little lovin' on the side."

"So, there I was, fifteen years old with no job, a landlady harpin' on me to pay my rent and no man in sight who was willing to sweep me off my feet and take care of me. What was I supposed to do? Then, one day, I run into a girl who used to live at the orphanage with me. I tell her what a pickle I'm in and she says, 'Look, honey. I went through the same thing until I figured out that when the goin' gets tough, a lady can always fall back on her womanly ways as long as she's halfway decent lookin' and men ain't satisfied with what their girlfriends or wives are puttin' out.' That's when she introduced me to Rick and the rest is history."

"But you still coulda gotten married, couldn't you?"

"Yeah. A few johns proposed but I wasn't interested. I like my freedom," Margaret shook her head.

Yeah, like Rick ain't callin' all the shots, Edward thought, but said out loud, "Well, how did I get here?"

"You gotta be kiddin'!" Margaret stared at her son and

chuckled.

"I don't mean *how, how*. I mean, who is my father?" Edward said in frustration.

"To be honest with you, hon, I can't exactly remember," Margaret lied, purposely fixing her gaze on the lights of the Brooklyn Bridge to avoid looking at her son. The truth was, she had very vivid, bittersweet memories of Edward's father. He'd been a handsome stockbroker with bright blue eyes that melted her heart the first moment he looked at her. He was the first customer she'd ever serviced. When he realized she was a virgin, his love making had been very sweet and gentle.

God, how she adored him! She was flattered when she learned that he was one of Rick's best paying customers and only wanted to see her.

But, Nathan Styles was also a married man and in the naivete of her youth, she'd allowed herself to believe he'd leave his wife and marry her because in the heat of passion, he always whispered that he loved her. When he found out she was pregnant with his child, he tossed her an extra fifty dollars and wished her good luck.

Rick was apoplectic because a pregnant prostitute was a liability. Eventually, he calmed down. After Edward's birth, he realized that Margaret's previously childish figure had miraculously blossomed into a more curvaceous, womanly one and was a definite asset to his business.

Every time she looked at her son, she was reminded of her first love. He was the spitting image of Nathan.

"How come you don't remember him?" Edward persisted.

"Because it was a long time ago and it gets harder to remember stuff when you get older," Margaret lied again.

"Well, you'd think you could at least remember who my father is," Edward mumbled. His melancholy tone broke her heart.

"I'm sorry. I'll think about it more and maybe I'll remember something," Margaret promised.

"Yeah, sure. And, how come I ain't got no brothers or sisters?" Edward continued.

"Believe it or not, you almost did," she replied, her voice becoming distant at the memory.

"And what happened?" Edward asked, turning to look at his mother curiously.

"It was born feet first and the stupid midwife Rick sent over didn't know what the hell she was doin'. The poor thing got choked by the umbilical cord and died and nearly killed me in the process. After that, I couldn't have no more kids. So, you better count your blessings that you came first," Margaret said, wagging her finger at him.

"Was it a boy or a girl?"

"A boy."

"Did he have the same father?"

"Nope."

"Did ya name him?"

"Yeah. We had to have something to put on his grave. I named him Nathan," Margaret replied, softly, her eyes suddenly beginning to water. She blinked back the tears and said, "Now I got a question for you. Are you ashamed of what I do?"

Edward was caught off guard by her query and took a few seconds to formulate his response. He was afraid that if he said yes, he might hurt her feelings. But then again, maybe if he told the truth and she realized how humiliated he felt because of her profession, she might finally try to find a more dignified way to earn a living.

"Well..," he began, nervously rolling the empty pop bottle between his palms, "yeah, kinda. I mean geez, ma, it's kinda embarrassin' when I see a friend's father comin' to the house to do, uh, you know... And the other kids are always makin' fun of me and calling us names. It ain't fair that I always gotta be defendin' your honor," Edward replied with brutal honesty.

His impassioned response shocked Margaret. How long had he felt so strongly about her chosen profession?

As she noted her son's somber expression, shame and guilt began to surface, emotions she never allowed to emerge. Without total emotional detachment, it would be impossible for her to tolerate the degradation she felt every time she serviced a john.

This sure ain't the life I dreamed of havin', Margaret thought. Then, she reached over to wrap her thin arms around her son, resting her chin on top of his head.

"Look, Eddie. I'm really sorry. I never meant to hurt you. You're all I've got in this lousy world. But I don't know what else to do. We gotta eat and have some place to live, don't we? I'm doing the best I can." Lifting his chin with her fingers, she looked into her son's sad blue eyes and said, "I love you with all my heart, Eddie and don't you ever forget it. We may not live like them rich people you seen in that movie but you got nothin' to be ashamed of. And don't let nobody tell you different. You hear me?"

"Yes, Ma'am," Edward nodded. Then, on impulse, he reached up and planted a kiss on her pale cheek.

"Aw, geez, Eddie," Margaret's voice cracked and she began to cry.

He rested his head against her heaving bosom in as she wept.

A few minutes later, when her tears subsided, she released him and smiled, playfully ruffling his hair.

"Look, enough with the questions. You got me blubberin' all over the place like a baby," Margaret said, drying her face with the end of her shawl. "We'd better go in. It's gettin' late.

After that evening, he never broached the subject again. He figured, if it didn't bother her, why should it bother him? But during quiet moments at night as he lay on his mattress, he would replay in his mind's eye the images of the perfect family he'd seen in the film that impressed him so much.

The Eighth House   Karen Sealy

* * * *

As their financial situation continued to deteriorate because of Rick's insatiable greed, Edward's resentment and anger rapidly escalated.

He finally reached his breaking point the night he was forced to watch helplessly as Rick brutally assaulted his mother when she begged him to allow her to take the night off because she felt ill.

When Edward tried to defend her, Rick directed his savagery toward him.

Later, after an out-of-control Rick finally stormed out of the apartment, Edward rushed to his mother's side, ignoring his own painful injuries. With tears of defeat streaming down his face, he gently tended to his mother's wounds and vowed to once and for all alleviate their suffering.

* * * *

By age fifteen, Edward could no longer tolerate being at home while Margaret serviced her men.

But, he put aside his feelings of disgust for his mother's occupation and stayed home on the morning he planned to confront Rick.

He was extremely agitated as he leaned against the kitchen sink with his bony arms folded across his chest, waiting for his mother to finish having intercourse with her customer. When the doors of her bedroom finally swung open, her gaunt face was expressionless as she slipped on her tattered robe. Racoon eyes, stringy hair and a pasty complexion were evidence of a broken body and shattered spirit. She looked much older than her thirty years.

The man, who was wearing an expensive suit, pulled a gold watch on a chain from his vest pocket to check the time.

"Thanks a million, doll," the gentleman said, as he handed Margaret a small wad of bills.

"Anytime, darlin'." She took the money and quickly slipped it into a pouch under her mattress.

Edward's hostility was more than evident but the man ignored him as he passed through the kitchen on his way to the front door. Edward studied his face as he walked by and wondered for the hundredth time if this man might be his father. But he wouldn't dare ask his mother again.

"I'm goin' to the bathroom, Eddie. I'll be right back," Margaret told him as she left the sweltering apartment to use the community lavatory down the hall.

Good, Edward thought, wiping sweat from his forehead with the hem of his soiled T-shirt. This would give him an opportunity to execute his plan.

Shortly, there was a knock on the apartment door.

"Just a sec," Edward called out. He rushed to his mattress, reached beneath the covers and pulled out a .22 caliber pistol. It had been given to him by the bouncer at the corner bar just in case he or his mother needed to protect themselves from an unruly john. He shoved it into the waistband of his knickers and pulled down his T-shirt to conceal it before opening the door.

"Hey, kid. How's it goin'?" Rick said, swaggering into the apartment.

"Okay," Edward mumbled.

Right on schedule, his mother's pimp had arrived to collect his portion of the previous night's earnings.

Edward glared at him with revulsion. Rick's jet-black, greasy hair was plastered to his scalp. He wreaked of the cheap, sickly sweet cologne he insisted on drowning himself in. His double-breasted, pin-striped suit hung loosely from his skinny frame. Edward was willing to bet he'd gotten it from the pawn shop around the corner.

Shoving him aside with indifference, Rick entered the bedroom. Edward seethed as he watched him reach under his mother's mattress for the pouch. He pulled out the thick wad of bills and counted the money with a look of satisfaction.

"What the fuck are you lookin' at, kid? Mind ya damn business," Rick snarled when he finally noticed Edward standing in the doorway of the bedroom.

"This *is* my business. Put the money down," Edward said, eyes blazing.

Slack jawed, Rick stopped counting and stared at him.

"What did you say, punk?"

"I said put the money down. You didn't do shit to earn it so you ain't got no right takin' it. It belongs to us," Edward declared, his voice quivering with rage.

"Get outta my face before I beat the shit outta ya." Towering over Edward's 5'7" body, Rick took a threatening step toward him.

Folding his arms over his chest, Edward brazenly said, "Go ahead and try."

Rick lunged at him but stopped dead in his tracks when Edward suddenly whipped out the gun from his waistband and pointed it at him.

"You must be crazy! You can't shoot me, you little punk!" Rick shouted, backing away from Edward.

"Put the pouch down and get out," Edward demanded, trying his best to sound tough. But the slight quivering of the gun in his hand revealed his nervousness.

Rick noted Edward's uncertainty and lunged for the gun. A startled Edward wrestled with the pimp, their movements resembling a strange dance.

A loud "pop" brought their struggle to an abrupt halt.

"Oh shit!" Rick shrieked as the bullet tore through his groin. Clutching his crotch, he doubled over and fell onto the bed, a dark, red stain quickly spreading between his legs.

The Eighth House

Karen Sealy

Edward was in a daze as he stood over Rick who was writhing and whimpering in pain. The pool of blood grew wider. Rick's body jerked spasmodically off the bed. After a final shudder, the pimp's body grew still.

Stunned by what he was witnessing, Edward didn't notice when the gun slipped from his sweaty hand and landed with a thud on the floor.

An overpowering wave of dread mixed with exhilaration washed over Edward, his face ashen. This wasn't how it was supposed to happen. Rick should have just dropped the pouch and left the apartment. But it was too late now. Rick was dead. He had to make things right again.

Something died in Edward at that moment. He was no longer just a juvenile delinquent who committed petty crimes. Now, he was a murderer.

He felt somehow detached from himself–as if a darker, more powerful side of him had emerged, replacing the young man he had been.

With a calmness that contradicted his previous actions, a look of deep concentration etched his face. His mind raced. The deed was done. Now, he had to act quickly.

Edward spun around on his heel when the front door crashed open and his mother ran in. The acrid odor of gunpowder drifted through the apartment.

"Eddie! What was that noise? Are you all right?" Margaret shouted, running toward her son. Then, looking over his shoulder, her eyes widened in horror when she spotted Rick sprawled on the floor. She had to clamp her hand over her mouth to stifle the scream that threatened to escape her lips.

"Oh my God! Rick!" she croaked, warily bending down to get a closer look. She stared in morbid fascination at the blood-soaked body and backed up when she could barely control the sudden urge to vomit.

"Oh Eddie! What have you done?" she wailed.

"It was an accident. I was only defending myself," Edward lied without hesitation. "Rick tried to rape me so I shot him. Pull yourself together. We gotta get him outta here before someone sees," Edward commanded, as he roughly pulled the chenille bedspread over Rick's corpse.

"But Eddie--"

"Look!" Edward growled between clenched teeth. He took her by the shoulders and shook her. "He was a pig! What was I supposed to do, just give in? Besides, we ain't givin' your money to nobody no more. We don't need no pimp tellin' us what to do. We can be partners. Me and you can open our own brothel and be partners. You don't have to work no more. I'm gonna take care of you."

Margaret was speechless as she stared at her red faced son. Then, she shook her head as if to clear her thoughts and pried away his fingers, releasing his painful grip on her arm. Pulling her hand back, she smacked him across the face, sending him tumbling onto the floor.

"My God, Eddie! Have you gone *crazy*? *You just killed Rick! You're gonna go to jail, Eddie! Oh God, my baby's gonna go to jail!* Margaret burst into tears and collapsed onto the floor in a heap, her body convulsing as she wept.

Edward crawled over and put his arms around her.

"Please don't cry, ma. That ain't gonna happen. Everything *is gonna be okay. You'll see. I promise. I'm gonna take care of you.* Everything is gonna be okay. Please get up. Come on. Please get up," Edward begged his mother.

Suddenly, Petey rushed through the open door. He had to fight his way through the throng of curious neighbors who were craning their necks to see what was going on in the apartment.

"Holy shit, Eddie! What the hell happened?" Petey stared in disbelief when he spotted Rick's bleeding corpse.

Edward sprang from the floor. "I'll tell you later. Run down the block and get Numbers and Bricktop," he instructed, pushing his friend toward the front door and slamming it shut after he left.

Then, he returned to his mother.

"Come on. Ya gotta get dressed. I sent Petey to get Bricktop and Numbers. They'll take care of the rest," Edward said, gently helping her up from the floor.

Margaret continued to shake uncontrollably as she struggled to put on her shabby dress. In a few minutes, Petey returned with two burly looking men. The taller one was Bricktop, the bouncer from the corner bar. He had acquired his nickname because he remained unscarred in spite of the bottles that were constantly thrown at his head during bar room brawls. Numbers, the shorter man, was the local number runner.

As soon as they spotted the body, they sprang into action. Once Numbers had wrapped Rick in the spread, Bricktop hoisted the body over his shoulder and without so much as a grunt, carried it out of the apartment.

"Don't yous' worry. We'll take care of everything," Numbers said, patting Margaret's tear stained cheek.

"Nice job kid," Bricktop gave Edward the thumb's up as they left the apartment.

Margaret, still in a daze, tugged nervously on her stringy hair as she stood in the middle of the kitchen and watched the door close.

"Come on, ma. We gotta clean this place up. Petey, get the mop and pail from under the sink in the kitchen", Edward directed, immediately taking charge.

His mother, with Petey's help, mechanically scrubbed the bedroom floor. Edward took a moment to sit at the kitchen table to count the cash in his mother's pouch along with what he'd taken out of Rick's pockets while they waited for Petey to return.

He shook his head in awe when the final count totaled five hundred dollars.

"That lyin', thievin' bastard," Edward swore in anger. "And I bet there's plenty more where that came from," he muttered, fingering the pile of greenbacks.

"We're all done, Eddie," Petey announced as he dumped the last bucket of bloody water down the sink.

"Good. We got some other business to take care of," Edward said. He got up from the table and returned to the bedroom where Margaret sat on the edge of the blood-stained mattress, holding her head.

"Listen, ma. I gotta go out for a second. You gonna be alright? Ya want Petey's ma to come sit with ya?"

Margaret looked up and nodded, her eyes red-rimmed and swollen, her face ghostly white. "You go. I'll be alright."

"Okay," Eddie said, turning away. Then, on impulse, he backtracked and knelt down in front of his distraught mother.

"It's gonna be okay, ma. I promise. You'll see," he said, softly, and kissed her on the cheek.

* * * *

"Where we goin', Eddie?" Petey asked as the two boys rushed down the crowded sidewalk. The street was a symphony of sights and sounds, from the pushcart vendors hawking their wares, bustling housewives scolding cranky children as they shopped, and the clang of horse drawn trolley cars, winding their way down the avenue.

"To Rick's house," Edward replied.

"Gee, Eddie. I can't believe you actually killed that bastard!" Petey cried, breathlessly, as he tried to keep up with his friend.

"He had it comin'."

"Well, gee. How did it feel when you pulled the trigger?" Petey asked, the excitement bubbling over in his voice.

"I don't wanna talk about it," Edward shook his head.

The Eighth House

Karen Sealy

"Okay. You really got guts, Eddie. I don't know if I coulda done what you did," Petey admitted.

"Forget it. We got more important things to think about." Edward replied with false indifference. Inside, he was bursting with energy. The initial shock of what he'd done had turned into pride because he'd finally taken steps to change his miserable life.

When they reached the pimp's rundown tenement building, they sprinted down the stairs to his basement apartment.

"How we gonna get in?" Petey asked when the doorknob wouldn't budge.

Edward surveyed the garbage strewn steps until he found what he wanted. He bent down and retrieved a medium sized rock. Without a second thought, he smashed the grimy window that was next to the door. Then, he carefully reached in past the jagged shards of glass and gingerly raised it.

"Yech! What a pig stye," Petey declared when they stepped into the one room apartment. Edward pulled the chain dangling from the ceiling to illuminate the single naked bulb. They nearly gagged from the heat and unbearable stench that hung in the air like a cloud.

The two boys could only shake their heads in disgust as they picked their way through the piles of papers, clothes and other debris strewn across the floor.

"Look at this," Petey giggled as he held up a bright, pink pair of lady's silk bloomers from atop a pile of old magazines. Then he cried, "Holy smokes"! when the cover of one of the magazines caught his eye.

"Lemme see," Edward said, snatching it from him. He could only shake his head in distaste when he flipped through the pages of the pornographic literature. It featured well endowed naked women in lewd and risque poses alone or with naked men. He handed it back to his friend.

"Stop droolin' over them dirty pictures and help me,"

Edward said as he began searching through a pile of clothes on the cot that served as Rick's bed.

"Whatta we lookin' for?" Petey asked, tossing the magazine back on the floor.

"Money. Rick's take from the girls gotta be somewhere around here. Now where would a pimp hide his money?" Edward paused, tapping his finger against his chin in contemplation.

"I don't know, Eddie. And with all this crap, it could take us days to find it," Petey shrugged his shoulders.

"Shut up a second and lemme think," Edward waved his hand.

Petey jumped when Edward suddenly stomped his foot on the wooden floor.

"Keep stompin' the floor like this and listen for somethin' hollow," Edward instructed him.

When they had engaged in the strange stomp and pause routine for nearly ten minutes, Edward shouted, "Got it!"

He dropped to his knees and pounded a spot next to his foot with his knuckles, confirming the hollow sound he'd heard.

"Gimme your pocket knife," he told Petey. His friend rummaged through his pockets and handed it to him.

Edward snapped open the blade and carefully stuck the tip into the narrow ridge between two floorboards. After a few quick flicks of his wrist, he was able to pry up the roughly sawed section of wood. He tossed it aside and stuck his hand into the dark hole.

Edward winked at his friend when his hand touched what felt like a small burlap sack resting on top of the earthen floor below the boards.

"Well, well, well. What have we here?" Edward smirked as he lifted the sack from its hiding place. Petey squatted next to his friend, holding his breath as Edward untied the sack and shook out its contents.

"I'll be damned! Petey whistled when three neatly bundled

piles of bills dropped to the floor with a firm "thump."

"I hope ya know how to count past a hundred 'cause this looks like a lotta dough, Petey." Edward could barely contain his delirium.

It took the duo nearly forty-five minutes to tally the money after a few miscounts. When they were finally done, Petey sprang from the floor and began dancing a crazy jig around the room, singing, "We're rich! We're rich! We're goddamned rich! Whatta ya gonna do with all this loot, Eddie?" Petey asked, his breath coming in short bursts.

"You'll see," Eddie replied, as he gathered the bills totaling five thousand dollars in his arms with a sinister look on his face. "You'll see."

CHAPTER II

Three days later, the back room of Malone's tavern was the location of an important meeting conducted by Edward. The eclectic group of attendees included; Margaret Hastings, seven of Rick's former girls, Numbers, Bricktop, Petey, and Sean, the tavern's owner.

The news of Rick's death spread through the neighborhood like wildfire. The precinct captain never bothered to send an officer to investigate the homicide. As far as they were concerned, a dead pimp was just one less criminal to worry about. And, even if they had been inclined to make an arrest, they would have been met with resistance and hostility from members of a community who had very little respect for the cops.

Nervous chatter permeated the establishment while the prostitutes waited for Edward to call the meeting to order.

"I guess you're wonderin' why I asked you to come here,"

Edward began, speaking with the authority and confidence of an adult rather than that of a fifteen year old. "Here's the deal. Rick is dead."

"And may the sonofabitch rot in hell," Velma, the oldest of Rick's girls interjected. A chorus of *"Amens"* punctuated her comment.

"Yeah. And now that he's dead, I'm takin' over his business."

This declaration was met with indignant cries of protest from the pimp's former employees.

"What the hell are you talkin' about? You're only a kid!" Rosie, the youngest of the group of women, exclaimed.

"That may be true," Edward said, jumping down from his position on the table where he had been sitting, to stand in front of the irate prostitute, "but I got the dough to back it up."

"What money?" she asked, skeptically.

"This money." Edward gestured for Petey to hand him the burlap sack. With all the drama he could muster, Edward dumped its contents onto the table and stood back to afford the group an unobstructed view of the loot.

Gasps of disbelief rippled through the crowd.

"How much ya got there, Eddie?" Numbers asked.

"Five thousand g's the bastard had stashed in his apartment plus another five hundred he had on him when he met his maker."

"So, whatta ya gonna do with it and what happens to us?" Velma asked.

"Well, I figure it this way," Edward began, returning to his perch on the table, "with this kinda dough, I could open one of them fancy bordello's like the ones uptown and we could start makin' some real money. We'd only cater to rich johns, no more hard luck cases. We'd offer the finest booze, entertainment, and the most beautiful women money can buy."

As Edward became more excited about his idea, he got up

and began pacing the floor.

"And, instead of bustin' your ass for peanuts, you'll get a percentage of the profits plus whatever tips the johns give you," Edward concluded, sounding like a legitimate businessman.

Shocked by Edward's proposition, at first, no one spoke. Then, the room was suddenly filled with excited chatter. Edward leaned back against the table with his arms folded across his chest and a broad smile appeared on his young face. He winked at his mother, pleased with the group's response.

Loretta, a plump, cherub faced prostitute with bright red hair, timidly stepped forward and raised her hand to get Edward's attention.

"Geez, Loretta, this ain't no school. If ya got somethin' to say, just speak up," Edward said.

"Well, um, I, um, I," she said, nervously wringing her hands with her eyes downcast.

"Spit it out, will ya," Edward said, impatiently.

"Well, what if a girl don't wanna do this kinda work no more? Like, what if she wanted to go legit?"

"Are you sayin' you wanna quit?" Edward asked.

"Yeah," Loretta replied, studying a spot on the floor.

"No problem. I'll give you what I think is a fair cut of the money you earned and you're free to do anything you want. And that goes for the rest of ya too. I ain't forcin' nobody to do anything they don't wanna do. I'm no bastard like Rick," Edward replied.

"Well, gee, that's real swell of you, Eddie. I was thinkin' maybe I'd go back home to Pittsburgh, if my folks will have me," Loretta said, with relief.

"Okay. We'll work out the details when the meeting is over," Edward promised. Then, he scanned the group and said, "Anybody else wanna quit? Speak up now."

"Nah. I wouldn't know what else to do. Besides, the kind of joint you're talkin' about sounds interestin'," Katherine, a voluptuous bleached blonde commented. The remaining girls shook their heads in agreement.

"That's it then. Now, since, like you said, I am just a kid, I'm gonna need some adults besides my ma to front for me. If you'd be willin', Numbers, I'd like you to help with the books."

"My pleasure, Eddie," the short man replied, tipping his hat in reverence.

"And since you're the only businessman I know, I'd like you to be my advisor on how to run things, Sean," Edward said, turning to the ruddy faced barkeeper.

"No problem, kid. I like your spunk," Sean grinned.

"Then that settles it. Bricktop has already been scoutin' out suitable places. I'll let him fill ya in on the rest," Edward said, jumping back onto the table.

"Ahem, er, well, there's this nice lookin' brownstone up in Greenwich Village available and the rent ain't too bad. Me and Eddie figured it would be smarter to rent out the place first and then when we make some more dough, we'll just buy it. Oh, and we ain't gonna hafta worry about the cops or nothin'. I already paid off the ones who might give us some trouble."

"Yeah, and when some of them police big wigs and politicians start comin' to the place, we really won't have no trouble," Velma said, causing the group to burst into laughter.

"Are ya gonna be servin' food there, Eddie?" Petey asked.

"Yeah. Why?"

"Cause I was thinkin' maybe my ma could be in charge of that, considerin' what a good cook she is and all," Petey said, hopefully.

"Sure. Why not," Edward agreed. "If nobody has any more questions, I guess that's it for now. We'll meet again in a couple a days after me, my ma and Bricktop take care of all the paper work to rent the place. Then, we'll hire somebody to decorate it all fancy. In the meantime, you girls take some time off. I'm gonna give ya some money to fix yourselves up. Buy some nice clothes and get ya hair done. Oh, and everybody has to go to the doc and get checked out. I want our place to have a reputation for havin' clean, healthy girls."

With that, the meeting ended. The young women bubbled with excitement as they eagerly gathered around Edward to receive their "allowance." Edward blushed bright red when they each planted a grateful kiss on his cheek as they left.

"I really appreciate this, Eddie," Loretta said humbly when Edward handed her a wad of bills.

"Don't mention it. Good luck to ya. And if your folks don't wanna let you stay with them, you're always welcome to come back."

"Gee, that's so sweet of ya, Eddie," Loretta gushed, her eyes filling with tears. Edward quickly stepped back to avoid her emotional embrace.

* * * *

"I'm really proud of what you're doin', Eddie, and I'm sorry that I didn't defend you against Rick. I never thought he'd try something like that," Margaret said, regretfully, when mother and son were finally alone in the back room.

"Forget it. Anyway, I told ya everything would be okay, didn't I?" Edward grinned.

"Yes you did. And to be honest with ya, I didn't know how long I'd be able to keep workin' like that. I ain't been feelin' so good lately," Margaret admitted, tiredly.

"What's the matter?" Edward said, alarmed.

"I just don't have no energy anymore, that's all."

"Well, you don't have to worry about nothin'. You're gonna be the madam and that's it. Whenever ya get tired, you can just sit around and relax," Edward said, hugging her.

"That sounds good to me," Margaret smiled, playfully ruffling her son's hair. "That sounds real good."

* * * *

Having the group's full cooperation expedited the opening of his bordello. While his mother was in the middle of directing two burley furniture movers as to the exact placement of a large mahogany armoire in her spacious bedroom, Edward interrupted her.

"Hey ma, come here a minute. I got somethin' for ya," he said, mysteriously, gesturing for her to follow him to his room across the hall.

"What is it, Eddie?"

"Come and see," he replied, a mischievous look on his face.

Margaret shook her head in resignation and entered the room. She was astonished by what she saw placed on her son's bed. There lay the most beautiful short sleeved, pale pink linen dress she'd ever seen. It had a high-neck collar made of delicate, English lace. Tiny pearls sewn in an intricate design adorned the bodice, ending in a full skirt with a wide, creme colored satin bow around the waistband.

Neatly laid next to the dress was a wide-brimmed straw hat with matching ribbon, off-white kid-leather ankle boots, elbow length white cotton gloves and a white, lace clutch purse.

"Oh my God, Eddie," Margaret whispered as she bent over to caress the delicate fabric of the dress.

"Get dressed and meet me in the foyer. I ain't finished surprisin' ya yet," Edward grinned.

In a few minutes, it was his turn to be shocked as he watched his mother descending the long staircase to the foyer. Befitting her regal attire, Margaret held her head high and her back ramrod straight as she strode down the stairs. With Velma's assistance, her auburn hair had been styled into a french knot, topped with the elegant straw hat. Bright red lipstick and pale pink rouge enhanced her normally sallow complexion.

"So, what do you think, Eddie?" Margaret asked, as she pirouetted before him.

Edward was speechless. His mother looked just like the woman in the movie who had invaded his dreams for so many nights. She had come to life right before his eyes in the likeness of his mother.

"You're the most beautiful woman in the world," Edward declared.

"Well, you don't look so bad yourself," Margaret noted, nodding her head in approval at Edward's well-tailored, white, linen jacket and knickers. Over his freshly cut hair, he sported a navy blue cap, which he wore tipped to one side.

"So what are we all dressed up for?" Margaret asked.

"We're going on a picnic in Central Park," Edward grinned.

Just then, Petey's mother, Bridget, entered the room carrying a large picnic hamper.

"Here ya go, Eddie - Oh Maggie, you look so beautiful!" she cried.

"Thanks to my wonderful son," Margaret said, proudly.

"Only the best for my ma," Edward grinned. "Let's go," he said, and mimicking the gentlemen in the movie, he offered his arm to his mother and picked up the basket with his free hand.

"Thanks a million, Mrs. Mulcahey. We'll see ya later," Edward winked and the handsome couple stepped out to enjoy the bright spring afternoon.

* * * *

Later, mother and son sat on a blanket under a large oak tree, surrounded by the remnants of their gourmet luncheon, admiring the beauty of the park. Edward asked, "Are ya havin' fun, ma?"

Reaching over to take her son's hands, her eyes brimming with tears, she replied, "Eddie, this has been the most wonderful day of my life and I'll never forget it as long as I live. I love you with all my heart, son. Thank you."

"You're welcome," Edward said, softly, his voice quivering with emotion.

At that moment, in the their oasis in the park, little did they know just how short-lived their happiness would be.

CHAPTER III

By August of 1916, Edward Hastings had become one of the wealthiest seventeen-year-olds on the Lower East side. His new image was a far cry from his waft-like appearance of two years earlier. He had transformed himself into a miniature version of a prosperous entrepreneur.

The Hastings' establishment became the talk of the town. Politicians, wealthy businessmen, and other members of high-society made up the list of regular patrons.

Edward, Margaret, and Numbers were astonished when their average weekly profits exceeded one thousand dollars.

But not everyone in the city was pleased with the success of Edward's bordello, especially when he decided to diversify their services to include loan-sharking.

This, along with other unforseen events, would prove to be Edward's undoing.

Although she no longer worked as a prostitute, the years of substandard living continued to take their toll on Margaret Hastings' health. She tried her best to conceal her deteriorating condition from her son. But a blind man would have noticed her

The Eighth House
Karen Sealy

rapid weight loss and chronic cough.

When the bordello's in house physician grimly announced that the source of her failing health was tuberculosis, Margaret swore him to secrecy.

Edward was just returning with Petey from completing an errand across town when, on New Year's Day, 1917, Margaret Hastings finally succumbed to the ravages of the disease. It was Velma who had the misfortune of finding her lying face down in her bed, dressed in her favorite party gown.

"How can we tell Eddie?" Velma wept, surrounded by the other distraught workers at the bordello.

"I'll break the news to him when he gets back," Bridget volunteered, dabbing her tear-swollen eyes with her apron.

Edward's spirits were high when he and Petey bound up the front stairs two at a time later that afternoon. They had successfully completed the purchase of a brand new car from a local gangster.

"Come on, Eddie. Ya gotta let me drive it!" Petey begged.

"Yeah, after you learn how to steer without runnin' up on the sidewalk," Edward laughed.

"Hey, where is everybody?" he called out when they entered the unusually quiet brownstone.

"Something's happened, Eddie," Bridget said, stepping into the foyer from the parlor.

"What's wrong?" Edward asked, alarmed by her distressed manner.

"You'd better come upstairs with me," was all she said.

As Edward headed for the stairs, she whispered to her son, "Go get a bottle of scotch from the bar and bring it to Maggie's room."

"Why?"

"Don't ask questions. Just do it," she said, sternly.

A few minutes later, the bottle crashed to the floor on the landing outside Margaret's room when the sound of bone chilling

The Eighth House
Karen Sealy

sobs filled the house.

Bridget Mulcahey could only stand by helplessly in tears as she watched Edward Hastings weeping uncontrollably over the body of his beloved mother.

"Ma! Oh ma! You can't leave me ma!" Edward sobbed over and over again, clutching his mother's lifeless corpse in his arms.

"Bridget, ya gotta do somethin'! Ya gotta get the doctor!" Edward leaped from the bed, his face contorted, his eyes bulging.

"It's too late, darlin'. She's gone," Bridget wept.

"Noo! Noo! Edward sobbed and fell to his knees, clutching his stomach and rocking.

"Oh, Eddie, I'm sorry. I'm so sorry," Bridget knelt down and gathered Edward in her arms.

"What am I gonna do? What am I gonna do?" Edward wept as Bridget tried to console him.

"It'll be alright, Eddie. We'll take care of you. It'll be alright," she crooned.

Petey, who had been standing in the doorway, turned away in sorrow, trying to control the flow of his own tears.

* * * *

It was nearly twilight when Edward's crying finally dissipated. He sat in the semi-darkness by his mother's side watching over her like a sentry as she lay in her bed. The only sounds that broke the eerie silence were an occasional sniffle or sigh.

Edward's exhausted mind was having great difficulty accepting that the only woman he'd ever loved was gone. Why did this have to happen now, when, for the first time in her life she'd been truly happy?

He continued to sit in the darkness. His heart began beating rapidly and his hands shook uncontrollably when he realized that now he was completely alone in the world. Edward started hyperventilating when the terrifying truth took hold of him. He leaned over and hung his head between his legs, gasping for air.

When he finally regained his composure, he slid from the bed onto the floor. Kneeling down, he took his mother's hand in his, ignoring how cold and lifeless it felt within his, and whispered in a voice that sounded much younger than his seventeen years, "I'm scared, ma. I ain't got nobody now. What am I gonna do?"

And at that moment, Edward Hastings wished he could forfeit all his wealth and return to the days when he was living in poverty. At least then, she was still alive.

* * * *

For the next thirty days, out of respect for Margaret's passing, the bordello remained closed. During that time, Edward was only a shadow of his normally confident and happy-go-lucky self. His grieving was characterized by sudden fits of anger followed by bouts of weeping.

Bridget kept a watchful eye on him when she noticed his drastic mood swings occurring more frequently and with greater intensity.

"Somethin' ain't right with Eddie," Petey commented one day when he was alone with his mother in the kitchen.

"I know. He held up pretty well at the funeral. It seemed like he was gettin' better, but now I'm not so sure. It ain't healthy for him to fly off the handle at the drop of a hat like that," Bridget said, nervously.

"What can we do?" Petey asked, concerned for his friend.

"Let him know we love him and we're all here for him, I guess," Bridget replied.

"I'm not sure that's gonna be enough, ma. I'm gettin' this bad feeling that he's gonna blow one of these days," Petey said, pessimistically.

"Well, it's all we can do," Bridget sighed.

* * * *

Bridget and Petey had correctly judged the extent of Edward's mental instability. He couldn't stop thinking about all the terrible things that his mother had gone through during her short life; the circumstances that had led to her untimely death. His blood boiled at the thought of all the years she'd been subjected to Rick's exploitation. If only he could have intervened sooner, Edward kept berating himself. But how could he when he was only a kid and didn't have any power at the time?

When he was extremely depressed, he'd blame his mother for their plight. Why did she have to be a prostitute? Why didn't she try to find something else to do beside selling her body to any piece of shit who threw a couple of bucks at her? If she'd had a decent job, they could have lived like respectable citizens. Wasn't it a parent's responsibility to take care of the child? Because she decided to be a prostitute, he ended up having to take care of her.

His conflicting emotions caused him to feel guilty about criticizing her. He began to suffer from excruciating migraine headaches that often left him incapacitated. He also suffered from bouts of insomnia. On those nights when sleep eluded him, he would sit in his mother's room, listening to the tune on the gold music box he'd given her for Christmas. Over and over again, the melody, "In The Good Old Summertime," played until he would drop off to sleep, finally succumbing to his exhaustion.

Most of all, he resented the sympathetic glances his employees and friends directed toward him. Edward soon realized that if he didn't regain control of himself, he might have a complete breakdown.

Finally, he decided to stop wallowing in self-pity. After all, he had a business to run. Whether he liked it or not, Margaret was

The Eighth House
Karen Sealy

dead and he was on orphan. And now, he had to take care of himself.

Shortly after normal business activities resumed, the threat his success posed to other neighborhood gangsters finally culminated in the destruction of Edward's growing empire.

February 10, 1917, on what would have been Margaret Hastings thirty-second birthday, Johnny Downs, one of the Lower East Side's most successful loan-sharks, made his move. As Edward's direct rival, he encouraged a disgruntled police detective who had been unceremoniously ejected from Edward's bordello for roughing up one of the girls, to contact the State juvenile authorities. The lawman then informed them that a certain house of prostitution was being run by a recently orphaned minor named Edward Hastings.

Edward was arrested and remanded into the custody of the State until the age of twenty-one since he had no known living relatives. Bridget tried to claim she was Edward's next of kin, but since she couldn't provide any proof, her efforts were fruitless.

* * * *

A month later, Edward sat on the bed in his tiny dormitory room, trying to comprehend the barrage of unfortunate events that had caused his life to take such a devastating turn for the worse. One minute his pockets were bulging with money, he was running *a successful business and his future and that of his mother's seemed so bright.* The next, he was confined to a room no bigger than a closet, in an institution where he had less power than the cockroach that was crawling past his foot.

Sighing, he walked over to the tiny window in his room and stood on his bed for a peek at the outside world. The Maple Ridge Home for Boys was designed to blend in with the surrounding countryside. The stone, ivy covered buildings resembled a college campus, except for the fifty-foot fence that surrounded the property.

Edward's sparsely furnished room included a bed, small table, lamp, chair and a chest for his clothing. To amuse himself, he began playing with the electric lamp while he tried to formulate a plan of escape. There was no way in hell he was going to sit there until he turned twenty-one.

Clicking the light on and off, he was startled by a loud pop as the bulb blew out, plunging the room into darkness. Reaching blindly down into the shade, he grabbed the bulb and twisted it. As he gave it one final turn, attempting to release it from the socket, it slipped from his damp fingers and fell onto the desk. Without thinking, Edward relaxed his fingers and before he could pull them away in time, they touched the live socket.

The powerful surge of direct current traveled up his arm and Edward thrashed wildly back and forth in a death dance with the lamp. His body felt as if it were on fire and a acrid odor of burning flesh filled the room. Finally, both he and the lamp crashed to the floor. With one final shudder, his eyes rolled to the back of his head and he was plunged into the darkness of unconsciousness.

CHAPTER IV

When he finally regained consciousness, Edward found himself lying on a cool, marble floor. The room was completely dark except for a spotlight that beamed down on him as if he were an actor on stage about to recite his lines.

Relieved that the burning sensation he felt throughout his body had subsided, Edward slowly sat up and looked around. The blackness of the room prevented him from seeing anything, but he had the distinct feeling that he was being watched.

Edward's breath caught in his throat when, suddenly, a

figure wearing a blood-red cloak stepped forward out of the darkness and began slowly circling him. The man was a very imposing figure to behold at nearly seven feet tall, with a lean but powerful body.

"Hello, Edward." The man's deep voice reverberated throughout the room.

"Who are you?" Edward asked, suspiciously. He shaded his eyes with his hands so he could get a better look at the old man who towered over him. His features were sharp, but handsome, with grey, almost colorless eyes, ruddy complexion, and prominent nose. Thin lips above a neatly trimmed goatee, and a crown of thick, grey hair that hung to his shoulders enhanced his appearance.

Unknown to Edward, Satan had altered his appearance to resemble what he knew the boy imagined the devil would look like.

"Who the hell are you, I said," Edward repeated, boldly.

Satan motioned for Edward to get up.

"Who I am isn't important right now."

"Where am I?"

The devil ignored his question and continued scrutinizing Edward a few moments longer, idly stroking his goatee with his long, thin fingers. Then, he abruptly turned away, his robes swirling around him. The movement of his cloak stirred the acrid odor of sulfur that clung in the air. He took a seat on a large mahogany throne, the solitary piece of furniture that occupied the room.

"Let's just say you're somewhere between here and there," the devil finally replied when he was seated.

"Well, that don't make sense. Look, I wanna get outta here. This ain't funny," Edward said firmly, trying to sound tough.

"You'll understand soon enough, my son. Come here. I want to show you something. Then, we must talk."

"Son? Are you my father?" Edward frowned.

"In a way, yes," the devil replied. I am Satan and I've been watching you. And now it's time for you to become the man you were put on Earth to be. But first, look over there," the devil commanded, pointing to a spot on his right.

Suddenly, a square patch of light appeared out of the darkness. It resembled a movie screen, mysteriously suspended in midair. Edward continued to stare in awe as dark, fuzzy images began to solidify in the middle of the screen. When they finally came into focus, Edward was startled to see a figure that bore an uncanny resemblance to him, lying face down next to a broken lamp on the floor of the room he had previously occupied.

"Hey, that looks like me! I don't get it," Edward shook his head. His eyes were beginning to hurt from the brightness of the light.

"Yes, it is you. Keep watching," the devil said.

Edward continued to study the film in silence as two men in uniforms, who he immediately recognized as guards, rushed into the room and began shaking him. When he didn't respond, one of them slapped him twice across the face, causing Edward to involuntarily flinch at the sight of being struck.

When the boy's eyes slowly fluttered open, the guards roughly pulled him to his feet and threw him onto the bed. A few second's later, another man entered the room, cleaned up the mess and replaced the lamp with a new one. Then, the picture abruptly faded.

The film shown to him a few seconds later made Edward shiver and turn his head away in shame. What he observed was a slightly older version of himself, his face battered and bruised. He had been brutally gang raped in a shower by four other inmates. Then, in another scene, he docilely allowed himself to be sadistically sodomized by two guards with hideously leering faces.

"Why are you showin' this to me?" Edward demanded.

"So you'll have a better understanding of what I'm about to say," Satan replied and with a snap of his fingers, the "screen" and its disturbing images suddenly disappeared.

"You've enjoyed being rich and powerful, haven't you?" he then asked.

"Yes."

"And tell me, how did it make you feel when you shot Rick?"

"How do you know about that?" Edward was dismayed.

"You'd be surprised just how much I know about you, Edward," the devil smiled. "Now, tell me how you felt."

He paused and then said, "At first, scared. But later, like I was, was..." Edward frowned as he searched for the right word.

"Invincible? As if you ruled the world?" the devil suggested.

"Yeah. That's it. But that's all over now. I'm locked up in some stupid institution for babies," Edward, replied, bitterly.

"And you've just seen what will happen if you remain locked up."

"Yeah," Edward replied grimly and shuddered.

"Well, all that can change, Edward. But only if you're willing to fulfill your destiny."

"Oh yeah? What's in it for me and what do I gotta do?" Edward asked, suspiciously. He didn't trust this strange guy in the red cape.

"Oh, you could live forever, and have unlimited wealth and power. Everything a human could ever want," the devil replied with an indifferent wave of his hand.

"You gotta be kiddin' me," Edward shook his head in disbelief.

"Oh no. I'm very serious. That's what you were meant to have, my son, as long as you do exactly as I say," the devil replied, his voice dripping with sincerity. "But first you have to make a choice."

"Yeah? What?"

"You can choose to follow me or go to the light."

"What light? What are you talkin' about?" Edward was

puzzled.

"The light that will lead you to your Heavenly Father. Where you'll be forgiven for all the sins you've committed and can live in eternal peace and happiness," the devil said, with mock reverence.

"Yeah? Well, that sounds like a pretty good deal," Edward replied.

"Yes, it is, but, before that can happen, you'll have to be willing to forgive all the people who've hurt you, like your mother's pimp. Do you think you'll be able to do that?" the devil asked, slyly.

A vision of the night Margaret was savagely beaten by Rick flashed through his mind, stirring up all the anger and hatred he'd felt as if it happened yesterday.

"Nah. I ain't never forgivin' that sonofabitch for what he done to me and my ma," Edward said with conviction.

"And you have every right to feel that way. In that case, I have no doubt that you'll find my proposition rather appealing," the devil smiled.

"Okay," Edward said, sitting back down on the floor cross-legged. "Start talkin'. I'm all ears."

"Good," the devil nodded with approval. He leaned back in his chair, lacing his fingers together across his chest.

"In exchange for my granting you immortality, unlimited wealth, and extraordinary powers, you must be willing to carry out a series of special tasks for me," the devil explained.

"Yeah, like what?"

"For one thing, murder, which I'm quite sure you'll have no problem with since you've already done that, and quite successfully, I might add," the devil smirked.

"What else?"

"Oh, just creating general mayhem. I want you to do everything you can think of to contribute to mankind's misery and suffering. Starve them. Infect them with diseases that will have them begging for a swift death. Provoke them into committing acts of barbarism against each other. Destroy their cities and their homes until they're reduced to living like animals." The devil's face had turned demonic as he spoke, his features taunt and twisted, eyes dark and blazing.

"Batter their souls and spirits until they no longer have faith in that God they worship and believe will lead them to salvation. Once they're brought to their knees, I will have the power to control them and they will become my slaves," the devil shouted, pounding his fists on the arms of the chair, his deep voice thundering throughout the room.

Edward was both frightened and mesmerized by the raw power he was witnessing. He hoped this strange man never found a reason to direct his wrath toward him.

He waited a few seconds to allow him to calm down before he posed his next question.

"But why would I want to do that to people who ain't never done nothing to me?" he asked, innocently.

"Why? You ask me why?" the devil was incredulous. "Perhaps you haven't suffered enough to appreciate the value of what I'm offering you. Look over there," Satan commanded and once again, the mysterious screen reappeared.

This time, the scenes that flashed across it were even more horrific than before. Edward gasped as he watched a twenty-year-old Petey Mulcahey, his best friend, cut down by a barrage of machine gun fire from police officers as he walked down the steps of the brownstone. The attack was led by one the of detectives who'd received bribes from Edward on a regular basis in exchange for allowing the bordello to operate.

Next, was a scene of Petey's mother being burned alive when, in a drunken rage, her husband smashed her in the head with a lit kerosene lamp, causing her hair and nightgown to burst into flames.

This was followed by an even more harrowing image, in which a very young Margaret Hastings was being savagely raped by a drug-crazed john. Edward felt sick to his stomach and wanted to turn away from the grisly scene but found himself immobilized.

"Is that enough reason, Edward, or do you want more?" the devil snarled. "No. I think you need just a bit more convincing."

Before Edward could respond, a powerful force gripped his body, hurling him through the darkness. In a split second, he was back in the institution, lying naked on the floor of the communal shower with four burley youths standing over him.

"Get up, punk," a pockmarked-faced boy ordered, while another twirled what appeared to be a broom handle menacingly in front of him.

"Leave me alone! Get away from me!" Edward tried to crawl away from the group, slipping on the wet floor.

"Get him!" the burliest of the boys shouted. Two of them grabbed Edward's arms, dragging him over to a low tiled wall that separated the stalls. The wind was knocked from his lungs when they slammed him onto the partition, his arms and face dangling over the side.

Edward's kicking, flailing and shouting turned to screams and whimpers when the attack began. He had never experienced such agonizing pain. The beastly assault seemed go on forever. When the group had satisfied their depraved appetite, they proceeded to pummel their victim with fists and feet. Edward howled when the bones in his face shattered and his ribs cracked. Then, cackling with glee, the ruthless group swaggered away, leaving him battered, bloody and semi-conscious.

For what seemed like an eternity, Edward lay on the cold, concrete floor in a pool of blood, writhing and whimpering in agony. Then, as abruptly as before, the powerful force grabbed him once again, hurling him through space until he was lying in the middle of the spotlight on the marble floor.

"What you've just sampled is an omen. Fortunately for you, I can prevent that rather vivid attack you just endured. As for what happened to your mother, it was out of my hands. I also cannot interfere with the tragedy that will befall your friends.

"But," the devil said, getting up to kneel in front of Edward, "I can give you the power to avenge their deaths, my son. Does my offer appeal to you now?" Satan asked, cooly, one eyebrow raised.

"Yeah. Yeah. It does," Edward nodded, emphatically, still unnerved by that frighteningly realistic episode.

"Good. I thought you'd see it my way. Come, then. We have much to discuss," the devil said, rising and extending his hand to him.

The moment Edward's hand gripped his, the unholy alliance between the innocent boy and the Angel of Darkness was sealed.

CHAPTER V

"Welcome to Hell, Edward," the devil said when they stepped through a doorway that had magically materialized.

Edward was astonished as he surveyed the strange new world that existed beyond the dark room. One and two story stone Romanesque-styled structures appeared across the rocky terrain. Sporadic patches of trees and brush also dotted the landscape. He glanced upward and noticed that the cloudless sky was a pale yellow, although the sun was not visible.

Edward squinted and rubbed his eyes because the colors of objects didn't appear as vivid as the hues he was accustomed to seeing on Earth. He felt dizzy and took several deep breaths of the unusually dense air. As he inhaled, his nostrils were invaded by a sharp, pungent odor. He would later discover that the sulphur pits located on the outskirts of the city were responsible for the

The Eighth House

Karen Sealy

unfamiliar smell.

"Come, Edward. I'll give you a tour of your new home. But first, you'll need a change of wardrobe," the devil said. Edward was dumbfounded when his institutional overalls were magically replaced by a heavy cotton, beige, knee-length tunic, belted at the waist with a braided leather cord. His ill-fitting boots were transformed into leather sandals.

"Hey! Gimme back my old clothes. I ain't walkin' around in no dress like a sissy," Edward protested.

"Do *I* look like a sissy to you?" the devil challenged, opening his cape to reveal a similar outfit.

"Uh, no. I guess not," Edward admitted, reluctantly.

"Good. Now come. We'll converse as we tour," the devil motioned for Edward to walk beside him.

"I got one question for you," Edward said, craning his neck to look up at the huge man.

"I'm quite sure you'll have many more, but go ahead. Oh, and you may address me as 'father' since, for all intents and purposes, that is who I am to you."

"Okay, *father*," Edward said, slowly. The word sounded strange coming from his lips. "Anyway, if I'm here with you, what about the kid layin' on the bed in the dormitory?"

"He only represents your physical, earthly body. The force that makes you who you are, which is your spirit, is here now. Since you made the decision to join me, you'll no longer need that body. The guards at the institution will eventually return to check on you and find that you've died from your injuries. Then you'll be unceremoniously buried in an unmarked grave somewhere on the grounds of the institution," Satan explained.

"Geez. That's pretty depressing," Edward said, gloomily.

"Cheer up, my son. None of that really matters now. That was another time and another place. What's really important is that you'll finally become the man you were meant to be. You'll also be able to pick a new earthly body when you return there to do my work," the devil said, patting him on the back, affectionately.

By this time, they had reached a huge amphitheater. They climbed its steep, granite stairs until they reached a tunnel. When they passed through it, Edward was astonished by what he saw.

Hundreds of tunic-clad men and women of all races, colors and ages sat alone or in groups on the tiered seats of the sloping gallery. In the center of the oval arena at its lowest level, the ground was covered with dirt.

"What's this place? Who are those people?" Edward asked.

"This is where my recruits are re-educated and are later given an opportunity to test their newly acquired supernatural powers."

"You mean all them people are dead too?" Edward asked as he sat down next to the devil on one of the tiers.

"Yes. And like you, they've endured great suffering during their earthly lives and have come here because they seek revenge against their oppressors."

"Is that why you're here?" Edward was curious.

"In a way. My story begins many centuries ago," the devil began, as he removed his red cloak. It was warm under the strangely diffused, but still powerful rays of sun that beat down on them.

"Have you ever heard of angels?"

"Yeah. Some preacher guy used to come to the house to try to get my ma to 'change her ways and seek God's forgiveness and salvation', as he put it. He said she had succumbed to the temptations of the 'Angel of Darkness'. Then he'd start mumblin' something about the 'fires of hell' and how she was just the devil's pawn. Hey, I guess he was talkin' about you, huh?" Edward smirked.

"Yes, I suppose he was," Satan smiled. "But, that preacher was incorrect when he said your mother was my pawn. Whatever she did was by her own free will, just as you've chosen to be here now."

"So, what about this angel stuff?"

"Some of this may be difficult for you to comprehend right now, but eventually it will all make sense. Many centuries ago, before the Earth existed, I was, what is called, an archangel. An archangel is a very powerful spiritual entity that never possessed a human form or walked the Earth. I was a loyal follower of the Heavenly Father, the creator of the Universe and us."

"So, what happened?" Edward said, fascinated by the story.

"To put it simply, I dared to challenge his power and disobeyed him. Then, I chose to come here along with others who sided with me against him. Since then, I've been on a mission to build my own army to rise against him in the future."

The devil's expression had suddenly turned dark as he'd spoken. "And that is the vengeance I seek, Edward."

"Well, if you told Him you were sorry, would He let you go back?"

"Yes, but I have no desire to return. I prefer to remain here where I am in charge and have power and control over others," the devil replied, then, turning to face Edward, his strange, colorless eyes suddenly turning a dark brown, he said, "In time you will learn that the hunger for power is an insatiable one. Once you have it, you will never want to give it up."

"But, that is enough philosophy for now," the devil's mood brightened. "I want to introduce you to your teachers. You'll have to go through years of formal education before you will be given supernatural powers. To be successful on Earth, the mind, body and spirit must be fully developed."

Edward followed the devil as he descended the steps to join a group of men seated on a tier just above the arena.

"Good day, my lord," the men bowed their heads in homage.

"Good day, gentlemen. I would like to introduce you to one

of my newest recruits. His earthly name was Edward Hastings. Edward, this is Apollon, who has taken the name of the Greek god of the arts, sciences, reason and inspiration. He will be your science, writing and literature teacher."

The slightly built man with a shock of curly red hair and green eyes nodded politely at Edward.

"This is Thelonious. He is a master mathematician."

"Hello, Edward," the narrow-faced, bespeckled man said as he studied the boy intently.

"Next, we have Zachary whose specialty is languages."

"*Bonjour, buenas dias,* hello," he grinned, his chubby face aglow as he jumped from his seat and grabbed Edward's hand, shaking it enthusiastically.

"Calm down, Zachary," Satan reprimanded him.

"Sorry, my lord. It's just that it's been so long since I had such a young student," the man gushed.

"And if you don't stick to the task you've been assigned he'll be the last student you have," the devil warned, his eyes narrowing. Then, turning back to Edward, he said, "Your classes will begin tomorrow. For now, you'll spend the rest of the day with me. Good-bye, gentlemen."

Satan dismissed them and gestured for Edward to follow him through an adjacent passageway.

"A word of warning, Edward," the devil said as they left the amphitheater. "Pay attention and learn as much as you can from your teachers but always be on your guard with them. They were pathetic, sneaky little creatures when they were on Earth and are no different here. Apollon was a mass murderer with over sixty deaths to his credit before he was executed in a Greek prison. Thelonious' favorite past time was setting fires. He's responsible for a massive blaze that destroyed an entire city in India. And Zachary was imprisoned after having a brilliant career as a linguist because he couldn't control his sexual cravings for children. He committed suicide in prison after the inmates learned of his crimes and decided to give him a dose of his own medicine.

"Jeez," Edward shuddered, recalling what would have befallen him had he gone back to the institution.

"No one here can be trusted except for me, Edward. Everyone has committed some horrible crime against humanity and because of their obsession with vengeance and power, they chose to join forces with me."

"Ain't you afraid they might turn on you and try to take over?"

"No, because I've been wise enough not to bestow anyone with supernatural powers greater than my own. And for those who might think of trying to seize control from me, I have a little surprise for them. Come, I'll show you," the devil glowered.

They were silent as they carefully navigated the rocky terrain that surrounded the city. Edward's breathing became even more labored as he struggled to keep up with the devil. He also noticed the strange odor in the air had suddenly become more intense.

When they finally reached the top of a steep hill, the land suddenly fell away into a deep, dark pit. Molten lava bubbled and steamed, releasing superheated sulfur filled vapor into the air. Edward gagged from the stench and his eyes burned.

"This is where those who dare to challenge me end up. So far, only a hundred or so people have been condemned to these eternal fires."

"But if they're already dead, what difference does it make?" Edward wheezed, tears running down his cheeks.

"The difference, my son, is that although the earthly body dies, the spirit lives on forever. The men who plotted against me are very much alive down there. It's just that they're not visible to the untrained eye. Take my word for it, they're in there. Aren't you, my pathetic souls?" the devil shouted sardonically into the crater. The response was a chorus of high pitched wails that echoed against the walls of the chasm.

Edward shivered.

"I think you've seen enough for now. Let's return to my palace. Are you hungry?"

"Not really even though the last time I ate must have been, gee, I don't know," Edward frowned.

"Approximately seven years ago, in Earth time; three hours our time," the devil explained and chuckled at the surprised look on Edward's face.

"I know. It seems crazy, doesn't it? But as I said before, in time, it will all make sense. You'll also find that the spirit doesn't require the nourishment that the body did. You may wish to indulge in a meal occasionally, though, because the spirit can still appreciate the pleasurable sensation a good meal arouses."

"Sounds good to me," Edward agreed.

When they reached the building where Edward had first made his unexpected entrance into Hell, he noticed that it was a large, four story, rotunda-shaped marble structure. As they stood outside, once again, the doorway magically appeared and he followed the devil inside.

The inky blackness of the interior had been replaced by a brightly lit room with a soaring sixty-foot high, domed ceiling. A better educated Edward would have recognized that Satan's residence was a smaller scaled replica of the Sistine Chapel in Rome. In the center of the enormous room was the devil's impressive solid mahogany throne which stood atop a gleaming, black marble base.

Along the perimeter of the circular structure was a series of solid bronze doors. Whereas the real Sistine Chapel was decorated with paintings, tiled murals, tapestries and statues with religious themes, the motif within these walls depicted raging battles and images of an obviously erotic nature. One statue in particular, which was an explicitly graphic reproduction of a couple in the throes of copulation, made Edward blush.

"Follow me, my son," the devil directed him and opened one of the heavy bronze doors to the left of the main entrance.

"Wow! Edward cried when he stepped into the room. Placed on a long, dark oak table lined with red velvet high backed chairs, was a gourmet feast of which he'd never seen before. The tantalizing aroma of roasted pork, beef, and chicken made his mouth water in spite of his earlier declaration of not being hungry. The roasts were accompanied by platters of fresh vegetables, potatoes and pasta. Edward's eyes grew wide when he spotted plate after plate of pastries at the far end of the banquet table.

"Sit here, Edward," the devil smiled, amused by the boy's reaction to the feast presented to him. "My wife will be joining us shortly."

Edward sat in the chair to the left of the devil who had seated himself at the head of the table.

"Go ahead and eat, don't be shy," the devil said and Edward began frantically piling his plate with food.

"May I offer you a beverage? I have water, wine, and spirits," the devil asked, playing the role of the perfect host.

"Maybe I'll try some of that wine," Edward decided, and the devil reached over to fill his silver goblet.

Edward took a cautious sip and immediately broke into a broad grin, nodding his head in approval. "This stuff sure tastes better than that crap we had at the bordello."

"That's because I only offer the best to my favorite guests," the devil replied, graciously.

As Satan relaxed in his chair, pleased with Edward's enthusiastic consumption of his meal, a door behind them opened.

Edward froze. Slack-jawed, his mouth stuffed with food and his fork paused in midair, he gawked at the woman who had just entered the room.

"Edward, I'd like you to meet my wife, Angelica." The devil stood, extending his hand to his mate.

Edward was rendered speechless at the sight of the raven-haired, statuesque, creature who stood before him. Her wavy tresses hung below her shoulders, hair that framed an oval shaped face with hazel, heavy-lidded eyes. Blood-red, full, sensuous lips held a pleasant expression as they were introduced.

"It's a pleasure to meet you, Edward," she said, reaching across the table to shake his hand. Standing up, he hastily dropped his fork and wiped his hand on his tunic before extending it. He was impressed with the firm grip from the slender, well-manicured hand.

"Me, me too," Edward stammered. When she reached across, he was afforded a clear view of her perfectly round, large breasts that threatened to tumble out of her revealing royal blue silk gown. Because of its snug fit, she probably wasn't wearing anything under it, Edward surmised. Then, he was horrified to discover that his less than virtuous observation had resulted in a very conspicuous arousal which protruded from beneath the fabric of his tunic.

Both Satan and his wife struggled to suppress the urge to laugh at the young boy's embarrassing predicament.

Edward's face was flushed as he abruptly sat down.

"I hope everything is to your liking and my husband hasn't been talking you to death, Edward," Angelica said, playfully.

"Uh, no ma'am. Everything is great," Edward replied, eagerly.

"So, tell me about yourself," Angelica said, as she accepted a goblet of wine from her husband.

During the rest of the meal, Edward engaged in casual conversation with the unusual couple. For a few hours, he actually forgot where he was and the tumultuous events that led to his new existence.

"Boy, am I stuffed," Edward declared when he'd swallowed the last piece of chocolate cake on his plate.

"Good. I think it would be wise for you to rest now. You've

had a long day," the devil suggested, rising from the table. Edward was startled when a man mysteriously appeared through one of the doors behind Satan.

"Joshua will show you to your room. When you've been properly trained, you'll find that your spirit won't need as much sleep as it did when it resided within your earthly body. But, that will come later. I will come and get you when I think you've had sufficient rest," Satan said. And to Edward's surprise, the devil reached down to give him a firm hug.

"I'm very happy you've finally come to me, my son. I have many plans for you. Good-night."

"Good-night, father," Edward replied, meekly, overwhelmed by this sudden expression of affection.

"Pleasant dreams, Edward," Angelica said, patting his arm as he walked by.

"Thanks for everything. I'll see ya later, I guess," Edward said and followed the man through the door.

Satan returned to his chair and sat back, stroking his chin as the heavy bronze door slammed shut with a thud.

"I think I've found the right man, my love," he said, confidently shaking his head.

"Perhaps you have, my dear. Perhaps you finally have," Angelica agreed.

* * * *

Edward was treated to another surprise when he entered his room and discovered that it was an exact replica of his bedroom at the bordello.

He sat on the side of the familiar bed and sighed as he removed his sandals. His head was spinning with unanswered questions. He was still having difficulty accepting everything that had happened to him since he "died". But for now, he'd just sleep and wait to see what tomorrow would bring.

His slumber was dreamless and restful.

Unfortunately, his young, inexperienced mind didn't have the capacity to understand the enormity of the agreement he'd unwittingly made with the Prince of Darkness. But, it was too late. For better or worse, his fate had been sealed.

CHAPTER VI

Edward's nap was interrupted a few hours later by a light tapping on the door.

"Time to get up, my son. I'll meet you in the throne room," Satan announced through the door.

"Okay," Edward replied and yawned, sleepily.

When he pushed back the covers to get up, what he saw beneath them made him cry out, "Holy smokes!"

Besides the fact that he was completely naked, somehow, while he had been sleeping, his five-foot seven inch, seventeen-year-old body had been miraculously replaced by that of a six-foot one inch, fully matured physique.

He scrambled over to the full length mirror behind the door for a better look. He was very pleased with the adult version of his old self and arrogantly strutted in front of the mirror like a proud peacock. But the question remained, how did he get that way?

When it occurred to him that his old tunic would no longer fit, he opened the adjacent closet in search of new clothing. He was relieved to discover several adult-sized tunics and pairs of sandals.

A few minutes later, his entrance into the throne room was met with enthusiastic applause from the devil.

"You look absolutely dashing, Edward. I take it you're satisfied with your new earthly image," the devil smiled, motioning for Edward to turn around.

"Yes," Edward said, surprised at the deep timbre of his adult voice.

"Good. It was necessary for me to accelerate your rate of maturity to aid you in fully absorbing the studies that you are about to undertake."

"Wow. This is really something," Edward grinned.

"I may make some minor, final adjustments to your appearance just before I send you back to Earth, but for now, we must concentrate on your mental development. Your instructors are waiting for you at the amphitheater. When you're done for the day, we'll have a meal together and you can tell me how things went," the devil said.

"Okay. I'll see ya later, then. And thanks. Thanks for everything," Edward replied with sincerity and left the rotunda.

* * * *

On his way to the amphitheater, he passed a few tunic-clad individuals who nodded pleasantly as he walked by. A few very attractive women also tossed approving glances in his direction, causing him to walk a little taller.

When he entered the amphitheater, Apollon was waiting for him where they'd met earlier.

"Hello, Edward. How are you this fine day?" his teacher called out as he made his way down the steps to the tier where he was sitting.

"Great. So what's with this school stuff? Do I get homework and all that?" Edward asked as he sat down.

"Yes. My methods are similar to what you would experience in an earthly school, except that the curriculum will be more difficult. Since, from what I've been told, you've only had a third grade education, we'll take things slowly. I'm confident that with your natural intelligence you'll do just fine," Apollon assured him.

"Why do I need to learn all this stuff anyway?" Edward asked a few minutes later when he'd scanned through his new textbooks.

"Because you'll want to be able to move about confidently as you carry out Satan's work when you return to Earth. The best way to accomplish that is by having the ability to assimilate yourself into any environment. You're already accustomed to a, how should I say, "simpler" way of life. So, now we will teach you how to conduct yourself as an educated gentleman would," Apollon explained.

"Okay. If you say so," Edward agreed and his first lesson commenced.

Two hours later, Edward rubbed his temples in exhaustion. His head was spinning from all the data he'd been expected to remember.

"I admit it's a lot for you to absorb but I think you did splendidly," Apollon beamed. "Now, I'm going to give you an assignment to complete on your own and we'll go over it tomorrow. Have a good day." The instructor then handed Edward a notepad and his books.

"I don't know about all of this," he muttered under his breath as the teacher walked away. In a few seconds, the empty spot was filled by Thelonious.

"Geez, don't I even get a break in between?" Edward complained when the teacher immediately handed him a thick textbook.

"I'm afraid not, my boy. In this world, time is of the essence. Please turn to page three and we'll begin with simple arithmetic," Thelonious instructed, briskly.

Sighing, Edward conceded that this was an unavoidable part of his agreement with the devil and threw himself into his work.

He was startled when the teacher suddenly announced that

the class was over. It was surprising how quickly the two hours had passed.

Edward took a moment to look around the arena and stretch his legs before he began his final class of the day. He noticed quite a few other students who he guessed were close to his age and wondered if he would have an opportunity to meet them.

"My goodness, Edward. You look wonderful!" Zachary's high pitched voice behind him interrupted his thoughts.

Yeah, right. You're probably disappointed I ain't no little kid anymore, you weasel. Edward smirked, recalling what the devil had said about the little man.

"Well, now. Are you ready to tackle the challenges of the spoken word?" Zachary said, making a production of arranging the text books between them.

"Yeah, I guess so."

"Good. Before we undertake the multitude of languages I've been instructed to teach you, first, we'll have to refine your somewhat colorful use of English."

"Oh yeah? What's wrong with it?" Edward asked, indignantly.

"Nothing, if you plan on returning to your old neighborhood and staying there. But, as I've been told, you'll be involved in some activities that will require extensive world travel and it's important that you be able to converse eloquently. Don't worry, when we're done, you'll still have the ability to switch back to your natural manner of speaking. *The trick is to be able to switch at will.*"

Leaning forward in a conspiratorial manner, Zachary then whispered in a gravely voice, "Between you and me, kid, I'm originally from da Bronx," and they both laughed.

"You're going to find that perfect diction can open many doors for you, Edward. Mark my words. Oh, I think I made a joke. 'Mark my words', get it?" the man chuckled with delight and Edward shook his head in amusement.

When the session was finally over, Edward had to admit that he enjoyed the sound and feel of the strange new words as they rolled off his tongue. He strolled along the road back to the palace and continued to practice.

* * * *

"So, tell me about your day, Edward," Satan said as they lounged in the shade under a patch of trees that surrounded a small lake later that day.

"Well, at first, it was kinda, um, I mean, I was a bit overwhelmed at first but now I'm looking forward to attending my classes," Edward said, pleased with his ability to correct himself.

"Splendid. With your natural intelligence as well as physical maturity, I predict that you should be able to complete your education within the next two days. Think of it, Edward; fifteen years of schooling in just two days!"

"No kiddin'? I mean, yes, that is amazing," Edward grinned.

"I think you'll be very pleased with your graduation present too," the devil said, mysteriously.

"What is it?" Edward was intrigued.

"Oh, just a little something that only a healthy, virile young man such as yourself can truly appreciate," the devil winked.

* * * *

The successful completion of Edward's formal education was marked by an informal party attended by his benefactor and his wife, along with other graduates and their instructors. The gathering was held in a garden adjacent to a patio at the rear of palace.

Edward was excited when he was finally able to mingle with his peers. He listened with interest as they described their earthly lives and how they became allies of Satan. Some were products of humble beginnings similar to Edward's, while others were the offspring of wealthy families.

All conversation abruptly ended when Satan climbed onto a low bench to speak.

"I would like to take this moment to congratulate all of you on your successful completion of the first phase of your training. Please give yourselves a round of applause. You deserve it," the devil said, scanning the sea of happy faces with pride.

"I know all of you are anxious to begin the next part of your education; when I endow you with your supernatural powers and you are given an opportunity to test them. But before that, you will be granted a few days of rest and relaxation. Amuse yourselves in whatever ways you please."

This comment was met with cheers and applause.

"Now, I would like to offer a toast," the devil said, reaching down to take a silver goblet from Angelica.

"To my beloved subjects and children. May your intelligence, loyalty and devotion lead to the successful destruction of humanity and the Kingdom of Heaven!"

"Cheers!" the group lifted their cups in salute.

"You may return to your rooms now where you'll each find a little gift that was specifically chosen for you. Enjoy yourselves and we will meet again at the amphitheater in two days," the devil concluded and as he stepped down from his position, he motioned for Edward to join him.

"I've given you an extra special surprise, my son. Have a good time," Satan beamed, his arm around Edward's shoulders as they strolled back into the palace.

Edward was as excited as a child on Christmas Eve when he hurried to his room. When he turned on the light, he didn't see anything unusual until he looked to his left. Reclining casually on the green velvet chaise lounge was a beautiful auburn haired woman.

"Hello Edward. I was wondering how long you were going to keep me waiting," the woman said, provocatively adjusting the edge of her red, silk robe that had slipped open, revealing a very shapely leg.

"Who are you?" Edward asked, stepping closer to her.

"I'm Jessica, your graduation present. I'm also here to teach you a few things I'm quite sure weren't a part of your formal education," she purred as she sat up. Edward began to perspire as her cat-like green eyes slowly scrutinized him from head to toe, lingering at his groin.

"Come closer. Don't be shy," she gestured. Edward obeyed, docilely.

"You're quite a handsome young man, Edward," she said and she stood up, her body only inches from his. "And so tall and muscular," she added, slowly caressing his bare arm.

Edward, who was in a trance as the woman's warm, sweet breath tickled his face, suddenly snapped out of it when Jessica's hand boldly slid under his tunic and made its way up to his groin.

"Mmm. Very interesting, she smiled as she fondled him. "I've been told that you ran a successful bordello when you were on Earth. Is that true?"

"Um, er, yes," Edward panted, beads of perspiration trickling into his eyes. His legs felt weak as the speed and intensity of her stroking increased.

"Then, you should be quite an experienced lover," she continued, purposely ignoring Edward's obvious distressed state of arousal.

"Nah. No. Not really," he stammered.

"You're a *virgin*? I can't believe it!" Jessica cried, throwing her head back in a hearty laugh. She stopped in mid-chuckle and said, "Oh dear," when Edward unexpectedly climaxed.

"Tsk, tsk. We'll have to do something about that," she shook her head, examining her damp, sticky hand.

"Take your clothes off. We have a lot of work to do," she ordered, pushing him onto the bed.

Before he could react, Edward found himself lying naked on his bed watching in anticipation as Jessica stripped off her robe and straddled him with her powerful thighs.

"Pay attention, Edward. There will be a test when the first lesson is over," she snickered and leaned over to smother his startled lips with her juicy, sensuous mouth.

For the next hour, Edward indulged in a variety of erotic activities he'd only vaguely heard discussed by the prostitutes at the bordello. When Jessica finally rolled off the bed to put on her robe, he could only continue to lie on the disheveled, sweat-drenched sheets, panting and exhausted.

"You just relax, Edward, while I get us some refreshments," Jessica said, stopping a moment to stroke his bare thigh with her long fingernails.

"Hurry back," Edward called out, lifting his head to enjoy the sight of her swaying, ample hips as she walked out of the room.

Jessica's expression turned serious as she stepped into an adjoining room where Satan was waiting for her.

"He seems to be a very willing student," the devil smirked, as the young woman joined her master in front of a two way mirror. Unknown to Edward, his earlier sexual activity had been fully observed by the devil.

"Yes. And by the next session, I should have him completely wrapped around my finger," Jessica agreed.

"Good. When you return, I want you to begin to tap into his subconscious guilt and hatred for his mother. I want to cultivate that rage into the driving force behind his hunger for revenge. He's still too complacent to properly carry out the tasks I plan on assigning him," the devil instructed, solemnly.

"Don't worry. I know exactly what to do," Jessica reassured

the devil and left.

As he continued to secretly observe Edward while he waited patiently for Jessica's return, Satan was confident that before he was given his supernatural powers, Edward would be a willing and cooperative ally. The young man was unaware that the pleasurable feelings his sexual experiences aroused were more intense than they would be if he still possessed a real, physical body. Upon his return to Earth, Edward would spend many years indulging in a multitude of casual and sometimes dangerous sexual liaisons in a futile attempt to recreate those unearthly sensations.

* * * *

When they had revived themselves with several goblets of wine, it was Edward's turn to play the dominant sexual role. He was rather pleased with his newly developed sexual prowess as he listened to Jessica's repeated cries of pleasure. In reality, he was now a victim of the same theatrics he'd found so amusing when performed by his mother when she was servicing a john.

"Oh, Edward, your mother taught you well," Jessica said slyly, watching through half-closed lids for Edward's reaction to her words.

"What did you say?" Edward's voice grew cold as he stared down at Jessica who was lying beneath him.

"I said, your mother taught you well. Didn't you watch her while she was working?" Jessica repeated, innocently.

"Oh course not!" Edward was incredulous.

"Well, weren't you ever tempted to find out why so many johns were willing to pay to have sex with her?" Jessica persisted.

"No!" Edward shouted, moving over to sit on the edge of the bed.

"There's nothing wrong with being curious, Eddie, considering you were only a child," she whispered softly in his ear.

"No. You don't understand. It wasn't like that. It wasn't any of my business," Edward shook his head adamantly.

"Come on, Eddie. You can tell me the truth. No one here is interested in judging you," Jessica urged him as she gently stroked his back.

Edward was silent, and then, his voice barely above a whisper, he said, "Well, there was one time when I was running the bordello."

"What happened?" Jessica coaxed him.

"It was a few months after we first opened. Some guy came to see her. I told him that she wasn't working anymore but he said if I told her who he was, she would make an exception," Edward began, his voice distant as the scene played in his mind.

"I didn't believe it but he was right. When I told her some guy named Nathan wanted to see her, she got all excited and told me to bring him up to her room right away."

"I was curious as to why she was so eager to see this guy, so after they were in the room together for awhile, I went upstairs and listened outside the door. At first, they were just talking and then when it got quiet, I peeked through the keyhole to see what was going on."

"And what did you see, Edward?"

Edward's back suddenly stiffened and his face grew taunt as he spoke.

"They were both naked and he was begging her to let him do it the way he always liked it. The next thing I know, my mother is climbing onto the bed on all fours and he's grabbing her ass, pumpin' her like there was no tomorrow. But the worst part was the look on her face. I could see it 'cause she was facin' the door. She looked like she was in heaven. Like she really enjoyed the way that bastard was doing it to her like she was some fuckin' dog," Edward said, bitterly, his speech momentarily reverting to its old pattern.

"How did that make you feel?" Jessica asked, quietly.

"What the hell do you mean how did it make me feel? It made me mad! I wanted to bust in the room and beat the shit outta the two of them!" Edward shouted, jumping up from the bed.

"But why, Edward? Surely you knew your mother enjoyed what she was doing. How else could she have been a whore all her life?" Jessica asked.

"Don't say that!" Edward spun around, his eyes blazing.

"Oh grow up, Eddie. Your mother was a whore because she wanted to be and you were naive enough to believe all that crap she told you about being a prostitute because she didn't know any other way to earn a living. She made a fool out of you whether you like it or not," Jessica shouted, cruelly.

"Shut up, you stupid bitch! You shut up!" Edward yelled, shaking his fist at her menacingly.

"I won't shut up. It's time for you to hear the truth so you can stop acting like a child and be a real man. Your mother was a slut who was an expert at doing everything we just did the past four hours. Those johns were willing to pay any amount of money to be with her because she never refused to accommodate them, no matter how disgusting or humiliating the act was. She loved every minute of the attention she got from those men and the power she had over them!"

"Stop it! Shut up!" Edward roared, clamping his hands over his ears in agony.

"But wait, Eddie. It gets better. Do you know who that man *was who she was so eager to see?* He was *your father*, Eddie. Nathan Styles was your father and she didn't even have the decency tell you!" Jessica shouted, grabbing Edward's hands and jerking them away from his ears.

"No. It couldn't have been," Edward shook his head wildly. "She would have told me. She knew I wanted to meet him. Why didn't she tell me?" Edward's voice shook as tears began streaming down his face.

The Eighth House

Karen Sealy

"Because the sad, ugly truth about your precious mother is that Margaret Hastings was a selfish whore who didn't give a damn about her beloved son. She did what she did because it made her feel good and she didn't care how you felt or what you wanted. And, it's about time you knocked her off that stupid pedestal you've had her on all your life and faced the truth. If you don't, you'll never be a real man, Eddie. You'll just be a sniffling little baby crying over his dead mommy," Jessica shouted, viciously.

Edward lunged at her so quickly, she didn't have time to brace herself against the blow that landed squarely on her right jaw, instantly knocking her onto the bed.

"If you don't shut up, I swear I'll kill you, you lyin' bitch," Edward's face was twisted with rage as he threw himself on top of her and grabbed her by the throat.

"I hate you, you bitch! I hate you! You lied to me! You said you loved me but you lied to me!" His hands squeezed tighter and tighter around Jessica's neck as she gasped for air, helplessly pounding her small fists against his chest.

"Go ahead, Edward. Let your hatred come to the surface. Feel the power in your soul. Think of how she and all the others have betrayed you. Think of the ways you can avenge your pain. Let the venom consume you," Satan urged, standing directly behind Edward.

"I'll get them! I'll kill them all! They have to pay for what they did to me. They're gonna pay!" Edward snarled.

Satan allowed Edward's savage outburst to continue for a few more minutes before placing the palm of his hand against the back of the head of the out of control man. He was instantly rendered unconscious and fell limply onto the floor.

Jessica rubbed her badly bruised neck and jaw as they slowly returned to their normal color. In a few seconds, all traces of the brutal attack had miraculously disappeared.

"You've done an excellent job, my dear. You may go now,"

Satan said, dismissing her.

Jessica retrieved her robe and left the room.

"Life is very cruel, my son," the devil said as he picked Edward up from the floor and gently laid him on the bed, covering him with a blanket. "But this had to be done in order for you to grow stronger. In time, you will come to thank me for this."

Satan took a moment to gaze sadly at his protege one last time before turning to leave the room.

Edward would remain in his unconscious state for most of the next day. When he finally did awaken, he would find that the Edward Hastings who still possessed the ability to forgive, in spite of his difficult childhood, was truly dead forever.

CHAPTER VII

"So, Edward, are you ready?" the devil asked.

"Yes, father."

Satan was pleased with the man who stood before him in the center of the arena. The normally pleasant, handsome face had been replaced by more severe and subtly cruel features as a result of the previous day's revelations.

"Good. Now, close your eyes and focus on the inner core of your body. Breathe deeply. Don't allow anything around you to filter through. If you do, the force of the electricity will be painful," the devil instructed.

Edward followed his instructions and closed his eyes. As he concentrated on slowing down his breathing, he pictured what he imagined to be a small, black box in the middle of his abdomen. In his mind's eye, the box rotated on its edge like a square-shaped top.

Satan approached Edward and carefully poked his arm with the tip of a small dagger. His failure to respond was the proof the devil needed that Edward had reached the level of deep consciousness that was required.

The devil then stepped back about thirty feet from Edward. Raising his arm, he pointed his long, thin finger directly at the man's head. His eyes narrowed. Suddenly, the sky grew unusually dark and a strong wind began to blow, swirling the dust on the arena's floor around their legs.

A loud boom followed by a crackling sound bounced off the walls of the arena when a blinding streak of light flashed from the tip of the devil's outstretched finger, striking Edward in the forehead.

On impact, Edward's body remained rigid but his temperature increased at an alarming rate, causing him to immediately perspire profusely. The strong stench of sulfur radiated from his skin.

In a few seconds, the winds subsided and the sky returned to its normal pale yellow.

Edward's eyes snapped open and he took a deep breath.

"How do you feel?" the devil asked, walking toward him.

"There's a tingling sensation in my skin and I'm hot," Edward said, his pulse racing.

"Good. That means the transformation was successful. Now we must test your new ability to manipulate electricity. I want you to close your eyes and focus all your energy inward again. When you feel a powerful force rising from deep within your gut, open your eyes and point to the white circle on that rock," Satan instructed.

When Edward felt a powerful energy force wash over his body, he opened his eyes and pointed. He was shocked when a flash of light suddenly shot from the tip of his finger, striking the dirt next to the rock and knocking him to the ground in the process.

"Don't worry, my son. It will get easier with practice. Come, try again," the devil chuckled, helping Edward up from the ground.

Edward closed his eyes again and this time when he felt the surge of energy, he narrowed his focus directly onto the white spot on the rock. Just before the streak of light exploded from his finger, he planted his feet firmly on the ground in preparation for the recoil.

This time, the bolt landed squarely in the middle of the target, causing a spray of rock chips at the point of impact.

"Bravo, Edward. Now, try again," the devil applauded.

With each attempt, Edward's aim and control improved along with his confidence.

"I have another target for you to practice on. I'm quite sure you'll find it to be very enjoyable but that will come later. Next, we must work on your ability to move objects by telekinesis. The energy you'll be using is similar to what you need to control the molecules of electricity but a little less of it."

"Close your eyes again and focus on a point deep within your brain," the devil directed. "Try to imagine the object that you want to move as it rises. Alright. Now, look at the rock again."

Edward stared at the singed piece of granite until his eyes began to water from the strain.

"Shit. I can't do it," Edward swore in frustration, shaking his head.

"Don't give up so easily. Try again and this time, you must not only see the object but try to imagine its weight and texture. Go ahead," the devil prompted.

Edward repeated the ritual. He was about to give up when suddenly, the medium-sized rock quivered and began to rise. He held his breath in anticipation as it slowly rose higher and higher into the air until it was about ten feet above the ground.

"Hold it, Edward. Hold it...Steady... Okay. You may release it now," the devil said and the rock crashed back onto the ground with a thud.

"Very good, my son. Very good," the devil patted Edward on the back. "Just keep practicing on different kinds of objects and it will get easier. Let's move on to changing your appearance at will. You'll find this one very amusing," the devil said. He strode over to retrieve a two foot mirror that was propped against a wall.

"The secret of this trick is to be able to bring yourself to the point of actually feeling like the person you want to turn into. The spirit has the ability to adopt the persona of all possible earthly bodies regardless of race, color, sex or physical attributes. Just focus inward and give it a try. To make it easier, I'll give you some examples."

When Edward was focused, the devil said, "Okay. This is an easy one. Try to transform yourself back into your ten year old body."

Edward smiled and pictured how he looked as a child. Then, looking into the mirror, he was amazed when, in a few seconds, his features began to soften and his height slowly diminished. When the transformation was complete, he was struck by an unexpected wave of sadness at the sight of the innocent little boy he'd once been.

"Very good. Now transform yourself into a very attractive woman," the devil instructed.

The image he immediately conjured up was that of the woman in the silent film he'd seen as a child.

Satan chuckled as Edward's boyish image began to elongate and develop provocatively shaped breasts and hips.

"You have excellent taste, my son," the devil smiled when the image stabilized.

Satan dictated a variety of images for the next few minutes until Edward was able to perform the change instantaneously.

"I told you it would be easy. The spirit is very flexible when not confined to a permanent earthly form. There's just one more exercise I'd like you to run through and then we'll end for the day," the devil said. Then, he turned to shout up at the mouth of a tunnel to their right.

"You can bring him out now," the devil instructed.

Edward's expression turned to one of shock and then anger when he spotted two men dragging a very reluctant man by the arms down the steps to the arena.

"Well, well. Fancy meeting you here you sonofabitch," Edward snarled into the face of his mother's former pimp, Rick.

"Geez, Eddie. You're all grown up now, ain't ya," Rick said, meekly, his eyes darting back and forth nervously beneath long, greasy black hair that hung over his forehead.

"Yeah, you piece of shit. And now I'm gonna finish what I started back at the house," Edward threatened, clenching his fists in preparation to punch Rick in the jaw.

"Not so fast, Edward. Why resort to such primitive methods of fighting when you can use this opportunity to test one of your very effective supernatural powers," the devil goaded him.

"Yeah, huh. I could use a little more practice," Edward smirked.

"Release him," the devil commanded and the two men let go of Rick.

"Start running while you can you skinny little prick," Edward said, a sadistic smile on his face.

"Aw come on, Eddie. Gimme me a break. You already killed me once!" Rick pleaded as he backed away.

"And obviously, you didn't have enough sense to stay that way, you dumb fuck," Edward yelled at the retreating figure of the gaunt man, his tunic flapping wildly around his body.

"Concentrate, Edward. Concentrate. Sometimes you may only get one chance," the devil cautioned.

Edward took a deep breath and extended his arm. In a split second, a bolt of electricity shot from his finger. It struck Rick in the middle of his back, the force of it hurling him into the air.

Rick cried out in agony when he slammed back onto the ground.

"Please, Eddie. I'm beggin' ya. Please don't hurt me. I'm sorry I did all that stuff to you and your ma," Rick whimpered, pathetically.

"Ah, so you ain't so tough now, are you? Get up, you piece of shit. Get up and take it like a man," Edward shouted, savoring the heady feeling of revenge and power that surged through him.

He raised his arm again as Rick frantically tried to crawl out of range. The next bolt struck him on the legs, followed immediately by another that caused his tunic to burst into flames.

Rick's tormented cries fell on deaf ears as Edward watched the man he'd despised all his life frantically trying to beat out the fire that consumed his body.

On the devil's signal, the two men ran into the tunnel to get two water-filled buckets and tossed them on the burning man.

"I think Edward is satisfied now. You can dump our pathetic target into the sulfur pits. He's no longer of any use to me," the devil instructed.

* * * *

"Now do you understand what I meant when I told you how satisfying and addictive power can be, Edward?" the devil asked as they sat at the long dining room table later that evening.

"Yes I do, father. And it's a good feeling," Edward agreed, taking a sip of wine.

"As good as sexual intercourse?" the devil asked, slyly.

"Well, I don't think it would be fair to compare the two," Edward blushed.

"Ah, perhaps not now but when you return to Earth, you may feel differently," the devil chuckled.

"Exactly when will I be returning?"

"Soon, I think. We just have a few more things to discuss and I want you to practice your new powers a bit longer until they become second nature to you," the devil replied.

"Whatever you think is best, father," Edward nodded and returned to his meal.

CHAPTER VIII

A week later, Edward stood before his father as he sat on his mahogany throne.

"Are you sure you're ready to go, Edward?" the devil asked.

"Yes, father."

"You realize that when I send you back, it will be your chance to prove to me that you should be the person assigned to commit the act that will cause mankind to finally destroy itself."

"I know and I appreciate the chance, father. You have my word that I'll use the powers you've given me to the fullest," Edward replied. He would do anything to prove his undying love and devotion to the man who he'd come to consider the father he desperately wanted and needed.

The devil nodded and gave Edward a look of genuine fondness. He was pleased with what he saw. His protege had grown into a handsome young man, a far cry from the scruffy child he'd been when they began their unholy alliance. Satan had no doubt that his chiseled good looks, muscular physique and warm smile, in the earthly body of a thirty year old man, would destroy the hearts of many women as he roamed the Earth, carrying out his diabolical tasks.

How fortunate that, as Edward drifted between the world of the living and the dead after his untimely death, he'd been able to *direct him* away from the light of forgiveness that would have led him to God and a very different afterlife, the devil mused.

"Good. Come to me, my son," the devil extended his hand.

Edward obeyed and approached the mahogany throne to kneel before him and kiss the large sapphire ring on Satan's left hand.

"Good luck, my son," he said, patting Edward's blonde head, gazing down at him with affection and pride.

Edward smiled and stepped back. In a few seconds, he dissolved into the darkness.

* * * *

EASTER SUNDAY, 1942

Now that his apprenticeship with the devil had been successfully completed, Edward was anxious to test his new powers on Earth.

He selected a Methodist church as his first target. Located in a small farming community, it would soon be filled to the rafters when the town's families attended the Easter service.

Hiding behind an elm tree, Edward calmly blew smoke rings into the unseasonably humid summer-like air as he watched the faithful arriving in cars and pickup trucks, dressed in their Sunday best.

Edward found his surroundings strange. Miles and miles of farmland, trees and streams replaced the big-city tall buildings, traffic, and crowd-filled streets he was accustomed to. When he first arrived in Balmville, Kentucky, he'd quickly changed his appearance from that of a city dweller to a country boy. The locals had nodded pleasantly in his direction as he strolled along the streets of the town, familiarizing himself with the area. What the citizens didn't know was that before Easter Sunday was over, Balmville's population would be reduced to the few heathens who hadn't felt the need to attend services that Sunday.

As the minister escorted the last congregant into the

building, Edward took one final drag on his cigarette, flicked the butt onto the dusty road, and continued to wait.

When the sound of hymn singing drifted across the road, he sauntered from the shade of the tree, stood in the middle of the deserted road and took a deep breath. He focused his gaze on the front doors of the whitewashed church. Just as his eyes started to tear from the strain, his ultra-sensitive hearing detected two faint "clicks", which indicated that he had successfully locked the front and rear doors of the church.

Smirking, Edward was pleased that his telekinetic powers were working well. Now, it was time for the main event. He took a few deep breaths to calm himself down and then closed his eyes. As he focused his attention inward on an imaginary point in the center of his gut that he envisioned as his core, his body begin a strange transformation. Every nerve ending tingled, causing the hair on his arms and the back of his neck to stand on end. As his temperature rose, his perspiration emitted a metallic odor.

Then, he opened his eyes, raised his right arm and pointed his index finger at the cross atop the church's steeple. His arm stiffened, and he was nearly knocked off his feet as the bolt of blue-grey light shot from the tip of his finger. It streaked across the road and struck the center of the cross with a deafening boom and a shower of yellow sparks.

Inside, the congregation had just finished the opening hymn, *Amazing Grace*, and was settling down to listen to the minister's Easter sermon.

Then all hell broke loose.

There was an eerie silence inside the church before its members finally reacted, in unison, to the rafters bursting into flames. The church was immediately filled with shouts and screams. Pews were knocked over as the worshipers tried to escape the flames, trampling each other in their stampede toward the two exits.

Having fully engulfed the rafters, the fire was now raining

burning debris onto the parishioners and snaking its way down the sides of the church. Thick, black smoke plunged the room into total darkness.

Frantic screams mingled with sorrowful wails of, "Help me Lord! Help me Jesus!"

Terror replaced panic and fear when the faithful realized that both exits were locked from the outside. While some were preoccupied with trying to beat the flames off their bodies, others used the pews as battering rams to break down the doors. When their attempts to escape proved futile, they flung themselves against the doors, only to collapse as the dense smoke mixed with searing heat incinerated their lungs. Those who weren't on fire or overcome by smoke continued to claw at the doors with bare, bloody hands in a desperate attempt to flee the inferno.

Edward coolly watched the carnage from across the street. Fully consumed by flames, the building gave one last roar and collapsed onto itself and its occupants, propelling a thick, black cloud of smoke and glowing embers into the bright, blue sky.

Edward took a deep breath and savored the putrid odor of burning flesh and wood that filled the air. The extent of the power he'd been given was far beyond what he imagined. He felt as though he was truly the most powerful man on Earth.

As promised, the devil had kept his end of the bargain. Edward was confident that he could fulfill his destiny.

CHAPTER IX

NEW YORK CITY, APRIL, 1955

Although it had been thirty-eight Earth years since Edward had last seen the building that once housed his bordello, very little seemed to have changed on his old block that was lined with stately brownstones. The buildings were still well maintained with colorful flower-filled window boxes and spotlessly clean front steps.

When he reached the place he'd once called home, Edward decided it would be less conspicuous for him to view it from across the street under the cover of a small maple tree.

A flood of memories coursed through his mind; the day he, Bricktop and Margaret came to pay the first month's rent and security, the grand opening of the bordello when limousines filled with the city's elite stretched down the curb.

The most grisly of his memories was that of the violent death of his best friend, Petey, as previewed for him by the devil. How tragic it was for the young man to have died on those very steps in a pool of blood, his body torn apart by gunfire.

He also recalled the day Margaret Hastings' coffin was slowly brought down the front steps by Numbers, Bricktop, Sean Mallone and Petey, on its way to the church and her final resting place.

He often wondered where she was now. He knew for a fact that she wasn't in Hell because he would have seen her. She'd probably followed the light of forgiveness and gone to Heaven. If she did, there was the possibility that he might meet her here in another earthly incarnation. According to what Satan had told him, a heavenly spirit had the option of returning to Earth to continue its mission to achieve spiritual perfection, just as inhabitants of hell were able to return to wreak havoc and seek revenge.

But at this point, he didn't give a damn if he ever saw her again. He despised her with all his heart for what she'd done to him. And, if by chance, their paths did cross and he was able to recognize her, it would give him great pleasure to torture and kill her so that she would suffer as he had.

When the front door opened and an elderly man in khaki overalls carrying a broom stepped out, Edward's curiosity peaked. He'd learned through earlier inquiries that shortly after his arrest in

The Eighth House   Karen Sealy

1912, the bordello had been shut down and the deed reverted to the previous owner. Since then, there had only been two other owners, the most recent scheduled to take possession on the first of May. Maybe the old man could shed some light on the brownstone's newest purchaser.

Edward casually crossed the street just as the old man started sweeping the sidewalk.

"Good morning, sir," he said, pleasantly.

"Same to you," the elderly man replied, skeptically peering over the top of his glasses at the stranger in the expensive grey fedora and beige trench coat.

"I'm an artist and was just admiring the fine architecture of this building. It's wonderful to see that structures such as these that are an important part of the city's history are so well maintained.

"Yeah, well, it didn't always look this good." The elderly man stopped sweeping to lean against the iron banister. "Rumor has it that back in the early 1900's, it was a pretty fancy whorehouse run by some kid and his mother. But, when the mother died, the kid got sent up river and it was downhill after that."

"Really? How fascinating. So, what happened?" Edward prompted the man who obviously enjoyed the attention.

"Well, then, the cops gunned down some gangster who took over the place. Sometimes when it rains, you can still see the bloodstains," the man added, nodding his head in the direction of the steps. "Then it was empty for awhile and that's when it got kinda rundown. Finally, in 1945, some banker bought it and restored it to its former glory. He died last year and now I heard some colored folks from one of them Caribbean islands just bought it. Wonder where they got that kind of money," the man grunted.

"Hmm. Interesting history. Maybe I'll come back another day before the new owners move in and take a few pictures. I'd love to capture this on canvas," Edward, pretended to study the structure.

"Yeah, well I guess that would be okay. Anyway, it was nice talkin' to ya but I got work to do," the man turned abruptly and returned to his sweeping.

"It was nice talking to you too. Have a nice day," Edward tipped his hat and walked away.

As he headed crosstown to Houston Street, Edward lamented over just how much he missed the city of his youth. How quickly things changed on Earth. Different clothes, cars, modern gadgets, even attitudes. It had taken some getting used to when he'd first returned. He finally understood what his teachers had meant when they stressed the importance of his ability to assimilate into any environment.

Edward was still deep in thought as he road the uptown bus that would return him to his modest hotel room. He would only be in New York for another two days before flying to Italy to take care of some unfinished business.

After testing his newly acquired supernatural powers on the Kentucky church, his immediate plans had been to return to New York to avenge the deaths of Petey and Bridget Mulcahey. But, unfortunately, too many Earth years had passed. Liam Mulcahey, who had cruelly burned his wife to death in a drunken rage, had died from sclerosis of the liver. The detective who had been responsible for Petey's death had been killed while on duty shortly after. He thought about going after the individual officers involved but later decided it wasn't worth it. He would probably meet his two main targets in Hell when he returned and would take care of them then, as he had Rick.

So, instead, he'd traveled the globe fueling the fires of hate in a world gone mad during the early 1940's.

When he'd finally had an opportunity to meet Adolph Hitler at a dinner held in his honor in Munich, Edward had surmised that when the obviously deranged leader of the Third Reich was returned to Hell, he could easily end up as one of the condemned souls banished to the boiling sulfur pits by Satan if he didn't learn how to control his preoccupation with absolute power.

Orchestrating so-called "natural" disasters, including fires, floods and deadly explosions that killed thousands, had occupied most of his time. He also indulged in the pleasures of the flesh that were readily available wherever he traveled. Life was good.

When he returned to his hotel room, Edward was preoccupied with thoughts of a particularly well-skilled prostitute in Rome named Francesca who he promised to visit while he there was on business.

In the privacy of his room, he stripped off his clothes, a normal practice of his, since he found earthly garments too confining in comparison to the loosely fitting tunic and sandals he'd worn in Hell.

Edward sat down at a small desk and reached for his journal. He'd begun keeping a diary shortly after his return to Earth. He thought it important to record all of his new life's work. He also wanted to remember every detail of his painful childhood; a childhood that was influential in his evolution into the man he'd become.

He'd written a narrative of his activities in the ancient form of Latin that Zachary had taught him. This tactic was employed to prevent someone from understanding the journal's entries in the event the book was ever lost or stolen. Additionally, his future plans were cleverly encrypted within a series of astrological charts. He'd learned that technique from an astrologer in Tunisia, with whom he'd carried on a rather torrid affair for six months. As Jasmine had assured him, only a highly skilled astrologer would be able to interpret the charts.

The thought of being with Francesca again excited him. Perhaps he wouldn't bother with conventional travel and would just transport himself directly to her location via the highly developed form of teleportation he'd been taught by Satan just before he left

The Eighth House

Karen Sealy

Hell.

  Edward scanned the room to see if there was anything of value he wished to take with him besides his journal. The only clothing he had at the moment was what he'd worn that day which he wouldn't need. During the process of teleportation, he could make himself re-materialize fully dressed.

  Deciding that he would travel light, Edward held the journal in his hands and closed his eyes. In a few seconds, he felt a strange tingling sensation deep within him and in a flash of light, he was gone without a trace.

  When he re-materialized, he was standing on the road in front of a nondescript two story building in a little village just outside Rome. This time, his manner of dress was less formal than when he was in New York.

  Slipping the journal into his jacket pocket, he tapped on the front door.

  "Ah, Eduardo! How wonderful to see you again!" Antonio Perelli, the proprietor of the bordello greeted him warmly, kissing him on both cheeks.

  "It's good to see you too. How are things going?" Edward asked as he followed Antonio into the large country kitchen. The aroma of freshly made pasta sauce filled the air.

  "Not so good, my friend. I am hoping that you will be able to help me with my little problem," he shook his head.

  The source of Antonio's 'little problem' was a direct competitor in the female escort business, trying his best to get rid of him. It was a running battle that had continued for nearly five years. Initially, the men had only traded occasional insults and idle threats against each other. Then, the feuding intensified. Each man attempted to seduce the other's prostitutes into working at his bordello with promises of higher pay and more fringe benefits. But now, with more money at stake, the dispute had escalated into physical confrontations.

The Eighth House

Karen Sealy

Upon learning of the situation, Edward could easily empathize with his friend, considering he'd gone through a similar incident as a bordello owner. And now, with his supernatural powers, he would have very little difficulty assisting Antonio with permanently disposing of his rival.

"Don't worry. By the end of the week, you'll have control over the entire district. And, here's the solution." Edward reached into his jacket pocket and pulled out a small amber colored bottle.

"What is this?" Antonio asked, taking the bottle and studying it.

"Oh, just a little concoction I made up. A few drops of that in your rival's drink should take care of everything. And the best part is that it's odorless, colorless and can't be detected in the human body. As far as anyone will be concerned, it will appear that a certain elderly bordello owner died from a sudden massive heart attack due to old age," Edward smiled.

"Amazing. How much do I have to put in his drink?" Antonio asked, staring at the bottle in wonder.

"Two drops will do. His death won't be instantaneous, though. It should take about an hour to hit him, which should give you plenty of time to get back here. That way, no one will connect you with his death," Edward explained.

"Hmm. This should be interesting. Let me call him now and tell him I've reconsidered and think it would make more sense to sit down and settle our problems like two gentlemen," Antonio smirked.

"Good luck. Oh, by the way, is Francesca here?" Edward asked, casually.

"Of course. She's waiting for you in her room. I told her to rest up in preparation for your visit. Enjoy. And thank you," Antonio said, shaking Edward's hand.

"Anytime. I'll see you later," Edward said and headed for the stairs at the rear of the building.

The Eighth House

Karen Sealy

"When I return, we'll have a good meal and some of my best wine to celebrate, if you're up to it," Antonio shouted after him with a chuckle.

"I'll try," Edward replied.

* * * *

When he entered Francesca's bedroom, she was standing outside on a small veranda soaking up the rays of the late afternoon sun. Her shoulder length, jet-black hair was tied loosely at the nape of her neck with a pink satin ribbon, and she was wearing a floral printed cotton dress. It clung to her body, enhancing her broad shoulders, narrow waistline and full, round hips.

"Hello, Francesca," Edward said, softly.

"Eduardo, my love! You're back! Francesca spun around with delight at the sound of her lover's voice.

"It's so good to see you again. I missed you so much," she said, rushing into his arms and kissing him. The sweet scent of her perfume and the soft touch of her lips against his mouth aroused him.

"I missed you too," Edward replied, pressing her closer to him.

"No more talk, darling. My body aches for you," Francesca said, huskily, frantically tearing at the buttons on her dress.

The two lovers were lost in their insatiable lust for each other as they made love. Francesca whimpered like a wounded animal as Edward's hands and mouth explored her body.

"Please, Eduardo. I cannot wait any longer. Please, do it now," Francesca begged, wrapping her legs around Edward's hips and thrusting her pelvis upward.

Francesca cried out as if in pain when they climaxed, and fell back limply onto the disheveled linens.

"You are an amazing man, Eduardo," she sighed, stroking

his damp hair as he rested his head between her breasts.

"And the best lover you've ever had," Edward added, playfully, lifting his head to look into her large, hazel eyes.

"Of course. Since I've been with you, I have lost all interest in being with any other man," Francesca declared.

"Good. And keep it that way," Edward said, rolling over and taking her into his arms.

"Yes, we'll rest awhile now, my love. And then later, I will treat you to a little surprise," Francesca said, reaching up to kiss him.

"Oh? What is it?" Edward was curious.

"You'll see," she winked.

* * * *

It was early evening when Edward was awakened by the need to relieve his bladder.

"Where are you going, my love?" Francesca asked, sleepily, when he got up.

"Nature calls," he replied, padding over to the bathroom.

As he bent over to flush the toilet, the world suddenly exploded around Edward in a flash of light. He tumbled through the air when the floor beneath him collapsed. The deafening sound of falling debris pounded in his ears. He crashed onto the basement floor of the building and was immediately buried by wood, mortar and glass.

It was pitch black and he gasped for air, choking on the dust created by the falling debris. There was an eerie silence except for the sound of his labored breathing.

From his position under the rubble, Edward could see straight through to the star-filled evening sky. A gaping hole was created where Francesca's second floor bedroom had once been.

He struggled in vain to free himself from under the large wooden beam that was crushing his chest. Although he knew he wouldn't die from his injuries, since he was immortal, he would still experience the pain and bruising of a normal human being.

As he was about to lose consciousness, Edward heard a familiar voice shout, "Oh my God! Oh God! Is anyone in there?" It was the frantic voice of Antonio.

"Over here," Edward called out, weakly.

"Eduardo! Francesca! Are you in there?" he called out again, climbing over the rubble in the opposite direction from where Edward was trapped.

Edward knew that his only hope for escape was to move the beam, even slightly, by using his telekinetic powers. He hoped he could muster up the necessary strength before he passed out.

He tried to ignore the agonizing pain that was now radiating from his chest down to his groin and focused inward. His body broke out into a cold sweat and he began shaking as the force within increased. But, due to his weakened state, he was only able move the beam a fraction of an inch. Fortunately for Edward, that slight movement triggered a chain reaction which caused a piece of mortar to tumble from the pile, attracting Antonio's attention.

"Is someone there?" Antonio cried, cautiously scaling the rubble where he'd heard the sudden disturbance.

"Yes. It's me," Edward called out.

"Oh my God, Eduardo! Hold on. I'll get help," the man said, frantically climbing over the debris onto the road.

In a few minutes, Edward heard voices shouting in Italian.

"There's an injured man here. Come quickly. We must get this beam off him," Antonio directed.

When the beam was finally lifted from his chest, Edward immediately burst into a fit of coughing and nearly choked on the blood running down the back of his throat.

"Hold on, Eduardo. You'll be at the hospital soon. Just hold on, my friend," Antonio took his hand, his voice filled with concern.

Edward could no longer tolerate the pain that now pulsed

The Eighth House   Karen Sealy

throughout his entire body and allowed himself to slip into unconsciousness.

* * * *

Three days later, Edward finally awoke with a start in his bed at St. Theresa's Hospital. It took him a few minutes to recognize his surroundings. When he tried to sit up, he was stopped by a nurse who was standing next to his bed.

"Please lie still, signore. You've been in a very bad accident," the woman said, gently pushing him back onto the pillows.

The memory of what had happened immediately rushed through his mind.

"How is the woman? Did they find the woman?" he asked.

"Yes. But I'm afraid she didn't make it. She died instantly when she was crushed in the explosion," the nurse shook her head, solemnly, and made the sign of the cross.

"Oh, Francesca," Edward whispered and turned his head away.

"You are very lucky to be alive, signore. The explosion completely destroyed the building," she informed him.

"It was an explosion?" Edward was puzzled.

"Yes. The police said someone had planted a bomb in the wine cellar.

"What about the owner of the building, Antonio Perelli? Is he alright?"

"I think so, signore. He was with you when you were brought here but no one has seen him since. You should rest now. The doctor will be in a little later to check on you," the nurse said.

When he was alone, Edward thoughts returned to the news of the death of his lover. He hoped she hadn't suffered. Then, he realized that one very important personal item was somewhere in the rubble--his journal.

"Shit!" Edward mumbled as he struggled to get up. The pain he was suffering now was nothing compared to what he'd experience if he didn't find that journal before someone else did.

He looked frantically around the room, hoping that Antonio had left him some clothes but found none. He sat on the bed a few minutes to allow his dizziness to subside. When his head cleared, he closed his eyes and concentrated on changing his appearance, which, fortunately, took only a few seconds to alter.

No one paid attention to the dark haired man dressed in jeans and a cotton shirt staggering down the hall and out the front door of the hospital.

Edward's weakened state didn't allow him transport himself directly back to where the bordello once stood, so he was forced to take a taxi.

When they pulled up to the gates of the house, Edward was shocked to see that the rubble had already been removed and in its place was a freshly plowed patch of dirt.

"Can I help you, signore?" One of Antonio's workers walked over to where he was standing, not recognizing Edward.

"Yes. I was looking for the owner of the house. He's a friend of mine."

"I'm afraid you just missed him, signore. He left shortly after the police told him that someone had tried to kill him by planting a bomb in his wine cellar," the man replied.

"Oh he did, did he? I guess he thought it was wise to leave before someone had a chance to try again," Edward said. *And the sonofabitch may have taken my journal along with anything else he could salvage, unless some other scavenger got it*, he thought.

Edward reluctantly returned to the cab, instructing the driver to take him to a hotel in Rome. He needed time to recuperate and think. How the hell was he going to track down his journal? Now the idea of recording his every move seemed like the worst decision he'd ever made in his life. At least he'd had enough sense to

The Eighth House   Karen Sealy

disguise its contents. But, what if his luck finally ran out one day and it accidently fell into the wrong hands? His ability to roam the Earth undetected would be seriously compromised.

Edward leaned his head against seat of the cab and closed his eyes. His only hope was that the devil was too busy to watch his every move. He needed time to search for his prized possession.

If he didn't recover it and the devil found out, there would literally be hell to pay.

PART II

TERICITA ELLIS
AND
AARON JACOBS

CHAPTER I

NEW YORK CITY, AUGUST, 2001

"This can't be right," Tericita Ellis mumbled, shaking her head while she looked at the astrological chart in front of her.

She reached for one of her reference books, flipped through the pages and squinted at the small type as she tried to locate the passage she wanted.

"Reading glasses, Teri. Reading glasses. They make a world of difference," she chastised herself and flipped them down onto her nose from their perch atop her head.

"Aha! Got it," she said, triumphantly, nodding in agreement with what she read. She swivelled around to the computer behind her to add the information to the report she was writing.

When she was sure the chart interpretation was complete, she pointed the mouse to the print icon and clicked it. While she waited for it to print, she stretched to loosen the stiffness in her neck, shoulders, and back. A warm summer breeze drifted through the basement window of her three-story brownstone, capturing the strains of the calypso tune playing on her stereo. Although the brownstone was located in the middle of New York City's Greenwich Village, its decor resembled her birthplace, the Caribbean island of Barbados.

Soothing earth tones were accented by a myriad of plants which gave the rooms a tropical feeling. On the walls hung watercolor prints depicting scenes of the islands, created by her father, Lawrence Ellis, who was a well known Bajan painter and sculptor.

Teri's stretching exercises switched to dance steps as the sensuous voice of favorite female singer resonated throughout the room.

She sang along in her deep soprano.

Her bold, vibrantly colored gauze skirt, designed by her mother, Isola, swung around her shapely legs as she sambaed around the room. The gold bangles on her arms clinked to the beat when she waved her arms over her head, her round hips swaying to the rhythm.

Her performance was interrupted when the phone rang and she turned to pick up the cordless phone from her desk.

"Tericita Ellis speaking. How can I help you?" she said, using a business-like tone.

"Hey sis. It's me," a slightly accented voice replied.

"Hi Andrew. What's happening?" Teri smiled, picturing her brother's handsome, brown-skinned face. He was the spitting image of their father; broad features, full lips always ready to break into a smile, his hair fashioned in a close-cropped afro.

"I know it's late but I'm calling to let you know I won't be able to make it to dinner. Something came up that I can't get out of," Andrew informed her. He closed the door of his office to shut out the noise coming from the busy cable newsroom.

"That's okay. Is everything all right?" Teri asked, loosening her french braid and shaking out her hair.

"Yeah. It's just something at work. Can I have a rain check for Sunday?"

"Sure. I guess I should be grateful I even get to see you twice a week since you got that fancy new job," Teri teased her brother.

At only twenty-five, Andrew had recently been promoted to assistant director at a cable station in Manhattan.

"You should be the last one to talk considering most of the time you're stuck like glue to that Prof. Jacobs. What's going on with the two of you anyway?" he asked, spinning around in his chair to look out at the Manhattan skyline.

"What are you talking about? We're just friends," Teri

replied, her attitude becoming defensive.

"Yeah. Right. That's not how it looks to me. Every time I see the two of you together, it seems like you can't keep your hands off each other," Andrew chuckled.

"Stop exaggerating," Teri said, her face becoming flush. She nervously twisted a lock of her hair. Even though she'd die before she'd ever admit it, his observation wasn't too far from the truth.

"I'm not exaggerating. The last time we had dinner together when mom and pop were up here, even they noticed. Every time you got up to go to the kitchen, his eyes were tracking you like radar and he kept staring at you with a love sick look on his face. And you? You were grinning wider than a Cheshire cat the whole night. Tell me I'm lying!" Andrew challenged.

"You're lying and besides, it's none of your business," Teri said, lightly, trying her best to mask her embarrassment.

"Sure. Well, here's a news flash for you, big sis. Your little, 'We're just friends', charade ain't working. When are you gonna admit that the two of you are in love, when you wake up with him next to you in bed, or did that already happen?"

"All right, Andrew. That's enough," Teri said, sternly.

"No, no. You're not gonna shut me up that easily," Andrew said stubbornly, tapping a pencil on top of his desk for emphasis. "I'm telling you sis, there's just so much a healthy, red-blooded man can take. He's gonna make a move soon, you mark my words. Don't be fooled by that "nerdy professor" facade he tries to hide behind. There's a lot of smoldering going on under the surface. Believe me, I can sniff out these things. It's a guy thing," Andrew declared, confidently.

"Hmph. He already did," Teri muttered.

"Yeah? When?" Andrew said, excitedly, leaning into the phone.

"Goodness. You are the biggest busybody," Teri clucked.

"Come on, sis. Fess up. You tell me everything else. Don't

get shy on me now," Andrew goaded her.

"Okay, okay, relax. It was a couple of months ago.

As she relayed the story, Teri picked up the 8x10 photo of her taken with Aaron in the garden of a jazz club they frequented. With his arm draped casually around her shoulders, Aaron's tall, thin, but muscular frame towered over her at five-feet-eight. The camera had done a good job of capturing his handsome olive-complexioned face, jet black, wavy hair, dark brown, heavy-lidded eyes and easy smile.

On their way home from the club that evening, they were caught in an unexpected summer downpour. Neither had an umbrella, so they were forced to seek shelter in the doorway of a store.

Aaron had squeezed his tall frame as far back as he could in the narrow space of the doorway so that they wouldn't get wet. When the rain started cascading down the store's awning, splashing on the hem of her dress, she was forced to lean back against him. She was both embarrassed and mildly flattered when she discovered that her nearness had sexually aroused him, a state he didn't seem inclined to alter. Trying to pretend that she hadn't noticed, she shifted her position slightly to the side which caused her to get her dress wet. Faced with the choice of either getting soaked or leaving well enough alone, she returned to her original position.

While they waited for the rain to let up, neither of them spoke, except for an occasional clearing of the throat or sigh. With her head just below his chin, Aaron was overcome by the aroma of her perfume and coconut oil she used to control her hair.

His hands, which he'd placed behind his back, shook as if afflicted with palsy, betraying his otherwise cool demeanor.

When Teri unexpectedly leaned forward to check the damage to her dress, causing her ample, round buttocks to press more deeply into his already smoldering crotch, he thought he would scream.

"Damn, I can't take this anymore," he'd mumbled,

surrendering to his frustration. In one swift move, he grabbed Teri by the shoulders, spun her around, and before the word, "Oh!" could escape her lips, he clamped his mouth over hers.

The intensity of the kiss caught them both by surprise. Teri clung to him like a drowning woman as he clamped his hands onto her thick hair, trapping her face against his.

When they'd finally separated, after what seemed like an eternity, they were both breathless and slightly lightheaded.

"Holy smokes, sis!" Andrew cackled into the receiver.

"Wait. It gets better," Teri smirked, rolling her eyes.

Still reeling from the passion of their first romantic kiss, Teri barely had a chance to close the front door of her house before Aaron grabbed her again, pinning her against the foyer wall. Grunts, muffled sucking noises and frenzied groans filled the hall as they kissed and groped each other. Before she knew what was happening, he was leading her by the hand upstairs to her bedroom, leaving a trail of her clothing behind them. It wasn't until she saw him unbuttoning his shirt that she panicked.

Still dressed in her slip, she sat down on the edge of the bed.

"I can't do this," her voice had shaken. Aaron stood in the doorway, red-faced and panting.

Andrew could no longer hold his tongue. "Oh no, sis. You didn't tell him that! I can't believe it! he howled.

"Yes I did. Hush up and let me finish," Teri said.

Astounded by her abrupt change in mood, Aaron had croaked, "Wha, why?"

"I can't. It's too soon. We need to slow down and really think about what we're getting ourselves into," she'd replied, turning on the light so they could see each other.

"You've got to be kidding! You get me all worked up like this and then wack me in the head with a bag of ice. Okay, I admit that right now, I may be a little delirious but I thought you were ready. I did read your less than subtle signals correctly, didn't I?"

Aaron had asked. His already flushed face turned a deeper shade of red.

"Yes. It's just that I'm not sure. This is still too new to me," Teri had shaken her head, causing her curly hair to shake wildly around her face.

"What? Sex in general or just with me?"

"With you, of course!" she'd sputtered, indignantly. Then, realizing how ridicules her statement must have sounded, she tried to clarify what she'd meant.

"Of course I've had sex before but this is different."

"What's different about it?" Aaron asked, sitting down on the bed next to her, his color slowly returning to its natural pallor.

"I can't explain it. It's just different," she replied, weakly, avoiding his gaze.

"Come on, Teri. You're making me crazy," Aaron said, rubbing his face with his hands.

"I know. I'm sorry," Teri said, softly, looking down at her hands folded on her lap.

Running his fingers through his hair, Aaron let out a long sigh.

"Okay. Look. I don't want to rush you into anything for whatever convoluted reason you have. Our friendship means a great deal to me and I don't want you to feel uncomfortable when we're together. So, I'm willing to slow down if that's what you want. For now," he added.

"Thank you," she'd replied, gratefully, noting the warning in his last statement.

"It's cruel and inhuman punishment but I guess I'll live," Aaron said, adjusting his clothes. "Do you want me to leave?"

"No! Stay for coffee," she'd said quickly.

"All right. But you'd better put something on if you want me to keep my promise," he grinned, motioning toward her closet.

Looking down at her slip, which left very little to the

imagination, she clamped her arms over her chest and scurried to the armoire to get her robe while he watched, with a look of amusement on his face.

For the remainder of the evening, they'd kept their conversation general, trying to ignore the sexual tension between them.

"You are one piece of work, sis, and Aaron has the patience of a saint. I hope you don't plan on pulling a stunt like that again. Thank goodness you're not *my* girlfriend," Andrew shook his head.

"I know, I know. You're right. It was very cruel of me," Teri admitted.

"Look, sis. You're almost forty-one, you're single, and childless. Don't you think it's about time you settled down? Don't you ever want to get married and have a family?" Andrew asked, with frustration.

"Of course I do!" Teri cried, indignantly.

"Then what's the problem?" he said, softening his tone. "I know it's not the race thing 'cause that's irrelevant nowadays," Andrew said, referring to the fact that Aaron, was white and Jewish. "So what's the problem? Since I don't see any other guys knocking down your door, don't you think you've wasted enough time?"

"It's not that simple," Teri sighed, running her fingers through her hair. "One of these days I'll explain it to you when I understand it better myself."

"All right, sis. Forget it. I didn't mean to upset you. It's just that I want you to be happy. You're always worrying about me. Now it's my turn to worry about you," Andrew spoke, in earnest.

"I know, darlin'. Look, I'd better let you go. I'll talk to you tomorrow. Take care."

"You too sis. Later."

CHAPTER II

Teri hung up and dejectedly slumped down in her chair.

"Ah, Prof. Jacobs. What am I gonna do about you?" Teri lamented.

Life would have been so much simpler if it weren't for the conversation she'd had with her maternal grandmother, Elizabeth Williams, twenty years earlier.

Teri was a professional astrologer and the basement of the house served as her office. Her parents had passed the brownstone on to her when they retired in Barbados. It was also where her maternal grandmother, Elizabeth Williams, had run her astrology business which she passed on to Teri before she died.

Teri missed Grandma Williams who had been her friend and mentor. She learned everything she knew about astrology from the wise old Bajan woman. When she worked at her old table and used Grandma Williams' books, she often felt that her granny was silently guiding her.

On her eighty-fifth birthday, Elizabeth sat Teri down to have a serious discussion.

"You've been a good student, Teri," the old woman had smiled proudly at her granddaughter. "I think I've taught you as much as I can. Now it's time for you to continue my craft on your own."

"Oh Granny. Don't start talking that nonsense again," twenty-year-old Teri admonished her grandmother.

Elizabeth patted her cheek affectionately.

"I don't mind goin'. I've led a long, full life and I'm satisfied with what I've accomplished. It's time for an old fossil like me to move on and leave a young person like you to continue my work.

The Eighth House   Karen Sealy

Besides, I miss your grandfather and we have some unfinished business to tend to," she added, with a twinkle in her eye.

"Shame on you, Granny," Teri giggled. "But seriously, what's all this talk about leaving? I can't imagine your not being here."

"Oh, I'll be around, don't you worry about that. You'll just have to work a little harder to see me."

Elizabeth reached around her neck to unclasp a silver chain holding a cross and handed it to Teri.

"I want you to wear this for the rest of your life. It was given to me by my *tanty* who was an astrologer too. If you ever need me, just hold that cross between your fingers and I'll be right there next to you."

Leaning forward, the old woman took Teri's hands and squeezed them.

"You have a rare and special gift, Grandbaby, that's been passed down for generations through the women of my clan. You're a seer, Teri. So's your mother but she chose not to develop the gift, which was her right. Not everyone can handle it. I admit that at times, it has been a heavy burden."

"What you consider your 'woman's intuition' is really a great deal more than that. The gift develops slowly and the more you use it, the sharper it gets."

"Never, ever question your gut feelings, Grandbaby. That's the gift talking. Do you understand?"

"Yes Granny," Teri nodded, solemnly.

"Good, because you're gonna need to follow it very closely one of these days. Oh, Grandbaby, I've seen a lot of troubling things in my dreams and charts," she continued, gravely. "There will come a time when the world will be plunged into such a state of confusion and unrest that it'll seem like nothing will ever be normal again. People will lose faith in God and themselves and become easily seduced by wickedness. It'll seem like indestructible forces of evil are walking the earth."

"During this time, you're gonna be faced with a monumental task, Grandbaby."

"Like what, Granny?" Teri was intrigued by the prospect.

"I haven't been able to uncover the nature of it, and Lord knows I've searched and studied every book and analyzed every chart I could create," Elizabeth replied with disappointment.

"This all sounds very ominous."

"I realize that, Grandbaby. But, I also want you to understand that your astrological ability is a gift and you must never use it to exploit or hurt others. People will come to you for guidance and you must respect the trust and faith they place in you and what you tell them. It should always be the truth as you see it and it must come from your heart."

"Sometimes your vocation will seem like a curse. You know that our profession is looked upon as Satanic by many religions, and at times, you may be forced to defend your beliefs. But no matter what others say, never lose faith in God or yourself. He gave you these gifts to be of service to others and this is the life-path you've chosen. Stay strong no matter what you're called on to do. Do you understand me, girl?"

"Yes, Granny," Teri nodded, thoughtfully, feeling slightly uncomfortable with the seriousness of her grandmother's words.

"I'm leaving all of this to you." She pointed to the books and charts in the room. "Use them wisely."

"You're making me nervous with all this talk of leaving." Teri knelt next to the old woman's chair so she could rest her head in her lap.

"I know, but these things must be said. I don't have much time left and it's important for you to be prepared."

For a few minutes the two women were silent, preoccupied with their own thoughts and emotions. Finally, Grandma Williams spoke again.

The Eighth House

Karen Sealy

"The stars have always fascinated me and I'll let you in on a little secret."

"What, Granny?" Teri asked, looking up at the face of the woman who's image was an older version of her own. Soulful, deep brown eyes surrounded by thick lashes were set into a chocolate brown, oval shaped face with high cheekbones. Full lips were framed by two perfectly round dimples.

When she was a teenager, Teri adopted her grandmother's habit of wearing her thick, curly hair in a French braid.

"If I'd been forty years younger, I'd like to have been one of those astronauts. Imagine being able to get that close to the stars, Grandbaby! It must be a wondrous thing," Elizabeth declared, her voice filled with awe as she stared at the painting of the solar system that hung over her desk.

"Anyway," Elizabeth continued, turning to look at Teri again, "My final bit of advice to you is to be very careful when you fall in love. You're gonna need a very special kind of man by your side to help you through those bad times. Don't chose in haste," the old woman forewarned

"I'll be careful, Granny," Teri promised.

"Good. Now, do an old woman a favor and bring her some ginger beer. I've talked myself dry," Elizabeth chuckled, patting Teri on the head.

A few days later, Teri's mother, Isola, found Grandma Williams dead in that same chair, an expression of peace and serenity on her unlined face.

No one in the family realized just how many people had been touched by Elizabeth William's wisdom and kindness until her obituary appeared in the newspaper. On the afternoon of her wake, nearly one hundred people of all races, colors and creeds passed through the brownstone to pay homage to the Bajan astrologer. At one point, the crowd filled the house and spilled over into the back yard and on the front steps. Some even made the journey to

Barbados where Elizabeth was buried next to her beloved husband and the rest of her family.

Six months later, Teri was still deeply depressed over the death of her grandmother. She could neither sleep nor eat. She knew that her deteriorating condition was of great concern to her family, but could do nothing to pull herself together.

She often sought solace in the basement office. One particular evening, as she sat in her grandmother's favorite chair, Teri had the uncanny sensation that she wasn't alone. Something made her turn her head toward the doorway of the living room and she was astounded by the sight of the faint outline of an apparition floating a few inches above the floor. The figure wore a long, flowing white dress that fluttered around her legs, stirred by an invisible breeze.

"Grandbaby, what's wrong with you?" the image suddenly spoke. "You can't go on like this. You've got to pull yourself together, girl."

Teri's shock turned to joy when she recognized her grandmother's voice. A few seconds later, the apparition solidified confirming it was her.

"What are you doing here, Granny?"

"I'm always here in spirit, Grandbaby and I've seen everything you've been doing. I came to you in human form this time because I think you need this manifestation to shock you into getting your life back on track. Stop grieving over me and get on with your life. You have to prepare yourself for important work."

"You told me that before, but, what *kind* of work?" Teri asked, her voice choked with emotion at the sight of her beloved grandmother.

"All I can say is that when the time is right, it'll be revealed to you. But right now, you must strengthen your body, mind, and spirit in preparation."

"But I can't do it without you!"

"Yes you can. Just remember everything I taught you and trust your gift." Elizabeth floated over to her grand daughter and motioned for her to get up. "I love you, Grandbaby, and I'll always watch over you," she engulfed Teri in her strong arms.

How strange it is that I can feel her warmth but her touch is a light as a feather, Teri thought, burying her face in Elizabeth's shoulder.

"Now dry those tears and get on with your life. Time is of the essence. God bless you and keep you, Grandbaby."

And, with those final words, Elizabeth lovingly kissed her granddaughter's forehead and let her go. As she backed away, she threw her a kiss and her image slowly faded into the darkness. All that remained was a faint breeze, the air permeated with Elizabeth's floral scent, caressing Teri's wet cheeks as it drifted past her.

That night, for the first time in months, Teri fell into a deep, peaceful sleep.

CHAPTER III

Now, years later, Elizabeth William's astrology business continued to flourish under Teri's direction. She'd been flattered when her Grandmother's former clients readily accepted her.

With the help of her Grandmother's training and a degree in psychology and human behavior, Teri had little difficulty providing her clients with advice and guidance. Some tended to believe that the complicated charts she produced contained the solutions to all of their problems. But she explained that astrology was only meant to be used as a guide. Nothing in the charts was written in stone and ultimately, a person had total control over the outcome of their lives.

"Well, Granny, I think you'd be proud of me," Teri said, as she stood before the painting of the solar system that still hung over her desk, tracing each planet with her finger. "And I hope you finally got your chance to touch the stars."

* * * *

Teri would have been very content with the direction her life had taken if it weren't for her grandmother's repeated dire warnings about the future. It was like an albatross around Teri's neck and the major source of her reluctance to allow Aaron completely into her heart.

How ironic that after following her grandmother's advice about dating, in the long run, it had ended up further complicating her life.

As an adult, she'd been very selective about the men she dated. Although the relationships started out fine, most ended in disappointment and frustration when the men could no longer hide their discomfort with her profession.

Initially, they found it strange and exciting. But, when she would construct a natal chart at their request and they discovered that she'd been able to uncover unfavorable information about their personalities and motives, the relationships quickly fell apart.

After awhile, she decided that dating just wasn't worth it and devoted all her time to her work. Everything was fine until she met Aaron.

Their initial attraction to each other had been purely *intellectual*, at least on her part.

She enjoyed taking adult education classes at Columbia University and decided to sign up for Ancient Religions and Prophecies taught by Prof. Aaron Jacobs. One day, after she had engaged him in a rather heated debate about the credibility of astrology, she stayed after class to have a private word with him.

"Have you come to pick over the remains of the rotting corpse, Ms. Ellis?" Aaron asked, dryly, looking down at her smug expression.

"No. I've come to extend the olive branch of peace and declare our latest debate a tie. I've also come to ask if I could treat the dying soldier to a cup of tea," she replied, cheerfully.

"I'm not sure I can muster up the strength, but I guess I could struggle if you promise there won't be any sudden verbal attacks."

"Oh no. I promise," she laughed, holding up her right hand as if to take an oath. "And please call me Teri," she extended her hand.

Once they were seated in a booth and ordered, she posed a question she was sure he wasn't usually asked.

"What's your birth date, time of birth and location?"

"I beg your pardon?"

"I said, what's your birth date, time of birth and location?" she repeated. When he gave her a puzzled look, she laughed.

"Don't worry. I'm not going to use the information to steal your millions in the bank. I just want to construct your natal chart," she explained.

"Why?" Aaron asked, guardedly.

"So you'll understand why we constantly butt heads in class. If I'm correct, you must be a Virgo. You strike me as the type of person who could analyze the print off a dollar bill, is very detail oriented and precise. I, on the other hand, am a Leo, full of fire and life."

"Are you suggesting that I'm a dull book worm who seldom comes up for air and lacks the interpersonal skills to function in the outside world?"

"Not at all. In fact, I think there's more behind those glasses than meets the eye. I also want to prove my point that astrology can help a person become aware of character traits they don't know they have. I believe that once a person has a clear picture of their potential, it allows them to decide how they can best go about fulfilling their destiny," she'd replied, matter-of-factly.

"Okay. I'll let you use me as a guinea pig to prove your point," Aaron agreed, tearing a piece of paper from his notebook to write down the information she'd requested.

"Good," she said. Glancing at it, she was pleasantly surprised to learn that he was only four years her senior. Then, she slipped it into her briefcase. "I'll have your chart ready by the time we meet for class next week."

"It'll take a lot to convince me. I hope you know what you're up against," Aaron said with a grin.

"Oh, I'm not worried. By the time I get through with you, you won't want to make decisions about anything before you consult with me."

"Isn't it kind of dangerous for a stranger to know such intimate details about someone?"

Leaning across the table, she'd looked around cautiously and whispered, "It depends on who has the information. Believe me. You can trust me with it. I'll take it to my grave."

The serious look on Aaron's face made her burst into a hearty laugh. When he realized she was kidding, he joined in. As they left the coffee shop, they promised to meet again the next week to discuss her findings.

Years later, Aaron admitted to her that during their next meeting, it occurred to him that their relationship might evolve into something more serious.

As it turned out, he was absent from class the following week. A note posted on the door announced that Prof. Jacobs was ill and the class was canceled for the day.

Without a second thought, she walked down the hall to the office of the Religion Department. Scanning the room, she spotted the receptionist and said, "Would you be so kind as to give me Prof. Jacob's home phone number? We had an appointment to meet after class and it's urgent that I speak with him."

Looking up at the imposing figure standing before her, the

young student shook her head.

"I'm sorry, but I can't. That information is confidential. If you'd like to leave him a message, I can put it in his mailbox."

"No. That won't do. It's important that I speak to him right away." Thinking quickly, she rummaged through her bag until she found one of her business cards. She handed it to the girl and said, "My name is Professor Tericita Ellis. I'm a visiting professor of astrology and I was supposed to meet with Prof. Jacobs to discuss a symposium we'll both be attending this Friday."

As the girl studied the card, Teri could tell she was debating whether or not she should comply with her request. Finally, she said, "Okay. I guess it'll be all right. Wait a second while I look it up."

She opened a small file cabinet on her desk and retrieved Aaron's number.

"Thank you very much, miss. You've been extremely helpful," she said, pleasantly, taking the paper.

Smirking as the door closed behind her, Teri headed for the bank of phones at the end of the hall and made the call.

Little did she know that a few blocks away, Aaron lay on the sofa bed of his cluttered apartment wishing he could somehow detach his head from the rest of his body until it stopped throbbing. How he'd managed to catch the worst head cold of his life was a mystery to him. With very little food in the house and even less energy to prepare it, the best he could do was lie flat on his back, trying to keep down what little liquid he'd managed to consume.

When the phone started ringing, it sounded to him as if the church bells from the cathedral down the street were in his apartment, signaling the beginning of mass.

"Damn. Why doesn't that damned machine pick up?" he groaned, flinching at the sound of each ring. Then, he remembered that, in his semi-delirious state, he'd forgotten to turn it on. Slowly climbing out of the sofa bed, he literally crawled on all fours to the phone.

"Hello?" he croaked.

"Hello, Aaron? This is Teri. My goodness, you sound terrible!"

"That's why I'm not in class today, Teri. What do you want?" Aaron sighed, leaning against the wall next to the phone with his head in his hands.

"I called to see how you were. Is there something I can do for you?"

"Unless you have the cure for the common cold, I don't think so. Now, may I please go back to my sofa so I can continue to suffer in peace?"

"No. At the rate you're going, you'll never get better. Tell me your address and I'll be right over," she replied, taking a pen and pad from her purse.

"Oh no. That's okay. I'll be just fine," Aaron said, in a rush.

"Nonsense. Stop actin' so bull headed and tell me the address. This is no time for a debate," she insisted.

Not wanting to prolong their conversation since the pounding in his head had grown in intensity as a result of his journey across the room, Aaron gave in.

In less than forty-five minutes, there was a knock on the door. Trying to make himself look as presentable as possible and then giving up when his efforts seemed fruitless, he shuffled to the door and opened it. He had to jump back as Teri stormed into the apartment in a flurry of colorful fabric and clinking bracelets, carrying two shopping bags filled with groceries in addition to her briefcase and large purse.

"Well, now I know I made the right decision, considering you look worse than you sounded on the phone. But don't you worry a bit. I've come to take care of business," she said, glancing at him on her way to what she assumed was the kitchen.

"Do you need my help?" Aaron asked as he staggered

behind her.

"No. Just go lie down and I'll take care of everything. Since people like you don't seem to be familiar with the four basic food groups, I brought along my own provisions."

Throwing his hands up in defeat, Aaron obediently returned to the sofa. Shortly, the clinking of pots and pans could be heard in his kitchen, sounds that reminded him of his ex-wife. He watched in amazement as Teri moved easily around the room as if it were her own. In a few minutes, the odor of chicken soup filled the apartment, making his mouth water.

"Here, sick boy. Sit up and have some of this soup. If your mother ever tasted it, she would swear it was prepared by a nice Jewish girl," Teri said as she handed him a bowl of the steaming liquid.

She stood with her arms folded as he took the first cautious sips of the pungent brew.

As the seasonings assaulted his taste buds, Aaron felt as if he'd died and gone to heaven. In a matter of seconds, the bowl was empty and he was unable to suppress a loud burp.

"Excuse me," he blushed.

"Don't worry. That's the greatest compliment you could pay a cook," Teri chuckled, taking the bowl from him.

"I don't know --."

Before he could say another word, his stomach rumbled.

"Oh, oh!" he said, clutching his stomach. He jumped from the sofa and ran to the bathroom. With tear-filled eyes, he watched the delicious meal he'd just consumed splash into the toilet.

"Tsk, tsk. I should have cautioned you not to eat like it was your last meal," she clucked, standing in the doorway behind him.

Later in their relationship, Aaron admitted that he'd been so embarrassed at that moment, he wished he could have flushed himself down the toilet after his meal.

She, on the other hand, was unfazed by the entire incident.

With the gentle touch of a mother, she helped him up and handed him a wet wash cloth to wipe his face.

"Do you think you have the energy to take a shower?"

Aaron shook his head, yes.

"Good. It'll make you feel a lot better if you clean yourself up a bit. While you do that, I'll clean up the kitchen," she suggested.

When he emerged from the bathroom dressed in a clean T-shirt and sweat pants, he was pleasantly surprised to find that she'd done more than just clean the kitchen. All his books were piled in neat rows along the edge of the floor and on top of his desk. His sofa bed had been remade with fresh, crisp linen that looked cool and inviting.

"Okay, gimpy. Let's try this again," she said, handing him a tray containing a cup of soup, glass of ginger ale and a slice of toast as he sat down on the bed.

"The soup will kill the cold, the ginger ale is to settle your stomach and the toast is to fill you up. It's an old West Indian remedy," she explained.

Balancing the tray on his lap, this time, he heeded her warning and proceeded cautiously, pausing between sips to make sure the soup was going to stay down. When the cup was empty, he handed it back to her and started on the toast and ginger ale.

"Ah. That's better. Now try to get some sleep. It'll take a few hours for the soup to work its magic but I guarantee that when you wake up, you're gonna feel like a new man."

"I don't know how I'm ever going to repay you for all you've done," Aaron said with sincerity, pulling the covers up to his chest.

"Eh, don't worry about it. I'm just lookin' out for my sparin' partner," she smiled.

When Aaron woke up later, the room was dark except for the glow from the lamp on his desk. Rolling over to retrieve his glasses from the end table, he saw that she was frowning as she turned the pages of one of his books. She was intrigued by the hundreds of books on various subjects, especially religion, that filled every available free space in his apartment.

"How do you feel?" she glanced at him over the top of the book.

"A hundred times better," he replied, noting that his head no longer hurt.

"See. I told you so."

"Is there any more of that magic soup left?" Yawning, he stretched his six-feet-four inch frame as he got up.

"Plenty. I made extra just in case you have a sudden relapse," she reassured him. Putting the book down, she followed him into the kitchen.

"I can't thank you enough for rescuing me from my own misery," he said as he lit the gas jet under the tea kettle.

"Oh, don't worry about it," she winked.

"By the way, how did you get my number? The receptionist isn't usually that accommodating."

"I have my ways," she replied, mysteriously. As she recounted her little charade at the office, they laughed.

"I brought your chart. Are you up to listening to my interpretation?" she said, changing the subject.

"Sure."

As promised, she was able to tell him things only he would have known about himself. Aaron was amused at how animated her face was as she explained the chart. Without meaning to, he found himself staring at her full lips as they articulated each slightly accented word she spoke. He wondered what it would be like to feel those full lips on his.

Although he tried his best to cover his embarrassment at the thought, she noticed his ears turning bright red and hoped that her face didn't betray how unnerved she was at having such an attractive man sitting only inches away from her.

"Do you have any questions or have I stunned you into

silence?" she asked, leaning back in her chair with a look of triumph.

"No. I hate to admit it, but you were right. What you said makes a lot more sense than what I read every day in the paper."

"Oh, that foolishness in the paper is rubbish. Every person under the same sign couldn't possibly have the same horoscope. Garbage like that gives astrology a bad name," she said, waving her arm in disgust.

The rest of the evening was spent discussing their professions. As they talked, they realized they had quite a bit in common since both were first introduced to their careers by a grandparent who had been an important part of their childhoods.

When she finally looked at her watch, she was shocked to see how late it was. Aaron insisted she let him call the car service he used when he came home late. As they waited for the doorman to call when the car arrived, she handed him a thick folder.

"What's this?" he asked, taking it from her.

"It's a detailed interpretation of your chart. I also took the liberty of printing a solar return for you. That will tell you what's going on in your life during the next year," she explained.

"Thanks. I'm looking forward to reading it."

Just then, the phone rang.

"The car's here. Thanks again for everything," Aaron had said, helping her gather her things. When he accidently dropped her briefcase, they both reached for it at the same time, causing their hands to touch. As they stood up, their gaze locked, causing Teri to blush.

She was the one who broke the spell.

"It's no big deal. Just hurry up and get better so I can whip your butt in class next week," she said, lightly, trying to regain her composure.

"Okay. But I'll be ready for you."

"In your dreams. Good night," she said and left.

Looking back, she had to admit that it had been pretty

brazen on her part to barge in on him that way but that was just the way she was. Whenever she sensed that someone was in need, she had to help them.

As time passed, their friendship continued to grow.

Although her parents liked Aaron, they wished that she'd gotten involved with someone black, especially of Caribbean ancestry. She reminded them that most men, regardless of race, were intimidated by her profession. Acknowledging that this was true, they decided that the most important thing was her happiness.

Since Aaron was an only child and his parents were dead, family opinion wasn't an issue for him. And now, after two years, Teri felt she was at a crossroad in their relationship. She loved Aaron with all her heart and had no doubt that they would have a wonderful life together. But, what about her grandmother's premonition? If it was as cataclysmic as she forewarned, did she have the right to involve someone else in it?

"Oh granny. What am I supposed to do?" Teri lamented, folding her arms on her desk and resting her head on them.

Without warning, Teri experienced a sudden flash of clarity that was like a nearly imperceptible tug at the back of her brain.

She decided, with no uncertainty, that after she and Aaron returned from her birthday dinner the next evening, she would have a frank discussion with him about her dilemma and let the chips fall where they may.

CHAPTER IV

Friday was Teri's forty-first birthday and greetings from family and friends poured in throughout the day. Unable to get any work done because of constant interruptions from well-wishers, she finally gave up and decided to relax until it was time to meet Aaron that evening.

She treated herself to a bubble bath in her large, antique bathtub. After applying lotion to her arms and legs, she stood in front of the full-length bathroom mirror and studied her image. Except for a few grey strands amongst the thick black waves, she basically looked the same as she had ten years before. She attributed her well-toned body to a healthy diet, daily yoga exercises and good genes.

After slipping into her robe, she started combing her hair. When she was satisfied with how it looked, she walked to the closet to get her dress. She knew the outfit she'd chosen was a little too sexy for a woman who was supposedly trying to maintain a platonic relationship with a man, but tonight, she didn't care. It was her birthday and she wanted to prove that age hadn't diminished her attractiveness.

* * * *

At 7:45 p.m., the doorbell rang and she let Aaron in. As he entered the foyer, he was speechless when he looked at Teri. Her sleeveless, low cut, black linen mini dress and high-heeled sandals, which showed off her fresh pedicure, more than complimented her figure and her long, shapely legs. He was proud to see that she was wearing the pair of silver dangling earrings and matching bracelet he'd given her last Christmas.

Teri noted how sexy he looked. His freshly cut hair complimented his handsome features. The black jacket, slacks and open-collared steel grey knit shirt, draped his body as if they had been specially tailored for him. He could have easily stepped from the pages of a men's fashion magazine.

"So, aren't you going to say anything?" she asked, coyly, as she walked slowly down the hall mimicking a runway model. On her way back, she had a sudden flash of deja vu. Why did it seem as if she'd done this before? She brushed the thought away and stood in front of Aaron with her hands on her hips.

Leaning against the door with his arms folded, he shook his head and smiled.

"Nothing I could say would be accurate. You've really outdone yourself this time, Teri."

"Why thank you Prof. Jacobs," she said, using his formal title affectionately. "And I must say you're looking rather dapper yourself this evening. I think we make quite a striking couple, wouldn't you agree?" she said, stroking the lapel of his jacket provocatively and reaching up to kiss him lightly on the lips. The musky scent of his cologne excited her.

"Yes I would. Let's go tear up the town," Aaron winked and opened the door.

* * * *

The play Aaron selected was a drama with enough tragedy in the plot to keep her sniffling throughout the entire first and second acts, much to his amusement. By intermission, she'd accumulated quite a pile of damp tissues which she stuffed into her small evening bag.

"Why in the world did you pick this play when you know how emotional I get?" she asked, blowing her nose and dabbing her eyes when the house lights came up.

"Because I get a kick out of watching you cry over the lives of fictitious characters. You shouldn't take the story so seriously," Aaron teased, when he noticed that her eyes were red and puffy.

"Hmph. You men never understand these things," she mumbled, as she checked her makeup in her compact's mirror.

"I need to stretch my legs. Would you care to join me?" he asked, getting up stiffly. The closeness of the rows of seats were torture on his long legs.

"No. I'll just sit here quietly preparing myself for the last act," Teri replied, waving him off.

Shaking his head in resignation, Aaron slowly made his way to the aisle.

While she waited for him to return, Teri put on her reading glasses and began casually leafing through her copy of the program.

When the chimes rang indicating that intermission was almost over, Teri decided to take a quick inventory of fresh tissues remaining in her purse. Noting her dwindling supply, she decided she'd just have to use Aaron's handkerchief which she knew he would find rather amusing.

While she was looking through her bag, she suddenly had the feeling that she was being watched. She looked up without moving her head and scanned the crowd. Her eyes focused on a fairly attractive man sitting a few rows in front of her. He was brazenly staring at her. Frowning, she returned his gaze with a steely one of her own, noticing how strikingly blue his eyes were. His only response was to nod and smile pleasantly as he turned his attention back to his female companion sitting next to him.

Satisfied that he'd gotten the message that she wasn't flattered by his rude behavior, she went back to the business of tidying her purse. A few seconds later, she could feel that he was staring at her again. When she was about to give him another dirty look, Aaron returned.

Distracted by the house lights dimming and the rising curtain, she dismissed the man's obnoxious behavior.

* * * *

Teri was still trying to recover from the play's sad ending when they reached the restaurant.

"We should have stopped to buy you another package of tissues since you've already run through several packets and my handkerchief," Aaron joked after they were seated.

"You're so cold-hearted. Didn't you feel anything for the characters?" Teri chided him, sipping her water.

"The only thing I feel right now is hungry. Do you think you could pull yourself together long enough to order or would you like me to pick something out for both of us?"

"You do it. I'm still too emotionally drained," Teri replied, rolling her eyes and resting her hand against her forehead, theatrically.

"I think you're in the wrong profession," Aaron said and began perusing the menu.

Teri's response was a discrete kick to his shin under the table and a broad smile, causing Aaron to wince.

After the waiter took their order, Aaron sat back in his seat to admire his companion. When they entered the restaurant, they were met with admiring glances from men and envious looks from women. Even though her eyes were still slightly red, which couldn't be seen in the dimness of the restaurant, Teri's beauty was breathtaking. He admitted that, as far as he was concerned, she would look beautiful in a potato sack but this evening, she'd taken out all the stops.

It wasn't just her beauty that attracted him. She was the only woman he'd ever met who understood his passion for prophecy and ancient religions. Her genuine interest in his profession brought them closer together.

Soon, his feelings toward her had become more romantic. He thought she felt the same until the night of their first romantic kiss.

He understood and respected her reluctance to become intimate with him, but he was unwilling to accept it. Tericita Ellis was everything he wanted in a woman. He loved her and tonight he would tell her exactly how he felt.

"I feel like I'm the main attraction this evening. There's a man at a table near the door staring at me," Teri discretely whispered.

"You should be used to it by now. Take it as a compliment," he said, without much concern.

"Well, I still feel a little uncomfortable, especially since it's the same person who was staring at me at the theater," Teri replied.

Shaking her head in disgust, she dismissed his presence when the waiter arrived with their food. While they were eating dessert, Teri looked up and saw the rude man leaving with his companion. For a second, their eyes met, causing her to shiver. Then, once again, he smiled pleasantly and turned away.

"Thank goodness that man left. He was giving me the creeps," Teri said, shivering again.

"You're becoming overly sensitive in your old age," Aaron chuckled.

"I don't think so. Are you gonna finish that?" she asked, pointing to the sliver of cheesecake left on his plate.

"No. You can have it since it's your birthday," Aaron replied, sliding his dish across the table.

"And it's been a wonderful birthday if I might say so. Thank you Prof. Jacobs," she said, as she popped the last piece of cheesecake into her mouth, savoring its rich texture and flavor.

"Oh, it's not over yet. I still have a few surprises up my sleeve," he said mysteriously.

"Really? I can't wait," Teri replied, slyly caressing his leg with her foot under the table. The atmosphere and two glasses of wine were bringing out her flirtatious nature.

"In that case, I'll ask for the check," Aaron winked and signaled for the waiter.

* * * *

When they returned to the brownstone, Teri immediately

opened the French doors in the basement to let in the cool night breeze filled with the fragrance of the hibiscus plants growing in her garden. Inhaling the floral scented air, she sighed.

"Are you having a nice time so far?" Aaron asked, putting his arms around her as he joined her in the doorway.

"Yes. Tonight's been wonderful," she replied, dreamily.

"Good. Then you'll really enjoy the grand finale," Aaron murmured, leisurely kissing her neck and shoulders. "Come inside so I can give you your present," he took her by the hand.

He sat down on the sofa and he pulled out a small package from his jacket pocket.

"Even though you haven't shown me one reason why you deserve this, I bought you something special anyway."

"What is it?" she asked, turning the rectangular package over in her hands.

"If you don't take all day to open it, you'll find out."

Making a face at him, she joined him on the sofa, carefully unwrapping the box.

"By the time you open it, we'll both be a year older," he teased. Then, she quickly ripped the paper off.

Inside was a book bound in rich brown leather. On the cover, the twelve signs of the zodiac were embossed in gold in a circular pattern. Upon opening it, she discovered that the pages, brown with age, contained text handwritten in Latin. Teri studied the book in awe.

"I can't believe I've actually rendered you speechless," Aaron chuckled.

"Oh darlin', this is so beautiful. I've never seen anything like it! Where'd you get it? This astrology book must be close to a hundred years old!"

"I bought it at an auction."

"An auction? When?"

"Last week. It was advertised in the paper and I decided to

go. Most of the items didn't interest me, but when I was about to leave, they brought it out. As soon as they described it, I knew it was something you'd like. The auctioneer said it was part of the estate of an Italian gentlemen."

"I hope you didn't spend a fortune on it. I know how ridiculously high those bids can get."

"Well, it wasn't cheap but don't worry about it," Aaron replied, hoping the expensive gift made her realize how he felt about her.

"I don't know what to say. This is the most beautiful gift I've ever received," Teri pressed her hand to her throat, her eyes beginning to water.

"A thank you kiss would be just fine," he smiled.

"Oh, you!" she laughed. Brushing away a tear that had rolled down her cheek, she reached over to kiss him. When she felt Aaron's hand creeping up her thigh, she pulled away while she still had the willpower.

"We have to talk," she said, quickly getting up and adjusting her dress.

"Yes we do. I have something I want to say too but you go first," Aaron replied, sitting back to look at her.

With his dark brown eyes watching her intently, she took a deep breath to help compose herself. For some reason, she was having difficulty remembering her prepared speech.

"I know my attitude about our becoming intimate is frustrating and seems a little ridicules to you and I think I owe you an explanation," she began, nervously pacing back and forth in front of him, her eyes downcast.

"I'm quite sure you're aware of my feelings for you," she continued.

"No, I'm not. Why don't you tell me?" Aaron said, nonchalantly, enjoying every minute of her obvious discomfort.

"I love you! I thought you knew that," Teri's head jerked up, surprised by his statement.

"Now I do. Go on," Aaron said, waving his hand, secretly overjoyed by her revelation.

"Well, as I said before, it's not that I don't want to have an intimate relationship with you. It's just that there are some things about me that I think you should know before we become more committed to each other," she continued, biting her lip nervously.

Pausing to take off her sandals, she stole a glance to see if his face revealed his reaction to what she'd said thus far. She was dismayed to see that he had removed his jacket and was looking very relaxed with his arms stretched along the top of the sofa and his long legs crossed. There was also a hint of a smirk on his face.

"Why are you looking at me that way?" she asked, annoyed that he could be so relaxed while she was a nervous wreck.

"How am I supposed to look while I'm listening to you?" he asked, innocently.

Ignoring his question, she resumed her speech.

"Some of what I'm going to tell you will probably be very confusing. And, to be honest with you, I still don't understand all of it myself," she said, as she sat down in front of him on the coffee table.

Suddenly, she was perspiring in spite of the cool breeze coming from the garden. She also felt anxious. What she was about to tell him would either end their relationship like so many others before or bring them closer together. But Aaron remained silent, directing his attention to the removal of invisible pieces of lint from his slacks.

"This is serious, Aaron. Are you listening to me?" she cried, throwing her arms in the air.

"Yes, Teri. I'm listening. Why don't you just say what you have to say?"

"Alright. When I was twenty, just before my grandmother died, she told me that sometime in the future, I'd be faced with a monumental task that would not only test my faith, but also my psychic gifts and my profession. She didn't know exactly what it would be but she assured me that it would be very traumatic. She also said that until that day, it was important for me to make sure that both my mind and spirit remained strong," Teri said, choosing her words carefully.

"What does that have to do with us?"

"Well, since I don't know exactly what's supposed to happen or how dangerous it might be, I'm not sure I have the right to involve anyone else. It seems as if this task is part of my destiny and can't be avoided. I thought it was important to be honest with you before we let this relationship go any further," Teri replied, gravely.

From the serious look on Teri's face, he could tell that this dilemma weighted heavily on her mind. Aaron sat forward and laced his long fingers together.

"Have I ever told you that I had a problem with your profession or your special gift?"

"No. In fact, you're the first man I've ever dated who was genuinely interested in it," Teri replied.

"Well, I guess then I should be completely honest with you too." He reached over to clasp Teri's hands between his.

"For awhile, after my first marriage ended, I doubted my ability to judge a woman's character. I wasn't interested in having a string of casual affairs. It just takes too much effort. Then, you came along and everything changed."

He glanced up and noted the look of apprehension on her face.

"You're the kindest, most unpretentious, self-sacrificing woman I've ever known," he continued. "You're also the only woman I've ever been involved with who wasn't trying to change me. Janet tried to make me into a suburban family man. That's why we got divorced."

Pausing to retrieve his jacket, he reached into his pocket and produced a small, square, velvet box. Snapping it open, he removed a simple, but elegantly cut diamond engagement ring.

Teri tried to remain cool as he took her left hand in his.

"I think I fell in love with you the day you came to my apartment to take care of me when I was sick," Aaron smiled at the memory. "Look, I understand your fear of involving someone in something that may hurt them but I don't care about that. None of us knows what life has in store for us and I'm willing to take my chances with you. And, whatever it is you have to go through in the future, I want you to know that I'll be right there with you every step of the way, no matter how bad it is. And having said that, Tericita Ellis, will you marry me?" he asked, slipping the ring on her finger.

Teri could only continue to stare at him and then the ring with her mouth hanging open. She was having difficulty sorting out everything he'd just said. She had no idea that he was planning on proposing that night.

Not wanting him to misinterpret her silence for rejection, she quickly replied, "Yes. I'd be more than honored to marry you, Prof. Jacobs."

Now it was Aaron's turn to be surprised.

"Really?" he asked, his grim expression turning into a broad grin.

"Yes. I may be bull-headed but I'm no fool. How could I pass up the chance to marry a man who isn't intimidated by my profession or my crazy premonitions?" Teri declared. "You have no idea how relieved I am by what you said. I was so afraid you'd react like all the other men I've dated. Then, I'd be alone again. I love you and I can't imagine what my life would be like without you," she added, gently caressing his startled face.

"Neither can I, Teri," Aaron said. He took her hand and kissed the dark creases of her palm. The touch of his lips sent a pleasant tingling sensation up her arm. Rejoining him on the sofa, she put her arms around him and planted light kisses on his forehead, eyes, the tip of his nose, and finally his lips. Then, sliding onto his lap, she reached behind his back and gingerly pulled his shirt from his waistband. Slipping her hand under his shirt, she slowly began stroking his bare back with her long fingernails as they kissed.

Aaron arched his back and uttered a low growl. Grabbing a handful of her hair, he pulled her head back and kissed her throat where her pulse was beating fast and strong, and then the velvety skin between her breasts. The sweet, tropical scent of her perfume filled his nostrils.

Teri's breathing became shallow as she lowered her head, forcing his mouth to meet hers again. Suddenly, all her doubts and fears seemed unfounded as they embraced. She relished the thought of fully giving herself to this man. Right here. Right now.

But, as she reached around and began unzipping her dress, Aaron grabbed her hand in mid-motion.

"What are you doing?" she cried, hoarsely, pulling away.

"Not so fast. You're not Mrs. Aaron Jacobs yet," he smiled, shaking his head in disapproval.

"What does that have to do with anything?"

"I think you deserve to experience just a little of the torture you've subjected me to all these months. You'll just have to wait until we're married before we're intimate," Aaron replied, trying to appear unruffled.

"But, but, you can't be serious!" she sputtered, eyes blazing.

"Oh yes I am," he replied, pushing her aside so he could get up. The sight of her curly hair sticking out wildly from her head, disheveled dress and the look of outrage on her face was comical.

"You seem a bit distraught. Let me get you something to drink," he said, coolly, as he tucked in his shirt and left the room.

When he reached the kitchen, he quickly grabbed onto the edge of the counter with trembling hands while he tried to regain his composure. Stopping himself at the height of his arousal had taken all the willpower he could muster but it was worth it. She had it coming.

When his heartbeat returned to normal, he took two bottles of water from the refrigerator and returned to the living room to find Teri sitting in her grandmother's chair, her arms folded across her chest with a murderous look on her face.

"I'm only taking your feelings into consideration," Aaron said, innocently, as he handed her a bottle.

Glaring at him, she snatched it and mumbled something he didn't quite catch. Smirking, Aaron returned to his seat on the sofa.

Opening the bottle with an impatient twist of the cap, Teri put it to her lips and drained it in one long swallow.

"Oh you're a sly one, Prof. Jacobs," she said, wiping her mouth with the back of her hand. "So when is this wedding supposed to take place?"

"Getting a little anxious, are we?" he chided, casually sipping his water. "Isn't that up to the bride?"

"Yes, but my schedule is more flexible than yours. Why don't we try to do it before you have to go back to school? We could have the ceremony in Barbados and honeymoon right there," she suggested, her mood becoming less agitated as she began sorting out the details.

Aaron could feel himself becoming aroused again as he watched her pace back and forth, her eyes narrowed in concentration. Her dress was still half unzipped and one strap was slowly making its way off her shoulder, revealing the curve of a very shapely breast. He decided it was time to go. If he didn't leave soon, he wouldn't be able to stop himself from making love to her right in middle of the living room floor.

"Oh, look what time it is," he blurted out, pretending to look at his watch. "Why don't you start working out the details and we'll talk about it tomorrow. I'd better be going."

"Oh? All right. I'll walk you upstairs," Teri said, absently, her mind still occupied with wedding plans.

* * * *

"Well, this has been some birthday. First a play, dinner, an antique astrology book and then an engagement ring. You really know how to treat a woman," Teri chuckled as they stood in the foyer.

"Well, I aim to please," Aaron grinned.

Suddenly pushing him against the front door, Teri put her hand on the back of his neck and pulled his head down to hers, planting a long, sensuous, open-mouthed kiss on his startled lips.

"You know I'm gonna get you for that stunt you just pulled," she whispered coyly into his ear, biting it lightly before she stepped back.

"I can't wait," Aaron grinned.

"I bet. Goodnight darlin'," she said sweetly, then abruptly pushed him out the door, closing it firmly behind him.

Standing on the front steps still grinning, Aaron shook his head.

"What in the world have I gotten myself into?" he thought and slowly walked down the stairs.

CHAPTER V

On Saturday morning, Teri lingered in bed while she studied the huge diamond ring. Her head was still spinning over the strange turn the previous night had taken. If it weren't for the sparkling jewel on her finger, she'd swear the entire night had been a dream.

She rolled over to wind the key on the music box on her night table. Grandma Williams had given it to her when she was a child. Soon, the room was filled with the cheerful strains of, *In The Good Old Summertime*.

Twisting her hand to trap the sunlight crossing her bed in the prisms of the stone, she chuckled. She couldn't wait until her parents and Andrew got the news, knowing her mother would cry while her father fanned her with a newspaper trying to calm her down.

Glancing at the clock, she saw that it was too early to call them. It was her father's Saturday ritual to go fishing with his brother while her mother went to the market. But she knew Andrew would be home.

She could barely contain her excitement as she dialed. In a matter of weeks, she would be Mrs. Aaron Jacobs, the wife of a college professor, premonitions or no premonitions. Nothing could dampen her spirits.

"Good morning baby brother," Teri said pleasantly when Andrew picked up.

"You sound pretty cheerful for a woman who's over the hill," he teased.

"Over the hill am I? Well, I've got news for you."

"Oh yeah? What?"

"Bring yourself over here as fast as you can and you'll find out," Teri replied, holding the ring up to the light again.

"Only if you promise to make me one of those old-fashioned Bajan breakfasts mom used to make."

"It's a deal."

"Good. Oh, I have something for you too."

"What?"

"Let's just say it's a very belated birthday present from someone special."

"Oh? That sounds interesting. Hurry up then," Teri said

and rang off.

* * * *

"Happy birthday, sis," Andrew said a few minutes later as he handed her a medium sized square box.

"What in the world did you get me?" Teri asked, taking the box from him as he sat down to eat.

"You'll never guess," Andrew said, bursting with excitement.

"I hope you're not tryin' to suck up to me so I'll run a composite chart for you and some girl."

"See, there you go again always thinking I want something from you. Can't you just take a gift and say thank you?"

"Don't lecture me. I'm still older than you," she said, placing the box on the table. As she unwrapped the gift, Andrew walked over to her stereo and placed a cassette in the tape deck. In a few seconds, the sounds of the latest reggae hit filled the room.

Teri let out a cry of delight when she opened the box and removed the tissue paper. Inside was an 14"x16" framed hologram of Grandma Williams. The three-dimensional image was so perfect, it was as if the old woman were alive inside the frame, suspended in time.

"Where did you get this?" Teri asked, her heart pounding with excitement.

"From Granny. She had it done years ago and asked me to give it to you on your forty-first birthday. She said this is when you would appreciate it most."

"I can't believe this. It's so beautiful," she said, rotating the picture in her hands. With each motion, she was able to see her grandmother's image from a different perspective.

"It's kind of spooky but cool. Where are you gonna hang it?"

"I'm not sure," she replied, looking around the room. Then,

she walked over to the wall next to her grandmother's chair.

"I think this would be the most appropriate place. When I'm working, it'll feel like she's watching over me," she said, removing the old painting and hanging the hologram in its place.

"It kinda gives me the creeps. It's like those pictures of Jesus that light up and it seems like the eyes follow you no matter where you walk," Andrew noted.

Suddenly, his favorite song came on and he started dancing around the room to lighten his mood.

"Come on sis. Let's dance," he said, grabbing Teri by the arm and pulling her in front of him. Laughing, she moved her hips to the beat of the music.

"Doesn't this remind you of the parties mom and pop used to have when we were little?"

"Yes. And they'd get mad when we'd imitate the old people doing that nasty dance, or windin' up, as they used to call it," she laughed.

"You mean like this?" Andrew asked as he rhythmically gyrated his hips in front of her.

"Oh Andrew stop! Granny's looking at you!" she giggled, nodding her head in the direction of the picture.

"Don't get all puritanical on me now. You used to do a pretty good imitation yourself." Andrew was slightly taller than his sister and his muscular body moved with the grace of a person who enjoyed dancing.

"And still can," Teri said, rotating her hips, matching him movement for movement.

When the song ended, they both collapsed into fits of laughter.

"Oh, god, those were the days," she gasped, throwing herself onto the sofa.

"They sure were," Andrew agreed, falling next to her. For a few minutes, they continued to shake their heads and chuckle in fond remembrance of their childhood.

"I kinda miss those days. We used to have so much fun. I felt like I didn't have a care in the world," Andrew said, pensively.

"Well, at least we'll always have those good memories. For that we have to be grateful. And thanks for the gift," she said, reaching over to hug her brother. Over his shoulder, she could see the hologram. For a second, it did seem as though her grandmother was looking directly at her. The expression on her face was so serious, it made Teri shudder.

"What's the matter, sis?" Andrew asked, feeling the slight tremble.

"Nothing. I'm just feeling a little emotional," she replied, trying to brush it off. Giving her brother a final squeeze, she got up.

"I hope you're not gonna turn out to be one of those old people who's always crying when they think of something sentimental," he teased. "So what's your surprise?"

Placing her left hand behind her back, Teri removed the ring from her pocket and slipped it on. Then she dramatically waved her hand in her brother's face.

"Check it out, baby brother," she said, smugly.

Andrew did a double take as he stared at the ring.

"Get outta here, sis," he said, letting out a low whistle. "Where'd you get that from?" He took her hand to get a closer look.

"What kind of question is that? Where do you think?" Teri was indignant.

"So Aaron finally made his move. Hey, congratulations sis," Andrew laughed, standing up to hug his sister. "When did this happen?"

"Last night," she beamed.

"Did you know he was gonna pop the question?"

"No. I'm just as shocked as you are. I still can't believe it," Teri sighed, admiring the ring for what must have been the one thousandth time.

"It's amazing what a guy will do to get a woman into bed," Andrew mumbled with his mouth full of food.

"Andrew!"

"Calm down sis! I'm just kiddin'," Andrew grinned. "So when's the big day?"

"We haven't decided yet. It'll be soon, though. I just have to coordinate the date with everyone's schedules. I was thinking we could have the ceremony back home. This way, we could honeymoon there too."

"Oh, the honeymoon. That should be a mess," Andrew snickered.

"Never mind," Teri shot him a dirty look and blushed. She'd spent most of the night tossing and turning, tormented by dreams that were filled with vivid images of she and Aaron making passionate love in a variety of places and positions.

"So my big sis is getting married. Isn't that something," he shook his head. It made him feel good to see her so happy. He had no doubt that Aaron would take good care of her and that they'd have a wonderful life together.

"It is amazing, isn't it? I guess Granny was right when she advised me not to chose a mate in haste," Teri said, glancing at the hologram.

"Are you sure he understands what he's getting himself into?"

"Yes. We've discussed Granny's premonition already. If he's willing to take a chance, so am I. Anyway, at this point, I can't imagine my life without him," Teri said, her mood becoming serious.

"Well, as long as you're happy, I'm happy. Do mom and pop know yet?"

"No. In fact, I should give them a call right now while you're here," Teri said, reaching for the phone.

"Good. I wanna hear when mom faints and pop has to run

to get water," Andrew laughed.

****

Just as Teri and her brother predicted, Isola Ellis nearly passed out after hearing the news of her only daughter's engagement. But she quickly recovered and started bombarding Teri with a million-and-one suggestions for the wedding. By the time she hung up, Teri had a headache and a bewildered look on her face.

"I think you and Aaron should discuss the possibility of eloping," Andrew said, amused by her dilemma.

"Don't give me any ideas," Teri said dryly.

"I wish you luck, sis. Anyway, I gotta go. I'm due at the station in an hour. Tell Aaron I said congratulations and if he needs any advice on how to keep you in line, he should feel free to call me," Andrew said, with a mischievous look about him.

"Thank you for the Andrew Ellis seal of approval," Teri said, swatting him playfully on the backside as she walked him upstairs.

"Take care sis. I'm really happy for the two of you," Andrew said, embracing her.

"And thank you for the hologram. It's really something, isn't it? But what made Granny decide to have it done?

"I don't know. I just remember going with her to a gallery when I was about four-years-old. I'll never forget it. It was like something out of a science fiction movie. The man at the place showed a film describing how holograms are created. After it was over, Granny had one made of herself." Andrew's eyes grew distant as he thought back to that day.

"When we got home, she gave it to me and said I was to guard it with my life until, as she put it, your birthday was a four and a one. Then, I was supposed to give it to you. Of course, that seemed like a million years into the future to me. Anyway, when I asked her why she couldn't give it to you herself, she said she'd be too busy. So I hid it in my closet. Every once in awhile I'd sneak a look at it but it used to give me nightmares. When I moved out on my own, I took it with me. And now, here it is," Andrew concluded.

"Oh, Andrew. How did I get so lucky to end up with a brother like you?" she said, grabbing him around the shoulders and hugging him, her eyes glistening with tears.

"Look, don't start crying all over my new shirt."

"Oh hush up," she said, kissing him on the cheek. "I'd better go."

"Okay. Later, Andrew. I love you."

"Later, sis," he replied, waving as he hurried down the stairs.

* * * *

From the position of her image inside the hologram, it appeared that the spirit of Elizabeth Williams was bursting with pride as she watched her two grandchildren in the basement of her beloved brownstone. Their close sibling relationship would soon play an important role in their survival.

They didn't know that she'd been sent back to watch over them but her power was limited. She was warned that if she interfered in the natural course of their lives too often, she would cause more harm than good. Fortunately, for now, all she had to do was watch. Hopefully, she'd adequately prepared Teri for what lay ahead.

* * * *

Returning to the basement, Teri couldn't resist standing in front of the hologram again. When she moved ever so slightly, it seemed as if Grandma Williams' dark brown eyes were looking directly into hers.

"I followed your advice Granny, and I found a good man. I hope you're happy for me," Teri said to the hologram. As she was about to walk away she could have sworn her grandmother's eye had winked. Shaking her head, she gave the picture a final glace and left the room.

* * * *

Teri was upstairs in her bedroom when she heard her business line ringing in the basement. Running down the two flights of stairs, she reached the phone just before her voice mail picked up.
"Good morning, Teri."
"Good morning, Aaron," Teri wheezed, breathless from her sprint to the basement.
"It's nice to know I excite you that much," Aaron chuckled.
"Don't flatter yourself," she quipped, staggering over to her grandmother's chair.
"So how did your family take the news?"
"Well, Andrew was speechless, my mother nearly fainted and my father was relieved," Teri replied, holding up her hand to admire the ring again.
"I hope you weren't up all night worshiping that ring."
"Of course not!" Teri lied, blushing, as she quickly put her hand down. "It *is* beautiful, though. It must have cost you a fortune. I didn't know college professors made so much money."
"We don't. Let's just say I was smart enough to invest my inheritance wisely."
"So you mean I'm about to become a wealthy woman? How wonderful. Maybe I'll be able to retire from the astrology business and become a lady of leisure," she teased.
"You will when we start a family."
"Aren't we getting a little ahead of ourselves, Prof. Jacobs? If you pull another stunt like the one last night, there may never be any children."
"Goodness, Teri. I didn't know you were a woman who held

grudges. But, don't worry. I promise I'll make it up to you on our honeymoon," Aaron said, lightly.

"Oh really? Well then I'd better get a batch of that herbal concoction my mother brews that's supposed to boost your energy. You're gonna need it," Teri quipped.

"We'll see about that. Anyway, the reason I called is to tell you to bring the astrology book I gave you when you come over tonight. I want to take a look at it."

"Okay. I'll --"

"Hold on a second. I'm getting a call," Aaron said when his line beeped.

"That's okay, darlin'. I have to go anyway. I'll see you around ten," Teri said quickly.

"All right. Bye," Aaron replied and clicked the receiver to pick up the next call.

"Good morning. May I speak to Prof. Aaron Jacobs?" a woman's voice said.

"This is he," Aaron replied, frowning at the sound of the unfamiliar voice.

"Good morning Prof. Jacobs. You don't know me but my name is Laurie Sanders. I'm the woman who was bidding against you at the auction last week," she explained.

"Hello, Ms. Sanders. What can I do for you?" Aaron asked, wondering why the woman was calling and how she'd gotten his unlisted number.

"I'm calling in reference to the astrology book. I was bidding on behalf of a client who's an avid collector of rare books. He was very disappointed when I was unable to outbid you. He suggested I contact you in the hopes that perhaps you'd be willing to sell it to him. He's ready to make you a very lucrative offer."

"Oh? That's interesting," Aaron replied, trying his best to cover his surprise at what the woman had just said. "And just how much is he willing to pay?"

"One hundred thousand dollars in cash."

Aaron nearly dropped the phone when he heard the amount. That was ninety-seven thousand dollars more than he'd paid! Why would anyone be willing to spend so much money for a simple book?

Trying to remain calm, he said, "It's a tempting offer but I'm afraid I'll have to decline. Unfortunately, I no longer have the book. It was given as a birthday present to someone who's also a collector."

"Oh, I see. Is there a possibility that person might consider selling it?" the woman asked, clearly disappointed.

"No."

"All right then, Prof. Jacobs. Thank you for your time," the woman said politely and hung up.

Aaron continued to stare at the phone. What a strange phone call! He couldn't wait until Teri came over later with the book. It hadn't seemed worth that much to him. Maybe they'd discover something after they read it.

"Well, I guess I'll find out soon enough," he sighed.

* * * *

"He said no," Laurie Sanders informed the man who was scrutinizing her with icy blue eyes as he sat across the room on the sofa.

"Are you still mad at me, sweetie?" she asked, shyly, joining him.

"Of course not. You did your best. Too bad, though. It would have made things so much easier," the man replied, shaking his head regretfully. "But that's all right. I'll just have to try to get it another way."

"Okay. Just tell me what you want me to do next," Laurie said, eagerly. She was anxious to make it up to him.

* * * *

Teri was in the middle of cleaning her office when the phone rang again.

"Tericita Ellis. How may I help you?"

"Hello, Ms. Ellis. My name is Laurie Sanders and I'd like to engage your services as a birthday gift for a friend."

"What type of chart would you like?" Teri asked, reaching for her calendar.

"A birthday chart interpretation."

"Do you mean a natal chart?" Teri asked, to be sure she understood exactly what the woman wanted.

"Yes, that's it. I know it's short notice, but would you be available tonight?" Laurie asked, hesitantly.

Teri made a face as she consulted her appointment book. She hated last minute bookings but private chart interpretations were very lucrative for her.

"Yes I am. What time?" she said, finally.

When Teri finished writing down the pertinent information, she was mildly amused at the woman's obvious relief that the arrangements were set. Apparently, the recipient of the interpretation was very important to her.

"All right, Ms. Sanders. I'll see you tonight at eight-thirty."

"Thank you so much, Ms. Ellis. I'm looking forward to meeting you. Good-bye," Laurie said and hung up. Then, turning to the man sitting across the room, she said, "Did I do okay, darling?"

"Yes. You did very well. Come here and let me give you your reward," the man replied, seductively.

"You're such a naughty boy," Laurie blushed and eagerly obeyed his command.

CHAPTER VI

Exhausted after having spent most of the night tossing and turning because of her excitement over her engagement, Teri decided to take a nap early that afternoon. As soon as her head touched the pillow, she fell into a deep sleep. When she finally awoke, it was nearly 7:30 p.m. and she was due at her client's apartment at 8:30. Scrambling from the bed, she ran to the bathroom, took a quick shower and got dressed. If she were lucky enough to catch a cab right away, she might be able to reach the party in time since she'd only have to go crosstown.

By 8:10, she was fully dressed. She ran to the basement and quickly grabbed the client's chart, stuffed it into her briefcase and headed for the front door. Just before leaving, she punched the code into the keypad on the wall, activating the alarm system. Satisfied that everything was secure, she locked the door and ran to the corner.

She glanced at her watch as she waved her hand in an attempt to flag down a cab. It was already 8:25. There was no way she could avoid being late.

When the light on the corner turned green, a taxi raced through the intersection, screeching to a halt in front of her.

"1015 East 23rd Street," she instructed the driver, reading the address from her pad.

As the cab eased back into the traffic, Teri suddenly realized that, distracted by the excitement of her engagement, she'd forgotten to run the computer generated interpretation of the client's chart. It was too late now. She'd just have to wing it.

In a few minutes, the taxi stopped in front of an upscale high-rise building.

The doorman, who had been standing in the lobby, rushed to open the door.

"May I help you?" the guard asked as she stepped up to the desk.

"I'm here for the Sanders party. My name is Tericita Ellis."

"Just a second," he said, running his finger down the list. "Okay, you can go up. It's the twenty-sixth floor," he said, putting a check next to her name and eyeing her curiously.

"Thank you."

While she waited for the elevator, the guard turned around to get a better look at her. She was dressed in a brightly colored skirt and blouse, her arms decorated with bracelets that reached the

The Eighth House — Karen Sealy

middle of her forearm. She didn't look like the type of person associated with the kind of people attending the party. He surmised that she must have been the astrologer he heard would be coming.

When she reached the twenty-sixth floor, she scanned the numbers on the doors in search of apartment "B". The plush carpet muffled her footsteps as she walked down the long hallway. Glancing up at the wall, she spotted an arrow indicating that letters A thru F could be found to her right. As soon as she rounded the corner, she could hear the sounds of laughter and music.

She rang the bell and took another deep breath. She smoothed her hair. The lock on the door disengaged.

"Miss Ellis, I presume," a stylishly dressed woman said pleasantly.

"Yes, and you must be Miss Sanders," Teri smiled, extending her hand. She estimated the young woman to be in her late twenties. "I'm terribly sorry I'm late."

"Oh, it's no problem, in fact, you're just in time. The party's just getting started," the woman said cheerfully, closing the door behind her.

As soon as she crossed the threshold, for a split second, Teri had a strange feeling that something unusual was about to happen. But she shook it off, attributing her feelings to fatigue.

From the expensive look of the decor, Teri assumed that the owner of the apartment was very wealthy. All the furniture was white, including the thick, plush carpet. The accessories could best be described as an eclectic collection of antiques from around the world. When she walked into the living room, she saw that a small round table covered with a black cloth had been placed in the center of the room. The long white sofa was pushed back against the picture window. She was overwhelmed by the unobstructed view of the Manhattan skyline.

"Come in so I can introduce you to everyone. Then you can help yourself to some refreshments if you like."

"Thank you," Teri said, flashing one of her famous dimpled smiles.

"Attention everyone! Attention! I want to introduce

tonight's entertainment. This is Tericita Ellis, the psychic," the hostess announced excitedly.

"Astrologer," Teri politely corrected her.

Scanning the room, she surveyed the other guests. Every race and nationality seemed to be represented. They were all elegantly dressed. But, there was something very odd about them. She also found it strange that there were no men at the party. Immediately, she became uneasy.

"Is there anything I can get you? The birthday boy is in the bedroom on the phone. I told him I thought it was very rude of him. But it's hard to stay angry at someone like him for long," the hostess giggled.

"Thanks. A glass of water would be fine," Teri replied.

"Okay. I guess you don't want your mind to be all foggy when you do your reading," she giggled again.

"That's right."

"By the way, I love the sound of your accent. Are you Jamaican?"

"No, I'm originally from Barbados," Teri replied, flashing another one of her full-dimpled smiles, a feat that was becoming more and more difficult.

"Oh, how exotic. Anyway, let me get your water," she giggled again.

Returning her attention to the guests, Teri was amazed at how artificial they all looked, like they weren't real people. Not one strand of their hair was out of place nor were the layers of perfectly applied makeup smudged. She also noticed that underneath their skin tight dresses, there must have been at least ten pounds of silicone per woman, straining to be released from low cut necklines.

Watching them closely as they conversed amongst themselves, she finally figured out what was so odd about the group. Although they were of different races and wore a variety of outfits, under closer scrutiny, the six women could have easily passed for sextuplets. The similarity of their features was uncanny. They also seemed to move in unison like a school of fish. When one lifted her glass to sip her drink, the other five followed. When another idly played with her hair, so did the others. But how was that possible? Was she hallucinating?

"Here you go. Why don't you mingle a little? Maybe you'll pick up some interesting vibrations," Laurie winked and handed Teri the glass of water.

"No, I'll just get set up. I assume that this table is for my use."

"Yes, and please let me know if you need anything else. I wasn't sure what a psychic might need," she giggled, obviously amused by her own joke.

Teri made a face as the woman walked away. When she pulled out one of the chairs, she accidently tipped over her briefcase, causing the astrology book Aaron had given her to slide under the table.

After she sat down, she reached into one of the compartments to get the chart. Since she'd forgotten to run the report, she was going to have to do a blind interpretation. It wouldn't be a problem as long as the chart didn't contain any unusual planetary configurations.

As she pulled out the computer sheet, she turned her head at the sound of the Laurie's voice.

"Finally, the birthday boy reappears. Come, darling. I want to introduce you to your birthday surprise!" she said, pulling him by the arm.

The gentleman was impeccably dressed in a designer suit. His hair, which was golden blonde, accentuated his baby blue eyes which were surrounded by long, thick lashes. His smile revealed perfectly shaped teeth; so perfect, he could have been in a toothpaste commercial. The average woman might consider him an example of her ideal man.

Teri was unnerved when she realized that he looked just like the man she'd caught staring at her in the theater and restaurant the night before.

"Miss Ellis, I want you to meet the birthday boy, Edward Hastings. Edward, this is Miss Tericita Ellis. She's a psychic," Laurie bubbled, excitedly.

The Eighth House

Karen Sealy

"My own personal psychic? How generous of you, Laurie. I'm very pleased to meet you, Miss Ellis," Edward smiled, extending his hand.

"I'm an astrologer, Mr. Hastings. Pleased to meet you," Teri said, trying her best to conceal that she recognized him as she shook his hand. When their hands touched, she felt a slight electrical shock, like static.

"That sounds even more intriguing, Miss Ellis."

"Why don't you two sit down? I can't wait to hear what dirt she's uncovered on you," Laurie said, pushing them both toward the table.

"What exactly do you plan on doing?" Edward asked Teri as he sat down across from her and the women gathered around.

"Well, I've created what's called a natal chart based on some information I've received from Ms. Sanders. It tells me the position of the planets on the day you were born. It's based on your time of birth, the location, month and day. The chart shapes like a pie and is divided into twelve sections, called houses. Each house represents an aspect of your life. For example, the first house represents your physical body, or how you present yourself to others."

"Inside each house you may find the planets of the solar system. And along the outside of the circle are the twelve signs of the zodiac. But all this depends on your birth date. The signs that the planets are in, enable me to predict what type of person you'll be and what kind of life you'll lead. You'll have a better understanding as we go through each house."

"I can't wait," Edward smiled warmly.

"Do you need any mood music, Ms. Ellis?" Laurie suddenly interrupted.

"No. What you're playing is just fine," Teri replied. Then, she picked up the chart which had been laying face down on the table.

When she looked down at the paper, Teri quickly stifled the gasp that nearly escaped her lips. The circle, which encompassed most of the page, was almost completely devoid of planetary signs except where the lines intersected to form what was known as the eighth house.

All the planets of the solar system and all the zodiac signs were crammed into that one house.

Her first thought was that her computer program had crashed or that she had been given the wrong birth information. The strange configuration was an astrological impossibility.

"Let me start by asking you a few questions," she said, trying to cover up her mental confusion. For the benefit of the rest of the guests, would you please tell us what your date of birth, time and location are?"

"August 23, 1960, 6:56 p.m., Dresden, Germany."

Well, she had gotten that much right, she thought, looking at the page.

"That means you were born under the sign, Virgo. If you look at the chart, you'll see that next to the symbol for the sun is the symbol for Virgo. Whatever sign the sun was in at your time of birth determines what your sun sign is," Teri explained, pointing an unsteady finger at the chart.

"How fascinating Ms. Ellis. Please continue," Edward said.

"You're a long way from home, Mr. Hastings. Were you, perhaps, an army brat?" Teri asked, saying the first thing that came to mind.

"Why yes, how in the world did you guess? And please call me Edward."

"I just had a feeling," she replied.

"Edward, you devil! I never knew that!" Laurie cried, clapping her hands in a childlike gesture.

"That's because you're not a psychic, isn't that correct, Ms. Ellis?" he said, looking directly at her.

"Yes," she replied, averting her gaze. The way he was staring at her made her skin crawl.

"Go on," Edward prompted her.

"Well, I see that you're a very ambitious man. This will help you become successful in business," Teri lied. "I'd say you were in some type of import-export business."

"Oh, I'm sticking with you, Edward," one of the women in

the group declared. Everyone laughed.

"Tell us about his relationships with women," another blurted out.

"Yes, please do," he said.

Glancing down at the chart as if she were really consulting it, she paused and then said, "Women find you very attractive and they especially like your air of mystery."

"What kind of women does he like?" someone else asked.

"Oh, he likes all different types of women," she replied. A collective 'ah' rose from the group.

"So what do you think the future holds for me, Ms. Ellis?" he asked, staring at her again. This time, their eyes locked and she was unable to drop her gaze.

"I predict that you are going to live a long and fruitful life," she said slowly, mimicking a line from a sidewalk gypsy.

"I've got to get out of here," Teri thought. She had never been so uncomfortable in her life. The longer she stayed, the harder it became for her to suppress the urge to just jump up and run. The stress of being in such a bizarre environment caused her to develop an excruciating headache.

"I'm very impressed by your accuracy." Then, holding her hand, Edward asked, "Perhaps you also read palms?"

The second their hands touched, they both inexplicably lurched slightly backward in their chairs. Teri's eyes clouded over when strange images and sounds began flashing through her mind. A dingy apartment. The smell of gunpowder. A pool of blood on the floor.

Edward's blue eyes turned strangely dark and distant as the faraway sound of his mother's voice echoed through his ears and the scent of her perfume filled his nostrils.

He found himself unable to let go of Teri's hand when they simultaneously snapped out of their trances. "It's not my area of expertise but I know a little about it," she replied, trying to keep the tone of her voice steady as her hand trembled.

"Well," he said, quickly regaining his composure and turning the palm of his right hand face up. "What do you see?"

The Eighth House
Karen Sealy

Teri was almost afraid to look down. His hands were very large. The nails of his slightly puffy fingers had a strange reddish hue to them. She noticed at first glance that there was an unusual shape to his Mount of Venus, near the thumb, and the Mount of the Moon, near his pinky. Both were extremely overdeveloped.

She was uneasy when she looked at his palm. Under normal circumstances, it was difficult to read the lines in the hand of a fair-skinned person because they were so faint. In his case, there was an even greater obstacle - his palm was completely devoid of lines, the skin as smooth as an egg. Teri thought she had finally lost her mind.

Struggling to remain calm, she had the distinct feeling that Edward Hastings was very much aware of her discomfort. While he waited for her response, she noticed a faint smirk had appeared on his lips.

"It's difficult to say because the lines are so faint," she said quickly.

"Maybe if I turn my hand toward the light that might help," Edward suggested, still holding her hand.

Teri's eyes widened in astonishment when she looked at his hand again. Lines were suddenly forming like cracks in a sidewalk. In a few seconds, his palm was filled with thousands of intersecting fissures that turned red like tiny rivers of blood.

Evidently, she was the only person who was privy to this phenomenon since there was no reaction from the other party attendees. They just waited silently for her to complete her reading.

"You have a very long life line and can look forward to living a happy and healthy life," she said quickly. When she tried to gently pull her hand away, he continued to hold on.

"Let me take a look at your hand, if you don't mind, Ms. Ellis."

Before she could respond, he turned it over.

"I predict that very soon you'll be embarking on a long journey that will be filled with excitement and mystery," he said, doing a very bad imitation of a fortune teller. Everyone in the room began to laugh and he finally released her hand.

"That was wonderful, Ms. Ellis," Laurie declared, clapping

and the rest of the group joined in.

"Yes, I can honestly say that your accuracy leaves me stunned," Edward said, his voice overflowing with charm.

"I'm glad you enjoyed my work," Teri said, nearly tipping over the chair as she hastily stood up. By this time, she was close to losing control entirely. All she wanted to do was get as far away from Hastings as fast as possible. While she gathered her belongings, she noticed the tip of the astrology book sticking out from under the tablecloth that hung to the floor. She quickly put it in her briefcase along with the chart.

"Perhaps I could come to you for a more private consultation in the future," Edward called out cheerfully as she walked away.

"I wish you'd stay a little longer, Ms. Ellis. You were very entertaining," Laurie said as she escorted Teri to the door.

"I'm sorry but I have another appointment after this," Teri lied.

"Oh, well in that case, let me give you your check. Wait right here."

Teri was about to tell her not to bother but thought better of it. It would seem rude. As she waited, she could feel Edward Hastings watching her from across the room.

"Here you are," Laurie said, handing her the check. Teri quickly shoved it into her purse without looking.

"Good night, Ms. Sanders."

"Good night Ms. Ellis. Thanks again."

* * * *

Once she was in the hall, Teri waited for the sound of the door closing before breaking into a run. When she reached the elevator, she impatiently jabbed the call button several times.

Taking deep breaths, she tried unsuccessfully to slow down her rapidly beating heart and began massaging her temples in a vain attempt to relieve her throbbing headache. Her deep breathing only left her feeling faint and lightheaded. If she didn't get some fresh air soon, she knew she would pass out.

After what seemed like an eternity, the elevator finally arrived, its doors gliding silently open. As it sped to the lobby, she paced back and forth like a caged animal.

"This is bad. This is really bad," she murmured, clutching the cross around her neck. In all her forty-one years, she had never been this frightened. Her intuition told her that whoever that man was, he was surrounded by a sinister and evil aura. And what were those strange images that flashed through her mind? She didn't want to think about him or them now. All she wanted to do was get out of the building.

She walked toward the sidewalk, her headache intensifying. She hoped she didn't look as badly as she felt.

Raising a slightly trembling arm, she hailed a cab. Within a few seconds, one pulled up.

"Where to?" the cabby asked as she sat down. For a minute she couldn't remember where she was going.

"Nineteen eleven, Riverside Drive," she said finally, giving the driver Aaron's address.

Glancing down at her watch, she noticed it was only 9:45. She felt as if she had been trapped at the party for days, when in reality, it had been a little over an hour.

She was grateful that for once, traffic on the West Side was light that evening. When the taxi stopped, she paid the driver and struggled to the entrance of Aaron's building. Franco, the night guard, was on duty at the desk.

"Hi, Ms. Ellis. Nice to see you this evening." When she got closer to the desk, he frowned.

"Are you all right?" he asked, with concern. She didn't look like her usual, light-hearted self.

"Hi, Franco. I think I'm just coming down with something," she replied, flashing a weak smile.

When she reached Aaron's apartment, he was already standing at the door. Pushing him aside without a word, she walked straight to the kitchen, opened one of the cabinets and reached for the bottle of Bajan rum she knew he kept there.

Aaron stared in confusion as he watched her put the bottle

to her lips and take a long swig, shuddering as the fiery liquid burned her throat. When she recapped the bottle and returned it to the cabinet, he asked, "Teri, what's wrong with you?"

Dabbing her lips with a napkin, she looked directly at him and simply replied, "Darlin', I think I've just met the Anti-Christ."

CHAPTER VII

"What did you say?"
"I said, I think I've met the Anti-Christ."
"You're kidding aren't you."
"I wish I were," she replied, gravely.
Aaron listened in disbelief as she described what happened at the party, omitting her strange vision.
"And you say this was the same man who was staring at you last night?"
"Yes, I'm positive."
Aaron frowned and rubbed his chin.
"Don't you think you should double check the chart before you jump to any conclusions?"
"I plan to," Teri said, picking up the phone on his desk to call a colleague.
"How long will that take?" Aaron asked when she hung up.
"About ten minutes or so. My friend has a computer that's fast. I want her to check the configuration."
"Tell me again about his hand."
"All right. Give me yours and I'll explain," she said, gesturing for him to sit down.
"The first thing I found unusual was the size. Your hand is large but in proportion to your height. His wasn't. His was abnormally large." Turning his hand so she could look at his nails, she continued. "See how your nails are a healthy pale pink?"
"Yes."
"Well, his nails had a red tinge to them and they were very

large and square. In palmistry, this is usually suggestive of a person who is cold and selfish with a violent temper. Then look at this," she said, turning his hand palm-side up. "Right next to your thumb is the Mount of Venus and opposite that is the Mount of the Moon. On your hand, they're slightly raised. On his hand, they were overly developed. This is indicative of a person who is hedonistic and possesses occult powers. But what disturbed me the most were the lines on his palms. One minute they were invisible. His palm was as smooth as an egg. Then all of a sudden, millions of lines appeared and started flashing like neon signs. And I could swear I felt an electrical shock when I shook his hand."

"Who requested the reading in the first place?"

"A woman named Laurie Sanders, who I assume is his girlfriend."

Aaron's eyes narrowed at the mention of the woman's name. Where had he heard it before?

Suddenly, the phone rang. Teri nearly tripped over Aaron's legs in her rush to answer it.

"Hello?" she said, her heart pounding. "Hi Regina. So what did you find?"

Aaron watched as Teri listened. He didn't like the look on her face.

"All right. Thanks Regina. And please don't tell anyone else about this. I'll call you as soon as I get a chance. Bye." Teri slowly hung up the phone.

"Well?" Aaron was uneasy.

Teri returned to the sofa and picked up the chart.

"It's worse than I thought. Regina ran another chart with the birth data I gave her and got the same results."

"Maybe he accidently gave you the wrong date of birth or he's lying."

"That's what I thought at first, so I asked him to repeat it. Maybe he is lying because there's no way both Regina's and my software can be defective. But why would he lie and even if he did, that still doesn't explain his hands. He certainly couldn't lie about them."

The Eighth House   Karen Sealy

"Okay. So let's say the chart is correct. What does all this mean?"

"It's complicated but let me try to explain," she began.

"First of all, it's an astrological impossibility for every planet to end up in one house. Most charts will have them scattered throughout several different houses. The next thing is the house they're in. The Eighth house is associated with regeneration, endings, the occult and death. Under normal circumstances, this wouldn't be that significant but all his planets fall in that house." Pointing to the chart, she continued.

"According to Edward Hastings, as he's calling himself, he was born August 23 which makes him a Virgo like you. The general characteristics of Virgos, as I explained to you when I did your chart, are that they're very modest, thoughtful, detail oriented, very fond of learning and rarely look their age. On the surface, that doesn't sound very sinister. But when you place the sun in the Eighth house, those characteristics also include a morbid interest in occult fields and issues of life after death. This corresponds with what I saw in his hand. Then, when you look at all the other planets in this house, it doesn't paint a very pretty picture. He's obsessed with death, has no feelings for anyone but himself, is sexually perverted, uses his good looks and charm to get what he wants, is obsessed with power, can regenerate himself and is very destructive."

"Okay. I'll admit he doesn't sound like a person you'd want to be friends with but I still don't understand why you're so upset."

"Because of this," she said, tapping the chart. "These are the symbols for Uranus, Neptune and Pluto. I'm sure you know that these are the outermost planets in the solar system which makes them the furthest from the sun, right?"

"Yes."

"Okay. And because of that, it takes these planets longer to complete one revolution around the sun. It's approximately one hundred years or so."

"And?"

"The last time these planets were in this position was in the 1800's. If this chart is correct, and it seems that it is, Mr. Hastings

The Eighth House   Karen Sealy

couldn't have been born in 1960 as he told me. Aaron, he has to be nearly 100 years old! That's why having all his planets in the house associated with regeneration is significant. The person I saw looked like he was in his late twenties to early thirties."

"This is all very confusing, Teri," Aaron said. He started pacing back and forth in front of her. "What the hell does all this mean?"

"You tell me. You're the expert on prophecy," Teri reminded him.

"Meaning what?"

"I'm not sure but look. According to Nostradamus, the third Anti-Christ was supposed to make his appearance in the early 1990's to begin his reign of terror that would climax with a bloody battle in the year 2000. Obviously, that was wrong since this is 2001 and so far nothing has happened," Teri said, pacing the room.

"And you're suggesting this is who Edward Hastings is? I thought you didn't believe that stuff."

"I don't but I know what I saw and how I felt. Granted, he doesn't fit the profile outlined in the quatrains since he's obviously not from the Middle East and the chart shows no political aspirations. He's also been around a long time. But what if Nostradamus was misinterpreted? Aaron, the person I've described is ten times more dangerous than any Anti-Christ. He's been able to assimilate into the general population. He looks normal. He's the all-American boy."

"Everyone thinks the world is safe now since nothing cataclysmic took place at the millennium. But, what if he purposely decided to come now when no one is paying attention?" Teri cried.

"Then why is he here and why would he reveal himself to you, of all people?"

"I don't know yet. Lord, this has been a crazy night and I've got a terrible headache," Teri sighed, rubbing her temples.

"Turn around and I'll massage your shoulders," Aaron volunteered, still puzzled by the explanation of her experience at the party.

She closed her eyes as his strong fingers gently kneaded the muscles of her shoulders and neck. Immediately, the tension and her headache lessened.

"After what happened tonight, do you think it's wise for you to meet clients at their homes for interpretations?" Aaron asked, cautiously. This was one aspect of her profession he didn't like. When he'd asked her about it before, she'd become very defensive.

"No. I should have followed my instincts and turned around and left as soon as I walked through the door. I was lucky this time that nothing bad happened to me," Teri replied, shifting her position so he could reach a spot on her back that was still tense.

Aaron was relieved that she hadn't given him an argument. Now, if he could only get her to stop seeing clients in her house. But it was best not to bring that up just yet. Maybe after they were married he could persuade her to stop.

"You missed your calling, Prof. Jacobs," she sighed.

"And just think, you'll have access to these magic fingers every night after we're married," Aaron smiled, pausing to kiss her neck.

"Mmm. I can't wait," she said, yawning. The lack of restful sleep was finally catching up with her.

"I'd better go before I can't get up," she said, patting his hands and standing up.

"You're not going anywhere. It's late. You can have the bed and I'll sleep on the sofa."

"It's tempting but I want take a look at that chart again before I go to bed and I need my reference books at home. I don't think I'll be able to sleep until I get a few answers," Teri shook her head, stretching and yawning again.

"Forget it. I said you're not going anywhere," Aaron insisted, taking her by the arm and leading her to the bedroom. Maybe a good night's sleep was all she needed.

"And speaking of books, I got a very strange call after I spoke to you this morning. It seems that the woman I outbid at the auction was there on behalf of a client who's a book collector. He's desperate for the book and is willing to pay me one hundred thousand dollars for it."

"I wonder why? Oh, by the way, it's in my briefcase. Maybe we should take a look at it now."

"No. That can wait until tomorrow too. Look at you. You can barely keep your eyes open as it is," he added. She was probably half asleep when she did the interpretation and imagined the whole incident, he thought as he watched her yawn again.

"If you think you'll be able to boss me around like this after we're married, you have another thing coming, Prof. Jacobs," Teri smiled, pausing to wag her finger at him as she took off her dress.

"I'm shaking in my boots. Lie down," he ordered, and helped her get under the covers.

"Thank you, darlin'," she said, wrapping her arms around his neck and kissing him before sliding under the blanket.

"You're welcome. Good night."

Before he could turn off the light, she was fast asleep. Slipping quietly back into the room, he stood over the bed and adjusted the covers. Even as she slept, her mouth slightly open, she was beautiful. Bending down, he gently pushed back her hair and kissed her forehead.

He turned off the light, closed the door and he smiled, anxiously looking forward to the day when they would be together every night.

CHAPTER VIII

Edward Hastings' mood was somber after a very frightened Tericita Ellis left the apartment. So she was the woman who now possessed his journal.

For many years after the bombing of the bordello, he'd been unsuccessful in locating Antonio Perelli. But his luck finally changed a week ago. By chance, he'd read in the newspaper that Antonio, who had relocated to the United States after the incident, had recently died. The contents of his estate were being auctioned in

The Eighth House Karen Sealy

New York City.

Hoping his journal might be among the items to be sold, he attended the preview and discovered, to his relief, that his journal was there. If it had been up to him, he would have just taken the book and left. Unfortunately, attempting to steal it would have brought too much attention to him so he decided to send Laurie to bid on his behalf.

After finally tracking it down, if that silly bitch had simply been able to outbid that pain in the ass Prof. Jacobs, he would have it right now. She'd assured him that because the book was of lesser value than most of the other items being auctioned that night, she wouldn't need to bid that high to get it. When Prof. Jacobs kept offering more, she'd become rattled and stopped at twenty five hundred dollars. Jacobs' bid of three thousand had ended the auction and the book was his.

If he had been there, he would have continued the bidding until Jacobs had given up. Obtaining the money wouldn't have been a problem. Laurie didn't know that he had the ability to manipulate electricity and could go up to any automatic teller machine and make it dispense as much cash as he wanted.

Now, as a result of his carelessness and Laurie's incompetence, it had fallen into the hands of the one person who had the power to interfere with his plans, Tericita Ellis.

When Laurie told him she was unable to get the book, he'd instructed her to do whatever was necessary to find out all she could about its new owner. Her inquiry revealed that it now belonged to Prof. Aaron Jacobs who taught ancient religions and prophecy at Columbia. At first, that didn't worry him.

It was when he had Laurie call Aaron with an offer to buy the book that he became anxious. Laurie's snooping had also uncovered the existence of Aaron's girlfriend, who was a well respected astrologer.

So now, his journal was in the hands of someone who might be able uncover the truth about him.

But, there was something else that was more troublesome about this unfavorable turn of events. He'd been very unsettled while in the presence of Miss Ellis. As he'd listened to her interpretation of his chart, her mannerisms and tone of voice had seemed vaguely familiar. And when he'd held her hand, why was he suddenly reminded of his long dead mother, Margaret? It was ridicules since this attractive black woman bore absolutely no physical resemblance to the woman.

"That damned book is making me crazy," Edward mumbled under his breath.

"What did you say, darling?" Laurie asked.

"Nothing. I want to spend some time alone with you this evening. Go put on something sexy," he said, whispering in her ear and licking it.

"Oh, Edward, you really know how to turn a girl on!" she giggled and hurried to the bedroom.

Looking over at the group of women across the room, he snapped his fingers and his party guests suddenly vanished. That little parlor trick of creating a hologram had worked well, even though he'd seen Tericita Ellis scrutinizing the women with suspicion. His hocus-pocus had been used to fool Laurie and Tericita into thinking that the "party" was legitimate. In actuality, the gathering was staged to test the astrologer's proficiency in her craft.

When he'd instructed Laurie to engage Tericita's services at his "birthday party", she'd been more than eager to after screwing up at the auction. When Laurie asked him who else he'd like to invite, he'd come up with the idea of the holographic guests, since he didn't really have any other friends to invite.

Too bad the holograms weren't real, he thought, with regret. It would have been interesting to have sex with all six of them and Laurie at the same time.

Group sex was one of his favorite pastimes. He never ceased to marvel at the promiscuity of twentieth century women. When he returned in the early 1920's after his apprenticeship with the devil, women were much more prudish and moral. Granted, there had always been women who were more than willing to satisfy his insatiable sexual appetite but they were nothing like the man-hungry women of the 90's. In the past, he'd been subjected to long courtship rituals before he could achieve his ultimate goal of having intercourse. But now, he could have as many women as he wanted, for as long as he wanted, with little or no effort. His charming manner and good looks sucked them in every time. It was so easy to wrap them around his fingers. Not even the threat of contracting AIDS altered their behavior.

Even Laurie hadn't protested about his having only female guests at his party. It was further proof of the humiliation some women were willing to tolerate in order to have a man in their lives.

For him, life in the late twentieth century with its drugs, sex and greed was like living in paradise. But now, since Tericita had his book, he'd have to put aside his pursuit of pleasure indefinitely.

"Ah, well, some other time," he thought.

"Where is everybody?" Laurie asked when she returned dressed in a transparent negligee.

"I told them I wanted to be alone with you and they just disappeared," Edward replied, casually.

"So what do you want to do now, darling?" Laurie asked, provocatively rubbing his leg with her hand.

"What do you think?" he winked. With a giggle, she grabbed his hand and led him in the direction of the bedroom.

It was decorated to resemble his former bordello. The king sized bed was covered with red, satin sheets. Naked bodies writhing in ecstasy made up the pattern of the wallpaper. A plush black rug covered the floor. Scattered around the room were candles of various shapes and sizes, all in black and red. But he especially enjoyed the huge mirror which covered the ceiling, affording him an unobstructed view of his sexual antics.

Edward was pleased to see how well he'd trained this simple-minded woman to participate in the sexual games he so enjoyed. Observing their images reflected in the mirror through half closed lids, he was more than satisfied with Laurie's erotic enthusiasm.

Sighing, he let his mind wonder back to the events of that evening. Watching the Ellis woman react to the chart's misinformation and the trickery of his hand, he knew she'd soon be able to uncover his true identity and earthly plans. He'd been surprised at how harmless she appeared. But looks could be very deceiving. At first, he thought he would be able to throw her off his trail by engaging in the same skullduggery he'd used on other astrologers. But Tericita was no idiot. He knew she was suspicious of him and admired how well she'd been able to conceal her nervousness. Oh, she was good, all right. And that was going to be her downfall. If she'd been like the other charlatans he'd dealt with in the past, he'd only have to concern himself with getting the book. Now, he would have to get rid of her permanently after he regained possession of the journal.

Edward's thoughts were suddenly interrupted when he climaxed. Laurie, now drenched in perspiration and panting, rolled over next to him and immediately fell asleep.

Poor Laurie. She didn't realize that he didn't care for her or any other woman. He only used her for sex. It was the only activity that could rejuvenate his more than one-hundred year old body.

Returning his thoughts to the problem at hand, Edward continued to review his options. He liked to think of himself as invincible, but he knew he wasn't. Satan didn't create henchmen who were more powerful than the devil himself. So, Edward had two weaknesses that could easily debilitate him. His first problem was with his lungs. In the early 1900's, before the industrial revolution reached its peak, the earth's atmosphere had been relatively clean. But now, because of modern factories, aerosol cans, cars and other pollutants, the air was filled with contaminates. Frequently, his lungs were unable to take in enough fresh oxygen.

His powers were also diminished significantly whenever he was in the presence of strong spiritual forces, a problem that Satan had cautioned him about. It was imperative that he avoid houses of worship or other places where the clergy might gather.

Fortunately, for him, Tericita Ellis was neither a member of the clergy nor living in a church.

Getting up, he reached for the cordless phone and left the bedroom. It was time to check on the petty thief who worked for him.

"Is she back yet?" Edward asked.

"Nope. The house is still dark," the man replied.

"Good. Go in and wait. The security system won't be a problem, will it?"

"Nah. Piece a cake."

"Okay."

"What should I do after I get the book?"

"Call me. I'll dispose of her myself," Edward replied, a sinister look on his face.

"Okay."

Satisfied that his plan was in motion, he returned to bed. A fiendish look crossed his face as he looked up at the faint image of himself in the mirror. "Ah, Miss Ellis. Have I got a surprise for you."

He'd been shocked when Laurie told him where Tericita Ellis lived. What were the odds of her living in the same brownstone that had once housed his bordello? His intimate knowledge of the *interior of his former residence made it even easier for him to prep* Lenny about gaining entry into the house without being detected.

Hopefully, the dilemma of the misplaced journal would soon be over.

* * * *

In spite of the disturbing events of the previous night, Teri awoke the next morning feeling refreshed. The aroma of freshly brewed coffee and toasted bagels filled the air. After she showered, she put on Aaron's bathrobe. When she entered the kitchen, he was at the stove scrambling eggs.

"Good morning darlin'," she said, wrapping her arms around his waist and reaching up to kiss his neck.

"Good morning. I trust you slept well," he replied, turning around to face her, grinning. "You were snoring loud enough."

"Liar!" Teri pinched his arm.

"Go in the living room, sit down, and behave yourself or you won't get breakfast," Aaron chuckled, pushing her through the doorway with an affectionate pat on her buttocks.

"You're setting me up, aren't you?" she asked a few minutes later.

"What are you talking about?" Aaron added a basket of bagels with cream cheese and jam to the eggs, freshly squeezed orange juice and steaming pot of coffee that were already on the table.

"Pampering me this way. Then after we're married, you'll probably grow an enormous beer belly, and expect me to wait on you hand and foot like a slave," she teased.

"You left out the barefoot and pregnant part," Aaron reminded her.

While he ate, Teri sat back a moment to observe him. He was clean shaven and his dark hair, still damp from his shower, was extra curly. He hadn't put in his contacts yet and was wearing his horn-rimmed glasses that made him look very serious.

Touching the ring on her left hand, it suddenly occurred to her that these little intimate moments between them would be part of their daily routine once they were married. She found the thought very comforting after having spent most of her adult life eating breakfast alone.

Watching him chewing his eggs and spreading cream cheese on his bagel, Teri was struck by such an overwhelming feeling of love for him, she got goose bumps.

"Something wrong?" Aaron asked when he glanced up from his plate and noticed she hadn't started eating.

"No," she shook her head, a broad, dimpled smile on her face.

"Then, what are you grinning at? Do I have something on my face?" he asked, reaching for his napkin.

"No. I was just thinking how much I love you and how I can't wait until we can have breakfast together every morning like this," she replied, softly.

"Oh," Aaron said, grinning.

"So what are your plans for today?" she asked, sipping her

juice.

"I was going to take a closer look at that astrology book. I still can't understand why anyone would be willing to pay one hundred thousand dollars for it," Aaron replied, leaning over to retrieve it from his desk.

"Neither can I. Maybe it's older than the auction house estimated."

"That's a possibility. There are quite a few astrological charts in here you might want to take a look at," he noted, flipping through the pages.

"Let me see."

The charts were quite different from the ones she was accustomed to working with. The symbols for the planets and signs were drawn in a very elaborate style.

"I'd like to put these coordinates in my computer and see what configurations come up. I wonder if the text corresponds with the charts?" she said, studying the strange words.

"I don't know. That's a form of Latin I'm not too familiar with. I'd have to compare it with a textbook I have in my office. Get your laptop computer when you go home and meet me at my office later. I'll bring the astrology book. If you analyze the charts while I take a stab at translating the text, we might be able to figure out what makes this book so valuable a lot faster," Aaron suggested.

"That sounds like a good idea. While I'm there I'll also take a look through your reference books on ancient prophecies. It might help me make sense of Hastings' chart. I still don't understand what's going on with it."

"Okay. Why don't we meet around three? Then, when we finish, we can go to that place around the corner for dinner."

"It's a deal," Teri said and began clearing the table. "No, no. It's the least I can do," she said before he could protest.

It was Aaron's turn to observe her while she briskly went about picking up the dishes. After each movement, she had to pause to adjust his robe, which kept slipping off her shoulder since it was three times too large.

"Come here," Aaron said, pulling her onto his lap as she was

The Eighth House

Karen Sealy

wiping off the table.

"You're a regular little homemaker, aren't you?" he grinned up at her.

"You're not too bad yourself, although the apartment could use a little sprucing up," she said, surveying the room and pretending to be displeased.

"Soon it won't matter because I plan on moving in with you."

"Oh really? That's news to me," she replied, one eyebrow raised.

"Of course. Why should I stay cramped in this little apartment when you have that big house all to yourself?" he said, matter-of-factly.

"Oh. So now you're finally showing your true colors, Prof. Jacobs, you fortune hunter," Teri chuckled.

"I thought you knew I was only marrying you for sex and money," Aaron said, pretending to be shocked.

"Hmph. If you're not careful, you won't be seeing much of either," Teri threatened.

"I don't think so, Miss Ellis. I know exactly how to keep you in line," Aaron smiled and kissed her bare shoulder where the robe had once again slid down. His mouth made its way to her breasts. Her breath quickened and she shivered.

"Oh, no. You're not gonna pull that stunt again," she said, pushing him away and getting up.

"What stunt?" Aaron said, innocently, a broad smile on his face as he watched her stumble into the bathroom.

"I fell for it once. The next time you get me all hot and bothered, I want some satisfaction," she cautioned, wagging her finger and slamming the bathroom door behind her.

CHAPTER IX

When Teri returned home, she was ready to tackle the mystery of Edward Hastings' chart and the astrology book. After checking her messages and taking care of a few things around the house, she would meet Aaron at his office.

While on her way to her bedroom, she was so deeply engrossed in sorting out her plans for the day that she didn't notice the darkly clad figure who had silently crept up the basement stairs and was only a few feet behind her. Just when she was about to step into her room, he attacked.

A leather-gloved hand grabbed her from behind, covering her mouth. Her first instinct was to stomp on the man's foot and grind the spiked heel of her shoe into it. Then, she felt the barrel of a gun in her back.

"Let's take it nice and easy, lady," the intruder threatened, forcing her back into the hallway. Noting that his voice sounded muffled, Teri assumed he must be wearing something to conceal his face.

Continuing to cover her mouth with his hand and holding the gun against her back, they slowly backed down the stairs. When he noticed her briefcase on the floor in the foyer, he motioned for her to pick it up. Twice on the way downstairs, she nearly fell and he roughly jerked her to her feet.

When they reached the basement of the house, Teri gasped. The living room had been ransacked.

Books, papers, clothing and other objects had been tossed haphazardly around the room. Her computer and other pieces of furniture had also been tampered with. Seat cushions and pillows were ripped to shreds.

Removing his hand from her mouth, the intruder grabbed her arm and pushed her onto a chair.

"Dump everything outta that bag onto the floor and make it quick," the gunman demanded.

When she emptied her briefcase, her personal items fell to the floor.

He kicked the bag in frustration and said, "Where's the book?"

"What book?" Teri croaked, her throat dry from fear.

"The book. The astrology book from the auction. Where is it?" he asked again, impatiently.

An image of the book sitting on Aaron's desk flashed through her mind. She replied, "I don't know what you're talking about."

Before she could react, he struck her across the face with the back of his hand, sending her sprawling off the chair onto the floor.

"Stop playin' with me, bitch. I ain't got all day. Where's the book?" he shouted.

Teri's ears were ringing and her vision blurred from the force of the blow. Trying to refocus, she shook her head and struggled back onto the chair.

"I told you I don't know what you're talking about. If I did, don't you think I'd give it to you?" she cried, her voice shaking. The taste of blood was filling her mouth from the cut inside her cheek and she could already feel the area below her right eye beginning to swell.

Without warning, he lunged at her and grabbed her by the hair. He kicked the chair from under her and slammed her against the wall next to the hologram of her grandmother.

"You wanna think a little harder about where that book might be?" the gunman sneered, his masked face only inches from hers. When he blinked, Teri was able to see that he was fair-skinned.

"Still can't remember? Maybe this will help," he snickered, and jerked her skirt up with the tip of the gun. Her entire body was shaking so badly, she had difficulty standing.

"I'm getting very tired of this," the gunman said, his voice rising. Placing the gun directly against her temple, he put his mouth against her ear and whispered, "If you don't start talking on the count of three, I'll blow your pretty little head off. One, two ---"

The countdown abruptly ended when the holographic image of her grandmother, hanging directly above them, suddenly came to life and spoke.

"You leave my granddaughter alone, you devil!" Elizabeth William's image shouted angrily, looking directly at the intruder, her eyes blazing.

"Wha, what the hell ---" the gunman stuttered, his eyes bulging.

Distracted by the talking picture, he had lowered the gun and stepped back. Without taking a second to consider the folly of her actions, Teri shoved him aside and sprinted toward the French doors.

She felt something whiz past her head, ending in a loud "plink" as a bullet shattered one of the small square glass panes of the door near her.

She kicked them open and was stumbling across her small yard when the second shot grazed her arm. Ignoring the pain, she climbed onto the wooden bench against the wall and hoisted herself over the top of the brick enclosure that separated her yard from her neighbor's. In the process, she ripped her skirt and skinned the palms of her hands.

After she cleared the wall, another bullet struck the top of it. She almost fell on Mrs. Klein who was pruning her rose bushes.

"Oh my God! Teri! What are you doing?" Mrs. Klein said, trying to help Teri out of her plant bed.

"Be quiet and stay down," Teri whispered, shoving her startled neighbor back onto the patio floor. After she was sure the gunman was gone, in a voice that sounded more calm than she really felt, she said, "We've got to call the police. My house has been robbed."

* * * *

While Teri sat trembling in Mrs. Klein's living room, her

neighbor had called the police and administered first aid. Then, while they waited for the police to arrive, she poured two glasses of brandy. They both needed something to help them calm their nerves. Her final act as the day's good Samaritan had been to call Aaron at his office.

"My god, Teri! Are you all right?" Aaron rushed to her side.

"I think so," she replied, her voice shaking.

He hugged her and she clung to him.

Stepping back to examine her physical appearance, he asked, "Are you hurt?" When he noticed the ugly bruise under her right eye and the bandage on her arm, he became alarmed.

"Do you want to go to the hospital?"

"No. The paramedics were already here. The bullet only grazed my arm so they gave me a shot of penicillin and left a cold pack for my eye. My hands and legs are a little scraped but they'll heal," she said, giving him a weak smile.

"Did you see who it was?"

"No."

"Did he say what he wanted?"

"No," she replied again. Then, glancing quickly in Mrs. Klein's direction and then back to him, she silently mouthed, "I'll tell you later."

Nodding his head discretely, he asked, "Are the police over there now?"

"Yes. They said they'll be back after they've checked the house."

"Okay. When they're finished questioning you, if it isn't too upsetting, we'll go back to the house so you can grab some clothes. You're coming home with me. Then you can tell me the whole story."

* * * *

Thirty minutes later, Teri was hugging Mrs. Klein, thanking her for her help.

"You're the best neighbor and friend a person could ever

wish for," Teri said, her eyes filled with tears.

"It was nothing. I promised your folks I'd keep an eye on you after they moved back to Barbados and I'm a woman of my word," she smiled.

"I'm glad you did," Aaron said, giving Mrs. Klein a quick peck on the cheek.

"My pleasure. You two go on now. You'd better take good care of this girl, Prof. Jacobs," she said, sternly, giving them both a motherly pat on the cheek.

"I will. Thanks again," Aaron said and joined Teri who was already sitting in the passenger seat of his Blazer.

* * * *

After they had driven a few blocks, Aaron said, "Mrs. Klein and the police filled me in on what happened but I think they're missing a few important details. What was the man looking for? How did you manage to escape?"

Shaking her head, Teri sighed.

"You're not going to believe either answer."

"Try me."

"Okay. He was looking for the astrology book from the auction. I was able to get away when the hologram of Granny yelled at him to let me go."

Aaron was so stunned by her answer, he nearly hit the car in front of him that had stopped for a red light. He quickly slammed on the brakes.

"What?" he cried, turning to look at her.

"You heard me."

"That's crazy!" Aaron shook his head.

"Look. Besides the fact that I'm on the verge of hysterics, I'm just as confused as you are," Teri replied, holding up her hands that were still shaking as proof.

"Well, since someone offered me one hundred thousand dollars for the book and I turned them down, maybe now they're trying to steal it. But this business with your grandmother's hologram..."

"It's a long story and when my mind isn't so muddled, I'll be able to explain it better. For now, you'll just have to take my word for it. If it's all right with you, I'd like to stop talking now. I have a headache, my arm and eye hurt like hell and I feel like throwing up," Teri said, bursting into tears.

"I'm sorry," Aaron said, reaching over to hug her with his free arm. "Hold on. We're almost there. As soon as we get upstairs, I'll give you something for your headache and you can go right to bed."

Teri unbuckled her seatbelt and leaned over to rest her head against his shoulder as she continued to cry. After such a wonderful morning, this was turning out to be the worst day of her life. She couldn't wait for it to be over.

* * * *

Edward Hastings slammed down the phone in disgust and cursed. Couldn't anyone do anything right? Lenny's attempt at getting the book had been unsuccessful. Then he'd had the nerve to blame a talking head of some old woman as being the reason for the screw up.

Pounding his fist into the palm of his hand, Edward's mind raced. Since Lenny couldn't find the book at her house, there was only one other possibility. The professor must have it.

Edward assumed that Aaron was still with Teri and the police at the brownstone. If he hurried, he could probably search the professor's apartment before he returned.

* * * *

When he arrived at Aaron's building, Edward was glad to find the lobby deserted with the exception of the guard at the desk. Before the man had a chance to question him, Edward raised his hand and pointed at the guard. Within seconds, the guard slumped over his desk, the victim of a fatal heart attack.

Edward's body underwent a strange transformation while he

rode the elevator up to his destination. When the doors opened on the tenth floor, his appearance had changed from a blonde hair, blue-eyed attractive young man, to a short, stooped over sixty-year old, dressed in a green maintenance uniform, complete with tool belt.

Edward glanced up and down the hall as he stood outside Aaron's apartment door. Satisfied that everything seemed normal, he quickly passed his hand over the deadbolt and heard a "click."

He wasted no time beginning his search. Tossing books, papers and furniture out of the way, he frantically looked for the journal. Still unable to find it, he became enraged. Where the hell could it possibly be? He kicked a chair out of the way and tried to think. If it wasn't at either residence, then they must have it with them!

"Shit! How the hell am I supposed to get it then?" Edward swore. He was tired and his lungs were beginning to fail him from being outside in the polluted city air too long. If he didn't return to the safety of his air conditioned apartment soon, he wouldn't be able to breathe, let alone chase after a book.

He picked up a newspaper and flung it across the room in frustration. He was about to open the door to leave the apartment, when, to his surprise, someone rang the bell.

Squinting through the peep hole, he cursed when he saw the face of an old woman. He took a second to compose himself and then opened the door a few inches.

"Oh! I saw you going into Prof. Jacobs' apartment. Who are you?" the old woman asked, craning her neck to look inside.

"I'm the new weekend maintenance man. I came to fix Prof. Jacobs' leaky faucet," Edward said, changing his voice to match his appearance.

"Oh? I've never seen you before. What's your name?" the old woman said as she tried to push the door.

"Irving," Edward replied and before the old woman could push the door again, he quickly stepped into the hall and slammed it shut.

"I'm Mrs. Lindsey from next door. I didn't know you could

get repairs done on Sundays," she said, eyeing him suspiciously.

"Only if it's an emergency" Edward smiled, revealing what looked like an ill fitting set of false teeth.

"Oh. That's too bad. I was gonna ask if you could maybe take a look at my stove. The pilot light keeps going out," Mrs. Lindsey said, disappointedly.

"I have another stop to make but for a nice lady like you, I could come back and take a look at it later," Edward winked, turning on the charm. "If this old bitch doesn't get out of my way, I'll electrocute her right here in the hall," he thought.

"Why that's very nice of you. I'll be home all day. It's apartment 10C, right here," she grinned, displaying an equally ugly pair of dentures as she pointed to her apartment.

"Okay. I'll see you in a few minutes," Edward promised and hurried toward the elevator. Fortunately, it hadn't left the floor.

"Good bye Irving," Mrs. Lindsey called out sweetly as the doors closed.

"Meddlesome old bitch," Edward mumbled and pressed the button for the basement. When the doors reopened, his appearance had returned to normal.

In the taxi speeding downtown, Edward tried to control his rage. Things weren't working out as he'd planned.

"The next time I see that astrologer and her interfering boyfriend, they're gonna regret it," Edward vowed.

* * * *

When Aaron turned onto his street, he was shocked to see two police cars and an ambulance parked in front of his building.

"Good grief. Not more trouble," he muttered, turning onto the ramp which led to the underground garage.

When they entered the lobby, they were met by two uniformed officers and a detective who watched a body, covered with a sheet, wheeled through the front doors.

"What happened?" Aaron asked, approaching the detective.

"Who are you?" he asked, eyeing them suspiciously.

In her semi-hysterical condition, Teri had to stifle a giggle.

She imagined how she must have looked to the police with her black eye, torn clothes and bandaged arm.

"I'm a tenant in this building and this is my fiancé," Aaron replied.

"Oh? And may I ask what your name is, sir?"

"Prof. Aaron Jacobs from apartment 10B," Aaron replied, curtly.

One of the uniformed officers had joined them and was now scanning a copy of the building's tenants list which was attached to a clipboard.

"It's here, Det. Williams," the officer nodded.

"Approximately what time did you leave the building today?" the detective asked, ignoring Aaron's tone.

"About an hour and a half ago. Why?"

"Was Mr. Donzetti at the desk when you left?"

"Yes. Why are you asking me all these questions?" Aaron asked, growing impatient.

Giving him the once over again, the detective sighed and finally said, "Because one of the other tenants found him dead at his desk about a half hour ago. We think he had a heart attack."

"What?" Aaron was stunned. "That's impossible. He was the picture of health when I left."

"That may be the case but he's dead, nonetheless. Did he ever mention to you that he had a heart condition?"

"No," Aaron shook his head.

"Well. We'll find out after the coroner performs an autopsy. I think you should go up to your apartment now. Your fiancé doesn't look too good," Det. Williams said, nodding in Teri's direction. At the mention of Franco's sudden death, her ears had started ringing. She unsteadily held onto Aaron's arm.

"I'm sorry, Teri. Hold on. We'll be upstairs in a second," Aaron said, grabbing her around the shoulders and leading her toward the elevator.

When they finally reached his apartment, Teri leaned against the wall, willing herself to remain upright while Aaron fumbled with his keys. Just as he turned the lock, Mrs. Lindsey opened her door.

"Oh, Prof. Jacobs! Isn't that terrible news about Franco?"

"Yes, Mrs. Lindsey. It's very shocking. Now if you'll excuse us---"

"What's wrong with Teri? She looks terrible." the old woman asked, when she noticed Teri's disheveled appearance.

"She was in an accident. Now if you'd excuse us---" Aaron said again, only to be interrupted once more.

"Oh, that's terrible. This city is getting more dangerous by the minute. I don't know why our stupid mayor can't do something about it," the old woman complained.

Teri felt herself fading fast and if Aaron didn't shut the woman up so they could get inside, she was going to end up on the floor, right at their feet.

"Yes it is, Mrs. Lindsey, Aaron said when he finally got the door open.

"Oh, by the way, that nice new weekend maintenance man stopped by to fix your faucet. He promised to check my stove but he hasn't come back yet. I wonder---"

"Good bye, Mrs. Lindsey," Aaron said, pushing open the door and dragging Teri inside. Before the old woman could say another word, he slammed the door in her face.

"What maintenance man?" Aaron mumbled and then stopped abruptly in the foyer.

"Oh shit! What the hell happened in here?" Aaron exclaimed.

Stepping from behind him to see what was wrong, Teri stared in shock. The sight of Aaron's ransacked apartment proved to be the last straw. Giving in to the buzzing that filled her head, she slowly slid to the floor, grateful for the tranquility of unconsciousness.

CHAPTER X

A few minutes later, Teri was awakened by the sound of Aaron's voice. His face gradually came into focus and she sat up, only to fall back onto the pillows overcome by another wave of dizziness.

"Just relax for awhile. You're in no condition to do anything," Aaron said firmly while placing a wet cloth on her forehead.

Teri acquiesced and closed her eyes, overpowered by tiredness.

It was early evening when she finally awoke. She sat up and was relieved to discover that her dizziness had subsided. But there was a dull ache where her arm had been grazed by the bullet.

Turning on the light next to the bed, she spotted her tote bag and rummaged through it until she found a pair of jeans and a T-shirt.

When she entered the living room, Aaron was sitting on the floor frowning as he tried to sort through the mess.

"Feeling better?" he asked when he noticed her standing in the doorway.

"Yes, but my throat is as dry as a desert. I need something to drink" she replied, running her tongue over her chapped lips.

"Sit down. I'll get it for you," Aaron said, and got up.

"No, that's okay," Teri waved him away and went into the kitchen.

"There's something very strange going on here," she said when she returned.

"No kidding," Aaron replied, shaking his head at the mess. "Oh, I called Andrew and he's over at your house with the people from the security company. They're trying to figure out how that guy got in without tripping the alarm."

"A lot of good it did. When I opened the door, everything seemed normal. What I don't understand is what's so important about that book that someone would resort to violence and vandalism to get it?"

"I don't know. How about taking a look at it now while I clean up?" Aaron said, handing her the astrology book.

"Have the police been here?"

"Yes. One of the officers in the lobby came up while you were sleeping. I still don't understand what happened to Franco. He was perfectly fine when I left this afternoon. I also wanna know what that maintenance man Mrs. Lindsey mentioned was doing in here. There's nothing wrong with my sink," Aaron replied.

"Do you think he may have been the one who did this?"

"Maybe. Mrs. Lindsey said we only missed him by a few minutes."

Suddenly, they heard the phone ringing somewhere in the room. Cursing, Aaron frantically searched through the piles of books and papers, finding it just before it stopped ringing.

"It's your friend Regina," he said, handing her the phone.

"Teri! My god! Are you okay? I called your house and your brother answered. He told me what happened," Regina cried, breathlessly.

"I've been better but I'll live."

"Thank goodness. Listen, this may not be the time to bring this up but I have some info I think you need to know."

"Sure. Go ahead."

"Well, that chart you asked me to double check last night was really driving me crazy. I wanted to see what that Hastings guy might be up to this year, so I decided to run a solar return on him. I used New York as the location. If you think the natal chart was weird, wait 'til you hear what I got this time," Regina said, her voice tinged with excitement and fear.

"I'm almost afraid to listen," Teri shivered, recalling her experience at the party.

"Well, hold onto your hat. His chart makes Hitler look like a choir boy. He has all of his planets in fire signs and not a drop of water. No Pisces, Cancer or Scorpio. This guy has no compassion for people. He's a regular stick of dynamite waiting to go off. If I didn't double check my software, I'd swear my computer had gone crazy!"

"There's nothing wrong with your software and what you found reinforces what I saw in his hand," Teri replied and described the results of her impromptu palm reading.

"Goodness, Teri. I hope you don't run into him again. I'm getting a really bad feeling about him."

"So am I," Teri agreed.

"Well, be careful. If I see anything that's important, I'll give you a call. Will you be staying at Aaron's?"

"Yes. I don't feel comfortable being in the house alone yet," Teri replied, recalling the raw terror she'd experienced when the man held the gun against her temple. She wondered if she'd ever feel safe in her own home again.

"Good. You take care, hon."

"Thanks Regina," Teri said and hung up.

"Now what?" Aaron asked, as he stuffed a handful of crumpled and torn papers into a garbage bag.

"It isn't good but at least I know I'm not going crazy," Teri sighed, rubbing her temples.

"We need less questions and more answers," Aaron said, shaking his head after Teri explained her friend's discovery.

"I don't know what's giving me a bigger headache, his chart or this book," Teri said, with disgust, holding both items in her hands. "Do you know anyone who can translate this text without having to look up every other word?"

Aaron frowned and mentally ran through his list of colleagues.

"There's a priest who was a member of a discussion group I used to belong to who I think is proficient in Latin. He's in a monastery in Albany. I'll give him a call," Aaron replied.

While he made the call, Teri perused the pages of the astrology book. There were six charts interspersed amongst the pages of text. She wondered if the text was an interpretation of the charts and if so, what it said.

Then, looking at Edward Hastings' chart, she recalled what Regina found in his solar return. Obviously, there was something very strange and dangerous about him. She'd never seen a chart where there were so many planets in fire signs. And to have the volatile planet Mars in fire meant that the person was prone to extremely violent behavior.

The image of the gunman came to mind again. The unknown assailant seemed very comfortable using violence to get what he wanted, Teri thought, touching the tender area under her right eye where he'd struck her. She had no doubt that if her grandmother's hologram hadn't distracted him, she could have been more severely injured or even killed. Were Hastings and the break-ins somehow connected?

Her thoughts were interrupted when Aaron hung up the phone.

"It's all set. Father Francis said he's willing to take a stab at it. Since it may take a day or so, he's invited us to stay at one of the hiker's cottages on the grounds. I think we could both use the change of scenery. We'll leave tomorrow morning," Aaron said and sat next to her.

"No. Let's leave tonight. There are too many strange things happening and I don't think we can afford to waste anymore time finding out what's in this book," Teri said firmly.

"Okay, if you feel up to it," Aaron replied, gently brushing her hair back so he could look at her eye. The swelling had gone down, leaving a nasty looking black and blue mark in its wake.

"I'm afraid to look in the mirror," Teri smiled, suddenly reminded of how badly she must look. Her hair was full of tangles and sticking out in every direction. Searching through the pocket of her jeans, she found a rubber band and tied her hair back into a make-shift ponytail.

"You look beautiful even under stress," Aaron reassured her with a kiss.

"Sure. I didn't mean to scare you by fainting like that. I think I've had a bit too much excitement for one day," Teri chuckled, patting the bandage on her arm.

"Well, you'll be able to relax at the monastery. It's peaceful and the grounds are beautiful."

"Good. Let me call Andrew to let him know where I'll be and then we can leave."

* * * *

Laurie Sanders turned over in bed and groggily looked over at the shadowy outline of Edward sleeping next to her. She stared at his almost lifeless body in amazement. He was the only person she'd known who slept like he was dead, barely showing signs of breathing.

Lightly tracing the outline of his muscular arm with her finger, she smiled. Although he was a very mysterious and unusual person, she had to admit that Edward Hastings was the best lover she'd ever had. His sexual techniques, and what he'd taught her, made her blush. Regardless of her mood, whenever he gave her that certain look, she became so horny that she'd have an orgasm even without him touching her!

Laurie reminisced about the day they first met. She was strolling through the farmer's market in Greenwich Village, depressed after an angry breakup with her boyfriend. Unknown to her, Vincent had been carrying on an affair with one of her best friends. When she stopped at the book vendor's table, Edward suddenly appeared next to her. They'd struck up a conversation and before she knew it, he invited her to dinner, stating he was new in town and perhaps she could show him around the city. Flattered that such an attractive man would approach her, Laurie accepted his invitation.

Edward wined, dined and charmed her. He made her feel beautiful and special. And he was very sexy. When dinner ended, she suggested he join her at her apartment for a nightcap. One thing led to another and before she knew it, they were in bed. It was nearly one o'clock the next afternoon when they finally ceased their lovemaking, exhausted and exhilarated. Two days later, Edward moved in.

After living with him for six months, she'd fallen madly in love with this unusual man, but she still didn't know very much about him. He vaguely mentioned that he was born in Europe and traveled around the world most of his life. When she inquired about his profession, he replied that he was fortunate and didn't really need to work. He had inherited a substantial sum of money when his parents were tragically killed in a car accident when he was younger.

But none of that really mattered to her since she believed they were a match made in heaven. She was just grateful that they were together and the envy of all her girlfriends.

Edward stirred in his sleep. She immediately became aroused and licked his ear. She slid her hand under the covers to caress him. He grabbed her wrist in mid-stroke.

"Be a darling and run a bath for us," he said, slowly opening his eyes to look at her.

"Oh! I didn't mean to wake you. But you looked so delicious I couldn't resist," she giggled.

"We'll pick up where we left off last night when we get in the tub, all right darling?" he smiled, squeezing her breasts.

"Oh Edward, you naughty boy!" she squealed and jumped from the bed.

"Silly bitch," he mumbled under his breath. Stretching, he yawned and sat up.

When he heard Laurie turn the water on in the bathroom, he made a phone call.

"What's going on?" he asked when Lenny picked up.

"They're at the Professor's apartment."

"Is the tracker in place?"

"Yeah. If they use the Blazer, I'll be able to follow 'em without them suspectin' anything."

"Good. Keep an eye on them while I figure out what to do next," Edward ordered.

"Will do."

Edward got up and went into the bathroom. Laurie was

already in the large, whirlpool tub lathering herself seductively with *bubble bath*.

"Come join me, darling. The temperature's just the way you like it," she purred, blowing bubbles at him.

"In a second. Nature calls," he replied and stepped around the wall that separated the toilet from the bathtub. When he was through relieving himself, he flushed the toilet and turned to gaze fondly at her as she washed her legs with a sponge.

He was about to join her in the tub when the phone rang.

"Yeah?" Edward whispered into the receiver.

"They just left the garage and are heading north on the West Side Highway," Lenny reported.

Where the hell were they going? He couldn't let them get away now, especially since he was more than positive that Jacobs had his journal.

"Okay. Follow them and don't let them out of your sight. I'll try to catch up with you as soon as I can," Edward said.

When he returned to the bathroom, he sighed. He felt badly about what he had to do next. But, he had no choice.

"Hurry, darling. The water's getting cold," Laurie said, playfully splashing water at him with her foot.

"We can't let that happen, can we?" Edward smiled, sitting on the side of the tub. Laurie purred when he stroked her breasts. Taking his hand, she rubbed it along her body under the water.

"Ah well. All good things must come to an end," Edward sighed, *ignoring his arousal. Without warning, a flash of white light shot from his hand into the water. The current of electricity traveled through the water.* Laurie Sanders bolted upright. Her body immediately began to jerk and thrash wildly, splashing water on the floor and wall. Her head banged against the side of the tub until it bled. Then, all movement ceased.

Standing over the tub, Edward was ambivalent. He had to admit that it was a cruel way to kill her but he'd enjoyed it nonetheless. He liked to be creative when it was time to rid himself of a problem.

"Goodnight, my sweet," he said, bending over to kiss her

forehead. He purposely ignored her eyes, which had rolled to the back of her head, and the blood trickling from her mouth.

When he finished dressing, Edward went through the dresser drawers and closets removing the few items of clothing he'd brought when he moved in. Gathering them in his arms, he stuffed them into a duffel bag and zipped it shut. He took one last look around the apartment and smiled, remembering the countless hours of sexual enjoyment he had experienced there. But this was no time to indulge in nostalgia. He had more important things to take care of.

Edward strolled past the guard's desk and paused to look at the man who was busy reading the paper. He was about to turn the page, when the guard stopped, his mind drawing a blank when he tried to think of what he had been getting ready to do. Then, he looked down at the page and recalled his original thought. Satisfied with the man's reaction, Edward walked through the lobby doors, confident that when Laurie Sander's body was discovered, the guard wouldn't be able to recall that Edward had ever been a tenant. He had erased the guard's memory of his existence.

Edward stood outside the building and contemplated his next move. He needed a car. Since he was going to be traveling, he wanted to go in style. Looking up and down the curb at several parked cars, he spotted a late model luxury sedan that was to his liking. He walked over to the car and passed his hand over the lock. The button immediately popped up. Then, placing his hand on the hood, he disabled the alarm.

The car's engine hummed as Edward directed the air-conditioning vents toward his face. He knew that the clear night air would be beneficial to his lungs.

He reached for the car phone to call Lenny again.

"They're on the thruway heading north. I'm about a quarter mile behind them," Lenny reported.

"Where the hell are they going?"

"I don't know but they won't get there without me findin' out," Lenny replied, confidently. The Blazer appeared as a green blip slowly moving across a computerized map of the area on the screen. It was attached to the tracking device mounted on his dashboard.

"All right. I'm about a half hour behind you. Call me at this number as soon as they stop or leave the thruway. I don't want to lose you."

"Okay," Lenny agreed.

PART III
REVELATIONS

The Eighth House   Karen Sealy

CHAPTER I

Teri and Aaron rode in silence for nearly an hour, the car speeding along the near-empty thruway. When he glanced over at her, Aaron saw that her eyes were closed but she wasn't sleeping.

"Explain that business about your grandmother's hologram again," he said.

"First, I have a question for you," Teri replied, opening her eyes.

"What?"

"Do you believe in life after death or reincarnation?"

Surprised by her question, he didn't answer right away.

"Well, there's a lot of Biblical and contemporary literature about it and most religions believe in some form of afterlife," Aaron said, carefully.

"You didn't answer my question. What do *you* believe?"

"To be honest with you, I'm not sure. I've never had the experience of having a dead person appear to me. Why?"

"Because if you did believe in it, you wouldn't find the incident with the hologram so strange. It's not the first time my grandmother appeared to me since she died," Teri said, turning to look at him through the darkness.

"Really?"

"Yes, the first time was a few months after she passed away. I was having a pretty rough time coping with her death. You know, she taught me everything I know about astrology. When she died, I felt as if I'd not only lost my grandmother but a very close friend too. Even though my mother and I have a good relationship, I always felt more comfortable talking to Granny about things that were very personal," Teri replied, touching her grandmother's cross around her neck as she spoke.

"Anyway, I was sitting in her chair in the basement and suddenly, she was standing there. She told me to stop grieving for her and to get on with my life. And she reminded me that *something important was going to happen and that I'd need all the emotional, spiritual and physical strength I could muster.* She also told me that she'd always watch over me and that if I ever needed her, all I had to do was say so and she'd come."

"What happened after that?" Aaron asked, fascinated by her story.

"Nothing. I graduated from college and took over the business. You know the rest."

"So tell me about the hologram again."

Teri shivered as she recalled the scene in the basement.

"The man had pinned me against the wall right next to it with the gun pointed at my head. He said he would give me 'til the count of three to tell him where the book was before, as he put it, he'd,'blow my pretty little head off.' At the count of two, the hologram lit up and Granny's image turned and looked him dead in the eye. She shouted at him to leave me alone. He was so startled, he took the gun away from my head and backed up. That's when I made a run for the French doors."

"I was so scared, I don't remember thinking about her or even praying. But maybe I did and she heard me. It's a good thing, too. I didn't think I was going to get out of there alive on my own," Teri admitted.

"Well, I can't understand it but if you say it happened, then I believe you. I know you're a very spiritual person and I know you aren't the type to suffer from hallucinations. I'm just glad someone was looking out for you, whoever it was," Aaron said, reaching over to squeeze her hand.

"It's funny that I even had the hologram. Andrew said Granny told him to give it to me on my forty-first birthday. She said that's when I'd really need it. I wonder if she had a premonition that something like this was going to happen to me, or was it just a coincidence?"

"I guess we'll never know. Anyway, I'm glad she's there for you when I can't be. But that'll change once we get married."

Teri nodded and reached over to kiss him on the cheek.

The Eighth House

Karen Sealy

* * * *

The Blazer pulled onto the grounds of the St. Thomas Aquinas Monastery shortly before 11:00 p.m. Father Francis opened the heavy wooden doors of the old stone building and waved, greeting his guests.

"Aaron! It's wonderful to see you!" the priest said, rushing over to his friend.

"I wish it were under better circumstances," Aaron replied, warmly, towering over the petite man as he shook his hand and hugged him.

"And this must be your fiancé, Miss Ellis," Father Francis said, turning to Teri. "I'm pleased to meet you. Well, let's go inside. Even though it's late, I took the liberty of having a light dinner prepared so you can eat while we talk. I'm as anxious as you are to find out what's in that book" he said, dropping Teri's hands and hooking his arm through hers. Aaron followed, carrying their bags.

The foyer of the main building was cool even though there were no signs of air conditioners. The twelve foot walls made of thick grey stones, were lined with stained glass windows along the top. Tapestry rugs covered the light brown marble floors and heavy lead cylindrical shaped chandeliers lit the way. The strong scent of incense that hung in the air reminded Teri of her grandmother.

When they reached the end of the hall, the priest turned left and opened a door. Inside was a small but comfortably furnished room. The largest piece of furniture was a heavy oak dining table where a buffet dinner had been laid out.

"Please, make yourselves at home," Father Francis said and ushered them in.

"Excuse me, Father, but could you direct me to the restroom?" Teri asked.

"Oh, I'm sorry. How silly of me. Of course you want to freshen up after your long trip. It's just beyond that door," he apologized, pointing.

"Thank you."

As she walked away, Father Francis stared after her and then turned to Aaron. "By the way, where is the book?"

"Here," Aaron said, taking it out of his bag.

The priest took the book and sat down across from Aaron. Turning it slowly in his hands, he caressed the smooth, leather cover.

When she joined them at the table, Teri studied the priest's small, wrinkled face. His reading glasses gave him an owl-like appearance and white, wispy hair framed his head like a halo. He was short in stature and his priestly garb covered a thin, frail body.

"Aaron, please tell me again how you came to acquire this book," the priest said, adjusting his glasses.

Aaron described the events at the auction.

"Did you happen to see the person you were bidding against?"

"No, but she did call me a few days later on behalf of her client. Her name is Laurie Sanders. It seems she represented an avid collector of rare astrology books. She wanted to know if I'd be interested in selling it to her for one hundred thousand dollars."

Both men where startled when Teri suddenly spilled some of the coffee she was drinking. Father Frances quickly handed her several paper napkins to wipe off the table.

"What did you say the woman's name was?" Teri asked.

"Laurie Sanders. Why?" Aaron asked, puzzled by her reaction to the name.

"Oh my God," Teri whispered. "That's the name of the woman who requested Edward Hastings' reading!"

Aaron was flabbergasted.

"Are you sure?"

"Yes. It's right here in my appointment book," Teri replied, frantically searching through her bag. When she retrieved it, she quickly turned to the page and showed it to him.

"If the person who attacked you didn't specifically ask for the book the day after you were at that party, I would think this was just a strange coincidence. Now, I'm beginning to think there's a connection between that woman's phone call, the man at the party and our places being broken into," Aaron said.

"What happened at the party?" Father Francis asked.

She described Hastings and the chart. The priest nodded his head, interrupting when he needed clarification.

"So, what do you think, Father?" Aaron asked when Teri had finished.

"Before I give my opinion, I must ask that the purpose of our meeting remain a secret among us. As you both know, the practice of astrology is condemned by the Church and I could get into serious trouble if any of my superiors found out that I was assisting an astrologer."

"Of course, Father. We both appreciate your willingness to help us," Aaron agreed.

"Good. Now as to your question, I agree that there may be a connection between this book and the weird man you met at the party, Teri. Maybe the answer is here," the priest said, opening the book.

Teri and Aaron anxiously watched as the priest slowly began reading the ancient language. After nearly twenty minutes, his expression became more serious.

"I'm afraid you're in a bit of trouble," the priest said, gravely. "There is a connection between this book and Mr. Hastings. According to what's written on the first page, it's his personal journal. He specifically encrypted everything in charts and an old form of Latin so that it would be difficult for the average person to read. It also says that if it should fall into the wrong hands, he'll stop at nothing to get it back."

"Then, it continues with a narrative about his childhood. It seems that his mother, Margaret, was a prostitute by trade and that his childhood was quite a wretched one. He then goes on to describe the emotional turmoil he experienced since he both loved and hated his mother because of her profession and how he felt neglected because of it."

"The next section is very disturbing. He gives a detailed account of how he accidently murdered his mother's greedy pimp, Rick. Then, he and his mother, along with some friends, opened a bordello of their own with the money he stole from the pimp. He describes how living in such a beautiful brownstone at 925 W. 4th Street made him feel like a king."

The priest was about to continue the translation when both Teri and Aaron shouted, "1925 what?"

"1925 W. 4th Street. Do you know that address?" the priest asked, puzzled by their sudden outburst.

"I most certainly do. That's where I live! That's the address of my house!" Teri exclaimed, grabbing the book from the priest to look at the text.

"That's crazy!" Aaron shook his head.

"Would you like me to stop?" Fr. Francis asked, upset by Teri's obvious distress over the revelation.

"No, no. Please continue. I'll be alright," Teri waved her hand and slid the book back over to him.

"As you wish," the priest said, hesitantly and adjusted his glasses.

Fr. Francis read in silence for a few minutes and then stopped, crossed himself and whispered, "Oh Lord."

"What is it, Father?" they said in unison.

Father Francis placed the book face down on the table and shook his head.

"Well, it seems you were right in your assessment of him, Teri. He goes on to describe how he 'died' at the age of seventeen in 1917. And, instead of going toward the light of forgiveness and our Heavenly Father, Satan intercepted him. He speaks fondly of how the devil took him under his wing and became the father he never knew. Satan promised him that in exchange for carrying out his diabolic tasks on Earth, Mr. Hastings would be granted immortality, unlimited wealth and supernatural powers. He was also told that by joining forces with him, he would have the ability to seek revenge against everyone on Earth who had hurt him, which seemed especially appealing to him."

"Then, he attended the devil's vigorous re-education program that would allow him to fully assimilate himself into any environment, thus enabling him to conceal his true identity wherever he roamed on Earth."

The Eighth House

Karen Sealy

"When this so-called re-education was complete, he returned to Earth in 1924."

The priest went on to describe Edward Hastings' account of what he'd been doing for the past seventy-seven years, starting with a church burning in a place called Balmville, Kentucky, that nearly wiped out the entire population. The most devastating entry was the description of the part he played in helping Adolph Hitler come to power.

"My god," Aaron whispered. Now he really wished he'd sold the book when he had the chance. What in the world had he gotten them into?

"It also says that Hastings, unlike his associates, has been given extra ordinary powers by Satan which will enable him to carry out some very specific tasks. He has a keen sense of smell that allows him to track people like an animal and he can manipulate electricity. He can also alter his outward appearance at will."

"But why would he reveal himself to me at the party?" Teri asked when she could finally bring herself to speak.

"I don't know. Perhaps he was testing you. He's written that astrologers who are good at their craft are his worse enemies. They would have the ability to interpret his charts and fully uncover what he's done in the past and plans to do in the future. He also may have been trying to scare you off."

"Well, he did a pretty good job," Teri said, dryly. For the first time in her life, she wished she'd chosen a different career path.

"There is some good news, though. He has two weaknesses. His lungs are failing him because the air is polluted and he can't enter holy places or go near members of the clergy. At least he can't harm you while you're here if he decides to come after you."

"I guess, at this point, we have to be grateful for small things," Aaron said, grimly. "So what do you think we should do now?"

"Well, I have quite a bit to read. It's late and I think the two of you have been through enough for one day. We can pick up where we left off tomorrow. Let me take you over to the cottage," the priest said, removing his glasses and rubbing his eyes.

"All right, Father. But before we go I have a request," Aaron said, taking Teri's hand.

"Of course. What is it?"

"Would you marry us?"

"What?" Teri cried, pulling her hand away.

"Look, Teri. From what Francis has told us tonight, we're in a lot of trouble. If Hastings comes after us, there's no telling what may happen. I'm willing to bet he sent that guy to your house to steal the book and obviously he gave him instructions to get it any way he could. I'm the one who got us in this mess and I'm going to do everything in my power to protect you. I don't want to wait until this situation is resolved before we get married. We've wasted enough time as it is," Aaron said, firmly.

Teri's mind was a jumble of thoughts. She didn't know what to do. She didn't need Father Francis to translate anything else to be positive that Hastings wasn't going to let a frightened thief discourage him from continuing his mission of retrieving his journal. And after what Regina had seen in his solar return, he would probably use violence if necessary.

Taking Aaron's hand, she finally said, "Well, if our days are numbered, I guess this is just as good a time as any to get married. It might not be legal according to the State but at least we'd have God's blessing." Then, turning to the priest, she said, "Would you please do us the honor, Father?"

"I'd love to," the priest smiled. Aaron let out a very audible *sigh of relief.* "Let me ask Father James and Father Matthews to be witnesses and we'll head over to the chapel," the priest said cheerfully.

* * * *

The chapel was small but designed as beautifully as a large cathedral. Standing in front of the small altar, Aaron and Teri held hands. Father Francis adjusted his robes and opened his missile. The two priests who would serve as witnesses stood nearby smiling broadly.

The Eighth House — Karen Sealy

"I know you would have preferred a more traditional ceremony but I think in the absence of time, you'll be pleased with this one," the priest said and began reading.

As he listened to the couple recite their vows, Father Francis was struck by what a truly significant event this was. Out of evil, came good.

"I now pronounce you husband and wife. Aaron, you may kiss your bride," Father Francis said happily, and closed his book.

Smiling, Aaron bent down to embrace his new wife while behind them, the two priests began to clap. Still beaming, they shook hands with Aaron and took turns kissing Teri.

A few minutes later, Father Francis happily directed them to follow him around to the side of the main building. When they rounded the corner, they spotted a small cottage at the far end of the property.

"We use this cottage as a temporary shelter for hikers who come through here from time to time. There's a very popular trail that begins at the southern end of the property," Father Francis said and pushed the door open.

Teri cried out in delight when she entered the cottage. Inside was a double bed surrounded by vases of freshly cut flowers. On a small table in the corner were two candles, a bucket containing a bottle of champagne, two glasses and a basket of fresh fruit.

"This champagne comes from one of our wineries further upstate," Father Francis said proudly. "I'm sure you'll enjoy it.

Teri was so astounded by what she saw her eyes began to water.

"I don't know what to say. Thank you so much, Father," she said, hugging the priest.

"You've really outdone yourself my friend. Thank you," Aaron agreed, shaking his hand.

"It's our pleasure," the priest said and walked toward the door. "There's a phone on the night table. Feel free to call us if you need anything else."

"Thanks again, Father," Teri said and closed the door behind him.

The Eighth House Karen Sealy

* * * *

Lenny was parked on the road just at the end of the driveway to the entrance of the monastery when Edward pulled up behind him.

"Shit!" Edward swore. He put the car in park and turned off the engine. His anger escalated when he read the sign next to the gate.

"St. Thomas Aquinas Monastery. Of all the fucking places, they had to pick a monastery."

Edward had run into a barrier he never expected. If he dared enter a place as sacred as this, his body would weaken, requiring hours of regeneration. And time wasn't something he had an abundance of.

"What'll we do now, boss?" Lenny asked, stepping out of the car and joining Edward.

"Nothing. I'll take over from here. You can go back to the city," he replied.

"Okay, boss. Good luck," Lenny said, yawning as he got back into his car. Before he pulled off, he handed the tracking device to Edward.

Edward smiled and watched the car disappear around the corner.

"Poor Lenny. He served me well. Too bad he'll never make it back to the city alive," Edward mused.

Edward returned to his car and drove it a few feet away from the driveway until it was concealed by trees while still affording him an unobstructed view of the entrance. As soon as Teri and Aaron left, he'd be right on them. Now all he could do was wait.

Resting his head against the back of the seat, Edward closed his eyes and began fantasizing about just how the astrologer and her boyfriend would meet their deaths.

CHAPTER II

The screen door leading to the porch in the rear of the cottage was open when Teri emerged from the shower. She slipped on her bathrobe and stepped out into the cool air that was filled with the scent of freshly cut grass and wild flowers.

"You're right. It is beautiful, even at night," she noted and pulled up a deck chair next to Aaron.

Puzzled when he didn't reply, she turned and noticed that he was cradling Hastings' journal between his hands. There was a dejected look on his face.

"What's wrong, darlin'?"

Aaron placed the book on the floor and leaned back in his chair, releasing a long sigh.

"I was just thinking how sorry I am that I was able to outbid Laurie Sanders and how I wish I'd sold it when I had the chance. If I had, we wouldn't be sitting here trying to hide from a madman who's trying to kill us for it."

"You can't blame yourself for what's happening. You didn't know the significance of the book. You were just trying to give me something nice for my birthday. Besides, I think there's enough guilt to go around. If I hadn't agreed to that interpretation, Hastings wouldn't have known that I was such a threat to him," Teri reminded him.

"I guess you're right. But what should we do after Francis completes the translation?"

"That all depends on what else he uncovers about Hastings. I still can't believe that I'm living in the same house he did," Teri shivered.

"Well, did your parents ever mention anything about the previous owners?"

"No, except that they bought it from the estate of a banker

back in 1955. I guess the title didn't include information about it having been a bordello back in the early 1900's."

"It's amazing how that beautiful house has such a sordid history. But, you'd never know from the way it looks now," Aaron said.

"No, especially after my parents had the place 'smoked out' shortly before they moved in."

"What's that?" Aaron was puzzled.

"It's a religious ritual where you have a holy person come in and literally walk through the house burning a specific kind of incense, saying prayers to rid the place of any evil spirits that might inhabit the home," Teri explained.

"That's very interesting. I've read about such rituals in my studies but I've never heard it referred to that way," Aaron noted.

"It's common practice in my culture. Anyway, I could try to tackle the charts after Fr. Francis completes the translation but it'll be difficult without my reference books. I was so distracted by the break in, I forgot to bring them with me when we went back to my house."

"We could go back and get them," Aaron suggested.

"No. We'd risk running into Hastings, which is something I definitely don't want to do," Teri shook her head.

"Maybe Andrew could bring them up for you."

"That's an idea. I'll call him in the morning," Teri agreed.

For a few minutes they were silent, enjoying the tranquility of the country evening. The sky was cloudless and the full moon illuminated the darkness with an eerie, white light. The spell was broken when Aaron uttered a low chuckle.

"This isn't exactly what I had in mind for a honeymoon," he said.

"Oh, it isn't so bad. We can always have another one later. What's important is that we're together," Teri smiled.

Aaron motioned for her to sit on his lap and held her in his arms. Her robe had opened and her skin, still damp from her shower, smelled of scented soap.

"Do you think maybe this could be the beginning of the premonition your grandmother was referring to?" Aaron asked.

"The thought did cross my mind. If it isn't, I'm afraid to think that something even worse could happen to us," Teri sighed, hugging him tighter.

"Don't worry. I'm going to do my best to protect you," Aaron promised.

"I know. I have the utmost faith in you," she smiled, kissing the top of his head.

"Well, I think I'll go take a shower. Every muscle in my body is aching from all this stress. Maybe it'll relax me," Aaron declared with a yawn.

"Okay. I'll join you inside in a few minutes. Without my hair dryer, this mess will take a few more minutes to air dry," Teri said, shaking out her hair that was still slightly damp.

Sitting alone in the darkness, Teri touched her cross and thought of her grandmother. How she wished the wise old woman were alive to give her advice. The situation with Hastings not only had her puzzled but fearful. When she thought of everything they knew about him so far, it conjured up a very bad image. They were safe for now, but what would happen if he found them? Could he be defeated and if so, how? She also resented that she might no longer feel safe or comfortable in her own home, not only because of the break-in but because such an evil man had once resided there.

"Ah, Granny. What are we supposed to do?" she asked the darkness. When the only reply was the chirping of crickets in the nearby brush, she sighed and got up.

* * * *

Standing in the shadows of the trees a few feet away from the cottage, Elizabeth watched her granddaughter with a heavy heart.

"Just hold on to your faith, Grandbaby. Just hold on," she whispered into the breeze and then dissolved into the night.

The Eighth House

Karen Sealy

* * * *

Teri was startled and, to her surprise, embarrassed when she entered the room at the exact moment that Aaron was coming out of the bathroom with a towel wrapped around his waist. Sitting on the bed rummaging through his duffel bag, he was oblivious to her sudden nervousness.

She blushed when it occurred to her that, in all the years they'd been together, this was the first time she'd seen him without a shirt on. She noted that, although he was very lean, his arms and chest were very muscular. She also observed that he wore a silver Star of David around his neck.

"Something wrong?" Aaron asked, looking up when he noticed her standing in the middle of the room.

"No. I was just thinking how much we have in common. I see you're wearing a religious symbol too," Teri replied, trying her best to appear relaxed. She found the sight of his nearly naked body extremely exciting.

"You mean this?" Aaron asked, tapping the chain. "I got it from Grandpa Jacobs as a gift for my Bar Mitzvah and I've never taken it off. I guess it has the same significance for me as your Grandmother's cross has for you. By the way, did you bring any of that aloe cream you always use? I forgot to pack mine."

"Yes," Teri replied, reaching into her bag and handing it to him.

"How about putting some on my back for me? I'll return the favor by rubbing some on those scrapes and scratches on your legs. They look pretty uncomfortable," Aaron said, pointing.

"They are," Teri replied, making a face. She motioned for him to turn around and knelt down on the bed behind him.

She gently massaged the cream into his back and shoulders. She could feel the taunt muscles under his smooth, olive-brown skin begin to relax. When she leaned forward to rub the cream on his neck and down his chest, he grabbed her hands.

"My turn," Aaron smiled, gesturing for her to sit down as he got up.

The Eighth House

Karen Sealy

She removed her robe and sat on the edge of the bed. In her haste to pack, she had mistakenly grabbed one of her older, sleeveless nightgowns. The cotton was worn and frayed, to the point of near transparency in certain places, which Aaron seemed to find very interesting from the look on his face.

With the seriousness of a professional masseuse, Aaron squeezed a drop of cream into his palm and rubbed his hands together. Then, he gently lifted her leg by the ankle and slowly smoothed the cream onto the scrapes along the inside of the calf and thigh of her left leg. When he could no longer see traces of the fragrant white cream on her velvety, dark, brown skin, he moved on to the other leg.

With the same slow, precise motions he used before, he began applying the lotion to her right leg. His expression remained blank as his hands crept higher and higher up the shapely limb, pushing up the hem of her nightgown in the process.

Teri closed her eyes and fought to control her breathing which was becoming more labored with every caress. Her temperature had risen and she felt as if all the nerve endings in her body were firing simultaneously. If this was meant to relax her, it was having the opposite effect.

Aaron smirked when his hands reached the top of her thigh and Teri jumped. She was clutching the bed sheets as if for support.

"Does that feel good, Mrs. Jacobs?" Aaron asked, relishing the sight of her obvious sexual arousal.

"Uhuh," Teri murmured.

"Good. I'm just warming up," Aaron winked and in two quick motions, he removed her nightgown and his towel.

Teri didn't have time to feel embarrassed. Before she could react, she found herself laying against the pillows panting with her eyes squeezed shut as Aaron slowly made his way down the length of her body, planting light kisses and caresses along her thighs. Each touch sent a wave of ecstasy flooding through her, making her feel faint.

When he finished kissing each of her toes, he retraced his route. By the time he reached her head, Teri's reactions had become audible.

"Try to control yourself, sweetheart. Remember, we're on sacred ground," Aaron teased and smothered her slightly parted lips with his mouth.

Teri dug her hands into his hair as he kissed her, his mouth tasting of mint toothpaste.

While he'd been concentrating his efforts on pleasing her, he'd been holding back his own burning desire, a feat that had finally become painfully unbearable.

Although this was the first time they'd ever been intimate, their bodies moved in perfect sync, as if their lovemaking had been choreographed. Teri was shocked by how sexually uninhibited she suddenly felt as she breathlessly urged him to thrust harder and deeper into her.

When they climaxed in unison, Aaron had to bury his face in her hair to stifle his cry of pleasure.

The night breeze that drifted through the window near the bed cooled them as they lay motionless, savoring the closeness of their bodies.

With her arms wrapped tightly around Aaron's broad back, his heart beating steadily against hers, Teri was filled with such an overpowering sense of inner peace, she began to cry.

"What's wrong?" Aaron asked when he felt the wetness of her tears against his cheek.

"Nothing. I'm just very, very happy that I met you," Teri smiled, holding him tighter.

At that moment, in that small cottage in the woods, Tericita Ellis-Jacobs felt as if nothing in the world could ever hurt her.

* * * *

While the newlyweds were enjoying their first night together, Edward Hastings continued to doze on and off in his car hidden amongst the trees. And, for some strange reason, the image of Margaret Hastings filled his dreams.

He shook himself awake and reached for the thermos of

coffee he'd gotten from Lenny.

"The fine citizens of the Big Apple will be enjoying my little surprise soon," he smirked and he peered at his watch through the darkness.

* * * *

New York City was still enjoying its last hours of sleep before the start of another busy work week. In Manhattan, traffic was light on the bridges that connected it to the outer boroughs and New Jersey. Few people crowded into the hot subway trains that ran underground. That was the reason the slight tremor went undetected as it caused large cracks to form in the underground pilings that supported the bridges and subway tunnels.

Everything would seem normal until thousands of unsuspecting commuters began to swarm into the city when rush hour commenced in a few hours. Edward wished he could be there to witness the result of his little trick. He'd just have to be content with watching it on television. Those blood thirsty reporters would have more than enough to talk about before the week was over.

* * * *

The eastern sky was just beginning to brighten when Teri awoke, feeling drunk with euphoria. Aaron's lovemaking was more than she'd ever imagined. It had also triggered a part of her sexuality she never knew existed.

She turned on her side, leaned on her elbow and silently observed him while he slept. He was laying on his back with his head tilted away from her. She felt like a voyeur as she studied his profile. His face was completely relaxed, making him appear younger than his forty-four years. She wondered what he was dreaming about as his eyes slowly moved from side to side beneath his heavily lashed eyelids.

For a second, the idea that this man was her husband didn't seem real. After sleeping alone for most of her adult life, it felt strange to have another person in bed beside her. She wondered if other newly married woman felt the same way or was she just being silly?

Would they always be this happy or would their marriage go sour after they got used to each other? Then, there was the Hastings dilemma. Would they be alive long enough to enjoy other intimate moments like this? The uncertainty of their future weighed heavily on her mind. She prayed that her happiness wouldn't be short lived.

She was startled from her thoughts when Aaron suddenly spoke.

"It's not polite to stare at people while they're sleeping, Mrs. Jacobs," he said as he opened his eyes and turned to look at her.

"Who said I was polite?" she chuckled, tracing the outline of his jaw with her finger.

"True. Well, I don't know about you but I'm thirsty. Why don't we break open that bottle of champagne that Francis was kind enough to give us?"

"But it's only five in the morning!" Teri reminded him.

"So, pretend we're in Europe. Get the bottle," Aaron said, pushing her out of the bed.

"I hope this isn't how you start every morning," Teri scolded him and reached for her robe.

"Don't bother with that. It's gonna be off again in a few minutes anyway," Aaron grinned.

Teri playfully swatted his arm and got up. As she crossed the room, Aaron turned on the light to watch her. Her body certainly didn't reveal her age. Her naturally firm breasts, wide hips and strong, shapely legs, were a tribute to her African heritage.

"Here. Stop giving me those lustful looks and open this," Teri said when she returned to the bed.

"My pleasure," Aaron grinned. He uncorked the bottle and filled their glasses.

"Let's see now. What should we toast? To the beauty of the human body or perhaps we should raise our glasses to the first people who indulged in the pleasures of the flesh?" Aaron said with a twinkle in his eye.

"How about something more traditional like love and continued happiness?" Teri said, sarcastically.

"All right, if you insist," Aaron sighed and tapped his glass against hers.

"Oh lord. I just remembered that a client was supposed to be coming over this afternoon. Remind me to call them when we meet Father for breakfast," Teri said, wrinkling her nose when the champagne bubbles tickled it.

"Well, soon that won't be a problem," Aaron said, casually sipping his drink.

"What?"

"Meeting clients."

"And why not?" Teri asked, suspiciously.

"Because you'll be too busy taking care of our kids and won't have time to run your business. I figure that with my teaching salary and investments, we could easily afford to have at least four kids," Aaron said, matter-of-factly. He could barely keep a straight face when he looked at Teri.

"What? You must be kidding!" Teri cried, spilling some of the champagne down her chest.

"Oops. Can't let that go to waste," Aaron said, leaning over to lick the amber liquid that had dripped down the tip of one of her nipples.

Teri's anger immediately dissipated when he continued licking and kissing her breasts.

"I think we'd better get started making those babies right now," Aaron said, huskily, putting the champagne glasses on the night table.

Teri pushed back the covers so she could straddle Aaron's muscular thighs.

"Not so fast. Now it's my turn to torture you," she said with a mischievous look on her face.

Aaron struggled to control his arousal as Teri's full lips covered his. He could feel the beat of his heart quicken as her hands deftly caressed and fondled him in ways he had never experienced before. When he tried to push her back onto the pillows, she wriggled from beneath him and returned to her position of dominance.

"Not yet. I'm not finished," she said, roughly pinning him against the headboard, seductively rubbing her breasts against his chest.

"Oh god," Aaron said, grabbing her firm, round buttocks and pulling her closer.

When his touch became less gentle and his kisses more forceful, she rolled over and pulled him on top of her. This time he wasn't interested in doing anything slowly. Teri was mildly shocked to discover just how strong and powerful his body was. She was also quite pleased with herself that she'd been able to arouse the usually cool and collected Prof. Jacobs, causing him to almost lose total control.

Aaron cried out shamelessly when he finally climaxed, his body quivering, then going limp. He was about to move from his position on top of her when she suddenly tensed her pelvic muscles, trapping him.

"Not yet," she murmured in his ear. She didn't release him until her orgasm slowly burned itself out, leaving her feeling pleasantly exhausted and relaxed.

"What the hell was that?" Aaron asked, dismayed by what had just occurred.

"Oh, just an example of what a person can do when they have total control of every muscle in their body," Teri replied, serenely. She reached for the bottle of champagne.

He snatched the bottle from her and took a long swig. "You're an amazing woman, Mrs. Jacobs," Aaron grinned.

CHAPTER III

A carbon-monoxide-filled haze had already begun to form over the city. Andrew tapped his fingers impatiently as his car slowly crept along the entrance ramp to the George Washington

Bridge. After spending nearly forty-five minutes crawling to the toll booth, the traffic continued moving at a snail's pace. He and hundreds of other motorists tried to make their way into the city.

"Sometimes I hate this job," Andrew sighed. After taking care of Teri's affairs, he'd had to rush to New Jersey to pick up a video tape from a freelance reporter. The segment was scheduled to air on his station in less than forty-five minutes. But, at the rate the traffic was moving, there was little chance he'd make it in time.

Sighing again, he shifted into neutral when the cars in front of him came to a dead halt. He hoped they wouldn't be at a standstill too long, fearful that his car might overheat. If it did, he'd have a lane of irate fools honking and cursing their heads off behind him.

At least the view was pleasant, he thought, gazing across the river at the Manhattan skyline. He had to admit he liked the city, with its bright lights and action. Granted, it wasn't as clean and peaceful as Barbados but then it wasn't fair to compare the two. He retreated to his family's home when he wanted to relax but New York was where he made his money.

Suddenly, his attention was drawn to one of the two huge spires that held the hundreds of cables that supported the bridge. Maybe the hazy morning light was playing tricks with his eyes, but the spires seemed to be swaying. Squinting to sharpen his vision, Andrew focused on the spire closest to him on the New Jersey side of the river. It too seemed to be moving. Then, as he continued to stare, the road shuddered beneath him.

"What the hell was that?" he muttered and jumped at the sound of the car horn honking behind him. He had been so engrossed in staring at the bridge, he hadn't noticed that the cars in front of him had moved.

He shifted back into drive. The roadway shuddered again. The other drivers in the vicinity seemed to be oblivious to the movement of the roadway. Easing his foot off the brake, he tapped the gas lightly to allow his vehicle to narrow the gap between him and the car in front. Then, the cars stopped again.

Andrew quickly looked up at the spires and was terrified when he noticed that the one on the New York side of the river begin to visibly sway. As it gained momentum, the cables connected to it began snapping one by one like the crack of a whip. Car horns honked frantically as the cables whipped around in the air, then came crashing down onto the cars directly beneath them.

On the westbound side, drivers slammed on their brakes in a vain attempt to avoid being hit by the snapping cables. Simultaneously, the road beneath them began to crumble.

Andrew felt his heart pound wildly. He held his breath and watched as the tower on the New York side toppled over and crashed onto the roadway. In what appeared to him to be slow motion, the road collapsed, plunging cars, buses and trucks into the river below, followed by tons of grey steel. On the New Jersey side, the spire, unable to withstand the weight of more than a million tons pulling on the weakened cables, swayed violently once more before it too collapsed into the water.

Andrew let out a strangled cry as he watched the line of cars in front of him disappear from view. When the dust cleared, only one car remained, teetering dangerously over the edge of the roadbed. Inside he could see a woman, the raw terror etched in her face reflected in her rearview mirror. She was clutching the steering wheel as the car pitched forward. He closed his eyes and screamed, unable to watch as it flipped over the side making a teeth shattering scraping noise, sending a spray of sparks into the air.

* * * *

Carmen Lopez was ready to use her pocketbook to slap the man who was rubbing up against her in the packed subway car. Almost every morning, she was subjected to the sick games of the city's sex perverts unless she was fortunate enough to get a seat, which wasn't often.

When the southbound train swayed as it rounded the sharp curve leading into the 14th Street station, Carmen lifted her arm and

The Eighth House

Karen Sealy

struck.

"Ouch!" the man cried when her heavy leather purse smacked against his back.

"That'll teach you," she snickered. The train doors opened and passengers spilled from the car onto the already crowded platform, only to be replaced by the same number of passengers. Before he could turn around to see where the blow had come from, she quickly scooted over to the door and stood between the cars.

Using her newspaper as a fan, Carmen wondered what the revenue from the recent fare increase had been used for. They surely hadn't used it to repair the air conditioning on the train. The temperature in that hot box must have been at least one hundred degrees.

Carmen swore and pulled open the door that separated the cars, hoping to at least feel some of the hot breezes that were whipped up by the train as it sped through the tunnel along the southbound express track. Then, she quickly slammed the door shut in disgust when the pungent odor of reefer was blown into her face from a man who was standing between the cars smoking a joint.

"Why must I live like this," she thought and she resumed fanning herself with the paper. "There has to be more to life than this." Five days a week she subjected herself to that torture, all because that beast she married left her and their three kids.

"I'm bustin' my ass at that damned office while he's probably in the Bahamas screwing my best friend," she thought bitterly. Two months ago, she had come home early from work suffering from a severe case of cramps and discovered her husband and the woman who was like a sister to her going at it in *her* bed like teenagers. The cheap bastard didn't even have the decency to go to a motel.

"God must be punishing me for something I did in my past life," she sighed.

Her train sped along the center track to the Brooklyn Bridge

The Eighth House   Karen Sealy

station. No one noticed that a crack along the ceiling of the tunnel was getting wider, dropping pieces of concrete onto the top of the cars and the track bed. In the tunnel just above it, the northbound local rumbled out of the Brooklyn Bridge station. Its weight caused the already weakened concrete track bed to break apart.

Back at the 14th Street station, another Number 4 southbound express was just pulling out. With nothing but green signals ahead, the motorman slowly pulled the L-shaped handle toward him, accelerating. In the hot, dimly lit tunnel, as the second southbound express approached the cracked ceiling, the walls of the tunnel vibrated. Little by little, chunks of concrete and plaster began falling onto the tracks causing a gaping hole to form. On the local track above it, a second northbound local approached. Unable to see more than ten feet ahead of him, the motorman didn't notice that the floor of the tunnel had dropped several feet, causing the tracks to buckle.

Passengers were thrown violently against each other when the front wheels of the first car dropped through the gaping hole. Panicking, the motorman pulled the cord for the emergency brakes, hoping to stop the train, which had been traveling at thirty-five miles per hour. Unfortunately, it continued moving forward, propelled by the weight of its ten cars.

With sparks flying, a deafening screech echoed through the tunnel. The first car crashed through the concrete floor, falling on the downtown express tracks. The remainder of the cars followed, instantly killing the motorman. Screaming passengers cried out in agony. They were violently pitched forward, piling atop each other. The track bed of the northbound local train continued to collapse beneath them. It was fortunate that the motorman of the ill-fated northbound local died instantly when the first car smashed into the express tracks. He was spared the horror of seeing the lights of the second southbound express speeding toward him.

On the street above the tunnel, the ground suddenly heaved,

followed by a deafening boom as the trains collided, their cars bursting through the pavement above like a volcanic eruption. Automobiles were tossed aside like toy cars. Pedestrians were thrown against plate glass storefronts. Steam, gas, and sewer pipes exploded when the trains collided.

Office buildings along the street vibrated dangerously, causing some of the windows to shatter. Pedestrians scattered like flies, screaming and frantically searching for a way to escape the exploding ground. Deadly shards of glass rained down on them.

Carmen Lopez screamed when the sound of the explosion echoed through the tunnel. Suddenly, her train screeched to a halt and the lights went out. The car was eerily quiet. The stunned passengers looked at each other in silence. Then, a deadly roar grew louder as it approached them. Before anyone could react, a huge fireball shot through the tunnel, engulfing the train. Carmen had only a second to make the sign of the cross as the window in the door next to her imploded, slicing her clothes and face. The flames that rushed into the oxygen rich car, leaped onto her body, turning her into a human torch.

The carnage had begun.

CHAPTER IV

Father Francis felt every bit of his seventy-three years when he left the monastery for his usual early morning walk after saying mass. He'd spent most of the night tossing and turning in his bed, recalling what he'd read in the journal.

As a priest, he had never questioned the existence of Satan. There were numerous examples of the forces of evil at work in the world. But the thought of coming face to face with one of Satan's disciples terrified him.

The Eighth House   Karen Sealy

For one brief moment, as he'd read Hastings' detailed account of how he was created and the wicked deeds he committed, he questioned his faith in God. Although he never really believed that Hell was a place filled with tormented souls writhing in eternal fires, Hastings detailed description of Hell with tunic-clad spirits and formal education was a foreign and disturbing concept to comprehend.

And what about Teri and Aaron? She had narrowly escaped death at the hand of someone working for the devil. What advice could he possibly give them that would protect them from such an evil force?

During mass, he'd offered a special prayer to God asking for guidance. He hoped he would get an answer soon.

He was just passing through the gates of the monastery when Edward spotted the black robed figure coming down the road in his direction. The priest was so deep in thought that he didn't notice the late model car hidden behind the trees.

Edward was tempted to let the man pass without stopping him since being in the presence of a holy man was detrimental to his health. But he needed to make sure that Teri and Aaron were really there.

Quickly getting out of the car, he trotted in the direction of the priest and caught his attention.

Startled by the sound of footsteps behind him, Father Francis stopped in mid stride and turned around.

"Excuse me, young man, but this is private property. Perhaps you're lost," he said, looking at the handsome blonde haired, blue eyed man with suspicion.

At first, Edward was silent. Then, breaking into his most charming smile, he said,   "Yes, I am. I was following some friends of mine and made a wrong turn. Would you happen to have seen an attractive black woman accompanied by a white man?"

"No, I don't recall seeing such a couple," Father Francis

replied, nervously fingering the wooden cross attached to his belt. The man bore a striking resemblance to the person Teri had described. Could this be Edward Hastings?

Edward's smile slowly turned into a sneer as he inhaled deeply. The smell of the priest's fear was so delicious.

"You're a poor liar, old man. Where are they?"

"I don't know what you're talking about," the priest said, slowly backing away from Edward.

Suddenly, Edward sprang forward like a cat and grabbed the priest by the neck.

"Don't lie to me! Where the fuck are they, you pathetic ass?" Edward growled, his eyes blazing.

"You're too late. They've already gone!" Father Francis cried, his frail body shaking uncontrollably.

"Do you realize I could snap your puny neck in the blink of an eye? Why don't you just tell me where they are and I'll go about my business."

"Go back to hell where you came from you evil bastard! You can't stop them now. You're too late!"

Enraged by the priest's words, Edward lifted him into the air and flung him to the ground like a rag doll, breaking his hip.

Father Francis cried out from the excruciating pain.

Edward laughed sardonically and stood over the priest. "You and your pathetic religion. You have no power over me or anyone else."

Father Francis shouted up at Edward's angry face as he slowly began crawling away, "God has the power to destroy you!"

Edward was about to respond when he heard the sound of an approaching car. While he peered down the road to see if it was coming in their direction, Father Francis continued to slowly crawl away in the direction of the monastery.

"I don't think so, old man," Edward said when he saw the priest's feeble attempt to escape.

Father Francis' body was hurled into the air when the bolt of electricity struck him in the back. When he hit the ground, he screamed in agony. The pain was unbearable. His heart fluttered uncontrollably. He couldn't breathe and gasped for air.

"Dear God, help me!" the priest groaned. He continued trying to drag himself along the dirt road. If he could only cross the gate, he knew he'd be safe.

Father Francis let out an inhuman wail when the second bolt struck his legs, causing his pants to burst into flames.

"Nooo!" the priest cried. Grabbing handfuls of dirt, he frantically tried to smother the flames that were causing his flesh to blister.

"Where's your God now, old man?" Edward shouted with glee as he watched.

"Please help me Lord," Father Francis whimpered, his face contorted with pain. When the bright morning sun began to fade, he know he was about to pass out. His lips moved in silent prayer. He turned his eyes upward and focused all his attention on the cross atop the huge iron gate. Suddenly, he felt a new surge of energy. He didn't know if it was a burst of adrenalin or the hand of God. He didn't care since he knew it would be his last chance to escape Hastings.

"Going somewhere, Father?" Edward gloated, coolly strolling over to look at the half-dead priest.

When Father Francis began praying aloud, Edward was struck by an invisible force that knocked the wind out of him. His lungs became constricted and he backed away.

The priest was oblivious to what was happening to Edward. He continued to stare at the cross and claw his way up the road toward the gate. He was now less than ten feet away from the invisible shroud of safety.

Edward could only seethe with anger and gasp for air as he watched the priest pass through the gate, out of his reach.

The Eighth House

Karen Sealy

Father Francis was on the brink of unconsciousness when he rolled over onto his back and looked up at the cross.

"Thank you Father," he whispered hoarsely and struggled to raise his arm to make the sign of the cross. He just managed to complete crossing himself when he finally passed out.

* * * *

"Father Francis will be joining you as soon as he's done with his morning walk," Teri and Aaron were informed by Mrs. Delaney, the housekeeper for the monastery. She finished laying out their buffet breakfast.

"Thank you," Teri said, warmly. The food looked delicious and for some reason, she felt exceptionally hungry that morning.

"A bit famished, aren't we," Aaron chuckled, watching her fill her plate. "I wonder what brought that on?"

"I have no idea what you're talking about," Teri replied, helping herself to a generous portion of eggs.

Aaron smiled and shook his head. When they'd finally managed to get out of bed, their departure from the cottage was delayed once again when Teri joined him in the shower. It was amazing the things two people could do standing up.

The newlyweds had just finished their first breakfast as husband and wife when Mrs. Delany burst into the room.

"Oh my God!", the woman wailed, hysterically.

"What's wrong?" Aaron said, alarmed.

"Look!" the housekeeper said. She turned on the small television that stood in the corner of the room.

Teri and Aaron could only stare in dismay at the pictures that filled the screen. Local programming had been interrupted by a live report about a catastrophe in New York City. Reporters were practically trampling onlookers as they rushed through the mobs of excited people and rescue teams trying to snag exclusive interviews.

The Eighth House   Karen Sealy

The TV news pictures showed wild packs of people, young and old, of all races, throwing bricks through the windows of some of the most exclusive shops on Madison and Fifth Avenues, grabbing handfuls of designer shirts, pants, jewelry, handbags and sneakers. When National Guardsmen attempted to stop them, they scattered like roaches.

Then, the camera zoomed in on the area where the subway cars had burst through the pavement after they collided underground. Gas fires continued to burn out of control as emergency workers frantically tried to cut open the doors of the train's cars. One bold cameraman was able to sneak past the police barriers and focus on the windows of one of the cars.

Teri, Aaron and Mrs. Delany stared at the images that flickered across the screen. They were captivated by the bloodied, burnt, and mangled bodies that were piled atop one another. Apparently, they had been tossed into the air like pick-up-sticks.

Then, the report switched to an aerial view of the Hudson River. Tears streamed down Teri's face as the camera panned the area where the George Washington Bridge had once stood. The roads leading to the bridge dropped off abruptly, leaving a gaping whole stretching from one shore to the other. Coast Guard and police boats could be seen combing the river. Divers made fruitless attempts at retrieving bodies from the piles of sunken cars, trucks and buses.

"When did this happen?" Aaron asked, leaning forward to examine the screen more closely.

"This morning during rush hour. Oh, those poor, innocent people!" Mrs. Delany sniveled, dabbing her eyes.

"I've got to call Andrew and see if he's all right," Teri said, her hand shaking as she dialed the phone. When a recording announced that the phone lines in the city were down, she slammed the receiver and began nervously pacing the floor.

"If you can't get through, try paging him. Maybe a few lines going out are still working," Aaron suggested.

Teri nodded and dialed again.

"Oh, Andrew! You've got to be all right!" Teri whispered, her heart racing. Once the call was complete, all she could do was pray.

"Does Father Francis know about this?" Aaron asked when he realized the priest still hadn't returned.

"I don't know. Come to think of it, he should have been back by now," Mrs. Delany said, dabbing her eyes.

"I'll go look for him," Aaron volunteered, pausing a second to kiss Teri on the cheek and whisper, "You hold on, sweetheart. I'm sure Andrew is just fine. I'll be right back."

Aaron quickly strode down the hall to the front entrance of the building. He didn't think he'd have a problem finding the priest. During his last visit, he'd accompanied him on his morning stroll and was familiar with his route.

He had only walked a few feet down the driveway when he noticed something dark lying just inside the gate. After he realized what he was seeing, his pulse quickened and he broke into a run.

When Aaron reached him, Father Francis wasn't breathing. He took a few quick deep breaths and knelt down next to the priest's frail body, immediately administering CPR.

"Come on, Francis. Breathe!" Aaron whispered as he rhythmically pressed down on his friend's thin chest. When he'd gone through the procedure for close to a minute, he rested his ear against his chest and listened for a heartbeat and checked for a pulse. To his relief, he detected a slight flutter.

Without thinking, he swept his friend into his arms and ran back to the monastery. He hoped an ambulance could get to there in time.

* * * *

Edward had retreated to the safety of his car's air conditioning when he spotted Aaron with the priest. Well, the old bastard had nearly killed him but at least now he knew the exact whereabouts of Jacobs and the astrologer. He'd continue to wait until they left.

* * * *

The monastery was thrust into a flurry of activity when Aaron burst through the front doors with Father Francis in his arms. Mrs. Delany directed him to the priest's quarters while another priest called an ambulance.

Father Francis was gently laid on the bed. They were horrified when they noticed the severity of his injuries. His pant legs were singed and torn, exposing raw, blistered flesh. Fearful that any attempt to treat his burns would only cause him more discomfort, they were forced to stand helplessly by his bedside and pray as they anxiously waited for the paramedics. When the ailing priest slowly opened his eyes, they gave a collective sigh of relief.

"Come closer," Father Francis whispered, slowly turning his head toward Aaron.

"What happened, Francis?" Aaron asked, clutching the priest's small, bony hand.

"He's here," the priest said, hoarsely.

"Who's here, Father?" Aaron asked, not understanding.

"It's him! The devil!" the priest cried, becoming agitated.

"Take it easy Father. Everything's going to be all right," Aaron reassured him.

"No! You have to go! It's Hastings!" Father Francis croaked, grabbing Aaron by the front of the shirt. Then, he fell back against the pillows, exhausted from his efforts.

Aaron heard Teri gasp at the mention of Hastings' name. Dear God, he'd found them!

"I beg of you, Aaron. Please go! You can't let him get you!" the priest said, his eyes filled with fear.

"All right. You just rest Francis. The paramedics are here," Aaron said when they heard the wail of a siren.

"Godspeed, my friends," Father Francis whispered and closed his eyes.

Aaron took Teri by the arm and motioned for Mrs. Delany to join them in the hall.

"What was he talking about?" the housekeeper asked.

"I can't explain. We have to go. Is there another way off the grounds that would lead us to the main road?"

"Yes. It's at the far end of the property. You can reach it by going around the back of this building."

"Great. Listen, I know this seems strange but I promise to call later and explain everything. Thanks for your help. You go back to Father Francis now," Aaron said, gently pushing the puzzled woman through the door. Then, turning to Teri, he said, "I'll bring the Blazer around the back while you grab our bags."

"Okay," Teri said, and they hurried down the hall.

Shortly, Aaron was carefully navigating the vehicle along the narrow dirt road running behind the monastery. When he reached the end, he slowly nosed it out far enough to check for oncoming traffic. The road was clear so he slammed his foot on the accelerator. The Blazer swerved slightly as the back wheels left the dirt road and made contact with the black pavement.

"So far so good," he commented, checking the rearview mirror to see if they were being followed.

"I hope Father Francis will be all right," Teri said.

"So do I. But now, where can we go?" Aaron asked.

"I'm not sure, but we have to get out of this area as fast as possible. Let's just head for the thruway," Teri suggested.

"Okay. Check the map and see which way we need to go to pick up Route 90."

Teri looked out the window for a street sign and then examined the map.

"Make a left at the next light and continue about a quarter mile. The entrance shouldn't be too far from there."

When they reached the intersection of the nearly deserted road, Aaron slowed down at the red light. Then, it turned green and as he was about to make the left, the sound of a car's racing engine and squealing tires could be heard. Looking in the rearview mirror, Aaron was dismayed as he watched the auto barreling down the road right in their path.

Making a split second decision, he accelerated and cut the wheel sharply to the left causing the back end of the Blazer to fishtail as the rear tires screeched and burned rubber, fighting to make traction. As the approaching car careened through the intersection, it just missed hitting the Blazer's rear bumper.

He pulled to the side of the road, his hands shaking as he shifted into park.

"Are you all right?" he cried, alarmed when he saw Teri clutching her forehead with her right hand.

"I hit my head on the window when you made the turn," she replied.

"Let me see," he demanded, leaning over and pulling her hand away. A thin stream of blood was trickling from the nasty looking knot that was beginning to form.

"Wait, let me get some water for that," he said and unbuckled his shoulder harness. He reached over to retrieve one of the bottles of water they had packed.

Taking his handkerchief from his pocket, he poured some onto the cloth and gently dabbed the area.

"Sorry," he apologized when Teri grimaced at his touch.

"I'll do it. Just get us to the interstate before whoever that was comes back," she said taking the cloth from him.

"Okay," Aaron agreed and strapping himself back in, shifted

into drive and continued down the road. Finally, he saw a sign indicating that the entrance to the highway was a few feet ahead.

"Do you think that was Hastings?" Teri asked as they entered the roadway and merged with the traffic.

"I hope not," Aaron replied, nervously glancing into the side and rearview mirrors. None of the cars nearby seemed suspicious.

"Oh God, what's going on?" Teri cried in despair. New York City was practically in ruins, Andrew hadn't returned her call, Father Francis was hurt and now Hastings was hot on their trail.

"As soon as I'm sure we've put enough distance between us and Hastings, I'll stop so we can regroup," Aaron promised, reaching over to squeeze Teri's hand.

"All right, darlin'," Teri sighed.

* * * *

Back at the end of the driveway leading to the monastery, Edward swerved wildly onto the main road in pursuit of the elusive couple. Then, he heard a loud pop come from the front passenger side of the car.

Slamming on the brakes, he jumped out to determine what the source of the noise was.

"Shit!" he cried in frustration as he watched the front tire slowly deflate. Something on the road had punctured the tire.

Clutching his hair, his face contorted with rage, Edward let out a blood curdling cry that echoed throughout the valley.

CHAPTER V

Andrew Ellis could barely stop his hands from trembling. He gratefully accepted a cup of coffee from one of the Red Cross volunteers. They were tending to the injured drivers on both sides of the river and had set up a temporary relief center in the gymnasium of a school located near the toll plaza of the bridge.

"If you'd like to speak to a counselor, just let me know." The middle-aged woman volunteer smiled sympathetically at Andrew and gave his shoulder a gentle squeeze before walking away.

Andrew nodded and looked around the gym. Nearly two hundred commuters had sought refuge there. Some were sitting on cots and chairs talking quietly, while others walked aimlessly around the room in a daze.

He knew exactly how they felt. As he sipped his coffee, the image of what had occurred replayed in his mind like a video stuck in a loop. No matter how much he tried, he couldn't erase the memory of the woman in the car directly in front of his. He kept seeing her terror-filled expression reflected in her rearview mirror as her car teetered on the edge of the roadway and finally went over the side. If he'd gotten through the toll booth ahead of her, he would have plunged to his death. The thought made him tremble.

He drained his cup and was trying to collect his thoughts when he overheard the Red Cross volunteers saying that New York City had been completely shut down. Manhattan had been sealed off from the rest of the boroughs and suburbs to allow emergency personnel to deal with the subway crash. Obviously, he wouldn't be able to return to his apartment that evening. He wondered if Teri and Aaron had heard the news. Thank God they'd already left for *the monastery before the bridge collapsed.*

Andrew opened his knapsack and searched for the most important document he owned, his passport, grateful that he hadn't removed it from the bag after his last trip.

"Excuse me, miss," Andrew called out to one of the volunteers.

"Yes sir?" the woman asked.

"Where can I find a phone?"

"Well, the phones in the school are probably swamped. You might want to try the ones that've been set up in the parking lot," the woman directed him.

"Thanks," Andrew replied and left the gym.

He had to wait on line nearly twenty minutes before he could make his call.

"Hello ma? It's Andrew," he said when his mother picked up the phone in Barbados.

"Andrew? Thank God! Are you alright? Where are you?" Isola asked, her voice filled with worry.

"I'm in New Jersey. I can't talk long. I just wanted to let you know I'm okay and I'm coming home," Andrew said, a lump forming in his throat.

"All right, baby. Have you heard from Teri?"

"No. She went out of town with Aaron last night so I guess she's okay."

"Well, maybe she'll call us here later when she can't reach you. What time do you think you'll be arrivin'?"

"I'm not sure. I'm gonna try to get the next flight out of Newark Airport. I'll call you as soon as I get a ticket," Andrew replied, looking at his watch.

"Okay. You take care, baby. We love you," Isola said.

"I love you too, ma. I'll see you soon," Andrew replied and hung up, feeling like a child who needed his mother.

He was oblivious to the chaos surrounding him as he walked back to his car which was parked a few blocks from the school. As he slid behind the wheel, he again recalled the image of the woman who'd died right before his eyes.

Distraught by what he'd witnessed that morning, Andrew rested his head against the steering wheel and wept.

* * * *

"We'll have to stop for gas soon," Aaron said checking the gage. They'd been traveling west on Route 90 for close to three hours.

"I think there's a rest stop not too far ahead," Teri said, studying the map.

"Here's the sign now," Aaron pointed. In a few minutes, they were exiting the highway.

After filling the gas tank, he parked and they headed for the restaurant.

"Do you want to try to reach Andrew again while we're here?" Aaron asked after they'd gotten their food and were settled into a booth.

"I don't know. We're too far away from the city for me to page him and I doubt if the lines there are working. Maybe my mother's heard from him. I'll try Barbados," Teri said, getting up.

"Thank god," she said with relief when she returned to the booth. "Andrew called and he's on his way down there. He didn't give my mother any details but it seems that he was in New Jersey when the bridge collapsed. I told her I'd call back tonight after he gets there."

"That's good. Now what are we gonna do?"

"I just took care of that. I called a friend of mine in Buffalo. She and her husband are astrologers. I explained the situation to her and she invited us to stay with them until things calm down. She said she was thinking of calling me anyway because she's been seeing some weird things in her charts too."

"I hope you told her that she was taking a risk by allowing us to stay there. Hastings could still be on our trail," Aaron reminded her.

"Of course I did but she said it doesn't matter. She agrees that something very strange is going on and wants to take a look at the journal too. I need their help since I don't have any of my books with me and at least we won't have to stay at a motel," Teri replied.

The Eighth House   Karen Sealy

"Okay. We should be in Buffalo by 2:00 p.m. I just hope we've put enough distance between us and Hastings so he won't know where we are," Aaron said, grimly.

"So do I. I think we've had enough trouble for one day," Teri replied. She was beginning to wonder if their lives would ever be normal again.

* * * *

Edward's mind was racing as the countryside whizzed past the window of the huge sixteen wheeler. After abandoning the car back at the monastery, he had walked along the main road until a trucker passed him on the way to the interstate. After flagging him down, the driver had been more than happy to give him a ride west. When asked how far he was going, Edward's response had been vague. Unknown to the trucker, Edward had the tracking device concealed in the duffel bag. He would ask the driver to let him out when Tericita and Aaron stopped. Then, he planned to commandeer another car so he could follow them.

The truck's owner, Seth Boone, who called Kansas City home, drove his rig twice a week. He usually hauled a load of packing materials up to New England from Chicago. It was a lonely job but he enjoyed the freedom. He could never picture himself sitting behind a desk.

When asked what type of work he did, Edward claimed to be a freelance writer who traveled around the country in search of interesting stories. He had changed his appearance to match his new identity. Now, he looked like a free spirit with shoulder length dark brown hair, brown eyes and a neat mustache and beard. His outfit, jeans, a T-shirt, denim jacket and hiking boots, gave him a rugged appearance. If someone had seen him at the monastery and gave the police a description of the owner of the car, he would bear no resemblance.

To Edward's relief, Seth Boone wasn't much of a talker. This gave him an opportunity to concentrate on the tracking device. For hours, Seth drove in silence, only making small talk about the scenery or something they passed on the road. When he noticed Edward periodically looking down at something in his bag, he told the trucker that it was just a video game called "Devil Chase". Seth had nodded and commented that it sounded like a game his kid had.

Hitching a ride gave Edward time to plan his next move. Time was passing quickly and he still hadn't caught up with Teri and the book. If he wasn't able to stop them, he'd face dire consequences.

"Mind if I turn on the radio? I like to keep up with what's goin' on in the world," Seth asked.

"Sure, go ahead."

Reaching down, he turned the knob and scanned the stations. After passing several that were playing country music, he stopped at one of the all news stations. When Edward heard what the broadcaster was reporting, he fought the urge to break into hysterical laughter.

"As we've been reporting all morning, New York City has been literally shut down after the devastating events that took place today at about 7:30 a.m. eastern standard time. The George Washington Bridge, one of the busiest roadways leading to the city, collapsed this morning, tossing hundreds of cars, buses and trucks into the deep waters of the Hudson River. Roads leading to the bridge have been closed, causing traffic jams stretching from Massachusetts, in the Northeast, and Pennsylvania, to the west. The Governor has also ordered all other bridges and tunnels in the area closed for fear that they too, may have structural damage that may have gone undetected. People in Manhattan are forced to remain in the borough and those who wish to enter the city are being turned away."

"Adding to the chaos, a few minutes after the bridge collapsed, two

The Eighth House

Karen Sealy

subway trains collided in a tunnel below mid-town Manhattan, causing a major gas line to explode. It's reported that hundreds of passengers were killed by the crash and the fireball that raced through the tunnel after the gas line was severed. So far, police and rescue personnel have been unable to determine how many people remain trapped underground or how many were killed by the series of explosions above ground that were triggered by the collision." "Members of the National Guard have been airlifted and brought in by boat to help control the crowds of people trying to flee the city and quell sporadic outbreaks of looting that have taken place throughout Manhattan. As we speak, the Governor of New York is asking the President to have New York City declared a disaster area. A news conference is scheduled for 2:30 p.m. at City Hall which we'll broadcast live. Now, we'll switch to..."

Seth's hand shook as he turned down the radio. "Well ain't that somethin'. And to think I just crossed that bridge earlier this mornin'. Christ, that coulda been me!"

"I guess that's why they say you have to live for the moment 'cause you never know what's gonna happen next," Edward said, pretending to be shocked.

"You got that right. Look, I gotta stop a minute. I'm shakin' so much I gotta pee," the trucker said. He signaled his lane change, slowed down, and pulled the rig onto the shoulder of the road. Jumping out, he ran over to a patch of nearby brush and relieved himself.

Edward remained seated in the truck and watched the man with amusement. If just hearing about the disaster was this upsetting to him, he could imagine how people all over the world were reacting to the chaos in the city. It was a shame he couldn't be there to enjoy it. He always found raw fear and panic as invigorating as sex.

"I tell you this world is gettin' crazier by the minute," Seth declared as he returned to the truck, mopping his sweat drenched face with his handkerchief. He sat on the step under the door, lit a cigarette and took a long drag. Edward turned his head away from the direction of the toxic smoke. Fortunately, a slight breeze was blowing, sending it in the opposite direction of the cab.

"First ya got those nuts up in the hills tryin' to overthrow the government, blowin' up buildings, and then the other fools plantin' bombs in planes. What the hell is next, poisonin' the damn water?"

"Not a bad idea," Edward thought. He'd have to give that some serious consideration. "Maybe this has somethin' to do with terrorists," he said out loud.

"Or maybe space aliens. You never know who's lookin' down at us plottin' all kinds of trouble. Maybe I should seriously consider retirin' and movin' me and my family to that cabin we got up in Montana. I like my job but I sure as shit ain't willin' to die for it. Now I'll have to figure out another way to get back to New England when it's time for my next run. Hell, I'll think about that later. I'm already shook up enough," Seth sighed.

Taking one last drag on the cigarette, he ground it out with his foot. Then, he climbed back into the cab, put the truck in gear and pulled back onto the road.

"If it's okay with you, I'm gonna pull over at the next rest stop so I can call my wife. If she heard the news, she must be havin' a fit thinkin' I'm one of them poor souls floatin' in the river."

"That's fine with me," Edward replied, although it wasn't. If they stopped too long, Tericita might go beyond the range of the tracking device and he'd never be able to find them. His only other choice would be to commandeer a car when the trucker stopped and follow them on his own sooner than he planned. In the meantime, he'd have to think of a way to slow them down.

"We sure been havin' some nice weather this summer," Seth noted, looking at the blue sky that stretched across the horizon. "One year I spent more time at truck stops than on the road 'cause every five minutes it was either thunderin' or hail big as golf balls were tryin' to bust my windshield. That's one of the bad things about bein' a trucker. If the weather don't cooperate, you ain't makin' a dime."

"I can imagine," Edward said absently. Seth Boone had just given him the solution to his problem.

"Oh, yes, Ms. Ellis. Do I have a surprise for you," Edward thought. He smirked and sat back to enjoy the scenery.

CHAPTER VI

Teri was relieved when they finally reached Marilyn and Steve Smith's Victorian house. They lived in a Black middle class neighborhood comprised of old but well kept single family homes. With only a few weeks of summer vacation remaining, the streets were filled with children enjoying their last days of freedom.

Aaron retrieved their bags from the back of the Blazer and Teri rang the doorbell. It was opened by an attractive Black woman *who's face hadn't aged a day since she and Teri had attended* college together.

"Tericita Ellis! Girl, it's so good to see you! Marilyn hugged her friend. "And you must be Aaron," she said when he joined them.

After making the introductions, Marilyn showed them to their room, located in the attic, which she explained had recently been renovated.

"When you get settled, come down to the kitchen. We'll have something to eat and talk. We have so much news to catch up on and there's so much Steve and I want to ask you. I'm so glad you called. These solar returns have been driving us crazy. If three astrologers can't get to the bottom of what's going on, nobody can," Marilyn shook her head.

"I hope so. We need all the help we can get. Thanks a million for inviting us to stay," Teri said, hugging her friend again.

"Anytime. *See you in a few,*" Marilyn said.

Aaron closed the door and Teri stood in the middle of the room absently fingering her grandmother's cross. " Y o u l o o k exactly the way I feel, tired and confused," Aaron said, taking her in his arms.

"That's the truth," Teri sighed, comforted by his embrace.

"I think I'll call the monastery to see if there's any news on Francis' condition before we join your friends. *I'm really worried about him,*" Aaron said, kissing the top of her head before releasing her.

"So am I. While you do that, I'm gonna freshen up. I must look a sight," Teri replied and went to use the bathroom.

When she returned, she was alarmed to find Aaron sitting on the bed with his head in his hands.

"What's wrong, darlin"? she asked, rushing to his side.

"Francis didn't make it. He went into cardiac arrest on the way to the hospital and the paramedics weren't able to resuscitate him," *Aaron replied, his voice choked with grief. He turned to look at her.*

"Oh, no!" Teri said. Her heart filled with sadness at the thought of the kind, old priest who'd tried to help them.

"If only I'd gotten to him sooner. Maybe he'd be alive now," Aaron lamented, his eyes glistening.

"Don't say that, darlin'. You did the best you could," Teri *reprimanded him as she took him in her arms and laid his head* against her breast. It broke her heart to see him that way.

"I know but I still can't help feeling I could have done more. He was in so much pain when I carried him back to the monastery," Aaron said, recalling the scene at the gate. "Do you think Hastings had anything to do with it?"

"Well, Father Francis did specifically mention his name. God bless him for warning us in spite of his own pain. *I just don't* understand how he found us," Teri said.

"God, how I'd love to get my hands on that bastard!" Aaron said, his grief turning to anger. He pulled away from her and stood up.

"That son-of-a-bitch and his god damned journal have caused enough pain and suffering! We've got to figure out a way to stop him before he kills someone else."

"We will, darlin'. We just need time to study the entire journal. I'm more than positive that everything we need to know is in it," Teri said, grabbing his hand to make him sit down again. "I know you're upset but you need to calm down. We have to be able to think clearly and rationally if we want to stay a step ahead of him."

"I wish I could just burn that damn book and be done with it," Aaron swore.

"I doubt that would make a difference now. Hastings probably thinks we know more about him than we actually do," Teri gently reminded him.

"I know. I know. I'm just tired and frustrated. Thank God we aren't stuck in New York City with him on our tails. At least on the road we have a better chance of avoiding him," Aaron sighed, his anger diminishing. "Let's go join your friends. The sooner we solve this, the better."

* * * *

Marilyn and Steve were shocked when Teri outlined their situation as they sat in the Smith's large country kitchen.

"This is unbelievable," Steve shook his head, flipping through the journal. "And you think this Hastings guy had something to do with your friend's death?"

"Yes. Here's Hastings' chart. Take a look at this and tell me what you think," Teri said and she handed it to him.

Steve stood behind his wife. She smoothed out the crumpled paper and examined it.

"I've never seen anything like this," Marilyn said. "Are you sure you have the right birthday?"

"Yes. That's what he told me at the party and I had an astrologer friend of mine in New York run it again for me and she got the same results. She also ran a solar return for him and saw some very disturbing things. I wouldn't be the least bit surprised if he didn't have something to do with the bridge collapse and the train crash," Teri said.

"I think the first thing we should do is run another computerized solar return so we can get a general idea of what he may be planning to do right now. Then, I'll input the coordinates from the charts in the journal and see what we come up with. Hopefully, we'll have a better understanding of who he is and what he plans to do in the future," Steve suggested.

"That sounds good. While you three tackle the charts, I'll take another stab at translating the text. Maybe the entries explain what's in the charts. If it does, we'll save a lot of time," Aaron volunteered.

* * * *

For the rest of the day and late into the evening, the two couples analyzed the charts and made notes. It was a grueling process. Hastings had taken great pains to disguise his personal thoughts and plans. By early evening, they'd only been able to decipher a small portion of the book.

At 8:30, Marilyn and Steve took a break so that they could put their two children to bed. Teri was deeply moved when the kids shyly walked over to kiss their guests good night. She wondered if the ordeal with Hastings would interfere with them having a family.

The Eighth House

Karen Sealy

* * * *

After reviewing Hastings' solar return and comparing it with what Regina had uncovered, they were positive that he was responsible for the disaster in New York and were able to confirm what his weaknesses were. They also uncovered information about his psychopathic behavior.

But, their most startling discovery was that Edward Hastings' time on earth was limited. In a few days, he would no longer have the power to regenerate his body and would disappear in the same manner he'd appeared in 1924.

It was close to midnight when they finally agreed on what disasters Hastings might have planned for the immediate future.

"He's going to tamper with something that all living creatures can't survive without," Aaron suggested as they went through the list of possibilities.

When Teri, who'd been deep in thought, suddenly whispered, "Oh, no," they all stopped talking and looked at her.

"What is it?" Steve asked, alarmed by the expression on her face.

"It's one of three things," she began slowly. "What are the three most important elements needed to sustain life on earth?"

Pausing a moment to think, a wave of fear swept the room when they all came to the same realization.

"Air," Aaron replied.

"Water," Steve added.

"And fire or heat," Marilyn concluded.

Teri reached for her grandmother's cross and prayed. If Edward Hastings was planning on manipulating any of those life sustaining elements, the entire population of the United States was at risk.

CHAPTER VII

The travel time between Albany and the outskirts of Buffalo should have taken only five hours. Since the trucker stopped at almost every rest stop on the Interstate to call his wife and reassure her of his safety, they arrived in the area nearly two hours later than scheduled. Along the way, Edward could barely resist the urge to shoot a few bolts of electricity up Seth Boone's ass when, once again, the trucker pulled off the road. He swung the huge rig between two other mammoth trucks in the parking lot of the Trucker's Delight roadside diner.

Often, during the trip, Edward had been tempted to just take over the truck or get out and commandeer another car. But since Seth knew the road better than he did, he'd saved precious time -- time he needed to catch up with Teri and Aaron. The delays still made him nervous. What if they drifted out of the range of his tracking device?

Jumping down from the cab of the truck, Edward checked the tracker's display. To his relief, the blip representing their vehicle hadn't moved in more than an hour. He assumed that Teri had probably stopped somewhere in Buffalo for the night.

"Let's get somethin' to eat. It ain't the best food in the world but it keeps ya goin' and the company ain't half bad either," Seth said, walking to the front of the truck.

"How far are we from Buffalo?" Edward asked, pointing to the lights of the city.

"Oh, about five miles or so. Is that where you want me to let you off?"

"Yes."

"Okay. Lemme grab a quick bite and call my wife and we'll

hit the road. I won't be stoppin' off for the night until I get a few miles outside Erie, Pennsylvania. There's a motel there I like to stay at."

"All right," Edward agreed and followed the husky trucker into the diner.

Inside, the strong aroma of steaks, fries and coffee made Edward's mouth water. Several truckers who knew Seth were sitting at the counter. After a few friendly hellos, they slid into one of the few vacant booths and sat down. A waitress immediately appeared with two cups and a pot of coffee.

"Am I glad to see you in one piece, Seth," the waitress smiled as she filled their cups. "I know you must've heard about what happened in New York. I was prayin' you'd already passed before it happened."

"The man upstairs must be lookin' out for me 'cause I just missed it by about two hours. I started out just a little earlier this mornin' than I usually do," Seth replied.

"Well, from what we've been seein' on the news, it's a big mess over there. They still ain't been able to tell exactly how many people are dead or hurt and to make matters worse, the police are fightin' looters and fools who're jumpin' into the East River tryin' to get out of Manhattan. I've never seen nothin' like it!" the waitress said, her eyes shining.

Edward watched in fascination while the woman was speaking. Although she tried to appear genuinely shocked and horrified by the disaster, he could sense that she was turned on by the catastrophe and secretly wished she were in the middle of the chaos. If he wasn't in such a hurry, he would have loved to spend some time with her. Women who were attracted to danger and the threat of death always turned him on.

"Oh, Ed, this is Charlotte. Charlotte, this is Ed. He hitched a ride with me back in Albany," Seth introduced them.

"Pleased to meet you," Edward said warmly and flashed his

most charming smile.

"Likewise," Charlotte replied, giving him the once over and liking what she saw. The intensity of his stare made her blush. "I'll give you a chance to check out the menu and I'll be right back. The specials are on the menu card on the table," she said and walked back toward the kitchen, her hips swaying in her snug fitting uniform.

"She's a great gal but she ain't got nothin' on my Ginger," Seth commented, chuckling over the look on Edward's face as he watched her walk away. "The specials in this place are pretty good. I think I'll try the pork chops."

Edward scanned the menu and decided to have the steak and egg platter. He hadn't eaten since the previous day and was famished.

Seth turned to face the television suspended from the ceiling in the far corner of the restaurant while they waited to order.

Edward smirked and he took a sip of his coffee. His torturous act had turned out even better than he'd expected.

* * * *

"I think we've done enough for one night. How about we turn in and start again early in the morning," Steve suggested, taking off his glasses to rub his eyes.

"Sounds good to me," Aaron yawned.

"You two go up. Teri and I will be up in a few minutes. We've got some gossip to catch up on that can't wait," Marilyn said, flashing Teri a look.

"Women," Stevie sighed and kissed his wife on the cheek. Then, he followed Aaron up the stairs.

"Okay, hon, what's wrong?" Marilyn asked Teri when they were alone.

"After all these years, you can still read me like a book," Teri smiled, tiredly, and accepted a refill of her cup of tea.

"Uhuh. *I could see in your eyes that you left out a few facts* when you were filling us in."

"Oh, Marilyn. I think there's more to this situation than a psychopath on a mission to regain his personal property. I can't shake the feeling that somehow I'm directly involved in this," Teri said, her voice filled with anxiety.

"You mean because of what your grandmother predicted?"

"No, it's more than that. It first struck me at the party. As soon as I walked in the apartment, I sensed that something wasn't right. And then when I met Hastings face to face, the feeling got even stronger. But it got worse when I held his hand to read his palm."

Teri leaned back in her chair and ran her fingers through her hair. "As soon as our hands touched, I fell into some kind of trance. Strange images started flashing through my mind; a squalid tenement apartment, the strong odor of gunpowder, and a pool of blood on the floor. And, it wasn't as if I was looking at those images *as an outsider*. I felt like I was actually *there*."

"Hastings also seemed to have had an unusual reaction when our hands touched. His eyes went vacant for a second and then he was staring at me with a weird look on his face. We both tried to play it off, but afterwards, I could tell that he was as rattled as I was." Teri paused to take a sip of tea.

"I was willing to brush the entire incident off as just a *figment of my imagination* until Father Francis' interpretation of Hastings' childhood. He lived in a run down tenement and shot his mother's pimp in cold blood in their apartment. Coupled with the fact that I'm living in the same brownstone that housed Hastings' bordello, how can I not think that there's some kind of connection somewhere?"

"There's one way we could find out," Marilyn said, hesitantly.

"I know, past life regression hypnosis. But, I'm not ready to go that far yet," Teri shook her head. Then she glanced across the table at her friend and said, "There's something else too but I'm kind of embarrassed to talk about it," Teri nervously cast her eyes downward and studied her fingers.

"Go ahead. You know you can tell me anything," Marilyn prompted.

"Okay. It's about Aaron."

"Well, you two seem very happy," Marilyn said.

"Oh we are," Teri looked up and smiled. "He's the best thing that ever happened to me and I love him very much. It's just that, well, last night was the first time we were intimate. I was a little nervous at first but then, when we... Forget it! I can't talk about this," Teri could feel the color rising in her cheeks and covered her face with her hands.

"Come on, Teri. Remember, I'm the roommate who'd listen to every detail of what happened when you'd come back from a date when we were in college," Marilyn gently reminded her.

"That's the truth," Teri chuckled. "Well, when we really got into it, somehow he tapped into a part of my sexuality that I never knew existed. It was like I was another person," Teri explained.

"Well, that ain't strange, honey. Being in love with the right man can bring out a lot of things in a woman, especially if it's been a long time between men," Marilyn chuckled.

"I know that but I was still a little embarrassed later. It's hard to explain but it's not only what I did but how I felt doing it. I felt so, so, free and powerful. Do you understand what I'm trying to say or do I sound like a complete fool?" Teri blushed.

"If you mean that making love with him brought out the vixen in you, so what? Honey, obviously you trust him and feel comfortable enough with him to let yourself go like that. And, if he didn't complain and you can keep that feeling alive throughout your marriage, you've got it made," Marilyn applauded her friend.

"I guess I'm just being silly. This Hastings business is driving me crazy. Thanks for listening, though."

"Come on. I think we've talked enough for one night. I'll see you in the morning," Marilyn said and they embraced. The two old friends ascended the stairs arm and arm, feeling like teenagers again.

* * * *

Aaron was sitting in a chair dozing when Teri entered the guestroom.

"You didn't have to wait up for me," Teri said, leaning over to kiss the top of his head.

"It's okay. What was so important that the two of you couldn't wait to talk in the morning?" Aaron asked, stretching his body with relish.

"Just girl talk," Teri winked. "Anyway, I want to call Barbados before we turn in. Andrew should be there by now," Teri said, sitting on the edge of the bed to use the phone.

"Are you gonna tell them we got married?" Aaron asked, as he undressed.

"No. My parents would ask too many questions that I'm not up to answering right now."

Aaron decided to take a shower while she was on the phone. When he came back into the bedroom, he saw that she'd been crying.

"I hope it wasn't more bad news," he said, joining her on the bed.

"No. Andrew arrived safely, thank God. But he's still in shock. Apparently, his car was just behind one that fell into the river. He was exhausted and crying when my parents picked him up from the airport. After he explained what happened, my mother made him go to bed. I wish I could be there for him!" Teri sighed and Aaron put his arms around her.

"You will be soon, sweetheart. Don't worry," Aaron said, stroking her hair.

"I know. I guess we just have to pray and take it one day at a time. Thank God we have each other," Teri said.

Aaron hugged her tighter and kissed her. The tenderness of his embrace was comforting.

"Come on. Bed time," Aaron said, turning back the covers.

"I'll be right in," Teri said and headed for the shower.

Refreshed from her shower, she changed into her nightgown and stepped in front of the sink. When she was done brushing her teeth, she took a minute to study her image. Except for the obvious signs of fatigue due to the stresses of the past forty-eight hours, the reflection in the mirror looking back at her was unchanged. But, for some reason, she still didn't feel like herself.

"You're getting overly paranoid in your old age, Tericita Ellis," she chided herself and turned off the light.

As soon as she slid under the covers, Aaron rolled over to snuggle against her back.

"This is a crazy way to start a marriage, isn't it," he lamented, his voice muffled by her hair.

"That's the truth. But, hopefully, soon this will all just be a distant, unpleasant memory. I know Fr. Francis is in a better place and at peace. We have to hold on to that thought," Teri sighed, turning over to face Aaron.

They were both silent, then, gently caressing and comforting each other in the quiet darkness of the room. When Aaron pulled her face closer to his, her lips immediately parted in anticipation of his kiss. Their deep kiss continued as Aaron helped her remove her thin nightgown.

Teri closed her eyes and relaxed against the pillows. She guided his hand to the secret places on her body that excited her. She felt her mind drift into another time and place when Aaron entered her and began moving rhythmically inside her.

Cloudy, distorted images floated past her mind's eye. Her nostrils filled with unfamiliar fragrances, her ears with foreign sounds. The size and furnishings in the room seemed to melt away, and for a fleeting moment, she imaged that she was in her bedroom in the brownstone. But, even that wasn't the same. Where were her tropical plants? The pastel walls? Her wicker armoire?

She murmured suddenly, and Aaron's mouth automatically sought hers. She grabbed a handful of his curly hair, her body coiling tighter and tighter like a spring as her orgasm intensified.

Aaron was too engrossed in the ecstacy of his climax to hear Teri's muffled cry of, "O God, Nathan!" that burst from her lips before she could stop herself.

Her eyes flew open in shock and embarrassment and she held her breath in anticipation of Aaron's reaction. She released a long, deep sigh of relief when he didn't respond.

Aaron only smiled down at her and kissed her forehead before rolling over onto his side. In a few minutes his was sound asleep.

*****

Later, she watched the steady rise and fall of his chest as he slept, still basking in the glow of their lovemaking. Her mind was a jumble of thoughts as she tried to sort out what had just happened. Who was Nathan and why in the world would she blurt out the strange man's name? What the hell was going on with her?

Mumbling in his sleep, Aaron suddenly turned onto his side and Teri repositioned herself, facing the window. With her back against the curve of his body, she laced her fingers through his hand. His arm curled around her shoulder.

She finally allowed herself to give into her fatigue and slowly drifted off to sleep. Soon, her breathing matched Aaron's. When she was just on the brink of deep sleep, she was suddenly aroused by a cool breeze lightly brushing her face and a nearly undetectable weight pressing down on the side of the bed next to her. Struggling to open her eyes, she was startled to see the image of a black woman sitting next to her. The apparition continued fading in and out of the darkness as if it were trying to stabilize.

Now fully awake, she nearly cried out when she realized it was her grandmother.

"Hello Grandbaby," Elizabeth said softly.

Teri was about to speak but hesitated.

"Oh, don't worry. He won't hear us. You can speak," she laughed softly, nodding her head in the direction of Aaron.

"I'm so glad to see you. How are you?" Teri whispered excitedly. Her grandmother hadn't appeared to her this way since she was twenty-one.

"I'm just fine, baby. You're grandfather says hello."

Reaching out to touch Elizabeth, Teri was surprised that even though her hand was able to pass through the image, she could still feel a sensation of warmth radiating from the woman's arm.

"I really miss you, Granny, especially now. I'm in a lot of trouble," Teri said sadly.

"I know. That's why I'm here. I tried to warn you about this a long time ago but I think you were still too young to understand. You've got a lot of work to do, child."

"But why? I don't understand what's going on," Teri said.

"The only thing I can tell you is that everything you need to know is in that journal and do not, under any circumstances let it out of your sight," Elizabeth cautioned.
"Let your astrological skills and your psychic powers guide you. You have the knowledge and power to beat him."

"But I don't feel I can," Teri said in despair.

"Since the safety and happiness of you and your family are at stake, you'll find a way," Elizabeth assured her.

Teri was silent as she contemplated what her grandmother said. Then she asked, "So what do you think I should do next?"

"Study those charts like I taught you. Don't overlook anything. The answers to all your questions are there. I know you have the strength to accept what you find," Elizabeth said, cryptically.

Teri's eyes were wide with fear as she looked into the worried face of her beloved grandmother.

Then, Elizabeth lovingly stroked her granddaughter's face. Her touch was as cool and light as a feather.

"I understand how overwhelmed and frightened you are, Grandbaby, but I have faith in you. Remember, I'm the one who taught you everything you know," Elizabeth smiled.   Tears flowed unchecked as Teri listened to her grandmother.

"Your husband is a good man," Elizabeth continued, glancing at Aaron.

"Yes he is. I'm very fortunate to have found him," Teri replied, humbly.

"Oh, Grandbaby. How little you know of the ways of the Creator. It has always been your destiny to meet but only if you were willin' to wait. You've been tested more times than you'll ever know. And as a reward, you've been blessed with this union and soon you'll be blessed once again."

"What do you mean?" Teri asked, puzzled.

"You're already makin' me a great-grandmother," Elizabeth said with delight.

Teri only stared at her grandmother in shock.

"Are you tellin' me that I'm gonna have a baby?"

"Not just one. Two!" Elizabeth beamed.

"I can't believe it," Teri whispered and she immediately put her hand on her stomach.

"Aaron's the kind of man I said you'd need when the bad times came. He truly loves you and will do everything in his power to protect you. You'll be triumphant against evil but only if you remain a strong and united force."

"Now, you have even more of a reason to fight. Do you want to condemn your children to a future controlled by people like Hastings?"

"No!" Teri cried.

"Then believe what I've been tellin' you. Have faith and look deep into your heart for the answers."

"All right, Granny," Teri promised.

"Good. One last thing. Hastings is gonna tamper with the climate of this country. You were right. I taught you well."

"But how?" Teri asked, shocked by her grandmother's revelation.

"He's gonna make it go up so high it's gonna feel like you're in hell. It won't last long but by the time it's over, many people will have died. Be careful."

"Thanks for the warning, Granny."

"You think I'm gonna let some devil mess with my grandbaby and her husband and not do somethin' about it? Just 'cause I'm not walkin' the earth doesn't mean the fight's gone out of me. I showed that burglar a thing or two, didn't I?" Elizabeth said angrily.

"Oh, Granny, it *was* you! But how?" Teri asked. At least now she was sure she wasn't losing her mind.

"I can't explain it but that's why I told Andrew to give you the hologram when you turned forty-one. I had a vision that something bad was gonna happen to you then," the old woman replied.

"Oh Granny, that's why I love you so much," Teri wept, hugging her grandmother.

"I love you too, Grandbaby. I'm gonna go now. You go to sleep and have sweet dreams. Remember, you can call me whenever you need me. I'm right here," Elizabeth said and leaned over to kiss her granddaughter. Her touch was like a cool breeze.

Rising from the bed, Elizabeth pointed toward the window.

"Look into the glass, Grandbaby, and you'll see all the people who are watchin' over you."

Teri sat up and peered through the darkness. As if someone had turned on a movie projector, suddenly, she was able to see an image of people standing in a group. The first person she recognized was Grandpa Williams who smiled and threw her a kiss. The sight of her grandfather, who had died when she was little, made her cry out with joy. Then, she saw other ancestors, who she didn't recognize, who waved. The image gradually faded.

"Good bye, Grandbaby. God bless you and keep you," were Elizabeth's final words as she dissolved into the darkness.

Teri's eyes immediately became heavy and she soon fell into a deep, peaceful sleep, filled with renewed courage and strength.

CHAPTER VIII

Two thousand miles away in the city of Los Angeles, Bertha Collins sat with her eyes glued to the television screen. She couldn't seem to get enough of the news from New York. It hadn't even bothered her when the networks preempted her soaps in order to provide continuous coverage of the disaster.

Feeling the temperature slowly creeping upwards, Bertha started fanning herself with an old newspaper. It had been a scorcher all day but the weatherman had promised that it would cool off by evening.

"That's how much those fools know," she grumbled and reached into the ice chest next to her feet to get another cold beer. Popping the top, she gulped down the chilled, amber liquid, letting it drip down her chin onto her already sweat drenched house dress.

She dropped the empty can onto the coffee table, belched loudly and hoisted herself off the sofa. Then she shuffled over to the rusty fan atop the television. Its oscillating motion was as sluggish as she felt.

"Piece of shit. I can fart harder than this damned thing can blow," she mumbled.

Returning to the sofa, she clicked the remote until she reached the twenty-four hour weather station.

"What can I say, folks," the weatherman shrugged his shoulders and smiled. "We're as baffled by this sudden shift in wind direction as you are. In the last hour, the temperature has continued to rise. At this moment, we're at the high for today, a steamy ninety-eight degrees and still rising."

"No shit!" Bertha swore at the screen. She had news for him. The temperature in her house must have been close to one hundred and five.

"Maybe there's something to this green house effect," the weatherman quipped to someone off camera.

Switching the channel in disgust, Bertha returned to the all news channel and resumed fanning, well aware of the swirling, hot breeze that was passing over her house in an easterly direction.

* * * *

"Nice ridin' with ya, Ed. Take it easy," Seth called out as he pulled away from the curb.

Edward looked down at the tracker and nodded his head with satisfaction. The blip was still stationary which meant he had been correct in assuming Tericita and Aaron were staying in Buffalo over night.

Slinging his duffel bag over his shoulder, he entered the revolving doors of the modestly priced hotel where he planned to rest for a few hours. His room wasn't as luxurious as he was accustomed to, but it was better than sleeping in a car.

He stripped off his clothes, padded over to the air conditioner and turned the dial to high. Breathing deeply, he inhaled the cold, filtered air but his lungs continued to feel slightly constricted. It was a sign that his time was really running out. No matter how much he rested, his body was beginning to lose its ability to regenerate itself.

Edward stretched out on the bed and began formulating a plan. That meddlesome bitch and that annoying Jew had to be caught. He needed to come up with something to stop them from leaving the city. It was a shame he couldn't pull a stunt like the one in New York. But maybe there was another way.

As Edward drifted off to sleep, he got an idea. Raising his arm, he pointed his finger at the window and a thin stream of light flashed across the darkness.

"That should be about right," he smiled and closed his eyes.

Edward's mind was filled with a myriad of strange images as he slept. One minute, the image of Margaret Hastings floated before him, her unlined face, youthful and vibrant. Then, it slowly faded into the likeness of Tericita Ellis. The images flickered back and forth several times until they finally merged into one, then abruptly disappeared.

His eyes fluttered open and it took Edward a few minutes to re-orient himself.

"What the hell was that all about?" he murmured in confusion. He continued to stare at the ceiling for a few minutes before drifting back to sleep, his question unanswered.

* * * *

Ten miles west of where Edward Hastings lay sleeping, Aaron was jolted awake by a flash of lightening crossing the sky. Waiting for the inevitable clap of thunder that would follow, he was surprised when the night remained silent.

Yawning, he rolled over, instinctively reaching for Teri, who continued to sleep.

Later, Aaron was awakened again by the sound of rain pounding on the roof above their room. Although it was sunrise, the morning sky remained dark, concealing the sun behind a thick cover of clouds.

Not wanting to disturb Teri, he quietly slipped out of bed and walked over to the window. Outside, the air was heavy. Huge droplets of rain fell straight as arrows from the sky. It was so heavy, he could barely see the sidewalk below or the other houses across the street.

Returning to bed, Aaron sat down next to Teri and watched her sleeping. Even with her hair radiating wildly from her head, she was still beautiful.

Suddenly she stirred, mumbling something in her sleep that made her smile. Aaron couldn't resist tracing the outline of her full lips with his finger. Feeling the warmth of her body next to his as he slept made him realize how much he missed being married. What a fool he'd been to wait so long to propose to her. What if she'd gotten involved with someone else? The thought depressed him. But that was irrelevant now. She belonged to him and no one was ever going to take her away from him, especially a demonic force.

Teri looked more rested than she had in days. He regretted having to wake her from a dream she was obviously enjoying but they had to resume their analysis of the journal as early as possible.

"Rise and shine, Mrs. Jacobs," he whispered and gently shook her.

"Mm?" Teri mumbled, opening her eyes.

"Time to get up."

"Already?" she asked, stretching her arms above her head and then around his neck.

"Yes, already."

The Eighth House

Karen Sealy

"Kiss me first," she commanded him.

"My pleasure," he smiled.

"That was better than breakfast," she declared and sat up.

"Why, thank you. By the way, what were you dreaming about just now? You were smiling in your sleep."

"I can't remember but it was probably about you," Teri grinned.

Aaron was about to kiss her again when a sudden flash followed by a loud clap of thunder rattled the windows.

"When did it start raining?" she asked, slipping on her nightgown and getting up to kneel on the window seat.

"Sometime after midnight, I guess. The lightning woke me up but there wasn't any thunder. Seems strange," Aaron said, joining her at the window.

"This is some storm. I think there'll be problems with flooding," she noted as she watched a river of water rush toward the storm drain on the corner.

* * * *

Teri and Aaron were pleasantly surprised to see the Smiths up and dressed when they entered the kitchen.

"Good morning, you two. This is some weather, huh? I don't remember hearing the weatherman mention anything about heavy rain today," Marilyn said, cheerfully. They sat down at the table.

"That's because it wasn't supposed to," Teri said, and silently wondered if Hastings had something to do with the drastic change in the weather.

"We need to finish deciphering what's in that journal as soon as possible. I don't want to put you in any more danger. The sooner we figure this out, the sooner we can leave," Teri said and Aaron nodded in agreement.

The Eighth House   Karen Sealy

"But Hastings will be gone in a few days. Why don't you just stay here?" Steve asked.

"Because we're afraid that if he does manage to track us down again, our being here might cost you your lives the same way it did Father Francis," Aaron said, gravely.

"Okay, then. Let's get started while we're eating breakfast," Marilyn replied. Steve went into the living room to get their reference books.

* * * *

To save time, Edward decided to rent a car instead of trying to steal one. He really had no choice because his little rain storm had resulted in fewer cars passing through the usually busy street outside his hotel.

Feeling rested, alert and thanks to room service, well fed, he was in top form and ready to tackle the problem at hand. Looking at the tracker, he pinpointed Teri's location and headed in that direction. After a few wrong turns, he finally reached the house and saw the Blazer parked in front.

From what he could see through the steamed up windows of his car, everything in the house was quiet. Maybe he'd be able to catch them off guard.

Not wanting to alert them to his presence, Edward parked a short distance from the house. Then, as he approached their driveway, he decided it was best to change his appearance. By the time he reached the front door, he had assumed the identity of an elderly priest.

Giving the door bell a firm buzz, he waited. Because of his keen sense of smell, he detected Teri's scent which hung thickly in the air. When no one responded, he buzzed again and peered through the glass panel at the side of the door.

"I wonder who that could be this early in the morning,"

Steve said when the doorbell rang. "I'll be right back." Edward could see a tall black man coming down the stairs. Making one minor adjustment to his appearance, he was already flashing an innocent smile when the door opened.

"May I help you?" Steve asked, startled to see the figure of an elderly African-American priest on his doorstep.

"I hope you can. I'm desperately trying to find a woman by the name of Tericita Ellis and I was told you might be able to help me locate her," Edward said, anxiously.

"Excuse me father, but may I ask who you are?" Steve asked, cautiously.

"My name is Father Thomas. I was sent here by a priest from St. Thomas Aquinas Monastery in Albany to deliver an urgent message to Ms. Ellis."

"Oh, you mean Father Francis?"

"Yes."

"But he's dead," Steve thought, frowning. His suspicions about the man intensified.

"What's the message?" Steve asked.

"I'm afraid I can't tell you. My instructions were to speak directly to Ms. Ellis or Prof. Jacobs," Edward replied, innocently.

Just then they were joined by Marilyn.

"Oh, hello," she said when she spotted the elderly priest.

"This is Father Thomas. He said that he was sent by Father Francis to deliver a message to Teri," Steve explained.

Marilyn frowned and stared curiously at the old man. She could tell he was genuinely distressed because he was nervously mopping perspiration from his brow. But something still didn't seem right.

"How did you know she'd be staying with us?" Marilyn finally asked.

"Father Francis told me," Edward replied.

"Oh?" Steve asked.

"Yes. Please, sir. We're wasting valuable time," Edward pleaded and in a last ditch effort to convince them, he said, "If you don't believe me, please feel free to call the monastery."

Steve looked at his wife and said, "Would you excuse us a moment father?"

Edward nodded as the couple closed the door. Placing his ear against the door, he listened to Steve and Marilyn debating whether or not they should cooperate with the priest.

"Hurry up and make up your minds, you idiots. I don't have all fucking day," Edward cursed under his breath.

"I don't like this at all. This could be that Hastings guy. I'll keep him occupied while you go warn Teri and Aaron that they'd better leave. Let them take our van and leave from the back of the house," Steve whispered urgently to his wife.

Marilyn nodded and hurried back to the kitchen.

"Who is it?" Teri asked. Then, noting Marilyn's obvious distress, she said, "What's wrong?"

"There's a priest at the door who claims to have a message for you from Father Francis. We think it might be Hastings in one of his disguises. You'd better go. Our van is in the back of the house. Go out that way while we stall him," Marilyn said in a rush. She handed Teri the keys and registration.

"You go upstairs and get our stuff while I get the van," Aaron said, and they both sprang into action.

Teri ran up the stairs two at a time. How could Hastings have found them again?

When she returned, Marilyn was waiting for her at the bottom of the stairs.

"You take care, Teri. Be careful," she said, giving her friend a quick hug.

"We will. Thanks for everything," Teri said, her eyes beginning to water. "I'll call you later to make sure you're okay."

When Teri got into the van, Marilyn joined Steve at the front door.

"I'm afraid you just missed them, Father," Steve said when Marilyn discretely squeezed his hand.

"I have? Where did they go?" Edward asked, trying to remain calm.

"Back to New York."

"But---"

Then, Edward heard the sound of a van speeding down the block. He turned to look and just managed to get a glimpse of a black woman sitting on the passenger side of the Caravan before it disappeared around the corner.

He could no longer contain his rage.

"You're gonna be very sorry you lied to me," he growled, his appearance gradually returning to normal.

Steve and Marilyn could only watch in fascinated horror when the elderly black priest was replaced by a blonde haired white man whose striking blue eyes were blazing with rage.

"Who's that, mama?" the Smith's five-year-old daughter, Brittany asked as she came down the stairs in her pajamas.

Before they could react, Edward lunged forward and grabbed the child who immediately started screaming.

"Let go of her, you bastard!" Steve cried.

"Take one more step and I'll brake this little bitch's neck," Edward snarled.

Steve immediately backed up and Marilyn took his arm.

"Now, tell me where the fuck they're going," Edward demanded.

"We don't know! Please don't hurt my baby!" Marilyn begged.

"This is a waste of time," Edward said, angrily. Since they had switched cars, he'd have to rely on his keen sense of smell to follow them and the more time he wasted there, the weaker the scent would become.

"Here's what you get for interfering," Edward said. Brittany Smith shrieked and fell to the floor when an electric shock surged through her body.

"Nooo!" Marilyn yelled and threw herself over her child's tiny body. It jerked spasmodically on the floor. Brittany was foaming at the mouth and only the whites of her eyes were visible.

Steve was about to take a swing at Edward when he too was struck by an electric shock. He fell against the stairs, clutching his heart.

Without glancing back to examine the condition of the Smiths, Edward ran to his car. Teri's scent was still strong and he was even more determined to stop the astrologer. He only had a few remaining hours on earth.

* * * *

Thirty miles outside Buffalo, Aaron focused all his attention on driving the Smith's van through the teeming rain. Thick clouds stretched as far as he could see, making him even more positive that Hastings was responsible for the inclement weather.

"I hope you have some ideas about what we should do next because I sure don't," Aaron said, glancing at Teri, who hadn't said a word since their abrupt departure from the Smiths.

"I'm thinking," Teri replied, anxiously. Her head was still reeling from the sudden turn of events.

Along the Interstate, the speed had been reduced to forty miles per hour. As usual, there were a few drivers who refused to heed the warning. When they passed the sign for Erie, Pennsylvania, the traffic slowed to a crawl.

Squinting, Aaron noticed a sign for a popular hotel that was located only a few exits from their location.

"There's a hotel not too far from here. Let's go there. It'll give us a chance to calm down and figure out what to do next,

The Eighth House
Karen Sealy

Aaron suggested.

"All right," Teri agreed.

* * * *

Six miles behind them, Edward darted in and out of the traffic leaving scores of angry motorists in his wake. He could have easily caused them to run off the road but it wasn't worth it. Teri's scent was so strong, it was as if she were sitting right next to him. His little rain storm had succeeded in slowing them down.

Pressing down on the accelerator, he swerved into the passing lane, then cut across three lanes to the right to avoid a slow moving car. From this vantage point, he was able to see that the traffic was slowing down a few miles ahead.

"Good. This should help me catch up to them," he thought. When he'd reached the area where the cars were nearly at a standstill, he pulled onto the right shoulder. Then, he rolled down his window and slowly passed each car, hoping to get a better look at its passengers.

Twenty cars up the line, Aaron switched on his signal, preparing to exit a quarter of a mile ahead.

Edward continued to scan the vehicles. The strong aroma of Teri's scent made him lightheaded.

"All right!" he shouted, his eyes darting excitedly, scanning the cars.

It was a trucker who finally allowed Aaron to move over toward the exit which was only a few feet away. He left the highway, leaving the trail of slow moving cars behind.

Edward's attention was inexplicably drawn to the vehicle that had just exited. When he realized it was Teri and Aaron, he jammed his foot down on the gas peddle in a frantic attempt to catch up with them. At the same time, a tractor trailer moved onto the shoulder, right in the path of Edward's speeding car.

The Eighth House — Karen Sealy

He was too slow to react and his car plowed into the back of the truck at forty miles per hour. The force of the crash automatically caused the driver and passenger side air bags to deploy, slamming Edward's body against the seat.

Motorists near the scene of the accident immediately jumped from their cars. The stunned trucker ran to the back of his rig to see what had hit him. Soon, two men were prying open the door and dragging Edward onto the grass next to the road. The smell of gasoline filled the air.

"Somebody call an ambulance!" the trucker shouted. The three men stood over Edward's rain soaked body.

He was conscious but his breathing was labored. His lungs felt as if they were filled with concrete. He was weak but he still had enough energy left to repair them. He just needed to make the good Samaritans leave him alone.

Turning his head, he motioned for one of the men to bend down so he could speak.

"Take it easy, buddy. The ambulance should be here in a second," the man said, patting Edward's arm.

Inhaling as much air as his battered lungs would allow, Edward hoarsely whispered into the man's ear.

"If you and your friends don't get the fuck away from me, I'm gonna detonate that bomb in my car and blow the bunch of you all over this road."

Jumping back, the man's eyes widened. At first he thought he might have misunderstood, but when he saw Edward's angry expression, he scrambled to his feet.

"He says there's a bomb in his car and if we don't leave him alone he's gonna blow it up! I'm gettin' outta here!" the man shouted over the sound of sirens and scurried back to his car. The other men looked at Edward and then at the retreating man and followed suit.

Hearing the approaching sirens, Edward knew he had to

work fast. He closed his eyes and he directed all his energy inward. In a few seconds, his appearance changed from blonde to brunette, tall and then short, until his body completely disappeared.

When the troopers and emergency technicians finally arrived at the scene of the accident, Edward Hastings was gone.

* * * *

"What was that?" Aaron asked.

"I don't know but it sounded like a collision not too far from the exit," Teri replied, turning around in her seat.

"Then we just got off in time."

Shortly, Aaron pulled the van into the parking lot of the hotel. In the lobby, a few heads turned and watched with curiosity as the interracial couple walked up to the registration desk.

"Afternoon, folks. What can I do for you?" the uniformed clerk asked pleasantly.

"We'd like a room for the night," Aaron said. He removed his wallet to retrieve his credit card.

Hesitating, the clerk, who wore a pin identifying him as Ted Campbell, looked at Teri and then back at Aaron.

"Uh, excuse me, sir, but I think maybe one of the motels further down the strip might have what you're looking for. We have a more, uh, family-like atmosphere here," the clerk said, his face becoming flush.

Teri was about to say something but changed her mind. She was curious to see how Aaron would handle what she knew was an inappropriate remark. He continued searching for his credit card and only replied, "That's fine with me." But the clerk's next statement was less tactful and Teri held her breath and waited for Aaron's reaction.

"Maybe you didn't understand me, sir, but we don't accommodate working women and their men here. We pride ourselves in running a respectable establishment."

Teri watched in silence. When Aaron finally comprehended what the man was implying, his eyes narrowed and his ears turned red. He leaned across the desk until his face was only inches away from the clerk's. In a strained voice, he said, "This may be too complex for your ignorant, small mind to comprehend but this 'working woman', as you so crudely put it, happens to be my wife. We've had a hard day, we're tired and we'd like to get some rest. If you don't give us a room, I'll make such a scene that all these nice families will be checking out faster than you can blink. Then, I'll sue you and this chain for discrimination and I'll be able to buy this piece of shit and you'll be working for me. Do I make myself clear?"

Teri turned her head to conceal the smirk on her face. The clerk turned bright crimson.

Fumbling with the papers on the desk, he said, "Please accept my apology, sir. I didn't mean to offend you or your lovely wife. It's just that we have a lot of problems, with uh, I mean, with the Interstate right here and all we --"

"Why don't you just give us a room and I'll forget what just happened. The name's Mr. and Mrs. Aaron Jacobs," Aaron interrupted the clerk and handed him the credit card.

"Why, certainly, Mr. Jacobs. You'll be all set in just a second," the clerk said nervously, and quickly typed in the information he needed into his computer.

When they walked to the elevator, Teri couldn't resist smiling. The people who had witnessed the scene quickly turned their heads and resumed their conversations.

"Jerk!" Aaron mumbled angrily as he unlocked the door and tossed their bags on the floor.

"Ah, Prof. Jacobs, you handled yourself very well. I'm proud of you," Teri said as she reached up to kiss her husband's scowling face.

"That guy had some nerve insinuating that you were a

prostitute and I was your john. Where does he get off saying something like that? I bet *if you were white he wouldn't have acted like that.* I bet you this place is full of one night stands," Aaron grumbled.

"Well, you took care of him so forget about it now," Teri said, trying to calm him down.

"What business is it of his anyway? That's what's wrong with people. If they'd spend more time taking care of their own business, the world wouldn't be in such a mess now," Aaron ranted.

"Look, just forget about it. We have more important things to worry about, like how Hastings managed to find us again," Teri said, tiredly. She threw herself on the bed.

"All right. I'll get us something to eat and be right back."

"Okay, darlin," Teri said. When Aaron turned to leave again, she stopped him.

"Come here a second," she said. Wrapping her arms around him, she gave him a hug.

"Thanks for defending my honor, Prof. Jacobs. I guess chivalry isn't dead after all," she said, smiling up at him.

"You're welcome, Mrs. Jacobs," Aaron grinned and closed the door.

CHAPTER IX

While she waited for Aaron to return, Teri stretched out on the bed and closed her eyes. She wanted to call the Smith's to make sure they were all right but she was afraid. What if Hastings had killed them? The thought made her stomach knot. But she had to be sure.

When no one answered after ten rings, she hung up. It was a bad sign.

"God, please let them be okay," she prayed and got up to get the journal from her bag.

She shook her head and wondered how such an innocent looking object could be the source of so much tragedy. What information did it contain that would cause Hastings to be so obsessed with stopping them? And most of all, what was the source of her sudden, strange sexual fantasies?

Her thoughts were interrupted when Aaron returned.

"Well, it's not gourmet food but it'll keep us going," he said. He placed a bag on the table next to the bed.

"I called the Smith's but there was no answer," Teri said. She joined him at the table.

"I hope nothing happened to them," Aaron sighed.

"I'll try again later. This just doesn't make sense," Teri said as she put the journal on the table. "What in the world could be so important in this book? Why is he trying to kill us? Okay. We know he was behind the disaster in New York but even if we knew about it ahead of time, we couldn't have prevented it. If he manipulates the weather, we won't be able to stop that either. So, there must be something else he's planning on doing in the future that we may be able to avert," Teri said, frowning.

"But what?" Aaron asked, agreeing with her line of reasoning.

"That's what we have to find out. The other question I have is, if I'm correct, when is this thing supposed to take place? If we've interpreted the text and charts correctly, this may be his last day on earth. That means, whatever catastrophe he has planned may take place between now and tomorrow morning."

"That doesn't leave much time for us to figure it out, assuming we can," Aaron sighed, running his fingers through his hair. "We need help with this, Teri. And we need it fast. We can't do it alone."

"I know, darlin'. But, I don't want to put anyone else in

danger by contacting them, and I've run out of people who might be able to help us," Teri said, dejectedly.

"I think I know someone," Aaron said, rubbing his face with his hands in deep thought. Suddenly, he had an idea.

"Let me make a quick call to a colleague of mine in Chicago," he said.

Teri flipped through the pages of the journal while Aaron spoke to his friend. Grandma Williams told her that everything they needed to know about Hastings was there. They would have been working on it right now if Hastings hadn't suddenly shown up on the Smith's doorstep that morning. She still couldn't understand how he'd found them. Was his sense of smell that keen? And if it was, it wouldn't be long before he found them again. They had to find some place to hide that wouldn't pose a danger to other people.

"Well, so far so good," Aaron said as he hung up and prepared to dial again. "I lied and told my friend in Chicago that I was doing some research on the prophecies of Nostradamus and was having problems with a particular quatrain on the Anti-Christ. He said he wasn't that familiar with them and suggested I call a mutual friend who he thinks might be able to help me. I'll phone him now," Aaron said.

Teri turned to listen to the conversation.

"Hello, Dan? This is Aaron Jacobs."

"Aaron! It's good to hear from you. How've you been?" Dan Black Elk said, delighted by the call.

"Well, I'm in a bind and I need your help. It's complicated though," Aaron hesitated.

Dan Black Elk looked down at the astrological chart of the United States on his desk and waited for Aaron to continue. He'd been studying it for the better part of the day and was very disturbed by what he'd seen. He'd also been picking up very strange psychic vibrations for the past month. If his intuition was correct, the disaster in New York was only the beginning of a series of events that were about to strike America. There was a strong demonic force living in the country and so far, he'd been able to conceal his identity.

"What I'm about to tell you is going to sound very strange," Aaron continued.

"I doubt it, my friend. Nothing is strange to a psychic," Dan chuckled. "Go on."

Dan's mood was somber as he listened to Aaron's story. What he was hearing was very similar to what he'd seen in his visions for weeks. But what connection did it have to his friend? Aaron's next statement answered his question.

"My wife is an astrologer and she's been pretty successful at interpreting most of the charts but we need help. We were wondering if you could take a look at the journal," Aaron said, finally.

"You don't have to explain anymore. Where are you now?" Dan asked.

"We checked into a motel just outside Erie."

"Good. It shouldn't take you that long to get here if you leave right now. You can stay with me."

"I don't think that would be such a good idea, Dan, although I appreciate your offer. We'll just stay at another motel and meet you someplace else," Aaron suggested.

"You don't have a choice, Aaron. Whoever this man is, I get the feeling he's still right on your tail. The sooner you get here, the better," Dan insisted.

"All right. Give me your address," Aaron agreed.

"I'm in a small town called Stormville just northeast of Buffalo. You may have a little trouble finding my cabin at night because it's pretty deep in the woods. You can reach it by way of a small secondary road just off of Route 90. Once you leave the Interstate, it'll be the first road you come to."

"Okay. We'll see you in a few hours, then. Thanks a million,

The Eighth House   Karen Sealy

Dan. You're a lifesaver," Aaron said, in earnest.

"Anytime. I'll wait up for you," Dan promised.

When he returned his attention to the chart, he couldn't shake the feeling that, before the day was over, the lives of many people would be changed forever.

*****

"It's a good thing you didn't bother to unpack. We'll be leaving again after we eat," Aaron said when he joined her back at the table.

"I hope your friend understands the risk he's taking by letting us stay with him," Teri said, picking up a sandwich.

"I'm quite sure he does. Dan's a Mohawk who's not only an expert on prophecy, but also an astrologer and a psychic. His grandfather was a medicine man. The two of you should have a lot to talk about," Aaron explained.

"You've never mentioned him before."

"I know. He slipped my mind. I've made a lot of friends through my discussion groups over the years and I'm not always able to keep track of everyone," Aaron replied.

"Well, he sounds just like the person we need to talk to so we can end this nightmare," Teri, said, rubbing her temples.

"I hope so. I don't know how much more of this I can take either," Aaron said. He got up and stood behind her to massage her shoulders.

"I guess we just have to pray and hope for the best," Teri sighed, closing her eyes. "You'd better stop before I get too comfortable. Let's go," she said, kissing his hand.

"Well, our departure should make the desk clerk happy, since he assumed we were only here for a quickie anyway," Aaron said, dryly, and picked up their bags.

"He wouldn't think so if he saw us in action," Teri winked

and closed the door.

When they reached the lobby, they looked out into the street and were surprised to see that the sky was filled with thick, dark thunderclouds.

"Maybe we'd better wait for the storm to pass before we check out. I'd hate to get stuck on the road in this," Aaron said.

"Alright. Let's go back to the room. I want to call my parents anyway," Teri agreed.

While she made the call, Aaron turned on the television to the all weather channel. He'd been wise to suggest that they wait. There was a severe thunderstorm warning and tornado watch in effect in the area for the next five hours due to the unexplainable severe heat wave from the west meeting a cold front from Canada. Then, the weatherman switched to the international report. When a map of the Caribbean appeared on the screen, Teri gestured for him to turn up the sound.

"The first hurricane of the season is making its way across the Atlantic towards the Caribbean. If it continues on its present course and velocity, it's scheduled to hit the northern coast of South America and the islands to the northeast by this evening. We'll continue tracking it and keep you informed," the weatherman said.

A few minutes later, Teri hung up the phone.

"So what did your parents say?" Aaron asked, noting the scowl on her face.

"Andrew's doing better, but now he's worried about the storm. Government officials are making preparations to evacuate the residents to shelters in the event the hurricane does reach them. I told him I thought they should go to Miami. My parents are too old to be dealing with something like that and he agreed. The only problem is they're so stubborn, they may just dig their heels in regardless. I'm praying Andrew's able to convince them to leave before it's too late," she replied, shaking her head.

"I'm sure they will. They've lived there long enough to

know how dangerous it is to be in the middle of one of those things," Aaron reassured her.

"I hope so. Anyway, I gave Andrew Dan's number so he can keep me posted. Maybe you should call Dan and tell him we'll be delayed because of thunderstorms, since he's expecting us to be there in a few hours," Teri said.

"Okay," Aaron agreed. He was about to pick up the phone when there was a loud clap of thunder. It rattled the windows and caused the lights to flicker.

"I think I'd better wait. It's dangerous to use the phone in a storm like this," Aaron said and he looked out the window. The sky was dark and they could feel the crackle of electricity in the air. Teri was about to turn off the television when the building lost power, plunging the room into total darkness.

"Well, I guess we'll be here for awhile," Aaron surmised.

* * * *

Day suddenly turned into night as the thunderstorm raged. Gail-force winds propelled debris across the road. Teri jumped when a flash of lightening streaked across the sky followed by loud clap of thunder that shook the window.

As Teri watched the swirling raindrops beat against the glass, she reflected on how in the span of five days, her life had become a living hell just because of a book. Father Francis was dead and there was a possibility that the Smith's had met a similar fate because they too dared to assist them. And now, a deadly storm was heading for Barbados. Could this too be the work of Hastings?

Touching her cross, she thought of her grandmother's visit the night before. She was anxious to share the news of her pregnancy with Aaron but thought it would be wiser to wait until it was confirmed by a doctor, whenever that would be possible. Who knew when they'd be able to return to New York.

The Eighth House Karen Sealy

Grandma Williams had also said that everything they needed to know about Hastings was in the journal and that she must have faith in God and herself, but it was difficult. If faith in God hadn't been enough to save a holy man like Father Francis, what chance did they have?

Teri shivered when another flash of lightening streaked across the sky. She had a premonition that something very bad was going to happen before the day was over and didn't have the power to stop it.

* * * *

Aaron wondered if Teri's thoughts were similar to his as she stared out the window. How in the world had he suddenly lost control of his life? A few days ago, his spirits were high in anticipation of their pending marriage. Now, one of his closest friends was dead and they were fugitives from a madman. He couldn't understand why this was happening to them.

He was glad they wouldn't have to stay hidden in a hotel while waiting for Hastings to leave, but were they, once again, putting a friend in danger by accepting Dan's help?

Another bolt of lighting illuminated the room and he looked down at his watch. They'd been stranded at the hotel for several hours and now it was late evening. And, so far, there was no sign of Hastings. Aaron felt anxious.

"It's late. I think we'd better go even though it doesn't look like the storm will be letting up anytime soon. If Hastings is still after us, I'd rather be a moving target than a sitting duck," Aaron said, joining Teri by the window.

"Alright," Teri turned to prepare to leave.

"Don't worry, sweetheart," Aaron took her in his arms. "Everything will turn out alright for us and your family. You'll see."

"I hope so," Teri smiled up at him and kissed his cheek.

Even though his words were meant to be reassuring, deep down in their hearts, they didn't believe them.

* * * *

Edward Hastings slowly rolled over onto his side and looked around. He was astonished to find that it was dark and he was in the middle of a forest. That meant he'd been unconscious for several hours and was a long way from the accident. Gusts of wind shook the trees around him and the atmosphere was filled with electricity, an indication that a thunderstorm was brewing. He cautiously sniffed the air, not wanting to aggravate his already aching lungs. To his surprise, Teri's scent was present and from its direction, it seemed that she was headed right toward him! Finally, his luck was changing.

Suddenly, he saw the headlights of an approaching car through the trees. Scrambling to his feet, he ran onto the road and started waving his arms. When the car slowed down, Edward quickly ran over to the driver's side and reached into the open window. The driver never knew what hit him before he died of an electrical-shock-induced heart attack.

Edward opened the door, pulled the dead driver out, and dragged his body into the woods. Then, he got behind the wheel and started down the road. His lungs were burning from the strain of disposing of the body. He needed to rest. But it was more important to find out where he was.

After he had driven along the dark, deserted road for nearly two miles, he finally spotted a sign, indicating that he had just entered the town of Stormville.

"Wherever the hell this is," Edward mumbled and pulled off the road. Turning on the overhead lamp, he pulled open the glove compartment and was relieved to find that it contained a map.

When he'd located his position, he stuck his head out the

window to sniff the air. Edward could barely contain his delight when he detected Teri's scent in the gusting wind. It had grown stronger since the last time he'd checked. According to the map, this was the only road in the immediate area. He was almost positive that she was heading in his direction on that very road.

He turned off the headlights and leaned his head against the back of the seat. Luckily, he would no longer have to pursue her in his weakened condition. He was scheduled to leave the earth at exactly midnight, which, according to the dashboard clock, was only forty-five minutes away. His master didn't make it a habit of extending anyone's time, so this would be his final opportunity to get the book from her. He needed to come up with a fool-proof plan of attack and he needed to do it quickly.

Edward looked around in the darkness and continued formulating his plan. In a few minutes, a sinister smile lit up his face. Teri and Aaron were in for the surprise of their lives.

CHAPTER X

ST. JAMES PARISH, BARBADOS

Andrew threw his hands up in frustration and turned away from the window. Thick, dark clouds filled the sky and the winds had already begun to increase their velocity.

"But Pop, the weatherman said we're gonna get hit hard. If we don't leave soon, we're gonna be stuck!"

"I told you ain't goin' anywhere. We've been through this a hundred times before and everythin' turned out fine. I've put too much work into this house and I'm not about to go runnin' off leavin' it because of some hurricane. If you want to leave, go ahead. You're a grown man. I can't stop you," Lawrence shouted angrily. He'd been arguing with Andrew about leaving since Teri had called

The Eighth House
Karen Sealy

earlier in the day.

"Can't you talk some sense into this bull-headed man?" Andrew cried, turning to Isola for support.

"Don't say that about your father. I agree with him. I'm not goin' anywhere either. We're gonna do just what we've always done in the past. Instead of arguing with your father, you should be helpin' him board up the windows and doors."

"Jesus Christ, I can't believe this. Didn't you see what happened in New York? Would you please listen to me? We have to get out of here before it's too late. Please, we're wastin' valuable time. Look at the clouds. Jesus, it's started rainin'," Andrew cried, hysterically, and rushed back to the window.

The waves of the Atlantic crashed violently onto the beach. If they didn't leave right away, they'd miss the last flight to Miami.

"If you wanna go runnin' like a scared rabbit instead of helpin' me, go ahead. Get the hell out of my house. I'm sick of arguin' with you!" Lawrence shouted. Grabbing his hammer and a box of nails, he angrily stormed out of the house.

"Please Mama. I'm beggin' you. Please come with me. I have a bad feelin' about this," Andrew pleaded with his mother, tears forming in his eyes. How he wished Teri were there!

"I can't, Andrew. This is our home. We have to protect it. We're too old to start over again. If you want to go, go. I'll understand," Isola said, with conviction.

"Okay, Mama. Please be careful. I'll call to see if everything's all right when I get to Miami," Andrew said, all the fight out of him.

"Take care, baby," Isola said, and he hugged her.

"I love you, Mama," he said and turned away. He picked up his bag before she could see that he was crying.

"I love you too, baby. Good-bye."

On his way to the car, Andrew walked over to his father who was in the process of nailing a board over the kitchen window.

"I'm goin' Pop. Please be careful."

Lawrence said nothing, his lips drawn in a thin line. He pounded a nail into the board.

Andrew shook his head dejectedly and ran through the rain to his car.

"God forgive me but I tried, Teri," he whispered. He took one last look at his parents in the rearview mirror as they struggled to nail a board over the front door.

* * * *

Dan Black Elk turned off the television and stood on the porch of his log cabin. The temperature had been rising all day and he could hear the distant rumble of thunder in the mountains. He hoped his guests arrived before the heavy wind and rain. He had a feeling that this storm would be different. The wind carried the signs that something bad was going to happen. He'd spent most of the day praying.

Turning to his Alaskan Husky, Scout, he said, "Come on fella. Let's take a walk."

Obediently, the dog followed him down the path leading to the road.

* * * *

Edward Hastings casually sniffed the air. The winds continued to carry Teri's scent. Closing his eyes, he resumed his nap. The electricity in the air temporarily rejuvenated his body.

* * * *

The Eighth House   Karen Sealy

MIAMI BEACH

Andrew's eyes never left the screen of the projection T.V. in the lounge next to the bar in the airline terminal. He had just made it to the airport in time to catch the last plane to Miami Beach. The flight had been a rough. The plane struggled to fly through the thick clouds created by the storm.

The all weather channel reported that the edge of the storm was approximately fifty miles east of the coast of Barbados and with the coarse it was taking, the island would take a direct hit sometime before midnight.

Looking at his watch, Andrew sighed. He'd tried to call Teri in Stormville, New York but all he'd gotten was an answering machine. Calling his parents had also proven to be futile. All the circuits were busy.

Signaling the waiter, Andrew asked for a refill of his drink. It was going to be a long night.

* * * *

STORMVILLE, NY

Edward's eyes flew open when a gust of rain-filled wind swirled through the car window. He estimated that from the strength of Teri's scent, she was only a quarter of a mile away and approaching fast.

His excitement was almost orgasmic. He quickly got out of the car, which he'd parked in a small clearing in the adjacent woods, and headed for the road. He wanted to strategically position himself. He'd only have one chance to execute his plan. He concealed himself behind a tree on the north side of the road and he laughed.

The Eighth House

Karen Sealy

* * * *

Less than a quarter of a mile away on the south side of the road, Scout stood and perked his ears. A clap of thunder rumbled through the mountains.

"What's wrong, boy?" Dan asked his companion. "Weather got you spooked too, huh?"

Walking over to the living room window, Dan peered into the darkness of the woods.

"Keep your ears sharp, Scout. I think we're in for some trouble."

* * * *

Teri turned on the overhead lamp in the van so she could read the directions to Dan Black Elk's cabin. According to what he'd told them, he was located only a few miles from the Stormville exit off Route 90.

"This is gonna be some storm when it finally breaks," Aaron said as a loud clap of thunder shook the van. It sounded like it was directly overhead.

"The turn should be coming up soon," Teri said. She switched off the lamp and peered out into the darkness. The only source of light was the van's high beams. Little droplets of rain sparkled like diamonds. The rain began to fall and the wind gusted through the trees, blowing branches and leaves across the road.

* * * *

The headlights drew closer. Edward adjusted his position until the large oak tree across the road was in his direct line of vision. His timing had to be perfect. He'd only have one chance.

The Eighth House

Karen Sealy

* * * *

Teri flinched when another clap of thunder boomed overhead. Without warning, the light rain turned into a downpour. Her body tingled and she felt anxious. Something wasn't right.

"Hmph, that's all we need," Aaron said and pressed the button for the wipers. Their effect was useless against the sheets of rain.

When the van was approximately one thousand feet away, Edward made his move. Raising his arm, he aimed his finger at the tree directly across from him. Suddenly, a bright stream of light flashed across the road. The bolt of lightening hit the base of the tree. It burst into flames sending splinters of wood in every direction.

"What was that?" Aaron asked, peering through the water cascading down the windshield.

"It sounded like lightening. I--Aaron, look out!" Teri shouted when she spotted the tree falling across their path.

Aaron slammed on the brakes and jerked the wheel sharply to the right to avoid hitting the deadly obstacle. The back of the van swung widely to the left, spinning one hundred and eighty degrees. Teri screamed when they skidded off the road into the forest.

The Caravan finally came to rest after it crashed into a large oak tree. Teri was slammed back against her seat by the force of the airbag.

She could hear the rain pounding on the roof of the van. The wind howled through the trees. Teri fought to remain conscious. Her left side was throbbing where she'd been thrown against the arm rest on Aaron's seat. Wincing, she turned to look at him.

"Oh no. Oh God!" she cried. Aaron was slumped against the smashed driver's side door, his shattered eyeglasses on his lap.

Frantically unbuckling her seatbelt, she leaned over to check his pulse. He was still alive but his pulse was faint. A thin stream of blood was trickling down the side of his face, just above his left eye.

"Oh God! Please help me! Don't let him die!" she prayed, hysterically. She was about to unbuckle his belt when her passenger door was unceremoniously yanked. And a hand reached in, grabbing her by her hair. Before she could react, Teri was dragged from the van and thrown to the ground.

"Hello, bitch," Edward sneered. Teri stared in horror into the rain-soaked face of the man she'd last seen at the party.

"Let me go!" she demanded. She was being pelted by the rain and wind. Her hair blew wildly around her head.

"I will as soon as you give me that fuckin' book."

"I don't have it!" she shouted at him above the howling wind.

"I don't have time for this. Give me that damned book!" Edward roared, grabbing Teri's hair. He roughly pulled her to her feet.

"I don't have it! I burned it!"

"Lying bitch!" Edward shouted as he threw her against the side of the van, causing the door to slam shut.

Stars flashed before her eyes when her head banged against the door.

"Please. I'm telling the truth. I don't have it," Teri pleaded.

"Get out of my way," Edward commanded and pushed her aside. Then, he slid the rear passenger door open. Spotting her tote bag, he grabbed it and dumped its contents on the ground.

"Shit!" he snarled. The book was no where to be found. He climbed into the van, and started throwing things out the door. When he still couldn't find the book, he jumped out and opened the front passenger door again.

Teri grabbed the handle of the sliding door and slowly pulled herself up. She had to do something to stop Hastings before he found her purse and the book. Taking a deep, painful breath, she lunged at him as he was leaning over to reach for her handbag where it had fallen between the front seats.

Then, she jumped onto Edward's back, wrapped her arm around his neck and tried to pull him from the van.

"Get the fuck off me," he growled, grabbing her arm.

Teri cried out in agony when a bolt of electricity shot up her arm, causing her to immediately release him. Pushing her off, Edward snatched the purse and tore it open. Throwing his head back, he howled gleefully. He emerged from the van, hysterically waving the book in the air and slipped it into his shirt pocket.

Aaron's head felt as if it were trapped in a vise. He drifted in and out of consciousness. He was vaguely aware of some movement to his right. Squinting through darkness and blurred vision, he turned to see what was going on. The sudden movement caused an explosive pain in his chest. He clutched his chest with his good arm. Gradually, everything dimmed. The sound of the rain pounding on the roof of the van faded away into nothingness.

* * * *

"Now I'm gonna take care of you once and for all," Edward said, turning to Teri. She tried to crawl away from him.

He snatched her roughly from the ground and pinned her against the side of the van with his body.

Teri stared into Edward's leering face. Then, unexpectedly, his expression relaxed.

* * * *

When Aaron opened his eyes again, his attention was drawn to the dark-skinned woman standing outside the crushed door of the van. He tried to focus. How could her white dress stay dry in spite of the teeming rain?, he thought. "Teri, is that you?" Aaron whispered, weakly.

"You have to come with me," the woman said.

"I can't. I'm in too much pain," Aaron groaned. His breath was becoming more labored with every word.

"Yes you can. I'll help you," the woman said, firmly, gesturing for him to open the door.

"Alright. I'll try," he said. Weakly reaching over with his good arm, he was surprised when the twisted remains of the door swung open with ease.

"Now just lean on me, darlin'," the woman instructed.

Aaron screamed in agony. A wave of excruciating pain struck him when he turned in his seat. Panting and sweating profusely, he carefully swung his legs around and stepped from the van. His broken arm hung limply at his side. He leaned against the woman in white for support.

They carefully made their way through the trees. He stumbled several times and had to fight to remain conscious.

"Come on, darlin'. Just a few more steps. You can do it," the woman said, guiding him with his right arm. Her grip was strong and cool to the touch.

When they were approximately one hundred feet from the van, they stopped and she helped him sit down with his back resting against a tree.

"Thank you," Aaron smiled, squinting up at her through myopic eyes.

"You're welcome, darlin'. Now you just sit here and rest," the woman said, gently patting his rain-soaked head.

"But who are you?" Aaron asked.

The woman merely smiled and backed away, vanishing into the darkness.

The rain continued to beat against him where he sat. He shuddered and drifted back into unconsciousness.

* * * *

"You've caused me quite a bit of trouble, Teri, but I must admit I've enjoyed having such an attractive adversary. It's a shame we didn't get to know each other under more pleasant circumstances," Edward smiled seductively, rubbing his body against hers.

Teri cowered against the van. His touch made her want to vomit.

"What's wrong, Teri? Aren't I good enough for little miss holier than thou? I guess your kind would never associate with me. Maybe I should knock you off your pedestal and show you what a slut you really are," Edward said, sardonically. He tugged at Teri's jeans.

The fear in her eyes turned to revulsion and terror, making Edward even more excited. Suddenly, an image of his mother's terror filled eyes flashed before him and the malicious words of the woman in Hell reverberated in his ears.

"She was a whore because she wanted to be one, Eddie. She loved what those men did to her! She didn't give a damn about you, Eddie. She lied to you. You were a fool Eddie! A fool....the bastard child of a whore....Nathan's bastard child conceived in lust like a dog...."

"NO! Edward shouted, shaking his head violently. Staring into Teri's face, the sudden, stunning realization of who she was struck him like a blow to the head, causing him to relax his grip.

Teri jumped at the unexpected opportunity to escape from his grasp and in one swift movement, she kneed him in the groin.

A sharp pain yanked Edward out of his daydream and he doubled over, clutching his groin.

Teri quickly stepped over him but slipped in a pool of muddy water caused by the teeming rain.

"Not so fast, bitch!" Edward shouted and lunged for her but her wet shirt slipped through his fingers.

Running blindly in the darkness, Teri frantically prayed that she would find somewhere to hide or someone would come along and help them.

She stumbled through the trees. To her relief, the road finally came into view. She was nearly ten feet away from it when a streak of light flashed through the trees. A bolt of lightening struck her, tossing her into the air. She hit the ground and heard the sickening crack of her ribs.

Edward stood over her and watched with sadistic pleasure. Her body twitched and she gasped for air.

"What's wrong, mother? Not feeling well?" Edward leered down at her.

Trembling, Teri struggled to turn her head and looked up at him in confusion.

"Come on, mother. Surely you recognize your loving son? I haven't changed that much, although I can't say the same about you," Edward snickered.

"I don't know what you're talking about," Teri shook her head in confusion.

"Think, mother. Think hard. Just because you followed the light of forgiveness doesn't mean you can't remember your past. Maybe this will jar your memory," Edward said. He dropped to his knees and roughly turned Teri over onto her stomach, smothering her face in the muddy ground.

"Doesn't this remind you of something?" Edward whispered slyly in her ear, thrusting his groin against her buttocks.

"Please stop," Teri whimpered and choked, her mouth filled with dirt.

"Don't tell me you've repented that much, mother. How convenient for you. Just go to the light and all is forgiven," Edward spat, sarcastically.

"Well, all isn't forgiven as far as I'm concerned. I think you deserve to feel the pain I've had to live with all my life because you wanted to be a whore," Edward berated her. "Come, so I can give you a reason to despise me as much as I've hated you," he said, ignoring her painful cries. He dragged her back in the direction of the van.

"You're really gonna love this one," Edward promised. Then, raising his arm, he pointed his finger in the direction of the van. A blue-white streak of light shot from its tip and hit the van, causing it to burst into flames.

"Nooooo!" Teri wailed. She had to save Aaron!

Edward snickered. She fought wildly to escape his grip. But his laughter stopped abruptly when she bit his hand. He loosened his grip. When she tried to run, he grabbed her by her hair again and slapped her across the face, knocking her to her knees.

Teri's choking sobs filled the air. She watched the bright, orange flames consume the van and her beloved Aaron.

"Oh Aaron!" Edward cruelly mocked her. "Where's your God now, Teri?" he whispered in her ear, kneeling beside her. "If He was as powerful as you believe, He would have saved your man. But He didn't and now poor Aaron is burnt to a crisp. How does it feel to be as powerless as I was when I was a kid?"

"Go back to hell where you came from, you son-of-a-bitch," Teri hissed.

"That's right. I am the son-of-a-bitch. I'm the son of a bitch of Margaret Hastings and Nathan Styles," Edward shouted, bitterly.

At the mention of the name Nathan, Teri whispered, "Oh my God, no!"

Edward reached out to caress her face. When she tried to turn away, he grabbed her by the neck and pulled her closer, roughly covering her mouth with his. Teri gagged at the acidic taste of his saliva.

"Before I go, I'm gonna leave you a little something to remember your loving son by," Edward sneered, pushing her onto her back and straddling her. Teri struggled in vain to get away from him. He ripped open her blouse and jeans.

"Please don't do this! I'm sorry for whatever you think I've done to you! Please, just leave me alone!" Teri pleaded.

"Shut up and just lay back and enjoy it like you always have," Edward smirked, unzipping his fly.

Teri stopped struggling and closed her eyes. Reaching for her cross, its metal now distorted from the heat of the electric shock, she prayed.

* * * *

At the sound of the first sharp crack of lightning only a few feet from his cabin, Dan and Scout bolted out the front door. Following the general direction of the sound, they ran as fast as they could through the dark woods, rain and wind beating against them.

They had nearly reached the road when they heard the screech of tires and the loud crunch of metal when the van skidded off the road into the trees. Running across the road, Dan was surprised to see the huge tree lying in the middle of the it.

"Go, Scout!" Dan shouted and the dog sprinted into the woods.

* * * *

"Shut up, hypocrite!" Edward cried in disgust. Teri continued to pray out loud. He was about to slap her when a huge dog suddenly appeared from the darkness and charged at him.

Edward was thrown onto his back when the dog jumped on him. Scout clamped his teeth onto his shirt, ripping it down the front. The astrology book fell to the ground.

Dan was astonished when he stumbled onto the scene of a man wrestling with Scout on top of him.

"Get off me!" Edward screamed and fought wildly to block the dog's snarling, snapping muzzle from reaching his neck.

Dan's hair stood on end when the air started crackling and

the wind picked up the strong odor of sulfur. A blinding ray of light flashed from the sky and struck the ground a few feet in front of him with a deafening boom. He was knocked to the ground.

When Dan's eyes readjusted to the darkness, he was astounded to see that Scout was now alone. The man had disappeared.

Relieved that his dog was apparently unharmed, he rushed to the woman's side.

"It's gonna be all right, miss. He's gone," Dan said, gently cradling the sobbing woman in his arms.

"Oh, Aaron!" Teri wailed, over and over again. It was then that Dan realized who she was.

"Don't worry, Mrs. Jacobs. Everything's gonna be okay," he reassured her and reached for the cell phone in his back pocket.

CHAPTER XI

ST. JAMES PARISH, BARBADOS

As Edward returned to his master, hurricane Anna struck the island with the force of a bomb. The two hundred mile an hour winds tore trees from the ground, tossing them across the island like twigs. The darkness hid the driving rain and flying debris.

Lawrence clutched his wife. She trembled in fear, sitting on the floor listening to the sounds of destruction around them.

"Maybe we should have listened to Andrew," Isola wept.

"We'll be just fine, darlin'. It'll be over soon," Lawrence reassured his wife.

Just outside the front door, a few hundred feet away, a mammoth wave rose above the beach, towering high above the little house.

Isola was torn from her husband's arms when the wave hit,

causing the living room wall to explode, letting in the ocean. When the water finally leveled off, Isola and Lawrence were gone.

＊＊＊

MIAMI AIRPORT

Andrew covered his face with his hands while he listened to the latest report about the storm. The weatherman could only speculate about what was happening on the island. Communication had been lost forty-five minutes earlier.

"Please let them be all right," Andrew prayed silently.

＊＊＊

Teri fought to awaken from her sedative induced sleep. Her dreams had been filled with images of a tree falling across a road and Edward Hastings' maniacal laughter. She had to wake up so she could find Aaron. Then, she remembered the burning van.

"I think she's waking up, Dr. Reyes," the nurse said, watching Teri's eyes flutter.

When the room finally came into focus, Teri tried in vain to speak. Instead, she coughed uncontrollably.

"Here. Take this," the nurse said. She gently raised her into a sitting position and held a cup of water to her lips.

"Just relax," Dr. Reyes said. "You've been in an accident but you'll be fine. You broke a rib and have a nasty bruise on your left side."

Dr. Reyes checked Teri's pulse and nodded with satisfaction when she found it to be normal.

"I want you to take it easy now. Try to get some sleep," the doctor advised, before she and the nurse left the room.

Teri closed her eyes and started to cry when she thought

about Aaron. Her life was meaningless without him.

She wouldn't allow herself to recall Hastings' horrible accusations about who she was. If she did, she would lose her mind.

She slowly turned on her side and continued to weep. Her body was wracked with pain and grief. She prayed she would die from her injuries.

* * * *

Outside in the waiting room, Dan cradled the phone against his shoulder and quickly scribbled the message from his machine at home. Someone named Andrew Ellis had left a frantic message that he was trying to get in touch with Teri. After the doctor allowed him to see her, he would return the call.

It had been quite a night, he thought, shaking his head. After the man had suddenly vanished, he'd called for an ambulance. Teri was in shock. Aaron, on the other hand, who he'd found lying unconscious against a tree a few feet from the burning van, was another story. Twice during the ride to the hospital, he'd gone into cardiac arrest and had to be resuscitated. Fortunately, he'd been stabilized by the time they reached the emergency room.

Dan poured himself a cup of water from the beverage cart in the waiting room and sat down on the hard, plastic chair. He still couldn't get over witnessing the sudden flash of light and the disappearance of the man on the ground. Could it have been the same man he'd seen in his visions? He was anxious to talk to Teri. There were many questions he wanted to ask, especially about the book he'd found on the ground. But that would have to wait.

Closing his eyes, he offered a silent prayer for the speedy recovery of Aaron and his wife.

* * * *

Twenty-four hours later, Teri continued to lay in her hospital room, exhausted and depressed. Her grief over Aaron's death was more painful than anything she'd ever experienced, including the death of Grandma Williams. And just as upsetting was the possibility that she had miscarried as a result of being struck by Hastings' lightening bolt. At least if her babies survived, she would still have a part of Aaron. All she could do was pray that the test results showed that her babies were unharmed.

Just then, she heard a light tapping on the door.

"Come in," she called out, hoarsely.

"I hope I'm not disturbing you," a handsome, forty-ish, Native American man said, hesitantly entering the room. He was dressed in a denim shirt and jeans that hugged his muscular frame.

"Not at all. Please come in," she replied, gesturing for him to sit down. "You're the man who saved my life, aren't you?" Teri said, studying the man's face. His complexion was golden bronze and complimented his mixed grey hair, worn in a braid down his back. His high cheekbones, prominent nose and strong jaw mirrored his Native American ancestry.

"You flatter me, but yes, I'm the one who called the ambulance. My dog gets the credit for saving your life. I'm Dan Black Elk," he replied, his dark brown eyes twinkling.

"Oh, I'm so glad to meet you," Teri smiled, offering her hand.

"I hadn't expected your arrival to be so dramatic," Dan said.

"Well, Edward Hastings obviously had other plans for us and now Aaron is dead," she said bitterly, her eyes filling with tears.

"What are you talking about?" Dan asked, puzzled by her statement.

"Aaron was still in the van when Hastings blew it up. Didn't you see it?" Teri said, her heart filled with pain.

"Yes, but Aaron wasn't in it. I found him unconscious, propped up against a tree a few feet away. He's in pretty bad shape down the hall in intensive care but very much alive," Dan informed her.

Teri gasped.

"I'll ask the doctor if you can see him now and if you're up to it, I'll wheel you down there myself," Dan offered.

Too dumbfounded to speak, she quickly nodded her head.

"Okay. I'll be right back," Dan said and left the room.

* * * *

Later that afternoon, Teri's heart beat wildly and she was in good spirits when Dan wheeled her to Aaron's room. Her beloved was alive and she'd gotten the test results back from her doctor. She was still pregnant and so far, everything was fine. The advances in early pregnancy detection amazed her.

The sight of her friend and lover with tubes running from his arm and nose and a cast on his left arm, was heartbreaking. Standing next to his bed, ignoring her own discomfort, she bent over and gently kissed his forehead near the bandage over his left eye. His right eye was bruised where the air bag had smashed his glasses into his face. But none of that mattered. He was alive!

"Hello, Prof. Jacobs," she said, softly caressing his face, tears of joy streaming down her cheeks.

Aaron slowly opened his eyes at the sound of Teri's voice.

"Hello, Mrs. Jacobs," he whispered.

"You look like hell," she smiled.

"So do you," he replied, grinning.

She pulled the wheelchair closer to the bed.

"How do you feel, darlin'?" she asked, holding his hand.

"Like crap. Are you all right?" Aaron asked, turning his head to look at her.

"Yes."

"What happened? The last thing I remember is swerving to

avoid hitting a tree that fell across the road."

Teri briefly filled him in, purposely avoiding the details about her encounter with Hastings.

"And is Hastings gone?" Aaron asked when she had finished.

"Yes. We're finally free of him," Teri replied.

"I hope so. What about the book?"

"I don't know. I guess he took it with him."

"Good riddance. Why are you crying? Do I look *that* badly?" he asked, reaching up to brush away her tears.

"No. I'm just so happy to see you," Teri smiled and kissed his hand. If he didn't remember what happened to the van, she wasn't going to bring it up, at least not now.

"I should have been able to protect you. But I promise you that I will from now on," Aaron vowed, squeezing her hand.

"I know you will, darlin'. Well, I have some good news," she said, changing the subject.

"What?" Aaron asked, anxiously.

"You're going to be a father," she beamed.

Aaron's mouth fell open.

"In fact, you're going to be a father twice," she added, chuckling.

"You mean --"

"Uhuh. Next May, you're going to be the proud father of twins," Teri declared.

"Oh my god, Teri. Are you sure?"

"Positive," she reassured him.

"But how? I don't understand."

"Now Aaron. What kind of question is that?" she teased.

Recalling their lovemaking, he smiled.

Are you all right?" he asked again with concern.

"Yes. I'm fine, they're fine and soon you will be too," she declared, kissing his hand.

"How long will it be until we can leave?"

"The doctor said you'll have to stay for awhile. Besides the broken arm, you suffered a concussion and internal injuries," Teri replied.

"What about you?" Aaron asked, caressing her face.

"Just a few bruises here and there. I may be checked out of the hospital tomorrow."

"But where will you stay? Who'll look after you while I'm stuck in here?" Aaron asked, becoming agitated.

"Don't worry yourself. I'll be staying with Dan. All I want you to do is concentrate on yourself so you can get well soon," Teri ordered, kissing him on the cheek.

"When can I see Dan?"

"Maybe later today. He's very anxious to see you too. I like him. He's a very kind and considerate person."

"I know. I want to thank him for rescuing us," Aaron said and suddenly grimaced in pain.

"Do you want me to call the doctor?" Teri asked, jumping up.

"No. It'll pass. Just lay next to me for awhile. You know I can't sleep without you beside me anymore," Aaron said. He gingerly moved over to make room for her.

Climbing next to him, Teri carefully positioned herself so that she could comfortably lay with her arms around him.

"Don't get any funny ideas. I don't think the doctors would approve," she teased, gently stroking his face.

"I love you Mrs. Jacobs," Aaron said, softly, gazing into her eyes.

"I love you too, Prof. Jacobs," Teri replied, a lump forming in her throat.

For the rest of the afternoon, the two survivors discussed their future with renewed optimism.

The Eighth House

Karen Sealy

* * * *

Andrew went directly to the hospital after his arrival from Miami Beach. Teri was scheduled to check out that day and he wanted to accompany her to Dan's cabin.

When he was sure Teri's and Aaron's conditions were stable, Dan Black Elk had returned his call and given him the details of the accident. When Andrew told him about the death of his parents in the hurricane, Dan suggested he fly up to New York as soon as possible to be with his sister.

Dan greeted Andrew with a firm handshake when he entered the waiting room.

"I really appreciate your inviting me to stay at your place, Mr. Black Elk. I don't know what to do anymore," Andrew said, tiredly.

"It's no problem. I have plenty of space. I'm very sorry to hear about your parents," Dan said, sympathetically. The young man's face, which was haggard and drawn, reflected the trauma he'd been through during the last seventy-two hours.

"Before I take you to Teri's room, I think I should warn you that she doesn't know about the devastation in Barbados. You might want to hold off on telling her until you get to my house," Dan cautioned.

"Okay, if you think that's best. When she asks why I'm here, I'll just tell her you called me after I left a message the other night," Andrew agreed.

Dan was touched by the sight of brother and sister greeting each other after such a traumatic week. It was good that Andrew had been able to join her. With Aaron still in critical but stable condition, Teri needed his support.

Although she was feeling better, Teri was relieved when they reached the cabin. It was three thousand square feet, with an open floor plan, tastefully decorated in a contemporary Native American style that resembled a hunting lodge.

She and Aaron would be staying upstairs in the small, but cozy loft apartment while Andrew occupied one of the additional bedrooms on the main floor. To give them privacy, Dan had moved into the studio apartment adjacent to the house where he maintained an office.

Teri was in good spirits, but the strain of the past week and the accident were still evident from the dark circles under her eyes and her slow gait. When they reached the cabin, Andrew insisted she immediately lie down and he would tend to her needs.

"This is a switch, huh sis," he smiled. She sat up in bed sipping the tea he'd made for her.

"What?"

"My takin' care of you for a change."

"Oh. Well, it's only a temporary situation. I have lots of things to do. I still can't believe Aaron and I have lost everything. But at least we'll be able to fly down to Barbados as soon as he's able to travel," Teri said, tiredly.

Andrew averted his eyes at the mention of the island. He dreaded having to tell her the truth but it couldn't be avoided.

"There's something I have to tell you," he said, glancing up at her and nervously biting his bottom lip.

"What is it, darlin'?" Teri asked, alarmed by his sudden apprehension.

"They're gone, sis. It's all gone," Andrew said, his voice cracking.

"What are you talkin' about?" Teri asked, frowning. She leaned forward and grabbed his arm.

"Oh God, Teri. They wouldn't listen! I tried to tell them to leave but they wouldn't listen!" Andrew said, bursting into tears.

"I still don't understand what you're talkin' about," Teri said, her pulse quickening.

"Mom and Pop were in the house when a huge wave hit it.

They got washed away into the sea," Andrew choked, unable to control his tears.

Teri heard a strange buzzing noise in her head and felt faint when she finally comprehended her brother's words.

"No. There must be some mistake!" she said. A lump formed in her throat. She couldn't breathe.

"I called Mr. Dunkley who lives down the road. He went over there and said the only thing left was the foundation. He said their bodies must have washed out to sea. The whole island is in ruins," Andrew said, tears streaming down his face.

Teri shook her head wildly. It couldn't be true. How could her parents be dead? She'd just spoken to them a few days before. She had to make herself wake up from this nightmare.

"I tried my best to get them to leave, sis, but they just wouldn't listen. I'm sorry!" Andrew cried, clutching his sister's cold, clammy hand.

Teri yanked her hand away and clamped it over her mouth. Her emotions were on the verge of exploding and her mind fought wildly to suppress the image of her beloved parents, trapped in the middle of the raging hurricane. When the horror of what they must have felt when the wave hit and the walls of the house came crashing in on them finally sunk in, she let out a wail that made Andrew jump from the bed.

Teri doubled over and rocked as she wept, her face contorted in anguish. All the pain, fear, uncertainty and anxiety she'd felt during their ordeal with Hastings was finally being released.

Andrew could only stand by the side of the bed shaking at the sight of his sister. He'd never seen her so out of control and it frightened him. But he had to comfort her. Brushing the tears from his eyes, he sat back down on the bed and took his sister in his arms, hugging her as tightly as he could. He crooned words of comfort and stroked her hair, just as she'd done so many times for him when he was a child.

CHAPTER XII

When she'd wept until she'd run out of tears, Teri fell back onto the pillows completely exhausted, much to Andrew's relief. He brought her a glass of water and adjusted the covers, instructing her to try to rest. Teri docilely complied.

When he'd gone, she slid down under the covers and buried her head in the pillow. Over and over she imagined what it must have been like for them to be trapped in the middle of that storm. Was this also because of the book? Had Hastings somehow found out about her family in Barbados and created the storm that killed them? Oh God, if only Aaron hadn't given her that damned book, she lamented.

The thought of blaming Aaron immediately made her feel guilty. It wasn't really his fault. How could he have known what the book contained and that Edward Hastings would come after them for it? Maybe it was really all her fault. If she hadn't accepted the job to interpret his chart at that damned party, maybe Edward would never have found her.

Teri could feel her throat constricting and her eyes beginning to burn again. Now she understood what her grandmother had meant when she'd told her there would come a time when her talent as an astrologer would seem like a curse. What good had it all done? She hadn't been able to foresee the accident or the hurricane that killed her parents.

And what about Hastings' description of her past life? If it was true, could this be her punishment for her past sins? For the first time in her life, Teri felt powerless. She'd always considered herself to be the kind of person who could tackle any problem. Now here she was, weak and useless while her husband was in the hospital and her brother was forced to deal with the greatest tragedy of his life without her support. They had no home or jobs and were forced to accept the charity of others.

When despair threatened to consume her again, Teri remembered the two innocent babies who were growing inside her. Even though she was so mentally and physically exhausted that she never wanted to get out of bed again, she knew she'd have to pull herself together at some point. If she couldn't do it for herself or Aaron and her brother, she'd have to do it for the twins.

Teri's hand automatically reached for her now misshapen cross and she prayed. She found the words comforting and relaxing. Soon, she drifted off to sleep.

But her dreams were not peaceful. They were filled with images of Edward Hastings' leering face. In the first dream, he was laughing and tearing pages from the astrology book and throwing them at her. Her second nightmare was of her final encounter with him. The repulsive sensation of his body against hers seemed just as real as the event itself.

Tossing and mumbling in her sleep, her eyes darted back and forth behind her lids. Next, she found herself in the middle of a hurricane swimming as fast as she could in a futile attempt to save her parents and Andrew. But a mammoth wave dragged them out to sea.

The final and most disturbing of her nightmares took place in the delivery room of the hospital. She was lying on the delivery table writhing in pain. Her contractions grew stronger and closer together. Crying out, she begged for someone to help her but apparently she was the only one in the sterile, cold room. When she felt as if her body were being torn apart, a man in white scrubs and a mask suddenly entered the room and stood over her. At first, she was relieved at the thought that finally someone would be able to stop her pain. Then, she became alarmed when the doctor strapped her arms and legs to the table. Moving toward her feet, he forced her legs open and reached into her womb as if to assist with the

The Eighth House   Karen Sealy

delivery.

Teri screamed when the mask slipped down revealing the face of Edward Hastings. She tried in vain to break free from the leather straps that imprisoned her. She could feel Edward's hand searching deep inside her for one of the baby's heads. Teri squirmed in pain. He roughly pulled out her son and held him up for her to see. Then, with his free hand, he reached in again, this time pulling out her daughter.

Holding her wailing children over his head by their feet, and laughing, she screamed again when she saw that the two infants were grotesquely deformed.

"See what happens when you sell your body to hundreds of men? See what happens...see what happens....see what happens..." his voice pounded in her head.

Teri awoke from the nightmare, shaking and drenched in perspiration. It was dark out and the house was silent. Turning over on her side, she peered into the darkness watching the moon gradually come into view through the window.

Her vigil came to an abrupt end when she felt a faint breeze on her neck. Reaching up to touch the spot, she was startled when she felt a hand.

"Hello Grandbaby," the familiar voice said softly.

Turning over, Teri's spirits soared at the sight of her beloved Granny's face smiling down at her.

"Oh, Granny. I'm so happy to see you!" she cried.

"I'm happy to see you too, Grandbaby. I know you've had some bad days since the last time we spoke," the old woman said, gently stroking Teri's hair.

"I've been a failure, Granny, and now Mama and Pop are dead," Teri bemoaned.

"Oh, darlin'. That's not your fault. It was their time to go," Elizabeth said, shaking her head.

"No, Granny. You don't understand. If I'd studied the

journal like you told me, I would have known what Hastings was gonna do next. But I didn't have time!"

"That's not true, Teri. It wasn't in your power to prevent it. Your parents chose to stay there. There was nothin' you or Andrew could have done to convince them to leave. That's the way it was supposed to happen. You can't keep blamin' yourself for the rest of your life."

"I just wish I could have at least said good-bye," Teri lamented.

"You can. They're right here," Elizabeth smiled and pointed behind Teri's shoulder.

Turning around in the bed, she cried out with delight when the images of Isola and Lawrence appeared before her.

"Hello darlin'," Isola said. Her image floated to the side of the bed.

"Oh mama! I'm so glad to see you! Are you all right?" Teri said, reaching out to touch the apparition.

"We're fine, darlin'. That's why we came. We wanted to show you that everything is all right and that it's time for you to concentrate on yourself and your family."

"You know about the babies?" Teri asked, excitedly.

"Yes, sweetie," Lawrence said, joining his wife.

"I wish you could be here when they're born so they could get to know you."

"Oh, we will be and you can tell them all about us, darlin'. That's why you have to accept that we're gone and get on with your life. We're very happy and we want you to be happy too. We're grateful that we left knowin' you'd found someone who loves you and will take care of you. And now you'll be havin' a family together," Isola said, proudly.

"And remember, Grandbaby, we'll always be watchin' over you and Andrew. Didn't I promise you that before?" Elizabeth said.

"Yes," Teri replied, nodding her head. Tears flowed freely

down her cheeks.

"Good. You take care now. If you ever need our help in the years to come, you just touch that cross I gave you and we'll be right there at your side, even though it's taken quite a beatin' it seems," Elizabeth chuckled and tapped the cross. "And no matter how bad things get, just remember that you've got the Creator and us protectin' you. All right Grandbaby?"

"Yes, Granny."

"And you must continue to seek the truth about your past, Teri. It's the only way you can forgive yourself and accept the second chance God has given you."

"I will, Granny. I promise," Teri said.

"All right then. God bless you darlin'. We love you," Elizabeth Williams said and kissed her granddaughter's wet cheek. Isola and Lawrence did the same. Then, their images faded away.

Teri continued to sit in the darkness for a few minutes, staring at the spot where her beloved family had appeared and basking in the glow of their love for her. Then, she turned on the light and picked up the phone. It was past midnight but she didn't care.

"Hello?" a groggy voice mumbled into the receiver a few seconds later.

"Hello Aaron," Teri said softly.

"Hello, Teri. How are you?" he replied, now fully awake.

"I'm okay, now. There's something I have to tell you."

"If it's about your parents, I already know. Dan told me this afternoon. I'm sorry, Teri. They were really good people," Aaron said, his voice filled with sadness. "I really miss you. It's lonely sleeping without you next to me."

"I know. It's the first time we haven't been together since we got married."

"Uhuh. And that means we'll have to make up for a lot of lost time, won't we?" Aaron grinned.

"I don't know about that, considering your broken arm and my delicate condition," Teri teased.

"Oh, yeah? Well, we may have to use our imagination when it comes to my arm but as for your 'delicate condition', I think we'll figure out a way around that too," Aaron chuckled.

"Shame on you. Are you trying to imply that I'm a wanton woman?" Teri laughed.

"You'd better be if you're gonna survive being married to an oversexed fugitive from the devil." Then, his voice becoming serious, he added, "At least we won't have to worry about him. Oh, I spoke to the doctor this afternoon. He said I may be out of this place by the end of next week," he added, changing the subject.

"That's wonderful," Teri said, delighted.

"All right. It's time for you to go back to sleep, you know, because of your condition."

"Don't be fresh. I'll see you tomorrow. Sweet dreams," Teri laughed, softly.

"You too. And Teri?"

"Yes, darlin'."

"I miss you and I love you."

"I love you too, darlin'. Good-night," she replied.

Hanging up the phone, she buried herself under the covers and thought how truly blessed she was in spite of everything that had happened.

* * * *

"Boy am I glad to be leaving here," Aaron said. He struggled to pull his shirt over his cast.

"I can imagine," Dan chuckled.

"I don't know how I'm going to repay you for all your help. This is a strange position for me to be in. The thought that Teri and I are literally homeless and without possessions is a bit overwhelming," Aaron sighed.

"Well, that's only until they start letting people back into New York City. And, from what I've heard on the news, it shouldn't be too long now," Dan replied.

"It seems like ages since we left New York," Aaron shook his head. "But at least we won't have to worry about Hastings and that damned journal anymore."

"I hate to be the bearer of more bad news but I wouldn't let my guard down just yet. He didn't take the book with him," Dan said, solemnly.

"What? Where is it?" Aaron said, turning to look at his friend.

"At my cabin. It fell on the ground when Scout attacked him and I picked it up. It's a little dog-eared but still readable. I took a look at the text and charts and saw some very disturbing things," Dan said, opening the door for Aaron.

"Please, don't tell me about it yet. I can't concentrate on that now. All I want to do is spend some quiet time with my wife," Aaron said.

"I think that would be best for now. Come on. She's anxious to see you too," Dan smiled and gestured for Aaron to sit down in the wheelchair.

* * * *

Teri had the opportunity to have a private conversation with Dan before he left for the hospital to pick up Aaron. She was somewhat relieved to be able to share her darkest thoughts with another astrologer and psychic. Dan wouldn't automatically dismiss her feelings and experiences as the rants of a woman on the verge of a nervous breakdown.

"What do you think could have suddenly triggered these memories?" Teri asked.

"It could be a number of things; stress, trauma, anxiety. Direct physical contact with the person you're connected to could also be a catalyst," Dan theorized.

"Like when Hastings and I first shook hands at the party?" Teri said, recalling the scene in her mind.

"Yes. The link between the two of you might have been re-established in that brief moment," Dan agreed.

Then, they were both silent. Teri reflected on his statement.

"You're aware that the only way to confirm your suspicions is through hypnosis," Dan said, gravely.

"Yes. But I don't know if I'm ready to face the possible truth just yet," Teri replied with honesty.

"I can understand that. It's a frightening prospect but I would be willing conduct the session for you when the time is right. Considering the stress you've been through, I think it would be best to wait until after you've had the twins. We don't want to subject your mind, body and spirit to anymore unnecessary trauma," Dan suggested.

"I agree. Thank you so much, Dan. I don't know what Aaron and I would have done without you," Teri said, reaching out to embrace her new friend.

"That's what we're here for, Teri. To help our earthly brothers and sisters," Dan replied.

* * * *

"You're makin' me dizzy pacing back and forth like that, sis. If you don't sit down, you're gonna wear out the man's porch," Andrew said. Teri passed in front of him for the tenth time.

"Oh hush. I can't help it," Teri replied, waving her hand impatiently.

She'd spent most of the morning changing her clothes and fixing her hair in preparation for Aaron's arrival as if it were their first meeting, and in a way, it was. This would be the first day of their married life without the threat of Hastings hanging over their heads and she was nervous.

To allow them total privacy for a few days, Dan had invited Andrew to go on a fishing trip with him. After the stress of the past few weeks, he was eagerly looking forward to the distraction. He hadn't gone fishing since the last time he'd been with his father when he'd visited Barbados six months earlier.

A fresh wave of grief swept over him when he realized they'd never be able to do that again. The idea that his parents were dead still seemed unreal to him. The realization usually struck him late at night when he was in bed. Unknown to Teri, he often cried himself to sleep, which greatly embarrassed him.

He had to admire how Teri was able to hold up so well, considering everything she'd been through. When she'd finally given him the details of their experience with Hastings and the journal, he'd been too stunned to comment.

He was grateful to have his strong, proud sister to lean on again. He was also delighted by the news of her pregnancy. He couldn't wait to become an uncle.

"Here they come!" Teri cried, excitedly, when she spotted Dan's pick-up coming up the driveway.

Dan walked over to the passenger side to assist Aaron. For a few seconds, Teri and Aaron stood in front of each other in the middle of the driveway in silence, oblivious to what was going on around them. Their intense love and devotion was reflected in the way they gazed deeply into each other's eyes.

Both Andrew and Dan felt like intruders as they watched. It was time for them to go.

"If you don't need anything else, right now, Andrew and I will be leaving," Dan said, breaking the spell.

"Oh, okay, Dan. Thanks," Aaron said, briefly tearing his gaze away from Teri. "Have a safe trip," Teri said, and hugged Dan and her brother.

When they were alone, Aaron took Teri's hand and they entered the cabin.

* * * *

"You have no idea how happy I am to see you," Aaron said, standing in front of her in the bedroom, drinking in her beauty with his eyes.

"For awhile, I had my doubts this day would ever come," Teri looked up at him, her eyes glistening. "But I don't want to talk about it now. I just want to pretend it never happened."

"So do I," Aaron, said, softly, stroking her thick, wavy, hair.

Reaching up, she took his hand, rubbed it against her cheek and kissed it.

They didn't need words to express their feelings. They undressed each other, ignoring the bruises that were a testament to the terrifying ordeal they'd survived.

Aaron never took his eyes off of her when he led Teri to the queen-sized bed, covered with a thick, brightly colored quilt. She laid against the pillows. His caresses were halting, almost shy at first. But when he finally kissed her, the familiar softness of her lips against his unleashed his passion for her.

Their lovemaking was intense in spite of Aaron's injured arm. Their hunger and desire for each other was insatiable. Aaron *wanted to drown himself in her scent, the softness of her skin and the warmth of her body.* Teri did nothing to suppress her cries of pleasure as he kissed and caressed her. She clung to him like a drowning woman and urged him on. He tried to devour her with his body.

No strange thoughts or images intruded her subconscious this time. It was just she and her soul mate re-united in love. When they finally climaxed, the raw energy of their lust for each other flowed between them.

Aaron buried his face between her breasts. Teri locked her arms and legs around his muscular body, their hearts still beating rapidly. They were silent for awhile, exulting in the joy of being alive and together again.

"I hope I didn't hurt your ribs," Aaron grinned. He raised his head to look at her.

"I don't think I would have noticed if you did. I'm just so happy to be with you, it doesn't matter," Teri replied, huskily, as she stroked his hair.

"I'll be glad when I can get rid of this," Aaron frowned, tapping his cast as he rolled over next to her.

"It'll be off before you know it, although it didn't seem to hinder you," Teri teased. She sat up, leaning on her elbow.

"It's wonderful not to be on the run for a change. I'm glad we took Dan up on his offer to let us stay here for awhile. At first I was kind of ashamed to have to accept someone's charity but I guess we don't have a choice at the moment," Aaron said, his tone becoming serious.

"Don't fret over it, darlin'. Our situation is only temporary. The most important thing is that we're both alive and well. We may not have material things now but at least we have each other," Teri said, tracing the outline of his lips with her finger.

"You're absolutely right," Aaron said. He tried to suppress a yawn. A wave of tiredness came over him and he couldn't keep his eyes open.

"Let's just rest now. We can think about all of that later," Teri said. She pulled up the quilt and snuggled against him.

She was just beginning to drift off to sleep when Aaron spoke again.

"I love you with all my heart and soul, Teri, and I promise that I'll never let anyone hurt you again," Aaron whispered in her ear.

Teri's only response was to lean over and gently kiss him on the cheek. She was at a loss for words to express her feelings for him.

CHAPTER XIII

"I bet you forgot today is your birthday and I have a surprise for you," Teri announced, mysteriously, standing at the foot of the bed later that night.

"It certainly did slip my mind. What's the surprise?" Aaron smiled.

"It's in there," Teri winked, nodding her head in the direction of the bathroom.

"This sounds interesting." Aaron struggled to get out of bed.

Teri's gift was to share a warm, luxurious bath with him in the large whirlpool tub. She had decorated the room with fresh flowers and scented candles. In the sink was a bottle of champagne on ice.

"Are you enjoying yourself so far," she asked, the warm, swirling water caressed their tired, battered bodies.

"Words escape me," Aaron grinned.

"Good. Now just relax," Teri said. She gently bathed his good arm with a soft, herbal scented sponge.

Aaron closed his eyes and sighed with pleasure while she continued to bathe him. Her soft caresses eased the memory of the terrible ordeal they'd been through.

Opening his eyes, he watched with pleasure while she bathed herself.

"Happy forty-fifth birthday," she smiled, kissing him deeply.

* * * *

"Feeling better?" Teri asked later, lying in his arms, idly playing with the fragrant rose petals that floated in the water.

"More than you can imagine. Your creativity never ceases to amaze me," Aaron sighed, kissing her cheek. "I wish our life could be like this forever."

"It could be but it may not be easy," Teri replied, softly.

"I know. I've been thinking about the journal too. I'm sorry Hastings wasn't able to take it with him. Then we'd finally be free of the burden," Aaron said, regretfully.

"That's true. But I still have a lot of nagging questions I need answered and the only way that will happen is if we finish translating the text and interpreting the charts."

"Dan said he took a look at it and found some very unsettling things," Aaron said, frowning.

"That doesn't sound too reassuring."

"I want you to promise me something before we touch that book again," Aaron said, taking her hand.

"What?"

"That you won't let any of this upset you so much that it jeopardizes your health or the health of the babies. I nearly lost you once and I'm not going to let that happen again," Aaron said, somberly.

"I promise, Prof. Jacobs," Teri smiled, lifting her hand as if to take an oath and dripping water on his face.

"Good. Now how about some of that champagne?"

Why of course," she said and reached for the bottle and a glass. Aaron chuckled when she struggled to open it. Since he only had one good arm, she was on her own. Teri cried out triumphantly when the cork finally popped out and landed in the water.

"And what should we toast to this time?" she asked when his glass was filled. She abstained since she was pregnant.

"To two healthy babies and a long, happy life," Aaron said without hesitation and he tapped glass against the tub.

The Eighth House   Karen Sealy

* * * *

Teri's stared up through the darkness at the beamed ceiling. She was unable to sleep although it was past midnight. Her thoughts were filled with the still unknown contents of the journal. It was as if the book were beckoning her.

Resigning herself to the fact that she wouldn't be able to sleep unless she deciphered at least one of the last two charts, she quietly got out of bed and retrieved the book from the dresser drawer. Closing the door behind her so she wouldn't disturb Aaron, she went into the adjacent room.

She sat at the desk, turned on the light and flipped through the yellowed, muddy pages of the book. The chart that interested her the most was dated the year 2003, which she was still able to read despite it being water stained.

Dan must have known she might be tempted to look at the journal because he'd conveniently left her a pile of reference books and his laptop computer which contained the astrology program she always used.

First, she plotted its location coordinates to determine the point of origin. She was surprised to see that it was Rome, Italy.

Next, she consulted the relevant pages of the books which showed that the person was born under the sign of Taurus. The rising sign was Cancer, the Moon was in Taurus in the eleventh house and he or she had Leo twice in the first.

A general interpretation of the planetary placements and signs in the chart indicated that the person was a humanitarian with leadership qualities. Having Taurus and Cancer placed in prominent houses meant that they were probably nurturing, loyal, intuitive, maternal and patient.

"Not bad," Teri thought out loud. One thing she could be sure of was that the chart definitely wasn't referring to Hastings!

With Cancer rising and the Moon in Taurus in the eleventh

house exactly conjuncting the person's Sun, they were also *genuinely concerned with the welfare of the people of the world.*

Teri sat back a moment to contemplate what she'd learned so far. Who, living in Rome, could the chart be referring to?

Teri's heart fluttered. Her excitement growing, she anxiously typed in the information that would allow the computer to run an interpretation of the chart and compare it with another chart already in the astrology program of the person she suspected it belonged to. She needed solid proof of what she'd discovered.

"Oh, no. This can't be right," she whispered.

Jumping from the chair, she ran to the bedroom.

"Aaron! Aaron! Wake up!" she cried, shaking him.

"What is it?" he asked, groggily.

"Get up! I need you to translate something," she said, her excitement mounting.

"Can't it wait until tomorrow?" Aaron asked, slowly sitting up.

"No. Come on," she replied, pulling him out of the bed.

"Alright! Alright! Wait a minute. Let me put something on," Aaron grumbled, slipping on his pajama bottom.

Teri ran back to the desk.

"This had better be good," he mumbled. She motioned for him to sit down.

"I've been interpreting a chart and the location of it turned out to be Rome."

"So," Aaron said, unfazed.

"I need you to translate that small section of text that comes before the chart," she said, breathlessly, and handed him the book.

"All right. Let me see," Aaron said, adjusting his new glasses.

Teri thought she'd have a heart attack while Aaron carefully read the text and wrote down the translation. When his finger reached a certain passage, he stopped.

Aaron's expression immediately changed from concentration to shock. Shaking his head, he turned back to the beginning of the page and read it again.

Teri nearly jumped out of her chair when he finally looked up.

"So, what does it say," she asked, leaning forward in anticipation.

Aaron closed the book and nervously ran his fingers through his hair.

"It's Hastings' description of how he plans to assassinate the Pope sometime during the year 2003 when he comes back."

"Oh my God," Teri whispered.

Aaron stood up, pacing up and down in front of her. How could this be true?

"I guess even though he was off by a few years, this proves Nostradamus was right when he foretold the rise of an Anti-Christ who would murder the last Pope of the century causing the destruction of the Roman Catholic Church. And unfortunately, we know who's going to do it," Aaron said, nervously biting his pen.

"But I don't understand why that would destroy the Church. Couldn't they just elect another Pope like they've always done in the past when one died?" Teri asked.

"Yes, under normal circumstances but maybe something else will happen that'll prevent them from doing that."

"Like what?" Teri asked, anxiously.

"I don't know."

"Well, according to my grandmother, it's all in the book. We just have to take our time and sort it out," Teri said, matter-of-factly.

Aaron remained silent, leaning against the doorway. Then he shook his head and looked at her.

"Wait a minute. Don't tell me you don't agree! We have to find out the rest. How else are we gonna be able to warn the Pope?" Teri cried, amazed by his attitude.

"And just how do you propose we do that? Write a letter to the Vatican saying we have information that confirms what Nostradamus foretold? Or maybe we should just fly over there and knock on the door and say, 'Excuse me, Holy Father, but my wife, who's a certified astrologer, has a book that describes a plot to murder you.' And what makes you think they wouldn't suspect us of being in on the conspiracy? The next thing you know, we'd be thrown in some Italian prison for our troubles and have the entire Christian world screaming for our heads," Aaron said with bitter sarcasm.

"I can't believe what I'm hearing, Prof. Jacobs. I thought you were the type of person who didn't hesitate to get involved," Teri cried, her anger growing.

"That was before we were nearly killed and I found out I was going to be a father. We can't just run off on a crusade to save the world. We have two other innocent lives to consider. My god, Teri. Look at us! We're homeless and both of us look like we've just come back from a war! Haven't you had enough? The Pope has the Vatican police and bodyguards to protect him, which is a hell of a lot more than we have!" Aaron shouted.

"I know that," Teri snapped, closing the books. "But we have to do something. I doubt that everything we've been through has been a coincidence. I believe that this information was revealed to us for a reason and we can't just sit back and pretend we know nothing!"

"So, you're willing to risk not only our lives but the lives of our children so that you can do what you think is God's bidding? Who died and put you in charge?" Aaron asked, trying his best to control his temper.

The tone of his voice made Teri stop what she was doing. She'd never seen him that angry before.

"I'm going to blame your inability to think clearly on the fact that you're pregnant and your increased hormonal level is clouding your judgement. Before we say things we'll regret later, I think it would be best if you put the book away and dropped the subject for awhile," Aaron said, coldly and abruptly leaving the room.

Teri fumed as she watched him go. His stinging comments had infuriated her and for the first time since she'd known him, she wanted to hit him. How dare he imply she wasn't thinking clearly? After the encounter she'd had with Hastings that nearly resulted in her demise, she was very much aware of the danger they were in. But it still didn't change the fact that the future of the world as they knew it was literally in their hands.

Straightening the desk, she turned off the light and stormed downstairs. She needed some fresh air and headed outside.

She threw herself down onto one of Dan's Adirondack chairs on the deck in the rear of the cabin and willed herself to calm down. Even though she hated to admit it, Aaron was right. She was no longer a free spirit who could just pick up and do as she pleased. She was now a married woman and soon to be a mother. There were other people to consider. But why had the book fallen into her hands? Grandma Williams had spoken of such an event years ago. Didn't that mean something?

Sighing, Teri placed her hands on her stomach. They already knew all too well the kind of power Edward Hastings possessed. If they didn't do something to stop him before 2003, what kind of future would she be condemning her children to? On the other hand, if they did get involved, what kind of hornet's nest would they be stirring if they dared to challenge Satan's diabolical plan? No. None of that mattered. Somehow, Hastings had to be stopped.

But, what if he *were* her son in a past life?

"Oh, Granny. What am I supposed to do?" Teri lamented, silently fingering her cross.

Well, she wasn't going to solve the world's or her own problems overnight. The best thing she could do was follow Aaron's advice and leave it alone, temporarily. As Grandma

William's had said, the only thing she could do was pray for guidance. If God wanted her to get involved, He would surely show her the way.

Looking down at the journal in the darkness, she frowned. It was amazing how such an innocent looking book could be the source of so many problems.

"This is a great way to start a marriage, fighting over world affairs as if we were diplomats," she muttered, returning to the bedroom.

Aaron was back in bed but she could tell he wasn't sleeping. She was glad because she had no intention of going to sleep without resolving their differences. Her loyalty and respect for him came before anything else.

Slipping under the covers, she leaned on one elbow facing him. Even in the darkness she could see he was scowling.

"I'm sorry, Aaron. You were right and I was wrong. I let my stubbornness get the best of me. Please forgive me," she said softly.

Teri waited anxiously for him to say something. Then, little by little, she could feel the tension in his body lessen. He regained his composure. Finally, he turned his head to look at her.

"Maybe you couldn't understand this before but since you just lost your parents, don't you realize how important you and our children are to me? You're the only family I have. You don't know how lonely and depressed I'd been since my divorce. Then, you came along and everything changed. All of a sudden my life has meaning. Someone finally needs me and loves me."

"You know I have a strong belief in God and justice and I have no problem doing whatever it is He wants me to do. It's the least I can do to show Him how grateful I am that He brought us together. But at the same time, I'm not going to pretend that I'm willing to sacrifice the people I love to save the world. Maybe my faith isn't as strong as yours but that's the way I feel," Aaron said, tiredly.

Teri wept as she listened to him. She was ashamed to think that for even a second she'd been willing to put her own blind spirit of adventure and sense of justice before the one person who'd stuck by her throughout their terrible ordeal. It was obvious she still had a lot to learn about being a married woman.

All she could do was cry. She put her arms around him and buried her face in his chest.

"I've already had a bath," Aaron smiled, hugging her.

"I'm such a stubborn old fool. I don't know why you put up with me," Teri said. She wiped the tears from her eyes with the sheet.

"I've been asking myself the same thing since the first day we met," Aaron grinned. Then, becoming serious again, he said, "Look. I'm willing to compromise. I'll finish translating the book but we have to agree not to make any definite plans about what we're gonna do until after the twins are born. After what we've been through, I think we just need to concentrate on being a family for now. If you're due next May, we'll still have plenty of time to tackle Hastings before he comes back and I'm sure Dan will want to help. Can you agree to that?"

"Yes," Teri nodded her head.

"You realize that no matter what we decide, our lives will never be the same. There's always the possibility that Hastings could send someone else to get us and the book. That's why we can't just rush into this thing without thinking it through carefully. We have to stick together. As it is, we'll probably always have to be on our guard," Aaron reminded her.

"I know," Teri replied and snuggled deeper into his arms. "It's ironic how even though Hastings is gone, he still seems to be terrorizing us," she reflected, and to herself, she thought, "*In more ways than you can ever imagine.*"

"Well, I'm going to try my best to make sure we don't play into his hands and fall victim to his power," Aaron said with resolve.

* * * *

In the darkness of the quiet evening, a tall figure stood behind a tree a few feet away from the house, casually smoking a cigarette. It was fortunate for him that the night was clear and the air was still. If it had not been, the pungent odor of sulfur that surrounded the mysterious figure would have been carried through the window of the bedroom where the unsuspecting couple were starting their new life together.